Looking Glass

I wouldn't hesitate to liken the masterful Glass House Trilogy to Tolkien's *The Lord of the Rings*
—Christine Spindler, German Physicist
and author of *The Rhythm of Revenge*

Looking Glass

Max & Ariana Overton

Mundania Press

A Mundania Press Production

Mundania Press LLC
6470A Glenway Avenue, #109
Cincinnati, Ohio 45211-5222

To order additional copies of this book, contact:
books@mundania.com
www.mundania.com

Cover Art © 2004 by Ariana Overton
Layout by Stacey L. King
Book Design and Layout by Daniel J. Reitz, Sr.
Production and Promotion by Bob Sanders
Edited by Audra A. F. Brooks

Trade Paperback ISBN-10: 1-59426-143-1
Trade Paperback ISBN-13: 978-1-59426-143-5

Hardcover ISBN-10: 1-59426-020-6
Hardcover ISBN-13: 978-1-59426-020-9

First Mundania Edition • January 2005

Library of Congress Catalog Card Number 2003114040

Production by Mundania Press LLC
Printed in the United States of America

10   9   8   7   6   5   4   3   2   1

ACKNOWLEDGEMENTS

No book is ever written by only one person. Even those authors who hole themselves up in secluded mountain cabins without a phone or computer write novels based on past encounters and interaction with other people. In addition, any author who bases their work on research cannot ever claim individuality in content. This book brings a tremendous amount of scientific research to the reader so we give credit where credit is due to those authors, scientists and researchers whose work gave this novel depth, credibility and insight.

Paul Cropper, Australian expert in Cryptozoologist and author of many books on the subject.

Tim 'the Yowie Man', a dear friend, dynamic field researcher and one of the most experienced trackers of 'mythological' beings on an international level. Tim has a book published by Random House that documents his travels in this field, as well as a movie titled *Yowie Man*.

Nathan and Ratana, Aboriginal students at James Cook University, Townsville, Queensland, who graciously allowed us to use their names and personas and generously let us pick their brains about Aboriginal beliefs and lifestyles.

A big list of scientists and researchers who published their adventures. (See the reference list at the end of the book)

Additionally, we owe a great deal to friends and publisher for their contributions of support, patience, suggestions and comments.

J.B. Scott, Sydney resident and true friend of many years. Without her help and support, these three books would not have come to the attention of the Australian reader as fast as they did.

Ken and Ardy Scott, of Townsville, our dear friends and supporters who put up with our lack of social skills while writing this trilogy.

Hundreds of list mates on the Internet who consistently supported and encouraged us to "Get the books written! We want more!", including the Allaboutmurder list, EPPRO, EPIC and other lists we haunt.

Finally, but the most important group of all, we want to thank our family. Without them, all of them, we may never have written any of the books we have completed. Their support and encouragement never wavered, weakened or failed.

Our son-in-law Byron, daughter Dani and two grandsons, Brandon and Jacob, are the backbone of our strength and determination to leave something behind for them to be proud of. Our books are always for them.

Our mothers, Nida and Cynthia. Need we say more?

Brothers, sisters and nephews. They all contributed to the support system we rely on.

Each other. Max and I are more than husband and wife; we are one.

FOREWORD

"Hold a looking glass up to your world. You will see familiarity magnified in minute, horrifying detail, but reversed."

~ Anonymous ~

PROLOGUE

Queensland, Australia
28,000 B.C.

The upper northernmost reaches of ancient Australia baked under a hot sun. The land lay steaming under a layer of thick, humid mist. Long stretches of thick fern groves under tall gum and flowering tropical trees made the landscape a primal forest of aggressive plants, each seeking to survive in a hostile world. A roar, loud enough to make the leaves shake, blasted through the foliage, shortly followed by the high-pitched scream of a terrorized, dying creature.

Oily water rippled softly, parting as the armored head of a large crocodile rose above the surface of a slime green pool next to the outer perimeter of the forest. Cold reptilian eyes scanned the muddy banks of the river and the small mob of short-faced kangaroos milling nervously near the water in the hot afternoon sun. The crocodile sank imperceptibly, a lazy flick of its tail moving it closer to the riverbank.

Massive, six-foot tall reddish brown kangaroos moved toward the water's edge, impelled by a growing thirst. In spite of their great size, they were nervous, scanning the river and the dense shrubbery along its banks for predators. Females nuzzled eager youngsters back from the water, unwilling to be the first to drink. A young buck gave a bark of alarm and leaped towards the cover of a stand of paperbark trees when a shadow swept over him. The shrill cry of a fishing eagle immediately reassured him and he turned towards the river once more. Dropping onto all fours, he slowly moved down to the water and, ignoring the other kangaroos, lowered his head to drink.

A surge of water rushed over his snout, death following so closely that the young kangaroo never even registered the fact. The head and chest of the animal disappeared down a yawning gullet as teeth ripped through its hide, crushing its rib cage. The momentum of the crocodile's rush carried it halfway up the riverbank, scattering the mob of kangaroos that fled screaming and barking for the undergrowth. Lying on the bank, the hindquarters of the kangaroo hanging from its mouth, the full size of the saurian became apparent. The young kangaroo stood six feet on its hind legs but the head of the monster alone matched that size. The crocodile ponderously swung its forty-foot bulk, slipping back down into the water and disappearing beneath the surface with a muddy swirl. The water calmed, leaving only a few tufts of hair floating near the bank and a splash of blood congealing on the grass.

The sun edged closer to the horizon. Gradually, life returned to the riverside. A family group of Diprotodons, huge cousins of the wombat, lumbered into the shallows, drinking thirstily. Smaller wallabies hopped cautiously in their wake, sipping quickly then leaping again for the relative safety of the forest. A lone thylacine drifted silently from the undergrowth to the bank, while peering suspiciously around, then it drank and faded back out of sight. The fishing eagle that had startled the young kangaroo, now past all caring, returned, circling the scene then settling onto a branch of a dead gum tree hanging over the water.

The bushes upstream from the dead tree parted and a scaly snout pushed through into the grassy clearing. The eagle turned its head, looking down with interest for a moment before returning to its grooming. The Diprotodons snorted and splashed ashore, herding the youngsters away from the intruder. Black eyes gazed impassively as the huge beasts walked back into the forest. The intruder pushed through the bushes with a sinuous motion, its immense bulk held high off the ground. The giant monitor lizard, *Megalania prisca*, dwarfed even its cousin to the north on the island of Komodo, reaching a length of over twenty feet. The lizard's flat head weaved from side to side, its long forked tongue flicking as it tasted the air. It made its way slowly down to the edge of the water where it drank. After a few minutes it raised its head and turned its ponderous head, tongue flicking again. Abruptly it erupted into motion, moving swiftly up the bank. It nosed hungrily at the patch of dried kangaroo blood. Casting about, it found nothing edible and moved on down river, tasting the air, following a trail of bare packed earth that held the impression of many feet.

Shrill voices chattered and screamed as Aboriginal children raced through the long grass, waving sticks as they ducked and weaved in some complex game. Motionless and unnoticed, the small figure of a young girl sat quietly on a termite mound near the edge of the grass. Pale-skinned but bronzed by the fierce sun, she was naked except for a grass loincloth and sun hat woven from grasses. She smiled as the children played, half wanting to join them.

Why do you not, then? A gentle thought wafted into her mind.

The girl sat still, recognizing the flavor of the mind that spoke. *I am no longer a child, Rima. I am twelve years old and can feel my womanhood rushing upon me. There is something I am called to do...* The girl's smile faded and she turned toward the figure behind her. Although she sat on a termite mound over five feet tall, she had to turn her face up to look at her friend and protector.

Gazing back at her was a huge, hairy being. A tall, conical head with a pronounced sagittal crest sat squarely on wide shoulders and a massive torso. Long arms stretched almost to knee level on muscular legs. Large pendulous breasts revealed the sex of the creature despite the thick silky hair that covered the whole body and face in a wave of brown with golden highlights. Large liquid black eyes peered out of the hair, the intelligence in them obvious and comforting.

The girl grinned and stood up, throwing her arms out to balance herself. Images danced through her mind of things never seen by her but remembered all the same. Gorilla, large African primate...Bigfoot, semi-mythical creature of the American northwest...Yowie, the Australian version of Bigfoot.

How wrong they were, she thought privately, locking away her thoughts from the mind of the creature before her. *They thought the yowie was a primitive, or a myth. Instead it is a creature created long ago—or rather, in years to come—for a specific purpose.* The girl opened her mind: *I love you Rima*, she thought fiercely.

A low rumble answered her as the yowie put out a massive hand to stroke her leg. *What brought that on, little one?*

I miss her, Rima.

The yowie patted her leg softly, nodding. *Your mother loved you, child. I believe she still does and will find a way to come for you. You were everything to her, her whole world. That is why she named you Gaia.* Rima chuckled softly. *She had to explain that to me.*

I can remember her, you know, although I was only a baby. Her mind was open to me and I can recall everything she knew. Gaia grinned suddenly. *Even why she still calls you 'Cindy', despite you having a name of your own, a name of your people.*

Rima shook her massive head, her silky hair swirling around her head like a cyclone. *That was the first time I came face to face with humans who were not of the 'others'. I liked her.* The yowie glanced up at the sun dipping behind the low hills. *We must go back. It is late.*

Gaia nodded and held out her arms. *Catch me then!* She bunched her legs to leap off the termite mound, then it hesitated. She dropped her arms and half turned toward the river. "Hunger," she murmured. "Great hunger and coming swiftly." Gaia turned back to the yowie with an urgent expression on her face. *Go, Rima. Quickly! Chase the children toward the camp. The great goanna comes.*

Rima nodded and dropped into a crouch, her long arms reaching forward as she flowed into a ground-covering gallop toward the playing children. She roared inarticulately, her mind screaming unheard warnings to the Aboriginal children ahead of her. They looked up at her approach and ran screaming, then turned and raced around her, laughing and throwing clumps of dirt and grass. "Rima! Rima!" they chanted as the yowie turned and weaved, trying to chase them away from the river.

A small boy, clothed only in a broad grin, ran close to the scrub leading down to the river. As he neared them a brown avalanche hurled itself at him, long jaws agape, saliva trailing in thick ropes. The boy screamed and fell over, his legs tangling as the giant monitor lizard raced closer.

Gaia stood atop the termite mound and watched the boy fall over. She closed her eyes, concentrating. The lizard halted abruptly, all four legs scrabbling at the dry earth, and froze in place only feet from the sobbing boy. It hissed, belching gouts of foul, saliva-specked air. It lashed its tail in a fury and backed up, still hissing. Suddenly it turned and raced off, its body raised and tail flying, crashing through the scrub.

Gaia opened her eyes, smiling. She jumped down as Rima ambled up with a questioning look. *I made it see a bigger lizard*, she grinned. *It got scared and ran off.*

Shouts erupted from the forest. Several Aboriginal men emerged from the trees, carrying spears and killing sticks. The children ran to them chattering excitedly, leading the still sobbing young boy.

Gaia put her hand in the giant hand of the Yowie. *Come on then, Rima. You can carry me back to the village. The medicine man needs us now.*

When the yowie frowned in confusion, Gaia added, *I can feel it. Something is going to happen and we will be needed.*

Chapter One

Molten rock, along with half melted machinery, twisted along the corridors and inside the great caverns of the Glass House Mountain complex. Strange, surrealistic sculptures of metal and rock now permanently decorated what was once a sterile, functional series of caves, each designed for a specific scientific purpose. The inner sanctum of the secret society that had watched over, and gently guided, mankind's development for centuries was effectively crippled but not destroyed.

Inside one of the smaller caves that still remained functional, Doctor James Hay and his wife Samantha stood behind the hunched back of a grey-skinned scientist who typed vigorously on a computer keyboard. They watched lines of data scrolling down the screen at an amazing speed. The dolphin-like scientist kept his saucer-round black eyes on the screen while he spoke in a high-pitched whistling voice. "When the yowie and Gaia tried to move through the portal stonesss, a backlash of incredible energy sssurged through with them. The mountain in California contained its own power sssource, not only from the Earth's core but from the Vox Dei machine your sssister built, Ms. Sssamantha."

The scientist glanced up at Sam's strained face and attempted a smile. The result was a split in his face that converted most of the lower half into a chinless monstrosity—full of teeth and thin-lipped. When Sam flinched and responded with a wan uplift of her lips, Doctor Xanatuo took that as encouragement and continued with his analysis, content that he was comforting the mother of Gaia, the one they sought.

"The combined power sssent them both back to a point in time that drew them like a magnet." He tried to scratch his bald head with a long, clawed finger but succeeded in missing the spot altogether. "How can I explain thisss to humans?" he murmured while trying to reach the spot again.

Sam reached over and gently scratched the top of his head while she said, "We don't need to understand the why or how, doctor. We just need to know if we can go back there too. We must find our daughter." Her hand froze on the last words and her voice came out choked and strained.

Xanatuo reached up and patted the hand still resting on top of his head. "There, there, my dear, we will find her. Ressst assured we are doing all we can. In fact, we do have great newsss for you." His round eyes stared up at James and Sam without emotion, but the shark's grin was back on his face.

"What?" James asked, aware that his heart was racing.

"A rock painting was discovered on the Atherton Tableland of a young girl, apparently with yellow hair, and a hairy monster being attacked by evil spiritsss, the Quinkan. Thisss isss believed to be Gaia and Cindy." The doctor continued to stare at them, clearly waiting for some response.

James sat down heavily on a chair, staring at the scientist. Sam looked puzzled. "How can you possibly think it is Gaia?" she said. "My baby is just that…a baby, not a girl."

"That is true, lady, but the coincidencesss are interesting."

James got to his feet again, his face tight. He towered over the seated grey, staring into his face. "This had better be good. I don't appreciate anyone getting our hopes up, only to dash them because of some fanciful notion." He gripped his wife's arm and added, "We've had too much of that already in the last six months."

Dr. Xanatuo looked up at him calmly. "Very well then, doctor…lady. Please be seated." He stood, turned, folded long-fingered hands into the wide sleeves of his white robe and took a deep breath. He stood looking at them as they slowly retreated to two office chairs. When he felt the couple was giving him their undivided attention, he donned his teacher's demeanor and began the lecture in the simplest terms he could think of.

"First, yellow isss a very rare color used in rock paintingsss. The pigmentsss are difficult to obtain and are only used in paintings of great sssignificance. We know from your genetic makeup that your daughter hass an eighty-seven per cent chance of inheriting blond hair."

"Yes, doctor, we know all this," James retorted with barely concealed irritation in his voice. His grey eyes bored into the smooth face of the scientist with an angry stare.

The grey smiled thinly as he continued. "Alssso, the monster in the painting can only be a yowie. There isss nothing else in Aboriginal legend that would fit." He paused, enjoying the expectant look on the faces of the humans. "But yowies were created only recently, by the sssame people who created this facility. They did not exist in prehistory."

I'm getting very tired of this pompous ass of a mutant treating us like we're imbecilic children, James thought just before he opened his mouth to protest.

"But my baby…how could she…?" Sam began, cutting him off

before he could start another argument with the creature that was trying to help them find their daughter.

"Last, the time frame," Dr. Xanatuo interrupted her, oblivious to the human's growing anger at his lecture. "The pigmentsss were analysed, carbon-dated using certain refinementsss. We also applied thermoluminescence techniques. The datesss are in close agreement. Those pictures were painted approximately thirty thousand yearsss ago, give or take five hundred yearsss."

Dr. Xanatuo held up his hand to pre-empt James's and Sam's attempts to interrupt his statement. "We have also calculated very carefully the power sssurge that made the two of them disappear. Based on their known massss, the energy involved, research into the archives and our theories on ssspace-time topologies, we can be certain they went back twenty-nine thousand nine hundred and four years."

The grey opened his mouth wide in a feral grin, displaying rows of peg-like teeth, sure that the humans would finally appreciate his great intellect and the information he now had to give them. "Taking all these factors into account we are tolerably certain your daughter sssurvived to become a young girl."

Sam felt stunned, unsure whether to rejoice or wait until the doctor finished his speech. Finally, a fragment of what the doctor said grabbed hold of her mind and stopped all thought for a moment. *A young girl?* she thought, while trying to wrap her mind around the alien image of her baby as a young girl.

James shifted in his seat. "You said these two images were threatened by something...the Quinkan, I think you said?"

"Yesss. That is an interesting point. The Quinkan are an Aboriginal embodiment of evil in the environment. They are believed to be thin black beingsss who live in crevices and cracksss in rocksss. They come out to cause mischief and harm." Dr. Xanatuo wrinkled his impressive expanse of forehead. "It is difficult to imagine these as real, however. It is more likely they represent sssome generalized threat. They were uncivilized timesss."

Sam raised her stricken face. "Then she could be in danger and we sit here doing nothing." The fiery red of her hair became a stark contrast to the paleness of her face. She stood up suddenly. "You stand there prattling on about your scientific discoveries, about how you think this and believe that, and all the time my baby, my Gaia, is in danger..." Her voice rose in pitch and volume. "...and you bloody well do nothing!"

Xanatuo took a step back. His thin neck vibrated with shock, and membranes flicked across his large dark eyes. "Lady, pleassse, control yourself. We are mindful of your emotional ssstate and we are working as fast as we can. We have a meeting this afternoon of all concerned partiesss. We promise you we will alleviate your concernsss. We will be outlining exactly what we can do then, if you wish, we can sssend you back to find her."

Sam's mouth remained open and she exhaled the breath she had drawn for another angry outburst. James stood and came to her side, gripping her arm tightly.

"Send us back? You can atually send us back?"

∽≈

Marc Lachlan stood by a pair of large French windows, gazing out into the night. A black, forbidding forest of pine trees pressed close around the cabin nestled between rocky spurs in the Colorado Rockies. He shivered slightly, watching dark shadows flicker and sway as the breeze moved the pine branches, occluding the light of the waning moon.

He could feel the tight muscles under his skin crawl with an unfocused dread. *So much for being a big tough guy*, he thought while watching what was left of the moonlight dim into more shadows, sending his six-foot-two frame shivering again.

A feminine voice, soft but insistent, insinuated itself into his mind. *Marc, my sweet hunk. Are you all right?*

He turned sharply, knowing even as he did so that the room was empty. A low log fire cast a dull red glow over the gleaming wood floors, overstuffed furniture and bookcases. He stepped rapidly to the open door between the living room and the kitchen, calling out as he did so. "Andi, I wish you wouldn't do that. You know it makes me feel uncomfortable."

A feeling of amusement swept over him. *That's not what you said last night. Let me see…if memory serves…"Oh, God, I feel part of you, I can feel you from both…"*

"Andi, please!" Marc cried out. "That's only for us." He concentrated his thoughts. *Andi. Those things are intimate things, between the two of us, when we're together. Anyone could be listening. I mean, anyone who…*

Oh, Marc. I've told you before. I can direct my thoughts to you alone. Not even my sister Sam can hear us and she's much better at this than I am. A figure appeared at the top of the stairs. His wife of three months, tall, long-legged, with the dusky dark looks that made his heart pound every time he saw her, stood majestically at the head of the staircase to his right. She smiled down at him, her green eyes flashing as they captured the firelight. The moment stood still while he gazed up at her and wondered, not for the first time, why she loved him.

Her smile widened with a mysterious uplifting of her lips. Then she glided down the stairs and threw her arms around him before kissing him lightly on the lips. "I love you because you're the right man for me, even if it did take a mountain blowing up and my near death to realize it," she whispered in his ear.

He wrapped his arms around her waist, snuggled his head into her neck and nuzzled her ear before nipping it lightly with his teeth. When she squealed and pulled back, he said, "That's for invading my mind again, you minx."

She laughed and stepped into his arms again. "I'm sorry, darling. But it's such a useful trick and I need to practice."

"Well, you can practice with your sister. Speaking of whom, how is she these days? Any word of Gaia?"

Andi's smile slipped. She shook her head and stepped back. "Not until today. I've been trying to contact her mentally of course, but for some reason I haven't been able to get through." She reached into a back pocket of her jeans. "Then this arrived."

"You didn't tell me a letter came. What does it say?"

"You were out walking when it arrived. I've been reading and re-reading it. It's not so much what she says as what she doesn't say. Here, see for yourself." She handed the plain white envelope to him.

Marc took the letter out of the envelope and unfolded it. Moving over to the lamp beside his favorite recliner chair, he rapidly scanned the single page of writing.

"Hmm. She sends her love...they've met up with Nathan and Ratana again...going into the Glass House Mountains...come to north Queensland immediately. She even gives exact latitude and longitude." He flipped the sheet of paper over, glanced at the blank back then peered at the postmark on the envelope. "Odd. There's no name of the post office, only a date and a year, '1770'."

"It's not a year, it's a place in Queensland. Apparently there's a small town called 1770 near the Glass House Mountains. It's just where it was posted from."

Marc grinned. "Why am I not surprised? Australia's full of weird animals, odd things in the rainforests and unpronounceable names. In fact, 1770 is refreshingly ordinary."

"The map reference is for a spot on the Atherton Tableland, just inland from Cairns in north Queensland. I looked it up in the atlas. Of course, I couldn't tell exactly where but we can look it up on a decent map when we get there." In spite of the casually spoken words, her face was serious and unsmiling.

"When we...we're going to Australia? When did you decide this?"

"I must go, Marc. There's something not quite right. Sam's over-whelming concern at the moment is finding Gaia. In all the conversa-tions and letters I've had with her over the last six months, she's talked of little else. Then I get this terse note asking us to go to some out-of-the-way spot, without any explanation or mention of Gaia. I'm wor-ried, Marc. I've got to go." Andi reached out to Marc. "I'm hoping you'll come with me."

Marc smiled wryly. "You don't imagine I'm letting you out of my sight, do you? Of course I'm coming with you." He frowned. "Not that

I'm particularly looking forward to going into the Australian bush again. I had some bad experiences there."

"I know you were there when Sam and James first met. Sam told me about the trip as far as the Glass House Mountains but said I had to ask you about the rest of it. You always said there wasn't much to tell," she stated with an expectant unspoken question woven within the words.

Marc fidgeted and looked away. "I wasn't completely honest about that, Andi. I forgot the details for a while but I gradually remembered. I know I saw creatures in the Australian forests that are not supposed to exist. Yowies, that's a type of Bigfoot, and lake monsters, though I didn't actually see one. The others say they did and I believe them." He turned back to Andi, gripping her hands and looking earnestly into her eyes. "It was only when you went to work for Morgan on that physics project in California that it all came back to me. That's why I know you saw those horrible shadow things and that incredible thunderbird."

Andi smiled and hugged Marc tightly. "And knowing these things exist you're still willing to get involved again? No wonder I love you, mister."

"Yeah, well...I always had more guts than sense, even when I'm scared shitless."

Chapter Two

Doctor James Hay and his wife Samantha hurried along a sterile-looking passageway deep within the Glass House Mountains. Despite months of feverish work to restore the complex, there were still many signs of the enormous and destructive energies that ripped through the installation months ago. In places, the very granite of the walls had melted, flowed, and now lay in weird congealed shapes around burnt-out machinery of uncertain origins.

Ahead of the pair of humans scampered a small grey technician, his short legs twinkling as he hurried the humans along. Every few seconds he turned his round, grey head with its huge, black almond-shaped eyes to reassure himself that they were following. The grey beckoned again, then pointed at a doorway set into a relatively unscarred section of the wall. He bowed, then raced back the way they came.

James stopped outside the door to catch his breath before entering. Sam patted her long, red hair and smoothed her pantsuit. "I wish they'd given me a chance to tidy up first," she muttered. "What's this meeting about anyway?"

"Search me," replied James. "All I know is our immediate presence was requested." He ran a hand over his hair and took a deep breath. "Come on then, love. Let's see what's up."

The room they entered seemed small at first glance, despite the number of people in it. James looked around at the mass of people and realized the lack of size was due more to the crowding rather than the actual dimensions. The room itself, James now saw, stretched over fifty yards in length and about half that in width. The ceiling soared above him, lost in darkness above the soft glow of suspended lights. Rows of seats stretched across the room, facing a raised podium with a large table and several chairs. A whiteboard ran behind most of the podium. To the right of the table and chairs stood a row of seats turned slightly away from the table and facing the audience.

Most of the seats were occupied and the faces he saw there immediately grabbed James's attention. Seated at the far left of the table was a pair of young Aborigines whose presence at once brought a smile to James's face.

Nathan, a stocky, muscular man from the southwest Queensland town of Cunnamulla sat relaxed in a comfortable looking swivel chair, his legs stuck out in front of him. He played with a pencil on the table in front of him, his repetitive motions the only sign of stress he displayed. His wife Ratana, a tall, slim woman from the northern tip of Cape York, showed the distinctive traits of a Torres Strait Islander background. She sat stoically, waiting to see what happened.

James grinned, thinking back to the last few years when, as a senior lecturer in Biology at James Cook University, he was instrumental in bringing Nathan to the College on a scholarship. The young man showed himself a mature, capable scholar and James took great pleasure in guiding Nathan through the rigors of his Bachelor's and Master's degrees. James also re-introduced him to Ratana, a recent Honors graduate, on a field trip into the outback two years before. Although related, and having been reared together for a couple of years, Nathan and Ratana were nearly strangers to each other. The pair fell in love and married only months later. Both remained close to James, assisting him many times with field studies.

Two empty seats separated Ratana from the only other person seated at the table. Doctor Xanatuo sat, back into a ramrod straight posture, hands folded primly in his lap, facing out into the room. James took the opportunity to study the scientist for the first time, despite his earlier discussion with the being. He was used to the small grey technicians who scurried around the complex, performing the many scientific tasks of the community. The small greys resembled nothing so much as the archetypal 'alien' of UFO abduction scenarios. The figure seated at the table resembled them, but only as a humpback whale resembles a dolphin. The skin was grey and the head swollen, bulging out in front like the domed prow of a cetacean. The eyes were large, black with no whites showing, and slanted. The mouth differed markedly from the small greys, however. Instead of small slits, rarely opened in speech, the wide lipless slash of mouth stretched across his face. James shuddered involuntarily when he recalled the rows of peg-like teeth that flashed when Xanatuo spoke. A long, mobile tongue flicked over the teeth, speaking English when required with an easy facility, though marred by an annoying, if slightly amusing, hiss. The scientist was tall, with long, spindly limbs and, when he moved, showed his dolphin ancestry in the flowing way in which his skin rippled beneath a pristine white laboratory smock.

Standing beside Xanatuo was a tall, old, Aboriginal man, his once-black hair and beard now greying. He stood with a stoop, clothed incongruously in a tee shirt, shorts and battered sneakers. James nudged Sam and inclined his head.

"It's Ernie," he whispered with delight. "Damn, it's good to see him again."

The sound of his voice rang through the silent room and James suddenly became aware of the audience when a sea of unfamiliar faces turned in his direction. He flushed and stood uncertainly, enduring the scrutiny of a host of human, near-human and alien-looking beings. The majority of the faces turned toward Sam and James displayed receding jaws, with large overhanging eye ridges and sharply sloping foreheads. Despite the experiences of the last year, James still felt his heart race at the sight of genuine Neanderthal men and women. Scattered through the white upturned faces of the 'cavemen' were several greys and a few other, stranger beings. Against one wall lounged a restless, moving mountain of hair. Several yowies, the ten-foot tall, gorilla-like beings specially created by the Neanderthal genetic program, turned their huge heads toward them. Intelligence glowed in their eyes, belying the fearsome aspects of protruding canines. A wash of interest swept over James's mind as they stared at him.

"Ah, Doctor Hay," said Ernie. "If you and Samantha would care to join us up here," he gestured at empty chairs at the table, "we can start this meeting."

James felt all eyes on them as he and Sam walked up the aisle, up the few steps, and onto the raised podium. He held a chair for Sam then sat down himself. James nodded and smiled at Ratana, while quickly shaking Nathan's hand. He leaned back when Ernie started talking again.

"Friends," he started, addressing the audience, "I asked you here for an important reason. Most of you have heard of Doctor Hay and his wife Samantha Louis." He nodded at the two. "They were central to the events of the last few months. I and the Council gathered here today felt you deserved to meet them and to hear for yourselves what we've decided."

James felt hot blood rush to his cheeks again and saw that Sam was also in the throes of embarrassment. He was used to public speaking but to be the focus of so much un-human attention was distinctly unsettling. He forced his attention back to Ernie's speech.

"…as Chair person of the Council, Garagh." The familiar figure of Garagh, the Neanderthal leader reputed to be older than Methuselah, smiled and sat down again. "Next to him is the Head of Physical Sciences, Doctor Qerentuo." A tall grey, showing the same dolphin-like features as Xanatuo, stood up and nodded at the audience before folding his long limbs into the chair again. "Doctor Fssthtok represents Biological Sciences." A small furry humanoid rose gracefully and inclined its head toward the audience, then toward the table before sitting down.

James knew of the incredible genetic manipulation programs that took place in this complex and probably in many others around the world. He had met and conversed with many of the results of this hybridising work. Doctors Xanatuo and Qerentuo shared a genetic ancestry with Neanderthals and dolphins; the small greys had monkey genes mixed in with dolphin and human. The towering yowies, known elsewhere as 'Bigfoot', 'Sasquatch' or 'Yeti', were also products of the Neanderthal genetic mill. The great apes, as well as humans and Neanderthals, contributed to their makeup. James stared at Fssthtok, trying to make some sense of his features. *Possibly otter*, he thought, *or maybe cat...*

"...and last of all, Coonabara, Head of Security." A huge yowie rose from his seat on the floor. Despite sitting on the floor of the stage, his head still towered above the others seated alongside him. Upright, the sagittal crest on his great shaggy head brushed the lights suspended from the ceiling. Coonabara smiled, baring huge canines, then turned and looked at James.

It is indeed otter, came a cool voice inside James's head. *He is quite sensitive about his appearance, though. Please do not stare at him.*

James flushed again and looked down at the table. *I...my apologies*, he thought back at the yowie. *I did not mean to cause offence. Please apologize for me if I...*

No apology is needed, came Coonabara's mental reply. *I merely stated facts for your future reference.*

Ernie glanced from Coonabara to James with a small smile. "Before we get down to the main business at hand," he went on, "I think we should summarize the situation for those of you who may have missed some recent events." Ernie paused and took a sip of water from a glass on the table.

"As you all know, our main work here in the Glass House Mountains, and in other places around the world, is to monitor and, where possible, guide the development and progress of humans." Ernie sighed. "Regrettably, humans have, despite our efforts, brought this planet to the edge of disaster. The environment, though outwardly still functional, is in danger of imminent collapse. It is too late for humans to correct matters. Nothing they do now will prevent massive climate change and extinction of the majority of animal and plant species."

A ripple of distress swept through the audience, with muted cries of dismay rending the silence.

"However," went on Ernie, in a quiet voice. "We appear to have been given a last chance. The 'Others' who guide us in our work have pinpointed a time in our distant past when a different choice could have saved us."

"We cannot change the past," cried a voice from the audience. "How does this help?"

"I shall explain this presently," said Ernie. "But first, a little background." Ernie walked out to the edge of the stage and stared into the audience. "Somewhere within the human and Neanderthal genetic heritage lies the cure for the disease that afflicts all life. We believed we found the necessary linkages in Doctor Hay and Samantha Louis. We drew them together, lured by a black carved stone in the forests north of the Atherton Tableland. We pointed them down to the Glass House Mountains. They came with friends and proved themselves worthy, despite many dangers. They became the parents of the child we believe will heal the world. The baby was born, a girl child, aptly named Gaia, which means 'World Mother' in an old human tongue."

Ernie frowned and stood silently for a few moments, obviously gathering his thoughts. "Then disaster struck," he went on. "A race of beings, incorporeal but deadly, guided an American conglomerate to devise and build a machine that could tap into the energies of the planet, wreaking havoc with the human mind. The forces released by this machine, the Vox Dei or Voice of God, almost destroyed this complex. It was only through great sacrifice that the menace was finally overcome. Unfortunately, the child Gaia was lost in the battle."

Ernie shook his head sadly. "Until recently, I believed she had died." He turned to James and Sam, who sat with stunned expressions on their faces. "Forgive me," he said. "I hoped she survived but I doubted it. It was my decision to keep you believing she lived." Ernie smiled wanly. "We now know she survived the blast of energy, being catapulted back along lines of weakness in the very fabric of time and space to the crossroad time specified by the 'Others'."

A hubbub of whisperings, squeaks and cries erupted from the crowd. Ernie waited for the noise to die down.

"Based on the evidence of the girl's survival and research by our scientists, we believe we can duplicate this accident. We intend sending a team back in time and space to achieve not only a rescue of Gaia but also to change the event that brought ruin to the world. The heads of departments have already been notified of the relevant aspects and will keep you fully informed of developments." Ernie raised his hands above his head.

"The humans gathered here will now enter into discussions with our Council and scientists. These discussions must remain private for the time being." Ernie smiled and swept his hand toward the seated Council members. "We all thank you for coming. Talk about what you have heard and ask your department heads if you have any questions."

After a moment's pause the crowd of humans, near-humans and other beings got to their collective feet, pushing chairs aside and shuffling along the rows. With several curious stares at the people on the stage, they filed out. Within minutes, the main body of the hall was deserted.

"Thank you...Ernie," said Garagh, rising. He turned to the other members of the Council. "Councillors, I ask your patience during the discussion to follow. Most of what you hear will be familiar to you. It is necessary that the humans here are made aware of the possibilities unfolding from our research." Garagh smiled at Xanatuo, who still sat upright in his chair, facing the empty room. "Doctor Xanatuo, I would be grateful if you would explain the theories of time travel to the people here."

Doctor Xanatuo got up slowly and sighed. He scratched the top of his head with his long, impossibly prehensile fingers before facing James and the other humans seated at the table. "I do not know whether I can explain thisss to you. You do not have the necesssary education." He held up a hand as James opened his mouth. "Yesss, Doctor Hay, I know you are educated for a human but you would need ssseveral lifetimes to comprehend the ssspatial mathematicsss alone. Then there isss multi-dimensional topology..."

"Doctor," interrupted Garagh. "Please keep it simple. None of us are likely to understand the mathematical complexities of your work."

Xanatuo inclined his head toward the Neanderthal.

"So what can you tell us? You said you would explain how we can get Gaia," Sam asked, trying to ignore the doctor's annoying sibilance.

The grey scientist pondered for a moment, his fingers once more seeking out the wrinkled, hairless dome of his head. "Perhapsss I can develop a sssimple analogy." He started pacing back and forth in front of the whiteboard covering the back wall of the room. "You are perhaps aware that ssspace has three dimensions? Those of length, breadth and height? And perhapsss, too, that time can be considered a fourth?" He gazed at the humans seated at the table, noting the look of understanding on their faces. "Good!" He nodded and smiled, showing rows of teeth between thin lips.

Sam shuddered at the sight but gave an encouraging smile in return.

"Imagine the creation of the universe as ssstarting like a child'sss toy balloon," Xanatuo lisped. "Our three dimensions will have to be represented as two on the sssurface of thisss balloon, because the inflation of the balloon represents time itself. Like thisss." Xanatuo picked up a marker pen and drew a circle on the whiteboard. "Let usss sssay that thisss point, here," he drew a small 'x' on the edge of the circle, "isss the moment we are concerned with, sssome thirty thousand years ago."

Xanatuo peered around at his audience. "And what do we know happened then?" he asked.

After a moment's silence, James sighed and said quietly, "Doctor Xanatuo, that is why we are here. To find out from you what happened then and how we can rescue our daughter."

Xanatuo frowned, his wrinkled grey forehead hanging low over his large dark eyes. "Very well, Doctor Hay. Will you pick up that marker pen on the table, please?"

James stared at the grey for a moment, then reached over and picked up the pen.

"Now tell me, Doctor Hay, could you have refusssed to pick it up?"

"Of course. What is this? What does this have to do with anything?" James threw the marker pen back onto the table, sitting back in his chair. Sam leaned forward and squeezed his forearm gently.

Nathan reached across and picked up the pen, looking quizzically at James and the grey scientist. "Are you saying this has something to do with predestination, or fate?" he asked.

"Not in the way you mean, young sssir. Every event, whether large, such as a volcanic eruption or political assassination, or sssmall, such as the cereal you have for breakfast..." Xanatuo grinned again, displaying his impressive dental array. "Every event carries choicesss with them. Future eventsss unfold differently depending on the choice made. Some eventsss have great effects, othersss affect the future only slightly."

James snorted. "Come on now, doctor. Are you telling me my decision to pick up that pen altered the future?"

"Yes, Doctor Hay, I am." Xanatuo held up his hand, forestalling a further expostulation from James. "The effect probably lasted less than a nanosecond. The universe isss self-correcting, though some decisions are easier to correct than othersss."

Nathan raised his eyebrows incredulously. "To correct, doctor? You are saying there is a plan to the universe?"

Xanatuo shrugged, his shoulders rippling oddly beneath his laboratory coat. "As a scientist, I can only report on what I can measure, what I can sssee. As a thinking being, a sssspiritual one perhapsss..." His voice trailed off into sibilant whispers.

Garagh coughed and leaned forward. "If I may make a comment at this point, Doctor? The issue perhaps is not whether there is some mysterious metaphysical plan in the mind of a hypothetical god, but rather whether there is a plan devised by other beings that can provide optimal conditions for human development."

"Not just human," growled the furry Fssthtok.

"Of course not," replied Garagh calmly. "But humans, like it or not, are central to the problem...and the cure. Please continue, Doctor Xanatuo."

Xanatuo blinked, and resumed talking. "Whether or not there isss a plan, the universe certainly works to remove the effects of some choices." Xanatuo turned back to the whiteboard and tapped the circle drawn on it.

"Imagine these alternate events as tiny bubbles that form on the surface of thisss sssphere of reality. They are like foam; infinitesimally sssmall particles that are constantly forming and bursting. They have no lasting effect, being sssubsumed into the multi-dimensional matrix of reality. Most last for fractions of a sssecond, though others are more long-lasting. A war or a political assassination may disssplay effects for a generation or more."

Doctor Xanatuo took a deep breath, held it for a moment, then exhaled in a long, musical whistle. "An event happened thirty thousand years ago in the Atherton Tableland of Australia that created a bubble, an alternate reality. We do not know what it wasss, or why it did not instantly collapssse. Instead the bubble increased in size, like thisss." The grey turned back to the whiteboard and rapidly drew another larger concentric circle. "Thisss representsss where our reality should be." He then drew in two other overlapping shapes touching the 'x' on the inner circle and the outer circle. "While these are the two dual realities formed from the event." Xanatuo turned back to his audience. "Do you sssee the sssignificance of thisss at lasso?"

James looked around at the others. Sam shrugged, looking faintly annoyed. Nathan was bent forward over the table, hanging on every word of Doctor Xanatuo. Ratana sat quietly, scribbling in a notebook. She looked up at Sam in the silence following the grey's question and smiled.

Garagh interposed again. "With respect, Doctor Xanatuo," he said, "we would appreciate a quick explanation. Time grows short and we do not have the luxury of listening to a lecture, fascinating though it may be."

The grey looked annoyed, his lips thinning almost to invisibility, his large dark eyes becoming hooded beneath his brows. "Very well." He turned back to James and Sam. "Asss I was sssaying, this event has created alternate realitiesss."

James shrugged. "So there's an alternate universe. Human scientists have postulated that sort of thing before."

"Indeed they have. Some human physicistsss have postulated what they call 'quantum wormholes' or a 'space-time foam' as if naming the phenomenon gave them a grasp of the meaning." Xanatuo wrinkled his thin lips into a brief sneer. "But they have taken a wrong turn and try to use this knowledge to weigh empty ssspace for their astrophysical theories. Even the greatest of human minds such asss Stephen Hawking from Cambridge and Dr. Coleman from Harvard have missed the greater sssignificance."

"With respect, Doctor, I can't see that this idea of alternate realities affects us at all. The other reality cannot be reached by us."

Xanatuo shook his head in agitation. "No, no, Doctor Hay. You have missed the sssignificance also. These bubbles of reality do not last, but we are on one of them. Normally an alternate reality is ssso small when it collapsesss the effectsss are undetectable. " He tapped the small shapes on the whiteboard. "Thisss large circle isss the reality that should exist. I do not know what will happen to usss, to our reality, when a bubble this large collapsesss."

Sam looked alarmed. "Is there any reason to think it might collapse? It's lasted thirty thousand years already."

"Lady, that isss why we are meeting here today. We mussst collapse the bubble to eliminate the topological stressessss..." The grey's speech dissolved into a hissing whistle. "If we do not, it isss posssssible the bubble that isss our reality will detach itself. The physical parameters of thisss daughter universe by itssself will be very different from the parent universe. I do not know whether life could exissst in it."

"Dear God!" Sam stood up suddenly, her chair clattering to the floor behind her. "You're saying we could die if the bubble detaches itself, but may not exist if it collapses?" She turned to James, tears appearing in her eyes. "I thought this meeting was to decide how to bring Gaia back to us, not to decide how we are all to die!"

James took her hand and squeezed it. He looked back at Xanatuo. "I thought so too, Doctor. What is the point of all this if we are doomed no matter what we do?"

"Your daughter existsss here, lady." Xanatuo extended a long finger to the 'x' on the inner circle. "When the Vox Dei machine overloaded our sssystem, the flashback of energy catapulted her back along the linesss of force to thisss point. We believe we can duplicate thisss procedure and sssend sssomeone back."

Sam turned and picked up her chair, then sat down wearily. "Then we would both be trapped in the past." She shook her head at James. "Of course I'm going, I'm not leaving my baby alone."

"And if you think I'm letting you do this alone..." He looked up at the grey. "Can you send more than one person back?"

Doctor Xanatuo nodded. "Yesss. Now that we know what happened, we believe we can control the processsss. We can insert a sssmall team within..." He paused in thought for a moment, "...sssay, ten daysss of the initial insertion. Of course, the processsss is extremely energetic, and even a sssmall miscalculation could result in missssing the target by yearsss."

"But then the team is trapped in the past?"

Xanatuo shook his head. "You misssunderstand, doctor. There isss no past as you would understand it. When humansss talk of the past, they talk as if events that happened are over, cannot be changed and are immutable. The past isss not yet finished, though it no longer existsss. We will be sssending you back to a reality that you should think of as different from our present one, not a past version of thisss one. It will, however, be very sssimilar to the past, as we know it. Perhapsss the differences will be undetectable, perhapsss not."

James swore, softly but colorfully. "Okay, I won't pretend I fully comprehend what you are talking about, but if not the past, then the team is trapped in this other reality?"

"Perhapsss. You and your lady will travel back to find your child, othersss will go to achieve the main purpossse."

"What purpose?"

"I thought I had made that clear at leassst, lady. The bubbles mussst be collapsed. That can best be done before the bubbles have grown."

"Then what will happen to us, in the past…in the other reality?"

The grey scientist shrugged again. "It will be interesting to find out. For you, it will depend on whether you are attached to thisss reality, or are firmly immersed in the other one." He tapped the whiteboard. "The inner circle. Or maybe you will rebound into the reality that should exissst at thisss point in time, the outer circle." He looked sadly around at his audience. "We cannot know beforehand and I will never know. Being part of thisss reality, when the bubble I am in collapses, I, and others in thisss complex, will ceassse to exist."

The Council members shifted uneasily, though nodding agreement.

Sam looked at him with a horrified expression on her face. Xanatuo smiled at her sympathetically. "It will be enough to know that life continuesss."

"Can you be certain of that?" she whispered.

"Life isss resilient, lady. Life pervades thisss part of the universe and I do not believe a collapse of reality, even a large one, will truly affect life as a whole. Individual organismsss maybe. We shall have to wait and sssee."

Sam turned to James, her hand shaking as she reached out to him. "Andi. And Marc. Your grandfather…they will all go too."

Xanatuo shook his head. "There is a difference, lady. I, and othersss here at thisss complex, were created by our mentorsss," he gestured towards Garagh. "As the reality that resulted from their actions ceasesss, their future, and oursss, will also cease to exist. The rest of the world isss extraneous and will continue to be. Your sssister and the othersss you mentioned should be largely unaffected. It isss with thisss in mind that your sssister has been brought here."

Sam shot to her feet, knocking over her chair again. "Andi's here? Where? When did she arrive? Why wasn't I told?"

"We called her in your name, lady. Ssshe is not here in the Glass House Mountain complex but will ssserve an esssssential purpose at the Atherton node in northern Queensland. We believe her presence there, and the bond that existsss between you two as sisters could establish a reference point that will guide you back to thisss reality. It isss important that she remainsss close to the starting point of your journey along the stressss-curvature."

James looked up sharply. "You're saying Sam will be able to return to the present-day…to this reality?"

"Together with any who choose to return with her, doctor. Ssshe will act asss a conduit." Dr. Xanatuo started pacing. "When the object of your journey hasss been achieved, you will have altered the future reality. We, here in this present reality, will find ourselvesss also altering. Asss we base our existence on the past error, we will cease to exist. However, we should have a sssmall measure of warning. When the sssigns are there, we will activate the mechanisms again to pull Msss Sssamantha back. Any who are close to her, in contact if possible, will be pulled back too."

Sam looked aghast. "But that could happen without warning. What if I'm alone and nobody can reach me in time?"

"You will have warning. The processssss takes sssome minutesss to develop. Just be sssure not to be too far from the othersss." The grey scientist flashed a quick, toothy smile. "Of course, we cannot know precisely what warning you will have. We have not done thisss before. I believe you will feel a tugging sssensation all over your body, followed by visual distortionsss." He shrugged, making his narrow humped back rippling. "Look for sssomething out of the ordinary."

"Thank you, Doctor Xanatuo," said Garagh, getting up. "I think we are all now aware of the extraordinary work you and your team have accomplished." He turned to the other Council members. "We must discuss a few last matters, my friends, before we leave. In the meantime," he added, turning back to James and Sam, "you must prepare to leave. If you would follow Doctor Xanatuo…"

Garagh strode across the stage and out of the room, Ernie and the other Councillors in his wake. James got to his feet, a bemused expression on his face.

"Well, love," he said to Sam, "looks as if things are happening at last."

"Typical bloody bureaucracy," drawled Nathan, getting up. "Months of inactivity then all of a sudden, frantic panic." He grinned at his wife Ratana. "At least we can't say things are dull all the time."

Chapter Three

Marc parked the camper van on a low grassy shoulder at the end of a long dusty road. The road ran along a low ridge, ending in a brief, but steep drop. A low fence constructed of rough wooden beams blocked the end of the road from a narrow trail winding down into scrubby vegetation.

Andi stood by the van peering at the map spread on the hood, her finger close to a carefully drawn 'X' just beyond the end of the road. "This is the place, Marc. I'm sure of it."

Marc looked around him, taking in the tangle of Australian tropical rainforest to one side of the road and the thick eucalyptus scrub to the other. Shadows from the drifting clouds wove a complex pattern across the vegetation. Desultory chirps and whistles of hidden insect and bird life were the only noises in an otherwise silent landscape. The hot air reeked of gum and dust. "Just as I remember," he muttered. "Any moment now some bloody great hairy monster will charge out of the jungle."

Andi grinned at him while folding the map and tossing it onto the front seat of the van. "Come on, you great coward. Let's see exactly where this important spot is." She clambered over the low fence and started down the steep track. "According to the map, there's a small clearing about a hundred yards away with some caves close by."

"Caves. Bloody great." Marc leaped over the fence and skidded down the slope, sending up clouds of dust. He raced past Andi with a laugh. "Come on then, yourself."

The two ran, dodging rocks and tree roots, and finally emerged into a small clearing. Their laughs died when they came face to face with a small, dumpy woman of indeterminate age dressed in ill-fitting khaki slacks, jacket and scuffed boots. Wispy grey hair poked out from a wide straw hat. A startled expression flitted across her face, giving way to a broad smile as she glanced at the two young people.

"Visitors!" she boomed in a very British accent. "Are you from the local university, or just interested in our work?"

Marc looked confused. "Er, I'm not...that is, we're not..."

"I think you must be confusing us with someone else," Andi replied. "We were just out here looking around. We had no idea you were here, Ms…"

"Simpson, my dear, Tilley Simpson. Stupid of me, really, I should have introduced myself at the start and not assumed you made the trip specifically to see us." She laughed, putting her hands firmly on her ample hips. "Now, who would you two Yanks be?"

"I'm Andi Lachlan and this is my husband, Marc. We're here on holiday, just exploring." She scanned the area, noting equipment and supplies discreetly packed on the side of the tent, and rolls of maps and stacks of notebooks inside the tent. Andi tilted her head to one side, smiling at the woman. "What are you working on that's so important?"

"Oh, just a little something that'll blow the archaeology establishment apart," she chortled. "Come have a look." She gestured behind her at the clearing, where Andi and Marc noticed a small tent and a trestle table. The table was stacked with more papers and equipment. A ring of stones surrounded a small kerosene stove on top of which a battered kettle emitted gusts of steam. "Have a cuppa too." She bustled ahead of them, calling out as she went. "Bertie, we have company. Bertie, where are you?"

The bushes behind the tent parted and a thin, cadaverous face peered out. Large brown eyes gazed over a hooked nose and an enormous handlebar moustache. An untidy mop of grey hair, thinning at the top, hung down to his shoulders.

"And who the hell would you be?" he rasped when he spotted Andi and Marc standing close to the camp table and inspecting the papers lying there.

"Bertie, that's no way to greet visitors who have come all the way from America just to see our work." She winked at Andi and muttered, "He's a bit of an ogre until he's properly introduced." She glared at her husband. "Now, dear, best manners please."

The face withdrew from sight then the bushes parted as a tall, lanky man stepped into view. Andi suppressed a giggle. The man looked like a caricature of a Victorian gentleman-explorer, right down to the baggy khaki shorts and solar topee he was adjusting. He walked stiffly up to the trio and, ignoring Tilley, drew himself up to his not inconsiderable height and stuck out his right hand.

"Good day. Allow me to introduce myself. I am Bertrand Simpson. Who might I have the pleasure of addressing?"

Andi smiled and firmly shook his bony hand. "Nice to meet you, Mr. Simpson. My name is Andi Lachlan." She half turned toward Marc and continued, "And this is Marc, my husband."

Marc reached over and shook the man's hand. "Pleased to meet you, Mr. Simpson."

"Well, now that we're all introduced, how about a cuppa?" Tilley bustled over to the fireplace and started rummaging around in an old canvas bag. "I'm sure I've got some extra mugs around here...ah, here they are." She pulled out two battered tin mugs and set them down next to two pottery mugs inscribed with the initials 'TS' and 'BS'. "Only teabags, I'm afraid, and no milk. We're rather short on supplies at the moment, and milk won't keep in this heat."

"That's fine, Mrs. Simpson," Andi responded with a smile. "We normally take our tea with lemon anyway."

Tilley frowned. "No lemon either, my dear. But we've plenty of sugar," she added brightly.

Bertie dragged over two folding canvas chairs from the tent and set them up near the fireplace, in the shade of a large gum tree. "Chairs for the ladies." He turned to Marc and twirled the end of his moustache with his right hand. "We chaps can rough it on the ground, what?"

"Er, yes. That'll be fine." Marc uneasily settled himself to the ground, after sweeping away bits of twig and stones. He accepted a mug of hot water with a teabag from Tilley, turned down the offer of sugar, and sat with a fixed smile on his face.

Bertie took his mug, briskly stirred in three heaped teaspoonfuls of sugar and sipped. He closed his eyes and murmured, "Sheer ambrosia, my dear. Nobody makes tea like you." He eased his tall frame to the ground and folded his long limbs about him, appearing like a contented giant stork come to roost.

Tilley smiled and sat down in a chair with her own mug in her hand. Turning to Andi, she remarked, "He does go on a treat, doesn't he?"

For a few minutes they sat and sipped their tea, Tilley and Bertie with obvious enjoyment. Andi drank politely and made appreciative noises to cover for Marc, who after one sip, screwed up his face and set his mug on the ground. The silence dragged on.

Marc coughed and cleared his throat. "I think perhaps we'd..."

Bertie set his mug down and looked up. "So, which aspect of our work fascinates you the most?" He gave Marc a piercing stare for a few moments before turning to look at Andi. "We haven't yet released our latest findings, so it can't be that. Perhaps it was my dear wife's brilliant work on diseases among the Neolithic Mammoth-hunters?" He smiled lovingly at Tilley. "Or maybe my modest attempts to categorize the use of stone artifacts in primitive religious ceremonies?"

Andi looked blank. "I'm sorry, I must admit I don't know anything about those things."

Marc's face showed interest for the first time. He waved his hands about as he stuttered, "Hang on...I remember reading...what the hell was it? Something about Neanderthals in India, I think. That was you, wasn't it? You're *that* Professor Simpson."

"Alas, ex-professor, my dear chap. The vice-chancellor decided my brand of enthusiasm was not in keeping with the hallowed tenets of accepted academia."

"What he means is his ideas were regarded as too outrageous and he was booted out," Tilley snapped with a grimace. "Those bloody twerps wouldn't know good scientific evidence if it bit them on their great, fat bums."

"That'll change now, my love," boomed Bertie. "Wait until we publish our latest findings. Incontrovertible evidence."

"Now, I remember your work," Marc shouted. "There was a huge debate about Neanderthals in the scientific journals. You really stirred up some ill-feeling but, boy, what a doozie of a theory you put forth! And the uproar..."

Andi looked puzzled. "What happened?" She glanced at Tilley and smiled. "I'm sorry, my field is physics. I'm not up on the life sciences."

"Well," Bertie replied, adopting the demeanor of a lecturer. He scrambled to his feet, dusting off his clothes. "To appreciate the controversy, we really need to start..."

"Keep it simple, Bertie," growled Tilley. "You're not in a bloody lecture theatre now."

Bertie blushed and looked crestfallen. "Sorry, my dear." He cleared his throat and paused, obviously searching for words. "You know that we humans are descended from a species that came out of Africa perhaps half a million years ago?" He glanced at Tilley nervously and continued. "Two species, or perhaps sub-species, arose: modern man and Neanderthal man. For a while they coexisted, then quite suddenly, about thirty thousand years ago, Neanderthal man vanished. Nobody knows what happened to them."

"There are theories, of course," broke in Tilley. "Some say modern man killed them off, others say they interbred with modern man and merged. Or they couldn't compete, or died of some new disease. Every year somebody adds a new wrinkle."

Marc opened his mouth, then closed it with a snap when an urgent voice invaded his mind. *Keep quiet, Marc! We don't know these people.*

Bertie nodded. "Until Tilley and I came across a fascinating series of sites in Europe, the Middle East and India. We believe we found evidence proving they migrated southeast, away from trouble. And now..." Bertie hesitated and glanced at his wife who nodded. "We found artifacts in Australia, right here in fact, that put Neanderthal man in coexistence with the Aboriginal tribes between twenty and thirty thousand years ago."

"Er...what sort of artifacts?" Andi asked, hoping they weren't going to show her buried bodies or worse.

Tilley beamed. "Would you like to see them? Of course, we can't show you everything just yet, but..." She rummaged in a rucksack by her feet and pulled out an old stained envelope. She emptied the contents in her lap and selected two color photographs. "Here, have a look at these," she said while passing them to Andi.

Marc rose and moved to stand behind Andi and looked over her shoulder. The first photograph showed a collection of old stone tools. Andi nodded noncommittally and turned to the second one. She gasped. "It's beautiful."

The picture showed crude paintings of animals long forgotten. The colors of the paintings looked like they were applied recently, seemingly leaping off the picture.

Bertie beamed. "Yes. Those ancient artists captured the essence of the beast, didn't they? It is almost identical in style to other cave paintings from France and Germany. There were others of course but this horse was perhaps the best preserved."

"Can you be sure it's genuine?" Marc asked with a sceptical crease in his forehead. "I mean, could it be a recent copy or even an Aboriginal painting?"

"Not a chance, old boy," Bertie chortled with a bray and a snort, while rubbing his hands together and hopping from leg to leg in excitement. "Aboriginal paintings are totally different in form and, besides, we have the first results back from the lab." He dug in his pocket and waved a piece of paper at them. "Carbon-14 tests on charcoal fragments in the black pigment. Twenty-five thousand years old!"

"And the clincher is the horse is totally unknown in Aboriginal art until the first white settlers arrived here only two hundred years ago," added Tilley. "So what do you think?"

Andi shook her head, looking at the two smiling archaeologists. "I think it's very convincing."

Marc pursed his lips. "Have you gotten any feedback from other scientists in the field?"

"Too early, old chap. We have yet to publish," Bertie said while stiffening his back and glaring down through ragged, thick eyebrows.

"We sent it to Nature magazine," grated Tilley, "but the sods rejected it out of hand. Sent it off for review and it was declined. Bloody bigoted, narrow-minded imbeciles." She sniffed then added, "I think we can get it in one of the European journals though."

"Do you have any other evidence?" Marc asked while avoiding Bertie's irritated stare.

"Good lord, yes, old boy! You don't think we'd storm the ramparts of accepted theory with only a few tools and paintings do you?" Bertie bellowed. He waved a hand around the site and added, "We've got a fabulous burial site with fragments of a skeleton and something else that vaguely resembles a humanoid, but we aren't sure of that one just yet. Interesting thing is it's obviously a Neanderthal burial, it appears to be a modern-type skeleton." He twirled his moustache with one hand while scratching the top of his head with the other. Then he noticed his wife's look of growing impatience. "Ah, yes, well, there must be a good reason for it. Points toward a mixing of the cultures, what?" Bertie glanced up at the sky. "Getting a bit late in the day, but if you come back tomorrow morning, I'd be delighted to show you round our dig."

Tilley smiled at her husband and got to her feet. She smiled in turn at Andi and Marc. "Are you staying nearby, dears, or did you two drive up from Cairns?"

Andi rose from her chair and gestured up the trail. "We have a camper van up on the road. We thought we might spend a few days hiking around here."

"Splendid. How about coming over for a nosh tonight?"

Marc looked puzzled. "A nosh?"

Tilley grinned. "Sorry. I keep forgetting about the differences in language between you Yanks and we Brits." She chuckled. "I meant a meal. How about I come and collect you when dinner is ready? Probably about sevenish."

After handshakes all round, Bertie ducked back into the bush and Tilley went into the tent to gather supplies. Andi and Marc set off back to their camper. After they clambered over the fence at the end of the road, Marc turned to Andi. "I was really looking forward to a few quiet days with you, babe."

"There's always the nights," she responded with a sultry smile. But before Marc could respond in kind, her smile faded. "Their camp is directly on the coordinates Sam sent. I wonder if she knew those two would be there? I wish I could get in touch with her and be sure."

Marc took her hand and said, "Look, James and Sam know what they're doing. If they wanted us to make sure the site was empty, they would have made it clear and they didn't." He drew her close. "Now, can we get back to our camper and maybe share the shower for an hour or two before we have to go entertain the geriatrics?"

Andi poked his side then walked briskly toward the camper, leaving Marc protesting at her sneak attack. She kept going and it didn't take him long to catch up. They both wore smiles of anticipation.

Chapter Four

Dr. Xanatuo ambled into the cavern at the head of a line of small grey technicians. He stopped in front of the group of humans gathered near the doorway, signalling for the technicians to proceed. His eyes, large and dark without a trace of white, regarded the group stolidly; his thin, almost lipless mouth was held in a tight line. After a moment of mental preparation, he inspected then addressed the group.

"Good, I sssee you are almost all here. We must prepare you for departure," he stated after scanning the cavern.

"The girl will be here in a few moments, good doctor." Garagh stepped to the front of the group. "Perhaps while we wait I might address the party?" he asked with a small bow of his head.

The grey scientist bobbed his massive head and backed away.

Garagh regarded the five people who were attentively watching him. "We are about to set out on an adventure into the unknown. What we must not forget is the serious side to our venture. Dr. Hay and his wife Samantha," he gestured at them, "will be searching for their child Gaia. Ernie and myself," he gestured toward the old Aboriginal man standing quietly behind the other four, "will be seeking to resolve the divergence in the space-time realities the doctor spoke to you about."

James smiled. "I think we are all aware of the gravity of our journey, Garagh."

"Indeed," agreed Nathan, drawing nods from Ratana and Sam, "we are all going into this with our eyes open."

Garagh sighed. "I know, my friends. All of this was discussed, but now that we are on the threshold, so to speak, I have some doubts. To all intents and purposes, we will be entering a primitive world filled with dangers and uncertainty. I have, of course, first-hand knowledge of the time, and my good friend Ernie, though through other avenues, is also intimately familiar with the time period of events that will unfold before us."

James took a deep breath and noisily exhaled it in disbelief. "First-hand, Garagh? We're talking about thirty thousand years!"

"That is so, my friend. I told you this before. Have you forgotten?"

James shook his head. "I think I assumed it was a figure of speech.

How could you have lived that long?"

"In the first place, my friend, I am not a human such as yourself. My Neanderthal people were always long-lived. Added to this are the life-force energies from those we term the 'Others'. The result is an extraordinarily extended lifespan."

Ernie coughed gently and interposed in a deep, gentle voice, "Perhaps we could leave this discussion for another time. We must prepare for our journey. We don't have time to discuss any of this right now, mate."

"Of course, Wandjina." Garagh bowed slightly to Ernie and then turned back to the others. "Suffice to say the members of our party were chosen for specific purposes. James and Samantha will search for their daughter, Wandjina will intercede with any Aboriginal tribes we come across and I will translate when we make contact with any Neanderthal people."

"What about myself and Ratana, mate?" inquired Nathan.

"Wandjina must be accompanied by servants in order to do what he is to do. You will act as his aides and protectors. His actions will be crucial to our success and so will yours." He gestured at the other member of the group who was almost invisible against the mottled brown of the cavern wall. "Wulgu here will be our main protector."

Every eye turned to the gigantic hairy figure standing immobile and silent behind Garagh's stocky body.

The yowie, covered from head to toe in a silky pelt of brown hair, stood nearly ten feet tall and was built like a gorilla, with huge arms and a slightly hunched back. His huge head, with its imposing sagittal crest, lent a menacing look of bestiality, belied by the unmistakable glow of intelligence within gentle brown eyes. A soft voice rippled across the minds of the humans. *It will be my pleasure to be of service to my human friends.*

"All of you have come across yowies before," went on Garagh. "They have proved themselves invaluable companions. We are fortunate Wulgu volunteered for this task."

It is too good an opportunity to miss; to actually see a time before my kind were created. The voice in their minds radiated amusement and eagerness. *Besides, Rima is my promised mate and I wish to find her.*

"Rima? Who is Rima?" Sam asked while searching Garagh and Wulgu's faces for a clue.

"You know her as Cindy." Garagh explained.

Sam smiled at Wulgu. "When we find my daughter, I am sure we will find Cin...Rima, too."

I will find her, Wulgu responded. His thoughts were tinged with something Sam couldn't recognize but suspected was passion.

"On the matter of protection," Nathan interjected. "Shouldn't we be carrying firearms of some sort? I mean, in case we meet a dinosaur or something."

James grinned. "It's only thirty thousand years, mate. No dinos, only mammals and the odd croc or two."

Garagh nodded. "We gave the matter a great deal of thought. We will only be back there for a few days and we feel Ernie and Wulgu will be able to protect us against any foreseeable danger. We run the risk of compounding the error that led to this reality split if we resort to violence to solve petty problems."

Garagh paused. Before anyone could form another question, he turned toward the doorway and said, "The remaining members of our party have arrived."

A young Aboriginal man entered the cavern, guiding a young girl by the elbow. Everyone openly stared at the pair. The contrast between the two figures was extreme. The young man was a full-blooded Aboriginal, dressed in the casual attire of young city people—tee shirt, sneakers and jeans. The girl was white, so white that her flesh seemed transparent, with long, blond hair and pale blue eyes. She was dressed in a pale green dress, full-length and gathered in folds at the waist, emphasizing her petite form.

The movements of the two also contrasted. The man moved smoothly and purposefully, with intelligence and humor radiating from his face. The girl, on the other hand, stumbled at the entrance and nearly fell. Her pale eyes remained fixed and vacant and her face expressionless.

"This young man is Narahdarn and the girl is Shinara." Garagh smiled while he made introductions. "Narahdarn, you have already met Ernie and Nathan. These others are Dr. James Hay, his wife Samantha, and Ratana, wife of Nathan and spirit-talker in her own right."

Narahdarn grinned and lifted a hand in greeting. "Gidday. Great day for a trip, ay?"

His smile was infectious and Sam found herself smiling with genuine humor for the first time in months. "Hello yourself," she said. She turned to Shinara. "Hello, my dear. Welcome to our little group."

Shinara gazed vacantly at Sam, with her mouth slightly open.

Sam turned to Garagh in concern. "Is she all right, Garagh?"

"She is in good physical health, Samantha, but her mind is elsewhere. We cannot reach her consciousness, even by thought."

"Then why is she here? You can't tell me she consented to come."

"That is true, Samantha," continued the Neanderthal elder. "I was given my instructions but not the reasons behind them. She will serve an important function, though exactly what that function is, was not revealed."

James interrupted. "Instructions, Garagh? Who told you what to do? I thought you were basically in charge around here."

Garagh inclined his head in assent. "Essentially, I have that honor.

However, the 'Others' guide us. We accede to their greater intellect and knowledge in all things, my friend."

"Who exactly are these 'Others'? We've all heard of them but nobody talks about them or sees them, that I know of anyway," James asked, remembering the months he'd lived in the complex and how every resident avoided the subject.

"Neither will I, Dr. Hay. Please do not pursue this topic any further. We are instructed to take Shinara with us and Narahdarn will accompany her to protect and guide her," Garagh responded with finality.

"Okay, Garagh. I'll say no more for now, but can you at least tell us who Shinara is? She looks completely human," James grinned, "and there are precious few humans in your organization."

Garagh hesitated then spoke slowly. "She is human." He glanced at Sam then continued. "You are aware that we are searching for a human genetic blueprint that will heal the negative effects of genetic error on this planet?"

Sam remained silent and waited.

Garagh took a deep breath and added, "We think Gaia might be just such a one. However, we are told something is missing in her, something present in Shinara."

"How can my Gaia and this girl have a similar genetic makeup?" Sam asked, taken aback by the line of discussion about her daughter and not sure why.

"Are you familiar with the concept of 'missing time'?" Garagh asked, lifting one thick eyebrow.

Every person in the cavern froze, aware that Garagh was telling them something of importance, something that would alter their circumstances.

"Oh shit." James turned away, running his fingers through his hair. He turned back, anger erupting on his whitening face. "If you are saying what I think you are saying, we were used, even abused."

"When you were a young man, Dr. Hay, you were taken by the 'Others' and a sample of your DNA excised."

When James unconsciously reached for the scar on his right shoulder blade, Garagh nodded. "Yes, the small triangular scar beneath your shoulder. Your genetic potentialities came to our attention then. Samantha came later, in the Glass House Mountains. She was abducted and an egg removed. This is a standard procedure for females. Then we made an exciting discovery. Your two DNA profiles matched those we'd been searching millennia for. We altered the egg slightly, fertilized it with artificial sperm raised from James's cells and gestated it *in vitro*."

"Garagh, this is not the time or place for thisss," Doctor Xanatuo rasped from the doorway. "Besidesss, these humans have no need to know our plansss or our reasons for doing what we do. All they need know isss we have worked for centuries to sssave them," he added with a cold, unemotional tone of voice.

Garagh held up his hand without turning around to see the doctor. "You are wrong, Doctor. They have every right to know the entire story. Please refrain from interrupting me again."

The doctor backed further from the room until he stood almost outside the door. Slipping his long-fingered hands into the billowing sleeves of his robe, he adopted a bland expression and stared at the floor.

Ratana and Nathan glanced at each other then at James and Sam with a look of unease.

James took two steps toward Garagh then stopped. "You didn't trust us to tell us? After all we've been through?"

Garagh sighed deeply. "It was not my decision. We had not met, nor did I think we would ever meet, let alone become close. Perhaps under other circumstances…"

Sam looked horrified. "You tampered with us?" She stared at James. "Then James…and I…?"

"Yes," said Garagh calmly. You are both the true parents of Shinara." His thick hand swept toward the young girl who showed no sign of understanding what was being said about her.

"What?" James blurted.

"You are both the true genetic parents of Gaia and Shinara, though there was a small addition of Neanderthal genetic information and a gene complex that the 'Others' gave us to insert into Shinara's gene code."

Sam moved closer to her husband and clung to him while staring in disbelief at the girl. Noting that she was shaking, James looked around the room and guided Sam to a chair against the far wall. Ratana followed and knelt beside her, stroking her arm while closely watching James as he moved back toward Garagh.

Suddenly, Shinara showed signs of life for the first time. She started singing softly to herself, a high-pitched wordless chant. Narahdarn moved to her in astonishment, touching her face and whispering to her. After a few moments, she lapsed back into silence but the interruption served to calm James's rage, though his anger remained unabated.

"Damn you! You had no right to manipulate us that way," James growled at Garagh then at Doctor Xanatuo, who stood like a statute beside the entryway.

"I am sorry, dear friend. I can only repeat that at the time I was acting on instructions and I knew neither one of you. Perhaps I should not have told you at all, but your curiosity concerning this girl is natural and sooner or later the truth would have emerged."

Sam wiped her eyes with a tissue and glared at Garagh. "I don't believe you," she said flatly. "Gaia is only a baby and this girl must be a teenager. How could they possibly be sisters conceived at the same time?"

"They came from two fertilized eggs by the same parents. Genetic manipulation preceded the use of an artificial womb, then implantation in a foster mother. We accelerated the growth of Shinara after she was born. She is only six months old chronologically but has the body of a twelve-year-old girl. After all, we could not take a baby with us into the distant past. Even this girl is too young. We could have preferred an adult woman, but...," Garagh shrugged. "We ran out of time."

"And all this for the greater purpose of your bosses." The sarcasm and hurt in James' voice was palpable. "I hope like hell you can forgive yourselves, because I'm not sure I can. If it wasn't for the fact that your venture is the only way we can rescue Gaia, I'd tell you just what you can do with your secret schemes and invasive actions." He turned away in disgust and returned to his wife's side. Turning his back on the uneasy group, he kneeled beside Sam and embraced her.

Garagh stood silently, his head on his chest. "I am justly rebuked. I feel the weight of my responsibilities ever more heavily with the passing of the centuries." He drew in a deep breath, let it out slowly then raised his face with a deliberate straightening of his back. "Dr. Xanatuo, I think it is time for you to send us on our way. In spite of our separate agendas and feelings, we still have a critical mission to accomplish."

The doctor slipped his hands out of his sleeves, straightened his back as well and nodded his great head in acceptance.

Chapter Five

Shadows clung heavily to the rocks and trees of the north Australian night. Though the evening was still and hot beneath a waxing moon, the lone man watched in fascination while darkness flickered and moved in the stillness. The forest was silent around him, the normal cacophony of insect and animal absent. The man paused, concentrating, feeling the fear hanging over the site, savoring it, knowing he was part of the fear.

A dry, slithering sound that reminded him of snake scales rasping on bark insinuated itself into his consciousness. The noise rose and fell, slowly becoming syllabic, until, eventually, he could make out words.

So, you have come at last. Why?

The man considered his answer. "You know why," he said slowly. "Your kind has remained with me ever since we used the Vox Dei machine to free you from your world. I kept my part of the bargain but you have not kept yours."

Yes. Your desire for power is unabated.

"Can you still offer me the power over my world you promised or am I wasting my time?"

We can. There is a danger, though.

"Oh? To you or to me? I thought nothing could hurt your kind, and if you kill me, you will never stop the girl. So, what danger could there be?"

Very little, but unmaking us would destroy us.

"You talk in riddles. Explain yourself."

Our foes seek to unmake our world. Should they do so, we are unmade also.

"So stop them." The man grinned. "Or is it that you cannot, and need more of my help?"

Yesss.

The man laughed out loud, the sudden noise sending echoes clattering amid the silence of the forest. He sat down on a fallen log, still chuckling as the shadows writhed and the dry rustling reached a crescendo. At length, he reached into his pocket for a cigarette and sat quietly smoking until the anger around him subsided.

We need each other, Ehrich, whispered the voice.

"Yes, I think we do. What do you want me to do this time?"

Our foes have found a way to return to the origins of our world and this world. They plan to destroy us by merging our worlds.

"How do you know this? I can't imagine them sharing these plans with you."

One of our kind still resides within one of the foe. When his brothers were cast out he remained. He has not been detected and he communes with us. They cannot keep their plans from us as long as our brother is watching.

"Interesting. Are you sure he is truly undetected? After all, I can feel the presence of you in myself."

Quite sure. We wish you to feel our presence.

The voice paused for several minutes. Ehrich waited patiently, secretly smug in the knowledge that the shadows would have to do things his way this time or be destroyed.

They will return to the origin very soon. The one who is hidden will provide the means for us to follow. We have no mass and will not affect their process. But we also have no form or structure. We need you to physically work our will on them.

"As you say, I'm very physical." Ehrich smiled, flexing his arms. "Won't my mass affect their machine?"

Yes. Added mass will affect the timing of their arrival. That is of no concern to us. We will be there to stop them and that is all that matters. They must be stopped. We need you to travel with them.

Ehrich contemplated the idea while lighting up another cigarette. He smoked quietly for a few minutes then, reaching a decision, ground the stub beneath his heel. "Very well, but I will need some guarantees. After all, you failed last time and I lost everything." He sneered at the rundown cabin nestled in the trees. "My exile does not sit well with me. I miss the power and money I had. So, I demand part of my reward now and guarantees of more to come."

You shall have what you ask.

Ehrich flashed an evil grin. "Good. The one you keep inside me can give me longer life, greater strength and no pain. I demand these things now." His grin broadened. "Later, I want power over the humans after you seize their world. I want to be absolute ruler over them. Absolute. Is that clear?"

It shall be so.

"Then we have a deal," Ehrich smirked.

The shadows moved and writhed through the trees. A feeling of wild excitement and cruel joy pervaded the atmosphere. Closer and closer they whirled to the man, then fell on him with a rushing, roaring sound.

Ehrich collapsed to the ground with a hoarse cry. "You gave your word!"

The sound of dry laughter echoed sibilantly in the night.

Chapter Six

"Pleassse remain outside the painted circle unlesss I instruct you otherwise."

Dr. Xanatuo turned back to the scurrying grey technicians, urging them to hurry. Small squeaks and grunts escaped their otherwise silent mouths as heavy equipment was pushed into place around the red-painted circle in the centre of the cavern. The small group of humans and the yowie stepped back to avoid their efforts.

Thick cables snaked across the floor. Pipes, smoking in the chill air, dropped flakes of white hoarfrost as liquid helium surged through them. A low humming sound that vibrated the organs within the humans' bodies rose and fell and the raw, chemical scent of ozone stung their nostrils.

"You will travel in two groupsss," hissed Xanatuo. "The first will act as a sssecurity unit. Garagh, Wandjina, Nathan and Wulgu will be in the first group. The sssecond group will be Dr. Hay, Sssamantha, Ratana, Narahdarn and Shinara. Both groupsss will have essential sssupplies, but, of necessssity, these were kept to a minimum. You will have knives and machetes but no killing weaponsss. You must be careful to sssselectively impact the environment." He gestured at the weight scales near one wall, where the greys were still unloading rucksacks and footwear. "Everything was weighed most carefully. As you know, massss and time are related. The amount of energy required to sssend you back was calculated based on your known massss. We are certain you will arrive within sssix months sssubjective time of the original event."

"A lot can happen in six months," said Sam quietly. "I know Cindy would guard Gaia with her life, but they could have moved anywhere in that time. Can't you send us back closer to the time they arrived?"

"The energy required increasesss as we get closer to the event, lady. We are already using every gigawatt we can muster." Xanatuo gave a high-pitched warbling cry that took Sam a moment to realize was laughter. "Indeed, we have connected to the local sssupply grid. We expect to black out partsss of Brisbane city when we sssend you off."

Sam gave a wry smile and nodded, disappointed and anxious.

Xanatuo continued. "You will feel sssome disorientation during the transfer. Do not be concerned—it should passss within a few minutesss. There will also be sssome interesting visual phenomena. Essentially, your three-dimensional bodiesss will become two-dimensional, then one and then, finally, you will effectively cease to exist in thisss universe. There will be a sssense of motion along the surfacesss of the bubble-universesss also. It might be sssensible to close your eyesss during the transfer unlesss you are curiousss." He warbled in a low, mournful tone. "I truly wish I could accompany you."

Garagh stepped up to Dr. Xanatuo and grasped his thin arm. "It is far more important that we can leave our safety in your hands, old friend."

Xanatuo's eyes glinted moistly. He nodded to the technicians, who signalled to him that the preparations were complete. "It isss time," he whispered.

The small greys bustled up, pushing the final power cable into the outlet in the outer ring of the painted circle. Ernie and Nathan took their places and Wulgu ambled over, putting a gigantic hairy hand on each of them.

Garagh looked around the cavern a last time, nodded, and joined them. "I shall see you in a very short while," he said to the others, who stood beside the computer console where Xanatuo was adjusting the settings.

Dr. Xanatuo flicked his long fingers rapidly over the keyboard, while closely watching glowing lines marching across a giant screen beside him. Another set of lines joined the first, then another. The lines grew closer, the humming sound grew higher in pitch and the chemical scent in the air grew stronger.

Sam watched as the lines merged on the screen. The lights flickered and she heard a gasp from Ratana beside her. She looked around and gave a small cry herself. The roof of the cavern was descending, pressing down on them. At the same time, the cavern walls were slowly receding, distorting. The figures in the centre of the circle wavered, as if viewed through a very thick lens. Sam grasped James's arm and glanced at his face. He was gazing around him in obvious fascination.

Always the scientist, she thought.

She smiled and turned back just in time to see the figures of her friends flatten beyond recognition. There was a sudden snapping sound and the disc of distorted air instantly contracted into a small glowing ball. Rapidly, it shrank, though she could not be sure whether it decreased in size or receded from her. There was a bright flash of light and the cavern returned to normal, except for the empty circle in front of her.

"Ye gods and little fishes," breathed James. "That was some show!"

Already, the greys were hauling more rucksacks into the centre circle. James took Sam's hand and walked forward. Ratana followed. Narahdarn took Shinara's arm and whispered to her. She gazed blankly at him and, stumbling, joined the others in the circle.

Xanatuo raised a hand. "May the force be with you," he solemnly intoned before breaking down with high warbling laughter.

"Silly bugger," growled James. "He's been watching too many movies."

"May you have good fortune on your venture," continued the grey scientist, becoming serious again. "It hasss been a privilege to know you, even for sssuch a ssshort time." He turned back to his keyboard.

A great silence descended over the group, the sound of the machinery falling away.

Sam turned to James in concern. "What's happening?" she tried to say, but she could not hear herself. She panicked and tugged his arm, yelling in her mind.

What's wrong? Why has everything stopped?

James hugged her. *Hush, darling. It's the process. Look about you.*

Sam looked around. James and the others looked normal but the cavern was being pushed and pulled out of shape. While she watched, the figures of the tiny greys stretched and grew until they towered over her. Abruptly, they disappeared into a pearly glow that surrounded the group and she felt herself being insistently tugged in all directions at once. The light increased and her insides lurched. She felt herself in motion, sliding with ever-increasing speed down a slippery slope.

The sense of motion increased. There was a bump, though none of them moved, darkness flitted above them and Sam caught sight of running figures, distorted out of all recognition. Someone crashed into her and she sprawled over the baggage. Waves of nausea hit her and the light faded into blackness.

෨෧

Andi examined her eyes in the mirror while deftly touching up her makeup. Marc moved behind her, putting his hands on her shoulders. Bending down, he flicked his tongue along the rim of her right ear. "Let's not go tonight," he whispered.

Andi laughed and moved her head away. "We have to, silly. Besides, Tilley or Bertie will be here soon. Do you want them to find us hiding inside like teenagers?"

Marc dropped his hands and chuckled. "Yeah, you're probably right. Later then. At least we don't have to stay too long."

Andi rose and pulled Sam's letter out of a drawer in the little kitchenette of the camper van. She opened it and scanned the contents. Frowning at the short message her sister sent her, she said, "I'm worried, Marc. Sam made it quite clear that we were to be close to the coordinates she marked but not to camp on them. The Simpsons have set up their camp exactly on the site."

"I wouldn't worry about it too much, babe. I mean, what can happen?" Marc grinned. "They'll probably just get an up-close and personal look at a yowie or some other monster."

"I wonder if we ought to try and persuade them to move their camp to another location?"

A loud, insistent tapping on the driver's side door and Tilley's booming voice interrupted them. "Are you in there, Andi...Marc? It's me, Tilley."

"Hi, Tilley," called out Andi. "We're in the back. We'll be right out."

Andi opened the door with a quick "Behave!" to Marc and stepped outside. Marc grabbed a flashlight and followed, plastering a smile on his face. When Tilley came around the van, Andi greeted her with a smile. "We're ready," she said, hoping Marc would behave himself.

"Hello, my dears. It's a lovely night isn't it?" Tilley smiled at the two then grabbed Andi by the hand and started walking toward the trail, waving the beam of a flashlight in front of her. "The radio said there are some electrical storms to the north but we should miss them here," she babbled. "Look at those lovely stars. I always think eating out under the stars is such fun, don't you, dear?"

Andi laughed. "Yes, it's a lovely warm night. I thought your husband might come to collect us."

"One cannot disturb the chef when he is creating, love. Terribly bad manners, you know. And, my Bertie takes great pride in his curries...I hope you both like curries?" she added anxiously.

"I'm not sure I know what they are, Tilley. I've heard the term but I've never eaten one."

"I have," Marc responded. "I was introduced to them when I was on assignment in India a few years back. They're fabulous when made correctly."

"Then I think you'll like Bertie's. He tries to use authentic ingredients whenever he can and there's a wonderful little shop in Cairns that has literally everything you can think of for international cooking."

Marc chuckled. "Funny how the Brits love a good curry." He directed a quick thought to Andi. *Maybe the evening won't be a total loss after all.*

The trio carefully scrambled down the slope, while the light from the flashlights swung wildly as they jumped over stones and roots. Reaching flatter ground, they moved off with Tilley leading and Marc bringing up the rear, sharing a flashlight with Andi.

Tilley prattled on while they walked down the trail. "Actually, we are using almost the last of our stores with the curry. We'll have to pop into town to pick up some more tomorrow. I can't say I'll be sorry to stay in a motel for a night or two." She laughed loudly. "God knows I need a good hot bath." She hesitated, head cocked to one side for a moment before resuming. "Bertie loves the wilderness areas. If he had his way we'd stay out here permanently, fossicking around in those old caves and hills...can you hear something?"

Tilley stopped dead in her tracks so suddenly Andi and Marc bumped into her. "What the hell...?" Marc exclaimed, almost dropping his flashlight.

"Shh! Can you hear a sort of buzzing? A faint crackling?" Tilley asked, her head slowly moving from side to side, like a radar dish seeking a source of sound.

Andi mimicked Tilley's head movements while gripping Marc's arm. "I think so. Can you tell where it's coming from?" She felt a shiver run up her back. "It's all around us."

Marc sniffed loudly. "It smells like something is burning." He sniggered. "Hope it's not the curry."

Andi shook her head. "That's not food burning, that's electrical. I've smelled it around high voltage lines. Ozone."

Abruptly, there was a bright flash of light that illuminated the scrub around them in a graphic contrast to the lack of color and light surrounding the area. Close on the heels of the light came a cry, abruptly cut off, and a thin clap of sound, like a door slamming.

A wordless cry erupted from Tilley. She plunged forward, bursting into the clearing. "Bertie! Bertie! Where are you?" she yelled, shining her flashlight wildly around, bringing various trees and objects momentarily into sharp focus in a drunken pattern.

In the circle of yellow light thrown off by a kerosene lantern, the only objects in view were the tent, two folding chairs and the semi-circle of stones. There was no sign of Bertie or his pot of curry. Tilley scurried around the clearing, ripping open the tent flap, crashing through the bushes, while calling out to her husband in a voice that became increasingly distraught.

Andi stood at the edge of the clearing, peering anxiously around and shining the flashlight in Tilley's direction.

"Perhaps it was just lightning," muttered Marc while he slowly moved toward the tent and shined his light into the thick brush behind it.

"I don't think so. Look at the sky, it's completely clear." Andi shivered. "I've got a nasty feeling it's got something to do with Sam's letter."

Tilley abruptly ceased her frantic searching and stood looking down at the semi-circle of stones. "Where's the bloody fireplace gone?" she wondered. "Bertie wouldn't have taken it with him, would he?"

Andi stood wordlessly just inside the circle of light from the lantern, uncertain whether she should say anything. Marc looked around him uneasily. "I can hear that buzzing again. I think we should leave." He raised his voice. "Tilley, come away from there. I think something..."

The clearing lit up like a flash grenade had gone off. For an instant, Andi thought she saw a group of people standing around Tilley then, as the darkness crashed in around her, she stood blinking with multicolored afterglows drifting in front of her eyes and obscuring her vision. When her vision cleared, the clearing was empty, except for the tent, two folding chairs, a semi-circle of stones and her husband, who sported the stunned expression of a holocaust survivor. The two archaeologists had disappeared as if they never existed.

Chapter Seven

Sam woke to utter confusion and dim images of creatures moving around her. She was propped up against a mossy tree trunk, with rough bark digging painful grooves into her back. She blinked, trying to clear her vision. She became aware that someone or something was rubbing her right hand. Finally focusing her eyes, she recognized James's face and a worried looking Ratana kneeling beside him. Sam smiled weakly, the smile fading when she looked beyond them at a black night lit by an occasional flash of lightning. The sound of drumming rain, the splash of water on a soaked ground and the tearing sound of raindrops on dense vegetation slowly seeped into her consciousness, along with the discomfort of damp clothing against her skin. She slowly became aware of other people moving around her and the sound of cries and a fierce argument.

Sam shivered in the cool air, her clothes damp on her body despite the shielding effects of the jungle canopy above her. "What happened?" she croaked.

"Lie still, love. At least we arrived safely." James hesitated. "Something happened though. We're not sure exactly what, but we seem to have picked up a couple of hitchhikers and…we can't find Garagh."

"Hitchhikers? Garagh? What are you talking about?" Sam grabbed James's hand and struggled to her feet. She pushed back her damp hair and peered into the darkness. "What's all the arguing about?" She raised her voice over the thunder of the tropical downpour. "Ernie, Garagh! What's going on?"

Nathan appeared out of the rain, soaked to the skin but grinning. "Hi, Sam. Good to see you're okay. As soon as this flamin' rain stops…ah, that's better." As he spoke the torrential rain eased to drizzle, then abruptly ceased. Patters of water still fell from the foliage, but the temperature began to rise almost immediately.

Ratana moved to Nathan's side and silently watched the figures across a small clearing arguing.

"Now, let's see about some light." Nathan banged the flashlight he held against his palm. It flickered then came on, throwing dancing shadows through the rainforest. He swept the beam around the small clearing. "I think what we all need is to dry out and get some food in us."

James nodded. "Sensible suggestion. It's amazing how even a small unexpected setback can totally alter one's perceptions." He rubbed his hands together. "Have we got the makings of a fire?"

Sam glanced at him in exasperation. "What the hell is going on over there, James? Where are we and what is happening?"

A dark figure detached itself from the trees and glided across the clearing toward the group. Sam gasped, then relaxed when Ernie's dark, rugged face caught the beam of the flashlight. "The wood is too wet for a normal fire, but I will see what I can do. There are matters to discuss and we cannot do this while our bodies cry out their discomfort." He rummaged in his backpack and pulled out a packet of fire-starters and a cigarette lighter. "Technology will have to lend a hand tonight." He smiled, his teeth gleaming white in the blackness. "We will discuss our situation and what we need to do now after we recover from that harrowing transport." He glanced up at Sam, imperceptibly acknowledging her anxiety with a look that promised she'd get her answers in good time.

Sam sighed and waited, watching the others scramble around the clearing and gather their packs under the shelter of the trees where she stood.

Quickly, Nathan and James found a few fallen branches and pieces of deadwood. The fuel was soaked, dripping water. James broke open a piece of the dead wood to feel the interior. "Too wet to fire," he muttered. "I'm not sure you are going to have much success with this, Ernie."

The old Aboriginal took the wood with a smile and, hunkering down, arranged it in a small pile. He inserted a couple of fire-starters among the twigs and lit them. They flickered with a low blue and yellow flame that sputtered against the wet wood. He held his hands over the flame, muttering. Gradually, the flame strengthened, then abruptly, the wood caught light, bursting into a miniature bonfire.

Within minutes, after the addition of more branches, the fire settled down into a steady blaze and sent out waves of heat. The flames lit the clearing with a warm glow, revealing ten figures.

Sam ran her gaze over the figures, mentally counting off the names of the group. "Ten?" she whispered. "There should only be nine. Where's Garagh? And who are they?" She pointed at two bedraggled people, a man and a woman, in khaki and standing shivering under Wulgu's withering glare. The man clutched a metal container in one hand and the hand of the woman in the other. The woman was staring around with a stunned look on her face.

"Our hitchhikers," Ratana replied with a note of puzzlement in her voice.

Ernie gestured to the fire. "Come, everyone. We must talk."

Slowly they gathered around the fire, pulling up some old mossy logs to sit on. Shinara stumbled into the firelight, with Narahdarn still guiding her. Wulgu rumbled menacingly and pushed the two strangers forward.

The tall, thin, elderly man with a huge handlebar moustache obscuring half his face turned angrily toward the huge creature. "Cease and desist, whatever you are. If you haven't the manners to treat a lady properly, I will have to teach you myself." He drew himself up and stared straight ahead at Wulgu's broad hairy chest.

The woman, nearly as broad as she was tall, and only as tall as the man's chest, clung to his arm. "Now, Bertie," she quavered. "I can look after myself. Don't antagonize it." She nervously glanced up at the creature that refused to budge from his position next to them. "I don't think it is intimidated, love." She shivered while her husband continued to glare up at the creature's wide face.

Wulgu rumbled again and Sam caught a hint of amusement when the yowie spoke to Ernie. *Does he wish to fight me?*

Leave us for a few moments, my friend. You are frightening them, Ernie replied.

Wulgu stepped backward into the shadows of the rainforest and vanished. The tall man shook the sleeves of his bush jacket out, gave a low "Harrumph!" of scorn and turned back to the group around the fire, with one arm circled protectively around the woman's shoulders.

James stepped forward with a smile and a welcoming hand thrust toward the stranger. "My name is Dr. James Hay."

The man lifted one eyebrow. The woman nudged him in the ribs. He sighed. "I am Dr. Bertrand Simpson, and this dear lady is my wife, Dr. Tilley Simpson." He looked around the group curiously. "Now, if you would be so kind as to tell us where the devil we are and how we got here?"

James frowned. "We were sort of hoping you could tell us."

Sam moved over to James's side. "Hello," she said. "I'm Samantha, James's wife. Whatever happened, you are welcome." She gestured to the fire with a smile. "Look, come and sit by the fire. We'll see if we can rustle up a bit of food and drink and see if we can sort this all out. I have a few hundred questions myself." She shot a look at her husband then at Ernie, who squatted next to the fire, ignoring the rest of them.

Tilley smiled hesitantly in return. "Thank you, Samantha. I must admit I'm feeling a bit faint. One moment I was entertaining guests, then a flash of light and Bertie disappears and the next moment I find myself in the grip of some horrible monster." She looked around apprehensively. "Or did I imagine that part?"

Sam took Tilley by the hand and guided her to a seat near the fire. "No, you didn't imagine it. His name is Wulgu and he is a friend."

Tilley's eyes grew wide. "It has a name? What is it?"

Ratana sat down on the other side of Tilley and introduced herself. "Wulgu is a yowie. You have probably heard of Bigfoot from America. Well, my friend, a yowie is a sort of Australian Bigfoot. He's intelligent and has a society and culture of his own. He's a friend and protector."

Bertie stood behind his wife, hovering over her like a bodyguard protecting a valued celebrity. "Yes, we know of these mythical creatures. Or, should I say, these creatures everyone thought were mere myths?" He twirled his moustache and looked thoughtfully at the fire. "Seems a lot of what we thought in the scientific community is wrong."

Ernie held up a hand to attract everyone's attention. "I think we should all be introduced first." He turned to Bertie. "My name is Ernie. Dr. James and Samantha have already introduced themselves. The young lady by your wife is Ratana, who in turn is married to my assistant here, Nathan. Our friend Wulgu you have met." He grinned broadly. "You really startled him when you stood up to him. Not many people would care to do that." Adopting a more serious expression, he went on. "As the others have already pointed out, Wulgu is here for our protection. He is only dangerous to those who would seek to harm us. Now, to complete the introductions…this young man is Narahdarn of the Euahlayi tribe and his young ward is Shinara, daughter of James and Sam."

Bertie nodded gravely at each person in turn then, when Ernie finished speaking, he said, "It is a pleasure to make your acquaintance." He looked hard at Ernie's now-solemn face. "I trust you will now explain the circumstances under which we find ourselves in your company."

"In a moment, Dr. Simpson. James, how about finding us something to eat?"

James sat down and rifled through his backpack and Nathan's. "I've already got a pot of coffee on the fire. Not much in the way of food though, I'm afraid. We will be living off the land as much as possible." He held up a loaf of bread and a big block of Australian cheddar. "Sandwiches anyone?"

Bertie coughed and held up the billycan in his hand. "Perhaps I may be allowed to offer some hospitality myself." He set the pot down by the fire and lifted the lid. "A rather nice beef curry, if I do say so myself. Actually more of a curry-stew as I had to make do with what was on hand, but it'll warm us up." He sat back, looking very pleased with himself while he twirled the ends of his moustache.

James leaned over and sniffed the contents. "A curry," he breathed. He took a spoon from his pack, dipped it into the pot, and tasted it. "And a corker at that." He grinned at Bertie. "You beaut. That'll go down a treat."

Bertie grinned. "I say, old man, you speak like a Brit. Are you one of her majesty's servants?"

James chuckled. "In a way, mate, I'm from Australia."

Before Bertie had a chance to respond, Nathan produced some tin plates and some spoons from his pack, dished out a heaped portion for everyone and passed the plates around. The bread was passed around and for several minutes, the only sound was the crackling of the flames, the clink of spoons against plates and the occasional gasp from Sam and Nathan when they dived for their water bottles.

Shinara accepted only one spoon of curry before spitting it out and throwing her plate to one side. She sat absently chewing on some bread and cheese as the others ate.

Narahdarn shook his head. "What a waste of good tucker, eh?"

Bertie looked up for a moment, catching Ernie's attention. "What about the big chap? What was his name, Wulgu? Won't he want something to eat?"

Ernie looked off into the night and sat silent for a few moments. "He will eat only vegetation. He will find what he needs."

Bertie looked at him quizzically. "You looked for all the world as if you were talking to the blighter."

Ernie smiled and turned back to his meal.

The last of the bread was used to mop up the gravy and the plates were pushed aside with grunts of contentment. Mugs of coffee were passed around and the adventurers sat back amid clouds of steam from their drying clothes.

"Damn good show, what?" said Bertie. "Now, I think it's time for a bit of a chin-wag. Who is going to do the honors?"

Ernie looked at James and nodded. *Be careful what you say, my friend.*

"Well, let me see. Where to start is the problem." James ran his fingers through his dark hair. "First of all, we are effectively about thirty thousand years in the past. We came back here for a specific purpose, namely to find our daughter, who was taken from us by accident. Our friends here agreed to help us."

"Oh, you poor dears," broke in Tilley, putting her arm around Sam.

Bertie twirled his moustache. "Thirty thousand years, eh? Sounds like a bit of a tall tale. Well, I'll return to that later. What I want to know is why my good lady wife and I are here with you. Did you kidnap us for a specific purpose?"

"God, no! I have no idea how you got mixed up in this."

"There is a small clearing on the Atherton Tableland at the end of Dunn's Road near the Chillagoe Caves," said Ernie quietly. "Do you know it, perhaps?"

"Why, yes. We were camped there doing some archaeological investigations."

"Then you were on the site of our transfer. I apologize, Dr. Simpson. We involved you completely by accident. We gave instructions to friends of ours to make sure the site was vacant but apparently they were unable to do so."

"Your friends wouldn't be a young couple by any chance? A young woman with black hair and green eyes and a tall, muscular man?" Bertie asked with a lift of one thick eyebrow.

"My sister Andi," exclaimed Sam, "and her husband Marc. Did you see them? Are they all right?"

"Oh yes, my dear. They were behind me when what ever it was snatched me away. They'd be here too if…oh, you mean…"

Sam smiled at Tilley. "It's just that I haven't seen her for about six months."

"Well, they were looking a bit peaky but I thought it was a result of their travel from America."

"Peaky? I'm not sure…"

James patted Sam on the arm. "Worn out, love. They're fine so stop worrying, okay?"

"They were both in good health when we…er…abruptly left," Tilley said.

"Yes, well, that leads us back to my questions," Bertie said, looking directly at Ernie. "What is going on here? And how did my wife and I come to be here?"

Ernie turned back to Bertie and James, speaking quietly. "All of your questions will be answered in time, my friend," Ernie replied. His gaze said far more.

"Sir, I demand…" Bertie stammered.

Ernie held up a hand, interrupting the man's objection. "Suffice to say, you and your good wife are here for a reason. For the moment, I do not know what that reason is so I cannot answer your question." He lowered his hand and addressed the others. "All of us are here for a reason. We must be patient until we find out what our unique contribution will be to this endeavor."

"You mentioned that our presence is causing you problems," Bertie said with a stiff back. "At least tell us why and how we can help." He scanned the faces of the others. "If we have no choice then we can at least be of help here," he stiffly added.

"Thank you, Dr. Simpson," Ernie said with a smile and a nod. "At the moment, our biggest concern is that it seems our friend Garagh was waylaid in the transfer."

"Who is this Garagh chap anyway?" Bertie asked before sipping his coffee and grimacing at the taste.

"A friend, and an expert in this period of prehistory," replied Ernie tersely. "Dr. Hay, you can confirm that Garagh departed with the rest of us in the first party?'

James nodded. "Yes, your departure was apparently uneventful."

"Then we must assume he was somehow exchanged during the passage through the transfer point." Ernie interrupted Tilley's and

Sam's whispered, but animated conversation. "Dr. Simpson, did you see another man in your campsite after your husband disappeared?"

Tilley ran a hand over her rumpled khaki shirt and flinched at the dampness before replying. "Call me Tilley, please. No, I didn't see anyone else. Not that I was looking of course, I was much more concerned with finding my Bertie." She flashed a loving glance at her husband.

Ernie looked troubled. "Then we are no nearer solving this particular problem. Though there is another question we can know the answer to." He addressed James directly. "You remember Dr. Xanatuo referred to the critical nature of the mass transported? It was important that the mass transferred matched the energy available. Well, we have picked up additional mass."

"How does that affect the transfer?" asked James.

"I cannot be sure but working with the formulae Xanatuo supplied, we arrived considerably later than we expected."

Sam looked at Ernie in consternation. "How much later?"

"It depends on the mass involved. Looking at our additional members," Ernie gestured at Bertie and Tilley, "and allowing for the absence of Garagh, I would say we are some five to seven years later than we planned."

"Oh, God! My baby! What might have happened to her in five years?"

James reached out to rub her shoulder. "Love, let's not panic before we have good reason to believe there's something to worry about." He gazed into her eyes, sending a message of comfort and strength to her.

Sam took a deep breath and let it out slowly. "Yes, you're right." A small, wry smile lifted her lips. "As usual, my love."

"Wulgu reported something curious too," Ernie said while watching the varied reactions of those in front of him. "He says that in the moments after our arrival he thought he saw someone hurrying into the forest. At the time, he thought it was Garagh, but he can detect no sign of him. Did you see anyone, Nathan?"

Nathan shook his head. "I was too sick. The transfer made me feel like throwing up."

"Neither did I, Ernie," Ratana added while dumping out the contents of her cold coffee cup.

"If there was somebody else, then we could be as much as ten or fifteen years later." Ernie shrugged. "I am sorry, Samantha. There is no way we can be certain." He looked sympathetically at her. "We know for a fact Gaia survived into at least youth, from the rock paintings." Ernie glanced at Bertie. "Her…companion will have protected her, you may be sure."

James stood, helping Sam to her feet. "Then we must begin the search at first light. I suggest we all get some sleep."

Chapter Eight

Drumming rain fell on the small Aboriginal village, extinguishing the night fires and turning the rich red volcanic soil into rivers of mud. Gaia lay awake on a bed of mosses and ferns beneath a thickly woven thatch of Pandanus leaves, listening to the rain and trying to remember her dream. Occasional flashes of distant lightning lit up the inside of the shelter, revealing puddles of water on the floor and the mountainous bulk of Rima curled up by the doorway, snoring loudly.

Gaia shifted uneasily, shivering slightly in the cool breeze that wafted through the shelter. *What was that?* she thought. *There is something familiar yet strange...*She sat up and cast her mind outward, following a stray thought teasing her brain. Outward, past Rima's mind, dreaming of her kind, past the minds of the dreaming Aborigines and sleepy watchmen, then out into the wilds of the northern Australian jungles. Savage hungers and fears impinged on her awareness as lesser minds swirled about her, intent on their own feral purposes. She felt a gentle tug, a pull toward the northeast, beyond the volcanic Stony Lands. Her mind slipped, bodiless, through the night, speeding down an emotional trail, following a psychic scent. *Who is that?* she called. *Who are you?*

The mind signature came closer, stronger. Gaia gasped in her shelter far to the southwest as recognition swept around her, drowning her in a rush of emotion and longing. Her mind snapped back to her body with the shock. She struggled to regain her composure and send her mind out again but something blocked her. She felt her mind sinking into a morass, a fetid pool that threatened to reach out and engulf her, body and mind. Gaia drew back with an effort and burst into tears, no longer an adult human with burgeoning mind-powers, but only a girl, exiled in a strange land, deprived of the mother she loved but only knew briefly.

"Rima, oh, Rima, wake up...please!" She sobbed aloud, scrambling over to the hairy bulk of the yowie. "Please, Rima. I need you."

The yowie grunted deeply and rolled over, instantly awake. *What is it, little one?* came a thought filled with love and concern.

"Rima, she is here. My mother is here and looking for me. I felt her, but something stopped me." Gaia sniffled and drew the back of her hand across her face. "I did feel her, Rima."

Little one, you know your mother loves you but...are you sure you did not just dream of her? Rima rose to her knees, towering over the young girl standing beside her. *I miss her too and often dream of her.*

Gaia shook her head. "I was dreaming, Rima. Then I caught this thought and followed it, far toward the north and east. It is my mother, I'm sure of it. She came to find me at last."

Rima stretched out a huge hairy hand and lightly caressed Gaia, drawing her close. *Can you feel her now?*

Gaia burst into tears again. "No, I can't!" She buried her face in Rima's arm. "I tried, but something stopped me," she cried indistinctly. *Rima, I didn't just imagine it.*

Hush child. I believe you. Rima patted Gaia's back gently. *We must wait and see whether she contacts you again.*

Gaia drew back and searched the yowie's broad face and gentle eyes. Her back stiffened with resolve and she dried her eyes before responding. "We shall see, but I am not waiting, Rima. I shall go to her immediately. Whether you come or not is up to you."

What do you mean child? How can you go to her? You do not even know if she is here. Where would you look?

"To the north and east, Rima. I told you. Beyond the Stony Lands and the rainforest down the Yanala River." Gaia set her face in a determined expression. "I shall leave at first light."

Rima knelt silently in front of the young girl, watching her eyes closely, reading her emotions and her body language.

The silence dragged on. Rima waited patiently, shielding her own thoughts. At length, Gaia's face softened and a pleading look came into her eyes. "Please come with me, Rima. I need you."

The yowie made a low rumbling sound deep in her throat. *I would be most happy to accompany you on your quest, little one.*

"Then you'd better go back to sleep, dear Rima, instead of keeping me up talking all night," giggled the girl. "We will need all our strength for our journey."

Rima grunted and cuffed the girl lightly on her head, almost knocking her over. She turned back to her spot by the door, grumbling to herself. She settled herself, watching Gaia settled down again and fall asleep almost immediately. The yowie continued to watch, thinking her thoughts, while the rain eased and the sky slowly lightened in the east.

෯෯

Far to the northeast, deep in the rainforest, Sam woke from a fitful sleep, uncertain about what woke her. She raised up on her elbows before dragging a small piece of twig from under her aching body. Pushing back the sleeping bag cover, she peered around the campsite. The glow from dying embers of the fire revealed bodies strewn around the clearing, most encased in sleeping bags or blankets.

Toward the far side of the clearing sat a lone figure, head bowed, a shadow almost lost in the stygian night. While Sam watched, the figure raised its head and she caught the faint gleam of flashing eyes. A hand rose in silent greeting before the man turned back to his contemplation of the surrounding jungles. Sam smiled briefly, glad that Ernie was on guard but still uncertain of the reason for her wakefulness.

So far away and so strange, she thought while the immortal jungle enveloped her senses.

She listened to the sounds of ancient Australia. A chorus of tree frogs, excited by the recent rain, sang shrill mating songs. The sound rose and fell, underlaid by a throatier, deeper booming sound coming from the lower ground to the east. Sam guessed it was some other type of frog. Insects broke in on the song, rasping their own incessant litany. Far away, Sam caught the scream of some unknown night hunter making its kill, or perhaps it was a cry of agony from its victim. Sam shivered, remembering that ancient Australia teemed with unfamiliar animals. She shifted on the hard ground, searching beneath her and removing another small twig, expanded out of all proportion by hours of lying on it.

Sam concentrated, closing her eyes, using all her senses to test the world around her, searching for a source of disturbance. A faint breeze brought the sour smell of ashes from the dead part of the fire, mingling with the stale odor of wet clothing and the green odors of burgeoning vegetation. A faint hint of curry still hung in the air, lending a human, domestic feel to the foreign scents of the rainforest.

Nothing. Sam lay down again, snuggling up against James, who immediately stopped his soft snoring and, half-wakening, muttered and turned over. Sam smiled again and prepared for sleep, forcing herself to relax.

Softly, faintly, as if riding on the zephyr that tickled her bare skin, came a feeling both familiar and strange. It grew stronger, awakening memories and fears, then abruptly vanished.

Gaia? Baby, is that you?

Sam opened her eyes in shock, struggling to re-establish contact.

Where are you, my darling?

She frantically sent her mind out, desperate to find her child.

Sam reached out mentally, searching for the mind signature she knew so well, and drew back in horror and disgust when a fetid, black entity touched her mind. She shook and almost cried out, feeling as if she had reached under an old rotting log or tombstone and encountered something dead and slimy. Blackness swept over her. She almost panicked when she heard voices that sounded like the whisper of a shroud sliding over the dry, flaking body of a corpse.

Control her.

Use her.

We must find her.

Destroy her.

Sam filled her lungs to scream then froze when a coruscation of light flooded her mind, driving away the blackness like a blast of fresh, sea air. A familiar mind washed over her. *Ernie, what was that?*

Do not be concerned, Samantha. The voice in her head paused, then resumed in an unemotional tone. *You must not try to contact your daughter again. It is very important. Now, sleep, Samantha.*

She heard Ernie's deep voice in her ears and, relinquishing her fears and worries, she slipped again into a fitful sleep.

Ernie sat and looked over the quiet campsite, a troubled look on his dark, craggy face. He looked out into the night again, remembering, searching.

Chapter Nine

"I can't go on. Not another bloody step."

Ratana leaned against a tree, with her long black hair hanging in wet tangles against her sweat-soaked shirt. She dropped her backpack and sank to the leafy forest floor with a sigh of contentment.

Ernie, who was leading the party in single file along an overgrown game trail, looked back and nodded. "Very well. Time is important, but it will not do for us to become exhausted. We shall call a halt for a short while." He immediately stepped off the trail and sat down, then quickly lost himself in thought.

James wandered back to the group of women sitting around Ratana sharing a water bottle. "How's it going?" he asked.

Sam looked up, wiping sweat from her eyes. "I forgot how hot it gets in the forests." She moved her leg and flinched. "And I think I'm getting a blister. We really should have broken these boots in before we left." She carefully moved her foot while glaring at the stiff leather boots.

"It'll be cooler when we cross the ecotone." He saw the incomprehension in her eyes and hurried on. "The zone where the wet rainforest changes to the dry sclerophyll forest. We will have more of a breeze there."

Sam unlaced her boot and pulled it off. She grimaced at the blood on her sock. "Damn. That's what I thought…and it's burst already…oh, yechh! What's that?" She pulled her hand back with a look of disgust on her face.

James squatted beside her, peeled her sock down and deftly cleaned away the blood with his handkerchief. "Yep, here's the culprit," he grinned, "leeches." He picked up a small black worm-like object and flicked it away into the undergrowth. "The other one has ruptured. Here," James rummaged in his backpack, "you'd better put some antiseptic cream on the wound."

"What revolting things!" Sam shuddered, looking nervously around her. "Can't we spray something on us to keep them off?"

"Just keep your socks rolled up over your trouser legs and check your legs whenever we stop. There shouldn't be too many more for a while, though, the ground is getting dryer."

Ratana and Tilley hurriedly rolled their trousers up, searching for other leeches. With cries of disgust, they picked off the small blood-suckers and squashed them beneath the heels of their boots.

"Rather a pity to kill them," observed James. "These forest leeches have a beautiful yellow 'racing stripe' down their sides."

Ratana shot him a withering look. "Sometimes I think you biologists are just too weird. Beautiful, indeed!"

Tilley eyed the pale form of Shinara sitting off to one side with her ever-present companion Narahdarn in close attendance. "What I'd like to know is how she gets away with it. I mean, look at her. The heat, these disgusting creatures..." She plucked another leech off the white skin of her ankle, quickly threw it to the dirt and stepped on it. She pulled her sock up and slipped her worn boot back on her foot. While lacing it up again, she glanced back at Shinara and picked up the thread of her thought. "...and all these barbaric discomforts. How does she do it?"

The others turned. Shinara sat sedately on a small, grassy patch in her pale green shift dress with open-toed sandals. Her overly white skin was unblemished, without even a scratch from the 'wait-a-bit' thorns they ploughed through to reach the small clearing.

Narahdarn sat beside her, picking leeches off his legs and swatting away persistent bush flies and mosquitoes. Shinara sat, untouched, in the midst of this activity staring blankly in front of her.

Sam called out to Narahdarn. "Does Shinara need anything?"

"No, Ms. Samantha," he replied, "I have given her water and a salt tablet. Bugs don't seem to bother her at all." Narahdarn grinned and shook his head. "She slipped through those thorns as if they weren't there."

"Bit of a rum do, what?" Bertie spoke quietly, as he walked up with Nathan. "I was watching her and if I didn't know better, I'd say those bloody thorn bushes got out of her way." He guffawed, twirling his moustache. He brushed his khaki shirt with his hand, straightened his jacket, and marched off up the trail toward Ernie.

Nathan grinned after him. "Handles himself well for a Pom," he remarked. "He must have walked three times as far as I did today, traipsing off to look at rocks and trees, and he's hardly sweating."

Sam looked puzzled. "What's a Pom?"

"A rather derogatory term for an Englishman," James explained. "It stands for the phrase 'Prisoner of Mother England', referring to the convicts that were the first colonists in Australia."

After a few minutes, Ernie called quietly for everyone to get ready to move. He gathered them together on the track and spoke softly. "I am concerned," he said. "We are being watched."

The others looked around at the surrounding jungle but could see nothing untoward.

"Wulgu can find nothing, but he feels it too," Ernie went on. "I do not like to split the party but I must drop back with Wulgu and see if we can identify the watchers. If Garagh were with us there would be no problem. He and I know where we are heading. As it is, I must give you directions."

"Perhaps we should just wait here," said James.

"No. We must be clear of the forest by nightfall." Ernie thought for a moment. "Follow this trail until you cross the ridge into the dryer forest. Walk down the ridge until you come to the two large boulders. You cannot miss them. Wait there. If I have not caught up with you by the time you arrive, I will by nightfall."

Ernie turned away then paused. "James, Nathan, Samantha, Ratana...one other thing. Guard your thoughts. Do not use them to contact each other unless your lives depend on it." He stared hard at them each in turn, then slipped into the undergrowth, disappearing in moments.

"Damn, but that blighter moves like a ghost," Bertie mused. "I wonder what he meant by that last remark? Ah, well. We'd best get started, what?" He marched off up the trail, hurriedly followed by the others.

The trail wound through the rainforest, slowly ascending. At first, everyone's eyes and ears were attuned to the vegetation around them, trying to spot the unseen watchers. After a while their attention wandered, the heat and humidity pressing in on them. Every now then the trail met another one or a faint path could be discerned branching off from the one they were on. It plunged off through the ferns and tangled vines toward the faint sound of rushing water far below. Whenever the canopy opened to let in shafts of sunlight, bright butterflies flitted along the edges of the openings, feeding off sprays of small white flowers high above them, or resting, wings open, in dappled sun-flecks.

The trail crossed a small trickle of water gurgling down a tiny ravine, spreading to form a muddy pool across their path. Footprints crowded the edges of the water and a distant crashing in the undergrowth told of some shy creature disturbed by their approach. They stopped for a few minutes, moistening handkerchiefs from the small stream or splashing water on hot faces.

"I say," said Bertie. "Look at that set of prints. That looks jolly like a cat of some sort, but a big one. I wonder what it is?"

James bent down and felt the pug marks with the tips of his fingers. "*Thylacoleo*. I'd bet on it." He stood up, brushing his hands against his trousers. "That's the extinct marsupial lion. Not overly large as cats go, certainly not as large as a modern lion, but still a deadly predator."

The others drew closer automatically. "No need for undue concern," James went on. "Just don't go wandering off by yourself."

The party halted a little after noon in the shade of a giant *Euca-*

lyptus grandis tree. The trees were sparser and tall grasses and shrubs grew in profusion between them. They found a bare spot covered by fallen leaves and sank down on the ground gratefully.

Tilley looked around curiously. "How come there's such a sudden difference in the plants?"

"This is what we call an ecotone," James said. "It's just the interface between two major vegetation types. The main difference is the rainfall. We've crossed the main mountain range into a drier area. We've passed through the rainforest and you'll find the walking easier this afternoon. It'll be cooler too, despite the sunshine. We'll get some coastal breezes, I think."

"Thank goodness for that," panted Tilley. "I thought I was used to the heat in the tropics...and the bloody bugs," she added, brushing away another hungry mosquito. She glanced over at Shinara sitting under another small tree, watched by her guardian Narahdarn. "What's her secret? She never seems to be bothered by bugs." Tilley shook her head and reached for her can of insect repellent.

Ratana got up and went over to Shinara. "Hi," she said. "How are you standing up to the heat? I've got some bug spray if you want it." She held out her can of repellent.

Shinara ignored her, lost in her own world. A mosquito, following the plume of carbon dioxide from the girl's breath, flew out from the surrounding bush and whined around her head. Her eyes flickered briefly, then resumed their unfocused gaze. The mosquito's whine ceased abruptly as the insect fell lifeless into Shinara's lap.

Ratana reached forward and brushed the tiny corpse from the girl's dress. "How did she do that?" she asked Narahdarn.

The young Aboriginal shrugged uneasily. "I don't know, Ms. Ratana. I try to get her to just make them go away, but she keeps killing them. I guess they're just bugs anyway."

After another few minutes, James got to his feet. "We'd better get moving. Ernie said our rendezvous point, the two boulders, was about eight kilometres from here." He looked back at the trail from the rainforest, then at the fainter trails leading into the grassland, indecisively. He hesitated, then pointed at the trail leading downhill. "That's the one."

They moved off slowly, brushing the tall grass out of their way, picking out a route between the shrubs and trees along the faint track made by animals. James looked troubled, searching his surroundings carefully. Within a few hundred yards however, the trail became better defined and James picked up the pace, confident again.

The path showed the prints of many animal feet, with occasional mounds of dried dung and evidence of grazing along the edges. Bertie squatted beside a large pile of droppings and poked at them with a stick. "They look pretty fresh, what? D'yer think the blighters might still be around?" He looked into the scrubland nervously.

"They're herbivores, professor, probably just kangaroos or wallabies," said James reassuringly, as Sam and Tilley cast uneasy looks
over their shoulders. "Keep to the path and we won't have any problems. Remember, they are more afraid of you than you are of them."

Bertie got to his feet and, throwing away the stick, moved off after
James. "Nearly got trampled by a herd of herbivores in India," he
muttered to himself. "Besides, where there's grazers, there's bloody
carnivores, and those I can do without. I don't fancy meeting up with
that *Thylacoleo* chappie."

Gradually the landscape opened out, becoming flatter as they
moved downhill. The trees became smaller, the great white-barked
gums disappearing, replaced by scrubby acacias and she-oaks. The
grass became more sporadic with expanses of red earth showing.

Despite James's promise of breezes, the day grew hotter and at
last he gave in to the increasing comments and complaints and pointed
off to one side at a stand of trees. "We'll take a break over there. Looks
like there might be some water, or a least some shade."

Leaving the path, they pushed through the grass towards the clump
of trees. Narahdarn paused. "I can smell water," he said, "and something else."

"So can I," agreed Nathan. "At least about the something else." He
wrinkled his nostrils in disgust. "Smells like something died..."

A sudden crashing in the bushes made them all jump and Tilley
gave a squeak of alarm as several red-brown bodies came hurtling out
of the leafy vegetation at the base of the trees.

Sam caught a glimpse of small rabbit faces and huge hind legs
balanced by sturdy tails as the animals exploded past them, bounding
off into the grass. "Wallabies!" she exclaimed, a grin on her face. "I've
been wanting to see them in the wild."

One animal raced off to her left, then abruptly changed direction,
leaping between Shinara and Narahdarn in its attempts to rejoin the
rest of its mob, fast disappearing into the grassland. It landed awkwardly, almost fell, then stopped and turned toward Shinara, shaking
its small head as if bothered by swarms of flies.

Shinara turned her head toward the wallaby and stared at it. The
animal stumbled and collapsed, twitching. A small trickle of blood
oozed from its nostrils and it shuddered and stilled.

For a moment there was a complete silence. "Jesus!" exclaimed
Nathan.

Sam looked down at the small corpse in horror, then at the blank
expression on Shinara's face. "Why? Why did you have to kill it? It
wouldn't have hurt you." She reached over and grabbed the young girl
by her arm. "Look at me, damn you. Why did you kill it?"

Shinara's eyes focused on Sam's face. Sam felt a small tickling
sensation between her eyes, then abruptly a savage stab of pain. She
gasped and stepped back, clutching her head.

"No, Shinara!" Narahdarn stepped between the two women, staggering as he looked into the girl's eyes. "No," he whispered, his hand rising to rub his temple. "You must not."

Her eyes became blank again and she turned away, looking at a tree as if it held some astounding secret.

The party moved into the shade of the trees, James and Ratana supporting a shaken Sam, the others maintaining a discrete distance from Shinara and Narahdarn.

Sam rubbed her temples, glancing at the young girl as she did so. "The pain's almost gone now, but for a moment I thought I was going to end up like that poor wallaby. Why did Ernie and Garagh insist on bringing her?"

The air was cool in the shade of the trees and they could hear the soft squabbles of a small roost of fruit bats high in the foliage above them. A stagnant pool pressed up against the paperbarks, the surface of the scummy water dimpled by the activities of innumerable insects.

"Not a very salubrious spot, what?" observed Bertie.

"Just a short break, I think," agreed James. "Make sure everyone's using plenty of bug spray. The last thing we need is some nasty tropical disease."

The broad expanse of drying mud around the edges of the billabong was covered in footprints. James could make out the two-toed imprints of the wallabies and numerous birds. Vague, more blurred impressions overlaid some of the wallaby prints and James searched the surrounding vegetation for any hint as to their owner.

Nathan, wandering off to one side, away from the pool and over a small rise, called softly. "James, you'd better have a look at this, mate."

James walked over the rise to see Nathan staring fixedly at what appeared to be a huge mound of fallen leaves. He opened his mouth in a query then closed it with an audible snap as the orange, fawn and green pile moved. His mind put together the fragments of the visual puzzle confronting him then rejected it as being too outrageous.

The mound rippled and slowly started to uncoil as a mottled python of gargantuan proportions raised its huge triangular head and focused on the men with a cold ophidian stare. A pulse of cold washed over James as he realized his head was on the same level as the snake's. A long, forked tongue flickered, tasting the dank air while a long soft hiss of air escaped the beast. Its head sank slowly downward and it moved effortlessly closer, its body pushing through the litter covering the ground.

James found himself rooted to the spot, staring in a mixture of fear and fascination. He realized his danger but pushed it to the back of his mind as his eyes drank in the awful beauty. *My God, it must be over forty feet. It must be that python they discovered the fossil remains of at Riverslea.*

A faint voice niggled at his mind. *James? What is it?*

Those colors, beautiful oranges, browns, greens. What's that behind it? A dead wallaby?

James? What's wrong? Remember Ernie told us to guard our thoughts. Sam's mental voice, though inaudible, registered concern.

I think there's a bulge in its stomach...I'm sure of it. It's in the middle of its meal.

James! Love! Answer me!

Prickles of panic invaded James's mind and he shuddered, coming out of his mesmerized state. He stepped back hurriedly, colliding with Nathan.

"For God's sake, let's get out of here!" James turned and ran, gripping Nathan's arm tightly. As they stumbled over the rise, he looked over his shoulder at the snake, now moving over the spot where they had been standing moments before, the last of its coils still unfolding. They charged into the group now standing near the pool around an agitated Sam.

She opened her eyes wide as James and Nathan appeared. James forestalled her query, calling out to them, "Get out of here! Hurry! There's a snake coming this way."

Bertie's eyes lit up. "I say, a jolly snake, what? I love snakes. Where...?" A gentle susurration, like a breeze through the treetops cut off his enthusiasm in mid-sentence. "Bloody hell!" he squeaked as the great triangular head of the python probed between the trees. "I...I think discretion, and all that, don't you know?" He retreated, spreading his arms wide to protect his wife.

"Get the hell out," James yelled. "Quickly!"

Everyone scrambled up the short rise and burst out into the late afternoon sun. They ran for about a hundred yards before they slowed and looked back. There was no sign of the reptile.

"'Strewth, mate. That was a flamin' close call." James's Australian accent broadened in agitation as he hugged Sam. "I figure the only reason we escaped was it was in the middle of its lunch."

Sam looked around. "Where's Narahdarn?" she queried. "And Shinara."

"I think they ran out over there somewhere," said Ratana, pointing off to one side of the thicket. "Narahdarn had to drag her, but they got away, I'm sure."

"Narahdarn! Where are you?" Nathan shouted. He paused, then tried again. Faintly they heard an answering cry and hurried towards it. They discovered the two standing in the middle of an open patch of ground. Narahdarn was picking twigs and burrs from their clothes while Shinara stood silent and still, staring into the slowly setting sun.

"Okay. That's enough excitement for one day. We'll have to leg it if we're to get to the rocks by nightfall." James started toward a faint trail in the grass, then hesitated. He looked around then started off down another trail before pausing again. "I think it was..." He turned to the others. "Does anyone remember which path it was?"

"We were travelling south and west," Nathan said. "More or less with the sun to our right, but I could have sworn the clump of trees with that snake was to our left. Now it seems to be to our right, if we orient ourselves with the sun."

"I think we should be going that way," commented Sam, pointing more towards the sun. If it's setting, that's west, so we should be heading over there."

"But the trees are in front of us," objected Tilley. "Did we come out on the same side as we went in?"

In growing consternation, they searched around them at the tall, waving grass, the intermittent clumps of trees and numerous faint paths, watching their shadows slowly lengthen as the heat went out of the day.

～～

Far to the west, in the overhang of two giant, weathered boulders, sat Ernie and the yowie, Wulgu. They watched as the short tropical twilight deepened to a clear black sky dominated by the sparkling swathe of the Milky Way and the fiery Southern Cross. The man and the hairy creature sat in the darkness, needing neither light to comfort them nor heat to ward off the chill of the night.

"They are not coming, my friend," Ernie softly replied. "Something has happened...and it is my fault."

The yowie rumbled softly. *You did what you must, Wandjina.*

"True, my friend, but I fear for their safety." A feeling of deep sorrow swept over him. "The shadow people are here." He shook his head. "They cannot be, yet, somehow, they are. Why they are here I do not know, but I fear that their desires run counter to ours."

Wulgu sat silently, guarding his thoughts, content to let the great Wandjina decide on a course of action.

Ernie sighed. "Our purpose is too important to risk by going back for them. Without Garagh I must fight alone." He sat silently for a long time as the stars slowly wheeled above them. "We must leave them to find their way alone, my friend. Tomorrow we head directly south to the meeting place of my people and Garagh's people." His gaze came to rest on one of the largest boulders surrounding them. He rose, stepped to it and put his right hand against the warm stone. He turned, walked back to the remnants of an old campfire, and picked up a small piece of black wood."

What is it you do, Wandjina? Wulgu inquired.

Returning to the boulder, Ernie answered, "Helping the only way I can, my friend. I'm leaving our friends a marker so they can find their way to us. It is all I can do."

They will find the place we go from this picture? Wulgu asked, curiosity rumbling through the thought.

"Yes, it is a map to the place we go," Ernie responded while using the charcoal to draw a map on the side of the smooth rock. "They will find us, have no fear. Now, it is time for you to sleep, Wulgu."

Wulgu grunted and rolled over onto his side, asleep almost immediately. Ernie sat alone, gazing out to the west, toward the intermittent glow of a volcano on the horizon and the black lava fields spread out around its base. His thoughts turned from his missing friends to the task that lay before him.

Chapter Ten

Gaia started the day in high spirits. The air was clean and fresh after the rain and bright butterflies swarmed around the flowering paperbarks along the river. She skipped along the path, singing a little food-gathering song to herself. She smiled at the thought of Umu, the old Aboriginal woman who had taught her the song, a grandmother many times over who had adopted her several years ago. Umu wept when Gaia announced her intention of leaving. The Aboriginal elders were upset too; Gaia was a valuable asset to the Tjalwalbiri tribe. Tjimi, the tribe's Karadji, or medicine man, looked troubled. However, the elders could think of no practicable way of preventing her, so they gave in with as good a grace as they could muster. The children, as usual, treated the whole thing as a game, leaping and chattering. They accompanied Gaia and Rima for over a mile before reluctantly turning back.

In her wake, Rima ambled along, keeping a watchful eye on the strip of riparian forest along the river. She had tried to carry Gaia at first, partly to protect her, partly to give herself some measure of control over an unwelcome situation. Gaia had objected, and when Rima tried to force the issue she found her muscles not answering her will. Only when she grudgingly agreed to do things Gaia's way had they set out.

After about half an hour, Gaia slowed her pace. The sun was climbing steadily, covering the land in a hot, dusty blanket of air. They had seldom been this far from the camp alone and the enormity of her venture was starting to register. The path they had taken wound along the Yanala River, sometimes passing within feet of its slow, oily surface; at other times the straggly paperbark trees along its edges were only just visible behind the tall grasses. Cicadas strummed and screeched incessantly, the noise rising and falling in waves in the still air. Occasional gurgles and splashes from the slowly flowing water told of unseen life beneath its surface.

As the wide expanse of loneliness crept in upon her, Gaia dropped back until she was beside the comforting bulk of the yowie. Her hand found Rima's and she squeezed it tightly. *I'm glad you came, Rima.*

The yowie rumbled contentedly, and, Gaia thought, a touch smugly. She grinned, disentangling her hand to punch the great hairy arm beside her then hugged her friend fiercely.

Just before the sun reached its blazing zenith, they stopped on a small hillock overlooking the river. Gaia sat down with a sigh of relief beneath a swamp Bloodwood tree, fanning her face with her woven grass hat. Several mosquitoes immediately homed in on the girl, only to lose interest under the influence of a tiny mental nudge. Rima insisted on taking the gourd down to the river for water, much to Gaia's amusement. She almost told her that there were no crocodiles in this part of the river but decided to let Rima think she was protecting her little friend. Gaia knew that she was probably safer wandering this land alone than even the powerful yowie.

Gaia opened a small leaf-wrapped package and munched contentedly on some baked roots and a small morsel of half-charred lizard. When Rima returned with the water gourd, she sipped the warm fluid gratefully, effusive in her thanks. She brushed the dirt carefully and lay down with the hat arranged over her face then she instantly fell asleep. Rima wandered around the hillock, always keeping at least one eye on the child, and picked leaves from some of the shrubs, stuffing them into her mouth. Breaking off a branch, she ambled back to the sleeping child and sat beside her, stripping the bark from the branch with her long canine teeth. After a while she dozed.

Gaia awoke to a feeling of being watched. She lay still, her eyes closed, reaching out with her mind to pinpoint the watcher. She felt no malice, only a semi-sentient curiosity. She opened her eyes and turned her head slowly. Ten feet away stood a large dog-like creature, light brown in color with a series of darker stripes covering its back and hindquarters. Her mind instantly started cataloguing and identifying it, turning over information learned in her first months of life.

No native dogs in Australia, only the dingo that arrived with man. This isn't a dingo. Stripes, with a thick, stiff tail and long head. Can only be a marsupial wolf, usually called a thylacine, she remembered, using her mother's lessons and her father's shared knowledge.

She grinned delightedly. *I've never seen one of those.* She raised herself on one arm, staring avidly at the creature. It jumped back as she moved and yawned impossibly wide, its thin jaws opening in a monstrous gape for a moment before it bounded down the slope and disappeared.

Gaia leapt to her feet, trying to catch another glimpse of the creature. She saw only a brief waving of the grass and felt its mind, unalarmed, moving off. Turning, she found Rima beside her.

Was that a striped forest dog, child?

Yes, Rima. It was watching us.

You tell me next time. It might have bitten you.

There was no danger, Rima. Gaia looked up at the sun, now sinking toward the horizon. *It is late. We have slept too long.* She picked up her hat and, setting it firmly on her head, set off along the path down the river.

The afternoon air cooled slowly as the pair moved further to the east. As the hot sun hovered above the line of smoking volcanoes strung out behind them to the west and north, Gaia halted at a fork in the path. One branch continued to follow the course of the river as it plunged into thick rainforest before forcing its way through dank-walled ravines, cutting through the low range of hills on its course to the sea. Gaia had never travelled this far but had listened avidly with the other children to hunters' tales. Steep paths, dense thorn thickets and fearsome beasts ranged the forest. She felt no real fear but hesitated, looking down each path as if for a sign.

The other path was fainter, less used by hunters as it led to the Stony Lands, a vast expanse of old black lava from some ancient eruption. It would be harder to move through this region and there would be no water, but it had the advantage of leading north. That decided Gaia. All day, a little niggling signal pulled her onward—a faint feeling that her mother was somewhere to the northeast. Now the call came from the north.

"Fill up the gourd again, Rima. We must leave the river now."

Rima rumbled deep in her throat. *Is that wise, my child? At least we know something of the forest path.*

Gaia scowled. "We must go that way. Now hurry up, Rima, it will be dark soon." She waited as the yowie stamped off down to the river, thrashing through the bushes and muttering non-vocal imprecations. Closing her eyes, Gaia concentrated on the distant mental signal. After a few moments she caught a faint impression of small brown animals fleeing in terror. A faint buzzing intruded on her thoughts and her hand automatically rose to brush away the annoying bushfly. Instead, the buzzing increased in volume and a tickle started between her eyes. Abruptly, she screamed aloud when a stabbing pain lanced through her skull.

It hurts! It hurts! Make it go away, Rima, it hurts! Gaia collapsed to the ground, writhing as the agony expanded. She was dimly aware of a screaming howl of rage and concern as Rima burst through the vegetation and swept the little girl into her arms, glaring all around for the source of the hurt.

As suddenly as it came, almost with an audible snap, the agony ceased, leaving only vague phantom pains skittering around her skull. Gaia hugged the silky body of her friend fiercely, crying in great wracking sobs. Gradually these eased to sniffles and Gaia raised her head to peer at the enraged grimace on Rima's face. *I'm all right, Rima. You can put me down now.*

Rima's hold on the girl tightened. *What is wrong, child? What is the cause of your pain?*

Gaia pushed against the encircling arms. *Nothing now. I think I just caught hold of the wrong thought. Maybe some animal dying. Let me down, Rima.*

Reluctantly, the yowie set Gaia down, though she remained hovering beside her, and still peered around for any potential threat.

"Come on then," said Gaia, rubbing her tear-streaked face with the back of a grimy hand, "We'd better get going." She resolutely started north along the faint track toward the lava fields. Rima grunted in exasperation and hurried after her, casting a watchful eye around her as she did so.

Nightfall found the two of them deep into the Stony Lands. The broken, jagged rubble of the old lava fields surrounded them, desolate and forbidding. They picked their way over the rocks, all hints of a trail having been lost within minutes of entering the region. At first there were signs of human visitation, rocks smashed and worn away where Aboriginal hunters had searched for obsidian flakes, the valuable volcanic glass that could be worked to a razor edge. Now there was just a vista of black, weathered rocks stretching before them, interspersed with small patches of scrubby vegetation eking out a meagre existence.

It was by one of these scrubby oases that Gaia and Rima decided to camp for the night. With an effort, the young girl had found some dry wood and managed to light a fire by twirling a stick in a small piece of crumbly wood. The small fire flickered and smoked, the dim light accentuating the blackness of the surrounding rocks. It cast shadows that danced and waved, catching the eye and disturbing the thoughts. Rima foraged in the low bushes for edible leaves and seedpods while Gaia washed down the few crumbs remaining of her earlier meal with tepid water from the gourd.

They settled down for the night, Gaia curled in the protective arms of the yowie, and lay looking up at the starry sky. The waxing moon rose rapidly, casting its pearly light over the landscape, as they fell asleep.

Gaia woke to find the moon nearly overhead. She looked around sleepily then snuggled closer to the gently snoring hulk of Rima. The air was chill, a faint breeze raising the fine hairs on her arms. When she closed her eyes, the feeling of being watched returned. She opened her eyes and stared into the darkness, searching for the source of her unease. Gaia got up carefully so as not to disturb Rima, stepped over the dying embers of the fire and looked north.

In the glow of the moonlight, a shadow detached itself from the blackness of the rocks and stepped out into the open. It spoke a phrase in an unemotional tone. Gaia stepped back in shock as she realized the figure had spoken in English, not one of the myriad Aboriginal dialects. She hadn't heard the language spoken since infancy but recognized it from her encyclopaedic memory.

"Hello, child." The man moved forward, the moonlight showing a short, stocky figure with a pale face and the remains of a business suit hanging from his body. "I've come to take you home."

Gaia shook Rima. *Rima, get up, quickly!*

Rima was awake in an instant and rose to stand beside Gaia. She stared at the figure of the man, her hair bristling. *I cannot hear it think. It is wrong.*

The man held out a hand. "Come, child, I will take you to your mother."

Gaia gasped and stumbled forward. Rima gripped her tightly by the shoulder. *Stay. I will bring him to us, and we shall see.* The yowie bounded forward over the rough ground, rapidly closing the gap. The man stood stolidly, arms by his side. Then, just before Rima got to him, he stepped to one side and vanished into the darkness. Rima roared and followed, also disappearing from sight.

Gaia waited anxiously as the roars of anger and clattering of stones got fainter. The moon slipped behind a thin wisp of cloud, the light dimmed, and black shadows slid out and over the girl. She reached up to brush them off and found her arms pinioned. She screamed once then felt herself falling as layer upon layer of fetid blackness swept over her, driving the air from her lungs and the light from her mind.

Rima raged in the darkness, following the figure flitting from one shadow to the next. She was panting with exhaustion when she heard the faint scream, abruptly silenced, behind her. With a howl she turned and charged back toward the campsite, oblivious to the cuts and bruises she suffered on the sharp lava boulders.

Rima burst into the camp to find it deserted. A single print of a boot in the ashes of the fire was the only evidence of intruders. She cast about in an agony of grief and self-recrimination. *Gaia, my child, where are you?* She threw boulders aside, searching in all directions, roaring with rage until the sweat ran from her body and her legs trembled. Blood puddled beneath her from the deep cuts suffered on the razor edges of the lava. Rima raised her head to the moon and howled as if her heart was breaking. The agonizing sound spread over the broken ground, echoing from the boulders until it was lost in the blackness of the silent night.

Chapter Eleven

Wulgu woke with agony twisting his insides and searing grief thundering through his heart. He groaned and sat up, feeling the gnarled hand of Wandjina on his shoulder. He turned his great shaggy head toward the human with a piteous expression. *Wandjina. It was a dream. Please tell me it was only a dream.*

Ernie shook his head. "No, my friend. It was no dream. Some tragedy has taken place and you heard the cries of one of your kind. It can only be Rima."

We must go to her, Wandjina.

Ernie looked at the huge yowie sadly. "I cannot. My purpose is too urgent for me to turn aside, even for you, my friend."

Wulgu wiped his face with his great hands. He looked thoughtful. *Then we abandon Rima? And what of the child? Where Rima is, so must the child be also.*

"It was explained to you before we left, Wulgu. My purpose is paramount; I must join the worlds again. If the child can be found as well then good. If not..." Ernie's voice trailed away.

Forgive me, Wandjina. The yowie's thoughts reeked of bitterness. *I thought you human, with a human's compassion.*

"You forget yourself, Wulgu," chided Ernie. His face softened as he went on. "I have watched humans for a long, long time and many times I have appeared as one and interacted with them, always for their ultimate good. If I do not display compassion, it is because I strive for a larger healing." The old Aboriginal man stood and stretched his arms, looking at the pink eastern sky. "I must depart. You are free to remain with me, or search for Rima. Or you may want to seek the others of our group and guide them back on to the right path."

Wulgu got up, towering above Ernie. *If it is truly my choice, then I will search for Rima.*

Ernie nodded. "Go then. Find her and rejoin me when you can." He flashed an image of a landscape at Wulgu. "The two tribes live here. Do not let yourself be seen, my friend." He raised a hand in farewell and set off down the trail slowly.

Wulgu grunted softly. *Farewell, Wandjina. I shall find Rima and*

I shall find you again.

⁓⁓

The first rays of the new day found James's little group exhausted. Unable to find their route, they had moved as far from the stand of trees with the billabong and its reptilian threat as possible before sunset and camped. They spent a restless night, none of them happy about the proximity of such a large predator. James alternated between pacing the perimeter of the little camp and sitting by the fire, fidgeting. The women, with the exception of Shinara, sat and talked softly. Shinara, in fact, was the only one rested the next morning. She had fallen asleep the moment she closed her eyes and not stirred until dawn. Bertie was wakeful but busy, talking earnestly with Nathan and Narahdarn then writing copiously in a small notebook with a blunt pencil.

After a cursory breakfast of trail mix and black coffee, James called everyone together and addressed them. "We have an important decision to make today. I believe I led you in the wrong direction after we came out of the rainforest. According to Ernie's directions, we should have reached his rendezvous point last night. Instead we are lost. It was my fault and I apologize." He smiled wryly and cleared his throat, averting his eyes from the group in embarrassment.

"So what should we do?" asked Ratana. The others nodded, making small noises of agreement.

"First, I think we need to find the trail we were on yesterday. We know it was near that clump of trees with the billabong, and being early morning, the sun should be on our left as we face the trees. With a bit of luck the dead wallaby..." he glanced at Shinara, "...is still there. We will know it's the right clump that way. Second, I think once we've found the trail we should retrace our steps back to the rainforest." He raised a hand as Sam and Tilley started to protest. "I know it's a long way but it's logical. We go back to the last place we can be certain of and start from there."

Bertie nodded, twirling his moustache. "Good show, what? Sound advice, eh chaps?" He looked around the group, beaming. "I've been thinking about our situation myself and I think I know where that dead beastie is."

They packed up their provisions and moved off in the direction that Bertie indicated, moving slowly in pairs, several yards apart. After about half a mile they changed direction slightly, angling to the left of a promising stand of trees. They circled the trees completely, finding no trace of the dead wallaby. Bertie looked chagrined and pulled out his notebook again.

"Perhaps we came further than I thought, last night. If we assume we did, we need to continue in this direction and try another clump of trees." He looked around, shading his eyes with one bony hand. "That one maybe," he said, pointing, "or perhaps those taller ones off there."

"Hang on, mate," said Narahdarn. "I've just remembered something. Remember we heard those fruit bats at the billabong yesterday?" He grinned. "It may be another roost, but I saw several flying toward those taller trees just before dawn."

"Nice one, Narahdarn. There won't be many roosts out here. Let's try those trees then." James smiled with relief, the strain showing in his face.

They moved slowly toward the distant trees, angling to the right and, by midmorning, were rewarded by the sight of the bloated remains of the dead wallaby. Small predators or scavengers had been at work during the night, but enough was left to satisfy them that this was the right carcass.

Orienting himself, James pointed back the way they had come the previous day. "Okay. Let's get moving. We should be able to get back to our starting point by lunchtime."

Early afternoon found them back at their point of emergence from the rainforest. A brief discussion and an examination of the area led to the discovery of three possible paths down the ridge. Two turned off quickly into the flat grasslands below, seemingly parallel to the path of the day before. The third led slowly downward, keeping close to the ridgeline. James was sure that this was the correct path.

After a brief meal and drink of warm water they set off along the path, keeping close together. Within a mile or two they started to encounter outcrops of grey sandstone, with loose rubble spilling down the slopes. Their footing became precarious and they advanced slowly, clutching at each other. They emerged from this area into a shallow basin. At the bottom stood a single boulder.

Nathan, in the lead, stopped by it with a low whistle. "Look at this. Narahdarn, what do you make of it, mate?"

The young Aborigine left Shinara with the other women, who edged away from her nervously, and joined Nathan and James at the rock. Under a low overhang, protected from the elements, was a cryptic design in red and white pigments.

"Dwarrah tribe, I'd say," said Narahdarn, running his fingers over the design. "This is a territory marker." He walked around the stone, looking closely at all its surfaces. "I think we will be entering their territory if we go further down the ridge."

James looked up as Bertie joined them. "Ernie told us to go this way, so I suppose they must be friendly."

"Quite possibly, Dr. Hay," said Narahdarn. "There was a good amount of hospitality shown amongst tribes at this time. And later," he added. "It was only if strangers were seen using the tribe's resources without permission that things got a bit hairy."

"Well, we've seen no sign of human activity. With any luck we won't need to test their hospitality."

"Not exactly," muttered Bertie quietly. "I didn't like to say anything in front of the ladies, don't you know, but I've spotted several artifacts today." He smiled smugly and twirled his moustache. "Trained eye and all that."

"What do you mean? What have you seen?"

"The most significant object was a tool-sharpening rock. Looked as if it had had recent use too. A couple of disused snares, some pieces of wood that looked a trifle artificial." Bertie looked thoughtful. "The most worrying object was one that could be perfectly innocent."

"Oh? What was that?"

"A broken branch. Just off the path and pointing the way we went yesterday. Maybe it was an animal, but it was missing today and the cut looked too clean for casual browsing by some passing animal."

James whistled softly. "So Ernie was right. We are being watched."

"Looks like it, old chap. What are you going to do?"

"Nothing much we can do. Go on, I suppose, and trust Ernie's knowledge of this area and the tribes." James called Nathan and Narahdarn over. He quickly told them about Bertie's sightings. "What do you think?" he asked.

Narahdarn looked troubled. "I'm worried that they are watching us instead of just openly contacting us. It's as if they have had trouble recently and are trusting no one."

"Then we had better press on to the rendezvous and hope that Ernie is waiting for us. Nathan, would you ask the ladies to join us? We must stay close and travel as fast as we can."

They left the shallow depression by the far side, following the track as it wound through a grove of she-oaks. James and Bertie led, followed by the women with Narahdarn and Nathan making sure that everyone kept up. They travelled at a brisk walk, aided by the gentle slope downhill and the sparse vegetation. Gradually the ground became stonier again as more sandstone outcrops ruptured the thin yellow soil.

"There," said James at last. "That must be it. The two rocks."

"I agree, old chap. Those are the only two large rocks around here and I estimate we are about the right distance."

"No sign of Ernie though." James was careful to keep a calm expression on his face as he turned to the rest of the group. "We've arrived," he called cheerfully. "Nathan, Ratana, would you please start a fire. I think we could all do with a breather. Tilley, would you help Sam brew up a cuppa?"

Ratana walked toward the two large rocks, unpacking her backpack as Nathan started picking up fallen she-oak branches. She bent over to gather a few round boulders into a circle for a fireplace. She straightened up and gasped as a dark figure stepped out from behind one of the large rocks. A lean Aboriginal hunter confronted her. He was clad only in a bark loincloth and carried a long, thin spear. His black eyes glinted as he stared at her from under jutting eye-ridges.

Ratana took a step back, tripped and fell. She sat down hard with a muffled squeak of alarm. Nathan looked up and, dropping his armful of branches, raced to her side. James and the others gave a shout and started forward as well, only to halt abruptly, as several other figures appeared, all armed with spears or boomerangs. Nathan helped Ratana to her feet and together they retreated until they were standing with the others.

James kept his eyes fixed on the Aborigines in front of him and spoke quietly. "Narahdarn, speak to them. Tell them we come in friendship."

"I can try, Dr. Hay, but there are over four hundred dialects and the ones I know may be just gibberish to them," he muttered. Narahdarn stepped forward, his hands spread at his sides. He called out a short phrase, followed by another. After a moment of silence he spoke again using different words.

The old Aboriginal hunter in front of him grunted and rattled off a polysyllabic reply. Narahdarn listened intently then spoke again, slowly. The hunter shook his head and pointed his spear at the group, talking again at some length. Narahdarn gave a short reply and turned to James.

"I can understand some of it, but the words he uses are archaic forms."

Bertie jerked his head sharply. "And this is surprising?"

Narahdarn grinned. "No, I guess not. Anyway, Dr. Hay, they are Dwarrah and they want to know who we are and why we are on their lands. What should I tell them?"

"Say we come in peace from a far-off land. Perhaps you should ask if they have seen Ernie. Use his Aboriginal name of Wandjina though…"

The hunters gave a great shout, some of them levelling their spears, others dancing back two or three paces, raising their boomerangs. Narahdarn spoke rapidly, his arms spread wide. The old hunter shouted back angrily. Narahdarn spoke again, his voice calm, repeating the same phrase over and over again. While he spoke, the weapons lowered and the hunters visibly relaxed.

"What happened?" asked James quietly.

Narahdarn spoke out of the corner of his mouth. "They thought you were invoking a great spirit force to overwhelm them. As you probably know, Ernie's Aboriginal name is the name of a mythological spirit from the Dreamtime. Apparently, here it means something a bit more literal. Please be careful what you say, Dr. Hay."

The old hunter gestured behind him and spoke forcefully. The other Aborigines muttered and half-raised their weapons again.

"He is inviting…no, more demanding, that we accompany them. I don't think we have much choice."

James nodded. "I don't think so either, but tell him we would be happy to come with him." He turned to the others. "Keep smiling, folks. Our lives may depend on it."

Narahdarn again spoke, smiling as he did so and pointing to each of the group in turn.

The old hunter grunted, scowling, then turned and walked swiftly past the two rocks and down the track. James moved after him, followed by the others in the group. The hunters loped alongside them, weaving through the undergrowth, keeping their spears at the ready.

Chapter Twelve

Gaia was dreaming. She sat in a large bark shelter, across a small campfire from a tall red-haired woman. They held what Gaia thought were teacups, though she had never seen teacups in her life. The woman talked about her plans to build a hut here and look after Gaia. The words made her feel warm and safe. She reached out to touch the woman but as she did so the light from the fire started to flicker and die. Dark shadows blossomed and the woman became indistinct in the murky air.

Gaia cried out and stumbled to her feet. *Mother! Come back! I love you!*

Blackness enveloped her and she groped in the darkness for her mother. Dimly she heard the sound of someone leaving. *She can't hear me!* Tears sprung from her eyes and she opened her mouth to scream out her mother's name. The darkness poured into her, forcing her scream back down her throat, cutting her off from her mother. She hurled herself forward but felt herself borne upward and backward. Something breathed heavily beside her.

The sense of motion became stronger and the breathing sound became more hoarse and distinct. Gaia opened her eyes to see the sweating, unshaven face of a strange man swaying above her. The man's eyes were blank and he breathed rapidly through dry and chapped lips. His arms were clutched firmly around Gaia as he ran, stumbling through the night.

Gaia pushed against the man's chest, feeling the unfamiliar textures of woven cloth. She tried to call out but her throat felt paralysed. She called out with her mind, *Rima! Rima!* Only a great emptiness answered her. For the first time in her life she felt alone, separated from those she loved. The arms about her clutched tighter and she buried her face in the crook of the man's arm. Then she sobbed, while her grief and her loss welled up to blind her. After a while the rocking motion and her own exhaustion combined to send her into a fitful sleep.

Gaia awoke in darkness. She lay still, her heart racing as she tried desperately to remember where she was and what had happened.

A pale, pearly light filtered in around her, dimly revealing an uneven surface of rounded boulders and mud. The air was still and dank, with a musty, disused odor. Faintly, she heard the sound of dripping water and the gurgling of a small stream, though she could not pinpoint the direction.

Gaia raised herself on one arm and peered about. *Where is Rima? She has let the fire go out.* She called out, her voice cracking. The thin echoes that bounced back at her from the rocky walls of the cavern and the damp boulders terrified her. She sat up, shivering.

"So you are awake at last?"

The dry, whispering voice from behind Gaia made her jump. She swivelled and stared into the dim light, vaguely making out a male figure seated about twenty feet away. "Who...who are you?"

The figure rose and approached, stumbling over the rocks. "We hope you slept well, little miss, and are quite rested. We will need to question you at length, we think."

"Who are you?" whispered Gaia. "I can't hear your mind."

"Our name does not matter." The corner of the man's mouth twitched and something unpleasant flickered in his eyes.

"Why do you keep saying 'we' and 'our'?" Gaia peered into the gloom. "Where are these others you keep talking about?"

The man laughed. "Things are not always what they seem, young miss. The figure you see before you..." He gestured at himself. "...sometimes goes by the name of Ehrich. You may call me that if you wish." The man paused and the grinning smile on his face slipped. "There are others here too." His voice took on an unpleasant whiney tone. "It's really not fair. I think I should be allowed sole use of my body, don't you think?"

Gaia sat silently, not sure how she should reply to this. She shivered and edged away from the man surreptitiously. "Why have you brought me here?"

"My friends want to question you. Will you answer their questions?"

"I suppose so. Will you take me back to Rima if I do?"

"Who is Rima?"

"My friend. She tried to catch you in the Stony Lands."

Ehrich nodded. "Ah, the great hairy beast. What is your relationship to this beast?"

"She is not a beast!" Gaia spat indignantly. "She is a real person, she's just a...a yowie. She's my friend and I love her."

"Very well, little miss. Answer our questions and we will take you back to your yowie."

Gaia took a deep breath. "What do you want to know?"

Ehrich sat down on a large rock next to Gaia. "We know you were born in a place and a time far from here. How did you get here?"

Gaia shrugged. "I don't know. I was only a baby. You could ask

Rima, I suppose."

Ehrich shrugged. "Perhaps we will. Your mother has come to find you, you know. But she has brought a lot of other people with her. Some of these are doing other things, one old Aboriginal man for instance." Ehrich glanced at Gaia expectantly. When she did not react, he went on. "Why have these others come? Who is this old man? Why are you so important?"

"I don't know. How could I know?" Gaia smiled weakly. "Please, will you take me back to Rima now?"

A change came over Ehrich's face. His pleasant smile disappeared and a look of horror twisted his features. "No," he gasped. "You promised."

Gaia turned a dismayed face toward the man. "But I tried to answer..."

Ehrich screamed hoarsely, his jaws opening so wide his joints cracked and popped. His wide, staring eyes flicked from side to side and his limbs trembled. A dusty, slithering voice issued from his gaping mouth. "Then you will answer to us."

Gaia's eyes opened wide. She got up quickly, backing away from the thing with Ehrich's face and body. The air of the cavern felt cold on her skin and goose bumps prickled her back and arms.

"Hold her," commanded the voice. At once the darkness of the cave walls shattered and flowed inward, enveloping the small girl as she struggled, yelling with fear.

In moments, Gaia found herself prostrate on the damp boulders, secured by cold, soft, sticky fingers of blackness. "Let me go," she sobbed. "Please let me go, I don't know anything."

She watched in horror as a misty shadow poured out of Ehrich's mouth and drifted across the boulders toward her. It flowed over her face. She turned her head violently from side to side, clamping her eyes and mouth shut. She felt it probing her nostrils and she panicked, screaming in terror as it flowed into her. Blackness swept over her mind, drowning her in inky nothingness.

Long minutes passed, then gradually the shadows withdrew from the pale limp body on the cavern floor. They swirled over the rocks and walls of the cave, pulsing and shivering.

She knows nothing. Anger crackled in the air.

Then she is useless. Kill her.

Yes.

Yet the old human, the powerful one, seeks her. Why?

She is important to his purpose.

What purpose?

Perhaps he seeks to use her to bind us, destroy us.

How?

Could she be unaware of her part in this purpose?

What then do we do with her?

Kill her.
No, guard her. She may yet be of use.
How?
The humans may be persuaded to abandon their plan.
Yes. Keep her alive...for now.
Agreed.

The shadows receded; the dark mist flowed back into Ehrich. The man jerked then trembled, with sweat breaking out on his face despite the cold dank air. He lowered his face to his hands and wept quietly. "Bastards," he muttered. "Fucking bastards."

After a few minutes, Ehrich fell silent and, raising his head, he sat looking at the body of the unconscious little girl. He sighed and got to his feet. "I suppose I'd better see about getting you some food. Can't have you dropping dead on me, can we?" He pawed through the tattered backpack at his feet, pulling out and discarding tins of food before selecting an energy bar. He dipped a tin cup into the stream and cradling the little girl in his arms, dabbed water on her face until she regained consciousness.

She lay in his arms looking blankly at the silhouette of the man bending over her.

Ehrich smiled at her and raised the cup to her lips. "Drink, child. Then eat. We must leave very soon." He raised his head and stared into the darkness at the rear of the cave. His eyes seemed to glow faintly as he stared. "We cannot wait for them," he muttered, under his breath. "We must leave while it is still night."

Chapter Thirteen

Ernie sat looking out over a rolling sea of eucalyptus scrub, remembering the future. From his vantage point, a grey limestone bluff towering nearly a hundred meters above the surrounding land, he could trace out meandering streams and the obvious signs of human habitation. Below him, lost from view in the crags and towers of rubble-strewn plains, were the caves that now sheltered the people he came so far to see.

The sun laid burning layers of air on his black skin, exposed now to the elements. Gone was the old, grey-haired, modern-day city Aborigine that travelled back to this place so recently. Gone were the tee shirt and shorts, the battered sneakers and dirty backpack. In their place, was an almost naked body, tall and muscular, and gleaming blue-black in the noonday sun. A loincloth was his only compromise with modesty. He knew many of his fellow Aborigines wandered this dry and dusty land in natural nudity but he was also sure his European companions were not ready for public nakedness.

He smiled to himself. He had seen and experienced many things in his long life, seen innumerable changes in beliefs and customs, but the one that gave him the most amusement was the white man's prudishness.

The first white settlers were the worst, he thought, *with their hideously constricting clothes and their savage attitudes to anyone they perceived as their inferiors*. He remembered several instances of their cruelty and unthinking hatred, though to be fair, some had shown a kindly, if somewhat paternalistic, face to the indigenous inhabitants of this great Southern land.

Where did it all start to go wrong?

Man had always shown a savage streak but that was to be expected in a hunting primate. There was nothing wrong with killing for food. Nevertheless, man could not, or would not, limit himself. The facility with which man killed, not only for food but also for pleasure, appalled him.

When had it started?

He could remember a time when the land was vast and people

were scarce, when groups of humans and near-humans cooperated. They lived, if not in friendship, at least with tolerance. Man was part of the environment, part of the planet's ecology. Now, they spread across it like a disease. Ernie had no name then, lived unseen and unknown to humanity, at one with the natural world. He wandered the Earth at will, going where he pleased, staying to watch generations come and go if the mood took him, living without any real purpose.

Where did I come from? He had no parents, he knew. *I was, I am.*

There was a moment when he was self-aware. *When was that?*

He remembered warmer climates and strange animals, then ice sheets and more familiar animals, far from these limestone cliffs. Hairy, naked men dancing around fires in draughty caves, looking up at the stars and, for the first time, wondering.

Their hunger and their need for a purpose, a reason for their lives, called me into existence.

There were others too, called by the energies of self-aware creatures as their numbers passed some critical point. He communed with these others, who divided the planet into zones of interest, and became involved with humanity. He had, in a very real sense, co-evolved with humans. As they grew and developed, so had he. But he rapidly outstripped them, growing in power and ability, as their short, hard lives condemned so much knowledge to be lost with each passing generation.

Am I then a god? Ernie smiled wryly. *Many would think so, but no.*

A deity was a being of immense power, of limitless knowledge, immortal and, of necessity, supernatural, beyond all earthly laws. He knew himself to be limited in power and knowledge. He had not fully tested his mortality, nor did he wish to. There might come a time when he would be prepared to give up his life, but that time had not yet arrived. As for being supernatural...he was only too aware how much a part of nature he was. Nature created him, not the other way round.

Many of his fellow creatures disappeared over the years. Just as a need and a belief had called them into existence, so too had growing knowledge, self-assurance and a lack of faith sent them back into non-being. Ernie knew he owed his continued presence to the people he had chosen to guide and support. The Australian Aborigines still had a deep connection with the land and a central core of belief in the Dreamtime, that ancient epoch when man, animal and spirit were one, were interchangeable.

He had been known by many names, Ernie being the most recent, a common name for the common identity he assumed. At other times, he had put on and taken off identities and names to suit his purpose. Some had called him 'Rainbow Serpent' after an early manifestation of his power. His favorite name was 'Wandjina', the name given to the mythical ancestral beings, the spirits of the clouds, makers of land, sea and human beings. He had lived as a spirit, as a being of the air and clouds and while he had not created anything, he was, in a sense, parent to the tribes who knew him.

Few people were aware of his true identity. James and Sam knew him only as a kind old man, wise in the ways of the Aboriginal people. Though, since the growth of their mind powers, they divined that there was something more to him. Nathan and Ratana, being of mixed ancestry, suffered great mental and emotional battles, trying to balance cynicism and faith. They believed him to be a leader, a guide in touch with the spirit world, though still human. Narahdarn, a young full-blooded tribesman from the central deserts, had an inkling of Ernie's true nature. He was always deferential, calling him Wandjina and obeying him instantly. Only Garagh knew him for what he truly was.

Ah, Garagh, my friend.

The disappearance of the old Neanderthal leader still puzzled him, though he thought he knew what must have happened. Time was a strange thing, particularly when one was forced to live through so much of it, and not all in a logical order. In many ways, he was outside time. Never having a separate existence outside the minds of those who created him, he was immune to paradox. He remembered being elsewhere at this very time he was now experiencing again, but found no conflict in the fact.

Garagh, on the other hand, existed as a physical body at this time. He had acted as a leader of the very tribe now residing in the Chillagoe cave system somewhere below him. Garagh had lived on, surviving into the twentieth century of the modern era, before he was sent back in time by the technology of the 'Others'. Despite what Xanatuo and the other grey scientists believed, this place was not just an alternate universe, it was indeed the past. If they weren't so locked into their own scientific delusions they would have predicted Garagh's demise. The universe had its own laws and would not allow a paradox. Garagh already existed in this time; he could not be in two places at once.

Ernie frowned, with a chill creeping over his skin, despite the hot sun. Though Garagh was not dead, it was as if he was dead. He had no doubt he would find a man called Garagh in the tribe below, but that man was the Garagh he once knew, a man guided to this spot by beings he called the 'Others', unsure of his future and his destiny. The Garagh he had forged a friendship with over the millennia was gone, vanished as if he never existed. Ernie mourned his passing.

And what of the 'Others'?

He had never seen these beings that guided Garagh. They were powerful, and knowledgeable, with a view of the universe that spanned millions of years. Perhaps they were gods, though Ernie doubted it.

They sometimes acted in a very arbitrary and high-handed way, with little regard for the feelings of the humans affected by their decisions. Maybe James was right in his suspicions that they were alien to this planet. If Ernie succeeded in healing this reality, in changing history, maybe he would have the opportunity to find out.

But first I must make contact. The beginning is so crucial. Ernie got to his feet and stretched. He ran his hands through his grey hair and paused. *What did I look like when first I was here?* His hair lengthened and became darker until there was only a hint of grey at the temples. *Better.* He picked up his spear with its fire-hardened tip and picked his way carefully down the bluff.

Emerging into the flatter land below the cliffs, Ernie walked along the base until he picked up a game trail. He carefully examined the path, while slowly moving along it. After a while he grunted with satisfaction and bent low over pellets of dung. He fingered them, rolling the droppings between finger and thumb. He sniffed the dung and grunted again. *A mature male. Good. And only an hour old.* It would be good to see his old friend again but he must remember the courtesies. Meat was always welcome to hunter-gatherer tribes.

He cast around for tracks and set off at a slow but steady lope into the plains. Several times he stopped to examine marks of grazing on bushes and clumps of grass, and once he spent some time scrutinizing the spoor of a predator. *Tiger cat,* he thought. He looked for, and found, the scat near a clump of pandanus palms. He was pleased to find it had eaten recently and would not be competing with him. Ernie noted the presence of ripe fruit on the pandanus and pressed onward.

He picked up his pace to a steady jog. The tracks led down to a small stream and, in the firm mud on the banks, he found fresh footprints of his prey. Water was still oozing into the prints and he knew he was minutes behind. He walked forward a few paces, checking the direction taken by the animal, then raced off downwind, curving in a circle toward a projected point.

Ernie stopped behind a small *Acmena* shrub, blending into the background. He snuffed the air, tasting the scent of the approaching animal. A soft thump-and-pause, thump-and-pause told of a creature at ease and unalarmed. He stepped out into the open, with his right arm cocked back and the fire-hardened tip of his spear steady in front of his eyes.

The kangaroo hopped slowly up the trail, leaning forward onto its short front legs then bringing its two huge hind feet up together with a muffled thump. It froze when it spotted the man standing motionless to one side of the track. After a moment, it raised itself to its full height and stared at the man, with its ears twitching forward.

Ernie called out to the beast, "I am hungry, bless me with thy death," launching his spear as he called. The kangaroo tensed at the sound and, when the spear flew, leapt forward in panic, driving the fire-hardened wood into its chest below its left front leg. It squealed and collapsed, its hind legs spurring wildly as if in flight. Ernie raced forward and, taking out a stone knife, stepped across the animal. Avoiding its hind legs, he drew back the head and cut its throat. The kangaroo shuddered and died. Ernie knelt beside it and stroked its head, while gazing into the glazing eyes. "Thank you for the gift of life, old one," he murmured.

꒜꒜

A small Neanderthal boy was the first to see the tall, black man striding toward the caves. He gave a squeal of alarm and, dropping the stick he was poking into a hollow log, scampered down the track, yelling for his parents. By the time the stranger reached the area of carefully cleared ground in front of the main cave, over forty men of varying ages were waiting, clutching spears and stone axes. Women hurried the children into the caves, cuffing the smaller ones and berating the older, more curious youngsters.

Ernie dropped the dressed carcass of the kangaroo in the dust at his feet, together with a small bag of ripe pandanus fruit. He stood silently; one foot raised and crossed over his other leg, balancing himself with his spear. He kept his face carefully neutral and shielded his mind from the babble of excited queries bombarding him.

At last, the crowd of men stirred and parted when a thickset, imposing individual pushed through to the front. The man's heavy eye-ridges gave him a permanent frown, belied by the broken-toothed grin below them. "Wandjina! Is it truly you?"

Ernie raised his hand in greeting. "I see you, Garagh, son of Uhlaht."

Garagh cocked his head to one side. "I had not thought to see you for many moons. You left here but a hand of hands ago, saying you were going walkabout."

Ernie felt a gentle but sharp penetration of his mind. He deftly deflected it and put a polite smile on his face. "I will tell you later what brought me here." He paused and looked around the group of silent men, who hung on every word, their minds ablaze with questions. "I brought meat in friendship. Am I welcome by your fires?"

Garagh clapped his hands together then spread them wide. "Wandjina is always welcome at the fires of the People...with or without meat." He grinned and gestured toward the main cave. "Come, my friend. Eat and take your rest. I would hear your words."

Chapter Fourteen

Wulgu found Rima where the black crumbled lava of the Stony Lands gave way to the edge of the rainforest. In the years since the last eruption, the shattered and burnt forests had regenerated, and the edges were now a tangle of vines and re-growth.

Rima looked up wild-eyed when Wulgu appeared from the forest before her. Her long silky hair was matted and sweaty and she bore crusted wounds on her feet and hands that still oozed blood. She wiped the hair from her eyes with one hand, while rocking back on her feet. A soft whimper escaped her lips when she eased the pressure on her cut feet.

Wulgu? Can it be you?

Wulgu approached her then rumbled deep in his chest. His black eyes flashed while he scanned her injured body. *What happened, Rima? I heard your call.*

I cannot believe it is really you. I had given up hope of ever seeing my kind again. It has been twelve years, Wulgu.

Wulgu lurched up beside Rima and stroked a hand gently along her cheek. *Too long, my Rima. But I am here now.* He turned the palms of her hands over, then frowned at the ragged cuts. *We must attend to these wounds immediately.*

Rima shook her head; droplets of sweat spattered the ground. *There is no time. I must find Gaia.* She searched the rainforest behind him. *Are you alone, Wulgu? Did no others come with you?*

Wulgu dropped her hand and stared into Rima's swollen eyes. *Others came, Rima. But I heard your need and came to find you.* He hesitated. *The child is here? Where?*

Horrible dark things took her. They came in the night. The yowie broke down into sobs. *I let them take her!* Rima moaned and rocked back and forth on her heels. *I must find her. I followed their scent, though it is very faint. It came here but I lost it. I must find it again!*

Wulgu dropped to all fours and snuffed the ground, pulling in a great lungful of air then loudly exhaling. He moved from side to side, casting about for a scent, like a bloodhound. At the edge of the lava boulders, he came across a faint scuffmark in the red volcanic earth and paused. *A footprint.* He gently cleared away the debris around it. *It looks like a boot. Was there a man with these dark things?*

Rima nodded. *Yes. A dark man. I could not read his thoughts.*

Wulgu sniffed again. *I have smelled this wrongness before. Strange creatures from elsewhere come here from time to time. They have a wrongness about them. The man that left this print has it too.* He shivered, while the hair on his back and head stood up, making his sagittal crest even more pronounced. He bared long canine teeth in a snarl. *I want to fight this man. His human smell is faint and he reeks of dangerous enemy.*

Rima groaned and let out another soft whimper when she put her weight onto her feet again. *I must go, Wulgu. Every moment I delay puts my Gaia farther away.*

Wulgu turned, his face softened. *I shall accompany you. First, we must do something about your wounds. Lie still and wait.* He walked into the rainforest, searching for familiar plants. A few minutes later, he returned to Rima, carrying an assortment of leafy branches, bark and grasses. He sat beside her while stripping the leaves and stuffing them into his cavernous mouth.

I could not find everything I needed, but these will do, he thought, while he chewed. *No doubt, we will find others as we travel.* Wulgu spat the green mass into his palm and poked at it with a finger. *It will do. Here, hold this on your cuts.* He picked up a slab of paperbark and shaped it roughly to Rima's foot. Stripping fibres from the grass, he expertly bound the paperbark over the poultice on her wounds.

It stings, Rima whimpered.

Good. Now sit here while I find the trail. Wulgu bounded off, scanning the ground minutely and sniffing deeply. He worked his way from the scuffed footprint near the lava field, across the small clearing, then toward the dense tangle of the rainforest. He plunged into the vines and disappeared. A few minutes later, he re-emerged and gestured. *Come, Rima, I have found their path.*

Rima got up gingerly and limped after Wulgu. Pushing through the boundary vegetation, she found the undergrowth under the rainforest canopy was much less dense. Wulgu was already only a vague shape glimpsed through the tree trunks. She hobbled after him, determined not to slow him down in their search for Gaia.

The trail ran straight through the forest, only deviating around large trees and rocks. Once, Wulgu led them around a large patch of lawyer vine, with its tangle of wicked-looking recurving spines, to find the trail again on the far side. He shook his head in wonder. *Why did he not go around? He must be driven by some great urgency.*

An hour later, he pointed out a mark on a fallen log. *He rested here.* Wulgu looked back the way they came then set out again. *We are losing ground,* he thought grimly. *He knows where he is going, but we must search for the path. Our only hope is to press on while he rests.*

Rima leaned against a tree, panting with the effort. Her wounded feet throbbed and the paperback bandage had worked loose on one of them, spilling out the poultice. She took a deep breath and limped after Wulgu. *As fast as you can, Wulgu. I can keep up. We must find my baby. She needs me.*

The land sloped down to a small, fern-choked gully. They carefully picked their way over rocks, searching the sides for any sign of their quarry having left the stream. Eventually, they picked up the trail again, leading up a steep slope. While they ascended, the vegetation thinned out and game trails became more evident. Soon, they were able to make better time, loping along on all fours. Rima ignored the pain in her feet and her sore arms and hands, happy to be gaining on the man at last.

They came to a long, low hill rising to a limestone bluff and followed the game trail along the slope, parallel to the cliffs. The trail was so well defined that Wulgu felt confident enough to pick up the pace to a run, only lowering his great head to the trail every few minutes to confirm they were still on the right track. So intent were they that they burst around a large boulder and came face to face with a herd of huge shambling animals, standing as tall as a man, but with the bulk of a rhinoceros. Coarse brown hair covered their hides. They were grazing on the shrubs and grass along the sides of the path.

Wulgu halted so abruptly that Rima collided with him. Together, they stood and stared at the beasts whose ears pricked forward in alarm, their great noses snuffing the air. A large male at the front pawed the ground, sending up clouds of dust. Behind him females and youngsters, milling around and bleating, edged slowly away. One female raised up on her hind legs, encouraging the young animal next to her to enter the female's pouch.

What are they, Rima? Have you seen them before?

Yes. Gaia called them Diprotodons. She said they are harmless unless they trample you.

Wulgu turned slowly to stare at Rima. He grinned. *Then we shall have to make sure they do not.* He raised himself up to his full height and took a deep breath, then let it out in an ear-shattering roar.

Rima joined in, ululating shrilly and thrashing a bush beside her. The large male diprotodon leapt back, startled. He bellowed, then turned and plunged back into the herd, scattering them before him. In a cacophony of shrieks and bellows and the snapping of branches, the herd crashed off through the undergrowth in a maelstrom of dust.

That worked rather well, thought Wulgu smugly.

He became less smug when he realized he had lost the scent of their quarry in the churned up ground of the stampede.

Chapter Fifteen

The men of the Dwarrah brought the group to a small encampment. The rough campsite sat next to a pool filled by a tiny rivulet trickling from a sandstone hill. Several rough lean-to shelters surrounded the ashes of a sprawling campfire. James was surprised to see no women or children but, after inspecting the site, decided that this was more in the nature of a temporary hunting camp.

The hunters escorted them to the shade of a gum tree near the pool and motioned for them to sit. Sam and Tilley gratefully collapsed to the sandy soil, shed their backpacks and fanned themselves with their hands. Bertie squatted beside them and mopped his face with a large red handkerchief. Nathan and Ratana were shepherded off to one side, nearer to the old ashes of the fire. The Aborigines tried to make Narahdarn sit with them but he refused to be separated from Shinara, shaking his head and repeating a denial. After a short but fierce argument, they let him rejoin the others.

"What was that all about?" murmured James.

Narahdarn shrugged. "They want to separate us dinkum blackfellahs from you pale spirit beings, I think." He frowned. "It seems they think you may be a threat. That's not a good start."

Tilley snorted. "The buggers must be blind. I mean, do we look like a threat?" She gestured around at the group sitting around in the sand, flushed from the heat and limp with fatigue.

"Interestingly, they've come across white people before, and that's why they are a bit leery of us."

Sam bolted to a sitting position. "Gaia! It must be Gaia. She's the only white person who could be here in ancient Australia." She gripped James's arm. "We must find out where she is."

"I don't think so," Narahdarn slowly muttered. "They refer to a whole tribe of pale people nearby. It seems there was trouble."

"By Jove!" interjected Bertie. "A white tribe? I've never heard of such a thing."

James glanced at the others before turning to Bertie. "It may be stranger than you think, mate." He grinned, enjoying his revelation. "I believe this is the group of Neanderthals we came to find."

Bertie opened his mouth then closed it with a snap. He frowned and raised a hand to twirl his moustache absently as he mused. "Neanderthals, you say? Assuming you are accurate, then this group at thirty thousand years before present time is possibly part of my postulated southern migration. Let's see, there was that site in Sirnak, Iraq, about fifty thousand years ago, Turbat in Pakistan about forty-five thousand…"

Tilley grasped her husband's arm and smiled at James. "I think you've made his day."

"…Java possibly, though the dating is suspect, probably Timor at thirty-eight, then the crossing to…here?" Bertie beamed at James. "It fits, by God, it fits!" He jumped up and let out a whoop of joy. "When I write this up, they'll…" He broke off. "We have got to go and see this tribe."

The Aboriginal hunters jumped up at Bertie's shout, before grabbing their weapons. The old hunter strode across to them, his spear held menacingly in his hand. He jabbered at them in a torrent of words, scowling fiercely at Bertie.

Narahdarn interposed himself between the warrior and James, holding his empty hands up and talking quietly, repeating the same phrases over and over. When the old man stopped shouting, Narahdarn gestured slowly at Bertie and spoke again at length. The old man lowered his spear and grunted, then turned on his heel and marched back to his fellow hunters.

"What did you say to him?" asked James.

"First of all, I was just asking him to calm down, to see that we offered no threat. Then I basically told him that Bertie was tracking these people, the Neanderthals, and had been for many years." Narahdarn gave a wry grin. "Sorry, mate. I sort of implied you have no great love for them. Sort of the old 'enemy of my enemy is my friend' routine." He shrugged. "Guess it might come back to bite us in the bum but, at least, it defused the situation for now."

Bertie snorted. "No great love indeed. Just spent my life studying the blighters."

James nodded at the young man. "I think you handled that well, mate." He sat down by the women again. "It does highlight an ongoing problem, though. If we can't understand each other, we're in for a great many misunderstandings. We need to learn their language, or, at least, get a working knowledge of it."

Tilley rolled her eyes. "I was never much good at languages, even as a girl. I don't know how I'm going to cope now."

Sam gave her a quick hug. "That makes two of us. Seriously, James, how can we possibly learn enough of their language in a short enough time to make a difference?"

James pursed his lips. "There is a way, I think," he said slowly. "Sam, do you know the value of the mathematical term pi?"

"Pi? What on earth are you talking about, hon?"

"Humor me. Do you know the value?"

Sam shook her head. "Somewhere around three, I think. I was no good at math in school."

Honey, the value is about 3.1415927. Aloud, he said, "Can you repeat it back to me?"

"Repeat what?" asked Tilley.

Sam looked thoughtful. "3.1415927. But that's not an exact value. It's the relationship between the radius and the circumference of a circle and it's been calculated to over a billion decimal places…" She grinned. "That might just work."

Tilley looked puzzled. "What might work? What are you two talking about? What has pi got to do with anything?"

Bertie wandered over and squatted beside his wife when she spoke.

James turned to Tilley and Bertie. "This may be hard for you to believe, but Sam and I…and Ratana, Nathan and Narahdarn…I'm not sure about Shinara…" Narahdarn nodded. "Anyway," James went on, "we can communicate by using just our minds."

"Bosh!" exclaimed Bertie. "What a load of twaddle. Those experiments by those parapsychology chappies put paid to all those ideas."

James smiled. "They did rather, didn't they? Nevertheless…" He looked at Tilley, who was quietly staring at Sam. "Tilley, talk to your husband. Come up with some little fact that only you two could possibly know about. Then whisper it to Sam."

Tilley and Bertie exchanged a long look. Bertie rolled his eyes and sighed. "I'm in the company of madmen. Well, my lovey-dovey, let's humor them." He leaned close to Tilley and, for a few moments, they whispered furiously. Tilley laughed, then turned to Sam and whispered in her ear. Sam laughed too and the two women smiled at each other.

"Come on then, old man," growled Bertie. "Do your party trick."

"When you were in India, in the northern hill country, you went to bathe in a small stream. You stripped off and jumped into a secluded pool, only to find the local women using it for their laundry. The angry men of the village chased you down the road and you were bare-bum naked."

Bertie's jaw dropped. "How the deuce did you do that?"

"I told you. We can talk to each other using just our minds."

Bertie rocked back on his heels and sat down with a thump in the dust. "I say, old chap, and I thought you were a scientist." He sat twirling his moustache and staring at James like he'd grown horns or two heads.

James shrugged. "To get back to my idea. We can communicate not only the direct facts, like pi, but also relevant ideas that sort of leak over with it. I suggest Narahdarn sits down and gives us a quick glossary of the Dwarrah nouns he uses and whatever he knows about sentence construction. We should be able to learn something of use."

Narahdarn pursed his lips. "A good idea on the face of it, doctor."

Sam smiled. "Let's get started then. You give us the English word, then the Aboriginal word and think it to us at the same time."

Narahdarn shook his head. "Not as simple as that, I'm afraid. Doctor, you know a bit of modern language I believe? Well, as you know, the grammar is very complex. They use a lot of hyphenated words that convey as much information as whole sentences in English. Verbs have three sounds for example, the first tells you who did the action, the second shows what the action was and the third shows when it happened. On the other hand, word order in the sentence is not as important as in English." He shrugged. "I still think it's a good idea, but don't expect too much from it."

James nodded. "Don't get disheartened. Even a few words will be of help. Give us a couple, Narahdarn, and let's see how it goes." He looked around. "How about the word for 'tree'?"

Narahdarn sighed. "See what I mean? It could be 'Gooree' or 'Bahal' unless you mean a specific type of tree or a tree in a particular place, or one where something happened. All of them are different and depend on the context syllables. Sorry, doctor," he said hurriedly, "try this then." Narahdarn projected the image of the tree overhanging the small pool of water, then an Aboriginal word for it. He modified the word by attaching action words to it. "I'm giving you phonetic pronunciations as best I can. The forms are archaic and are a bit surprising actually."

"What do you mean?" asked James.

"Well, I was led to believe that the general languages spoken at this time would be fairly similar, what's referred to as proto-Australian, with few similarities to modern dialects. In fact, I had a crash course in it before we came. Now, I'm from Central Australia, and my tribe has a very different dialect from those up here in north Queensland in modern times. But the Dwarrah dialect is more similar to my tribe's than to modern Queenslanders or proto-Australian. It's as if the tribes were moving around a lot. I guess a lot can happen in thirty thousand years."

"A problem for the language experts, if we ever get to talk to any." James nodded to Narahdarn. "But if what you say is true, a grounding in your tribe's dialect should help. Let's have another word. How about stream?"

The lesson continued. Lengthy silences were broken by short explanations to Tilley and Bertie, who repeated the words out loud. Bertie pulled out a notebook and jotted down some words using phonetic spelling. They contacted Ratana and Nathan, who sat close to the pool with the Aboriginal hunters. After a bit of reluctance on Nathan's part, they joined in, eavesdropping on the hunter's conversation and relaying it to Narahdarn for translation.

I'm not sure we should be doing this. Remember what Ernie said? He said not to use our mind-speech. Nathan looked uncomfortable. *Why do you think he said that?*

Ratana reached across and squeezed his hand. *He must have had a good reason, love. He did say we were being watched. Perhaps our thoughts betray our position in some way.*

So why are we using them now? Come to that, why can't we even detect Ernie's presence any more? Nathan looked across at the other group. *Sam? What about you? Have you detected Gaia since you arrived?*

Sam nodded uncertainly. *Yes, briefly. Something stopped me, something…nasty. Then Ernie said not to try to contact her. Since then, I haven't even felt her, or Ernie. It's as if everything is closing around me.*

Nathan slapped his knee with one hand, drawing quick looks from their captors. *That's it exactly. I'm finding it harder to reach out with my mind, even to people close to me, like you.*

You too, huh? James thought. *I was worried it was just me. I wonder why?*

I think Ernie did something to us, to stop us using our minds. He can be a bit high-handed that way.

Ratana gave Nathan a startled look. *He wouldn't do that, love. I'm surprised you'd even think it.*

Why? He's gone off on his own, doing God knows what, and left us at the mercy of these savages. You know he has no real interest in finding Gaia.

James was shocked by the undertones of bitterness in Nathan's thoughts. *Nathan, that's not entirely fair…*

Isn't it? You know he only came back with us to find a way to heal this supposed breach in the time-line. You weren't there when he discussed it with Garagh and the scientists. As far as he's concerned, finding Gaia is only a secondary goal.

No! I can't believe that. Sam suddenly stood up and stared across the campsite at Nathan. *It's not true, is it, James?*

No, love, it's not. James rose and held his wife tenderly. *Nathan, you know Ernie and Garagh had another reason for coming back here. But they spent a great deal of time and effort finding Gaia in the first place and arranging for us to come back and rescue her. Your comments dishonor the man.*

Nathan snorted then shook off Ratana's hand. *You think so? Then why do the Dwarrah react like this to him?* He turned to the tribesman near him and, displaying more ability with the language than the others thought him capable, addressed the man.

"Know that we are the emissaries of Wandjina. Holding us captive will incur his wrath. Release us at once."

For God's sake, Nathan, no! Don't use his name. James leapt to his feet in consternation.

Narahdarn also rose slowly. "Shit. That'll put the dingo in the chook house, for sure."

The tribesman yelled and shoved his spear at Nathan, who stumbled back with a stunned look on his face. The other Dwarrah jumped up, grabbing their weapons then running to surround Nathan and Ratana. The leader jabbered at them, shaking his killing stick in their faces.

Narahdarn listened, relaying a rough translation to the others in a hoarse whisper. "He does not recognize Wandjina as anything but an evil spirit...he does not fear him...he will do what he pleases." Narahdarn paused. "Damn the man...he intends to take Nathan to the elders...he will leave the white spirits...sorry, that's you...to die here."

The Dwarrah tribesmen hustled Nathan and Ratana off to one side while others grabbed Narahdarn and bound him with grass ropes. They picked up the backpacks and, pushing the three Aboriginal members of the group ahead of them, set off into the brush.

Sam hugged Tilley. "What are we going to do?" she asked.

James looked grimly at the others. "Survive. Somehow."

Chapter Sixteen

Rima became more and more restless as the day wore on. The diprotodon herd had ripped up the ground, spreading a pall of dust over the path and trees. The faint footprints and even more tenuous scent of wrongness they followed all day disappeared with the stampeding herd. Wulgu followed the devastation for over a mile before the herd slowed and veered off to one side, the memory of the initial panic seeping from their tiny brains. He carefully examined the untouched path for several hundred yards beyond, but he found no trace of their quarry.

Wulgu moved to the uphill side of the track and quartered the ground slowly, smelling the vegetation and examining the hard ground for any hint that the man had left the path. He moved wide around the churned up ground, then painstakingly tracked back toward Rima. When he reached her, at the spot where the stampede had started, he moved to the downhill side and worked his way forward.

Nothing. It is as if they have disappeared. Wulgu slumped down under a *Syzygium* bush, then stripped off a handful of the young leaves and crammed them into his mouth. He watched morosely while Rima limped up the path toward him.

She radiated concern and grief. *Wulgu, they must be somewhere. Could the herd have left the path at the point where the man left before them?*

That would be too coincidental. Let me think. Wulgu closed his eyes and sat motionless, chewing on a twig. After several minutes, he opened his eyes again and nodded. *Remember the patch of lawyer vine, Rima?*

Yes. What about it?

He didn't avoid it. He moved straight through it in a straight line. He moved directly toward these cliffs all day. The only deviation was when he followed this path. I think he has reached his goal and turned uphill toward the cliffs again. Wulgu stood and stared across the hillside of scrub at the line of low cliffs stretching out on each side. *But where? I didn't find any sign on the uphill side.*

Wulgu moved uphill and started covering the ground again slowly.

There must be some sign. He is human. Even those 'things' can't hide that. He moved patiently, with Rima limping along behind him.

Rima looked about her while Wulgu worked, misery in her eyes. She had lost Gaia, her whole reason for existence, through a stupid mistake on her part. What was she thinking, going off and leaving her alone in the night? Now she was in danger and she, Rima, was doing nothing to find her except tagging along while Wulgu did all the work. He didn't even know Gaia, yet he was tireless in his efforts. She could see the strain he was under. *Well, that will change,* she thought, feeling anger building in her. Together they would find her darling Gaia and rip that evil man limb from limb. Rima growled deep in her throat and bent low, snuffing the ground, searching alongside the male yowie.

I've gone over that area already, Rima. Move outward and see whether you can find anything there.

Then what's this? Rima stared down at a patch of bare ground. In the bare soil was a straight furrow, as if a stick had been poked into the earth then dragged forward. It pointed directly at the cliffs.

Wulgu grunted in annoyance and ambled over. He looked at the ground then bent closer. *I could not have missed this. I went over this area minutely only an hour or so ago.* He sniffed the ground, drawing in a great whiff of air. *The smell is different. Very similar, but different somehow. It smells more natural, less wrong.*

Perhaps you smell the stick. Rima sniffed, wrinkling her nose.

Wulgu looked toward the cliffs. He walked slowly in the direction of the furrow, stopping often to smell the ground. Fifty feet further on, he grunted again. *A footprint. And the old smell. We are on the trail again.* He set off at a slow run toward the darkening line of stone bluffs.

They passed into the shadow of the cliffs cast by the setting sun and picked their way through the rubble-strewn ground at the base of the limestone bluffs. The hills rose straight up from the scrubby hillside. The two weary yowies found the faint trail of their quarry leading to a high, slanting crack in the rock face. A small stream issued from the crack, forming a scummy pool that seeped away into the sandy soil. Numerous footprints in the wet sand around the edges told of the many animals that used the cave as a source of water.

Wulgu carefully examined the footprints, then pointed out the distinctive marks of a man wading through the pool into the depths of the cave. They bent and drank thirstily, cupping the water in their great hairy hands. Then, with a nod of agreement, they waded through the pool and into the dark cavern beyond.

Daylight faded rapidly to a faint greyness as they advanced. Despite their caution, rocks clattered when they picked their way up the gurgling stream in the dim light. A dry rustling noise crackled. They froze in their tracks until a faint chittering identified the source as bats lost in the gloom above them. Water dripped and splashed from the walls and the air smelled musty and uninviting.

It feels empty, Wulgu.

Wulgu peered around him, straining to see in the dark. *He was here; I can smell him. Also much wrongness.* He moved deeper into the cave, re-crossing the tiny stream. He groped among the rocks and grunted in surprise. *I was right. Somebody did come back with us.*

What do you mean?

When we arrived back in this time, there was confusion. I saw someone run off into the forest. Nobody else saw him and the others thought I was mistaken. Wulgu held up a small object. *Look Rima. A can of meat. A modern human has been here.*

Rima sniffed the can, before wrinkling her nose in disgust. *That is the evil man's smell.* She threw the can down and got down on all fours, casting about, seeking others scents in the gloom. She whimpered and pressed her face to the cold rocks. *Gaia! My Gaia was here. I can smell her.*

Wulgu joined her and inhaled delicately, savoring the faint odor. *So that is the child? I shall remember it.* He raised his shaggy head and peered into the darkness. *We must find the trail again before nightfall gives these things the advantage.*

In the mud near the stream, they came across another furrow ploughed into the soft surface. It pointed deeper into the cave. Rima smiled. *My darling is leaving a trail for us to follow.*

Wulgu shook his head. *There is no smell of her here. The man would not let her wander freely, and certainly would not let her mark the trail in his sight. Someone else has left this for us. But who?* He closely examined the mud. *There are faint tracks here but unlike any animal or human I have seen.* He shrugged. *We cannot delay.* He led the way deeper into the blackness of the cave, groping along the course of the stream.

Darkness rapidly became impenetrable night as the entrance to the cavern fell away behind them. The trail narrowed to the faintest of scents discernible on the rocks beside the tiny trickle of water. The two yowies crept along on hands and knees, their faces close to the ground, following the dissipating scent. After an hour and several hundred yards of crawling, they lost the trail completely.

Rima sat down on a rock and put her head in her hands. *We have lost them again,* she wailed.

Wulgu sighed deeply. *Rima, we need the strength of our race now, not wailing.* He searched the dim trail ahead. *They must be going somewhere. There must be another exit.* He stood up and peered deeper into the darkness. *The only thing we can do is go back, then work around the cliffs and look for another entrance.*

Rima, a grim look on her face, joined her inspection of the darkened trail to his. *The scent will have gone by then, Wulgu. It is faint even now.*

*I cannot see that we have a choice. If we hurry we...*Wulgu broke off when a rock clattered ahead of them. *Did you hear that, Rima?*

Yes. Is it them?

Possibly. What animal would come this far into a cave?

They crept forward, straining to hear, being careful to make as little noise as possible. A rock shifted ahead of them again. They moved on cautiously. Then a faint tapping sound came from one side, echoing off the high roof.

We must follow, Rima. We have nothing else to guide us.

They moved away from the streambed, which was now reduced to only a few damp patches of mud. The tapping sound receded from them as they clambered up a slope covered in large boulders, drawing them onward. The echoes changed when the cavernous space around them closed in. Soon, they crept through a smooth-floored tunnel, moving ever upward.

I think I can see something, Wulgu.

Wulgu stopped and peered ahead, rubbing his eyes with the back of his hand. *I see it too. A greyish light. We are close to the surface.*

The light slowly increased until they could just make out the walls of their passageway. The floor levelled out and the outline of a cave entrance came into view, lined with ferns and mosses. A shadow flitted across the grey light seeping in from the outside world.

Wulgu pointed then bounded forward. *There! Something moved.*

He burst out of the cave into dense forest, Rima on his heels. He turned, slowly searching the vegetation that was now darkening as the sun sank below the horizon.

What did you see? Rima anxiously asked while searching the area. *Was it the man? Was it my Gaia?*

Wulgu frowned and shook his head. *It was too small for a man and the limbs were too short for it to be the child.* He turned to Rima. *Here, I will share my memory of it.*

The yowies concentrated, Wulgu remembering every detail he could, pulling up the fleeting image into his mind's eye. Rima connected with him, sharing the image and storing it in her own memories.

I agree. That is not Gaia, and it is too small to be a man.

If I did not know that they never existed in Australia, said Wulgu thoughtfully, *I would call that a monkey. It was hairy.*

Well, it has gone now and the sun has set. Can we find the trail again?

There is no scent, said Wulgu flatly. *Moreover, we need light to look for footprints.* He savagely thumped a tree trunk alongside him, making the leaves shake violently. *We must camp until dawn and guard against these 'monkeys'.*

We have company, Wulgu.

Wulgu swung round to face Rima, then turned to look at what she saw. Standing in the deepening gloom of the rainforest was a small, hairy, man-like being. It stood about three feet tall, with disproportionately long arms and short legs. Its face drew out into a short muzzle, though the black eyes faced forward, staring out from under prominent eye ridges. It was covered in dense black fur that hid details of its body. Wulgu caught a swift movement beside it as another one appeared, then another. He glanced around them, seeing more shapes step out from the vegetation.

Wulgu edged back with Rima, until their backs were against the rock wall by the cave entrance. *They are many but they do not look like much of a threat.*

The figure they spotted first moved forward, not so much walking as darting in short, rapid strides from one tree to another. It raised its head and chittered at them. It seemed to be waiting for a response. Wulgu framed a careful thought and sent it out. *We mean you no harm.* The creature chittered again, paused, then said clearly, though in a high-pitched, squeaky voice, "The figure you see before you goes by the name of Ehrich."

Wulgu and Rima gaped. Wulgu shook his massive head. *Ehrich? That is not Ehrich.*

Who is Ehrich? Rima asked.

He is an evil man who tried to kill our friends, Wulgu replied. *If he is here, he is the one who captured Gaia.*

The figure squeaked again rapidly. "Ehrich," it said.

Another figure chirped in with, "You could ask Rima," in a young girl's voice.

Rima gasped and started forward. *That is Gaia's voice.*

The figures scattered before her, squeaking in alarm. She stopped and withdrew again, waiting until the little furry humanoids reappeared. When they did, she smiled at them and made soft hooting noises. *I wish they could hear us, Wulgu.*

It does present a problem. They seem incapable of mind-talk and, for once, I regret we have no capacity for audible language. Wulgu frowned in concentration. *I am unsure of what to do now, Rima.*

The figures gathered closer, making their high-pitched chirping noises while they moved. Abruptly, they started talking again, using incomplete phrases and obviously mimicking things they had heard.

"...you promised."

"Hold her."

"So, you are awake."

"...name of Ehrich."

"...ask Rima."

Wulgu's face lit up. *Ah, that's it.* He leaned forward and pointed at the figure that said Rima's name then he pointed at Rima. He did this several times while the figures stared at him in silence.

The tiny figure cocked its head to one side and spoke again. "Hold her...Ehrich...ask Rima."

Wulgu excitedly pointed again at Rima, while nodding and grinning. The creatures were silent again for several minutes then "Rima?" said the first figure.

Wulgu clapped his hands and pointed at Rima, who nodded vigorously and smiled. The creatures all pointed at Rima and called out, "Rima, Rima, Rima, Rima," squeaking in excitement.

One of them pointed at Wulgu. "Rima?" it asked.

Wulgu shook his head and pointed at Rima again. The creature pointed at Wulgu and asked "Ehrich?"

Wulgu shook his head sharply, his face twisting into an automatic snarl. He pointed back into the cave then out into the rainforest. He held his hand out at about six feet from the ground then pointed back into the cave. Next he held out his hand about four feet from the ground and whimpered softly. *This is hopeless,* he thought to Rima. *How do we convey a picture of the man and Gaia?*

There was a movement among the crowd of creatures in the gathering twilight. One of the creatures dragged forward a tiny figure that was straining at the hand clutching it, pulling back and wailing. The creature that was doing most of the talking pointed again at Rima and repeated her name in a decisive manner. He then pointed at the taller figure clutching the youngster and said, "Ehrich." He looked at Wulgu then at the youngster and said, "Child," in a firm voice.

Wulgu and Rima both nodded, excited that the creatures clearly understood that Ehrich was with Gaia and that they were searching for the two.

The creature stepped closer to the yowies and pointed into the cave mouth. "Ehrich. Child." He added another phrase, which made the others turn away, while making little snarls and mewls of displeasure. He then said "Rima," and pointed at both yowies. He picked up a stick and, bending over, drew a straight furrow in the leaf litter.

It was you, thought Wulgu. He pointed along the furrow and hooted softly.

The figure scuffed out the furrow with one hairy foot then turned and walked into the forest, beckoning with one hand.

I think he wants us to follow, Wulgu.

Yes. Do we trust him?

What have we got to lose? There is no trail and my instincts tell me these beings don't like Ehrich any more than we do.

Rima placed her hand in Wulgu's and they followed the small tribe of creatures into the forest.

Chapter Seventeen

"I'd say we are in a bit of a tight spot, what?" Bertie thoughtfully looked in the direction of the departing Aboriginal hunters. He slowly swivelled on his heel, taking in their surroundings. "I think we need a good chin wag to come up with a decent plan of action."

"Couldn't agree more, mate," said James. He turned toward where Sam and Tilley were talking softly with each other then glanced at Shinara. The girl sat alone in the hot sun, with the usual abstracted expression on her face. "Could you ladies see if you can persuade Shinara to join us by the billabong?" He smiled encouragingly at Sam and Tilley before turning away, his face taking on a sombre expression.

Shinara proved to be unexpectedly pliable, getting up and accompanying Sam and Tilley without any resistance. When they settled by the water, James addressed the group. "Okay. We have a major problem and we need to make some decisions fast. The first is, do we stay here or do we leave?"

"Forgive me, James, but why on earth would we want to just stay here?" asked Tilley.

"Several reasons. We are only some ten miles from the two boulders Ernie told us to wait by. I believe either he left us a message or he will come looking for us. If we remain in one spot rather than traipsing around the countryside, we stand a better chance of being found. We also have shelters here," James gestured at the rough lean-tos, "and a water source. We don't know the area or the resources it contains. Animals will be coming to the water. Perhaps we can kill some for food."

Bertie nodded. "Good point, old chap, but your argument carries a sting in its tail. From what we've seen of this place, there are a lot of rather hungry carnivores around too. By staying around the water we provide them with a snack as well as a drink."

"As I said, we have a choice to make. If we leave, where do we go?"

"Shouldn't we go back to the two rocks?" asked Sam. "If Ernie is expecting us to be there…"

James smiled at his wife with a softening of his gaze. "Can you point us in the right direction, love? I'm a bit lost myself and I don't fancy my skills as a tracker these days."

Sam looked around in dismay. She raised her hand, pointing, then hesitated and dropped it again. "I think it was over there but I'm not sure." She shook her head.

"All right," said James. "Any other suggestions?"

"Want Narahdarn." The soft, clear voice took them all by surprise. They stared at Shinara with open-mouthed wonder.

"By Jove, the lass can speak," breathed Bertie.

"Want Narahdarn," Shinara repeated, with a hint of expression enlivening her face.

"You know, I think she has a point," Tilley gently muttered. "There are arguments for staying and for leaving, but we can't abandon our friends. Nathan, Ratana and Narahdarn." She nodded at Shinara while smiling at the girl. "They've all been taken away. We must follow them. Perhaps we can rescue them." She plucked at her sweat-dampened shirt then glanced at Sam with an inquiring look.

Sam nodded. "Yes, Tilley. I agree. We must try and help them."

"Besides, we know these Dwarrah chappies live close to the Neanderthals. We have got to find them," Bertie added excitedly, giving a small hop from leg to leg then reaching down to pluck two tics from his exposed thigh.

Sam smiled at him then searched her arms and legs for biting insects while she added, "Yes, Ernie was going to them. If we can find the Neanderthals we may find Ernie."

James coughed to cover his amusement when every member began to unconsciously imitate his wife by inspecting their limbs for parasites. "I agree too, but I hope everyone else noticed those spears and killing sticks they carry. They may be crude weapons but they are efficient. And I don't think those tribesmen would hesitate to use them."

"Friends are friends, love," said Sam with a sigh. "Tilley's right. We must go after them." She got up and brushed off her slacks.

Bertie twirled his moustache. "If we are going to do it, then time's a-wasting, old chums. A fresh trail is a good trail and all that. I've done my share of tracking in Pakistan and India. I should be able to follow these blighters."

"Right then," agreed James, springing to his feet. "First, drink as much water as you can before we leave. Also, soak your hat or tie a wet hankie around your head. I just wish we had something to carry water in, I think we're going to need it. Find a good, stout stick too, if you can."

Shinara looked up at James, her face showing a degree of perplexity. "Want Narahdarn," she repeated.

"We'll find him, Shinara." He held out his hand to the pale young girl and helped her to her feet when she took it.

The five set out after the Dwarrah tribesmen. Bertie led the party;

his thin frame and long legs striding over the sandy soil like some oversized stork. He carried a gnarled gum branch that he used to circle the faint marks left by the hunters and their captives. "Someone's using the old noggin," he commented with an approving nod of his head. "Look at that scuff-mark. Obviously made by a shoe."

Tilley was next in line, her sturdy frame sweating already from the intense heat. Nevertheless, she kept a smile on her face and often turned with an encouraging word for the young girl behind her.

Shinara followed docilely, without being led. The absence of her usually constant companion Narahdarn had stimulated her in some fashion. Her eyes flicked over the surroundings instead of maintaining her usual fixed gaze. She didn't stumble as often as before either; Samantha only had to steady her a couple of times.

Sam noticed the girl was not sweating and wished she knew how she maintained such composure on a hot, dusty day. The sun burned in a cloudless sky but the humidity was high enough for her to feel real discomfort. Her shirt clung damply to her body and she found herself hopping on one foot when she removed an irritating piece of gravel from her shoe and another tic from her arm.

James brought up the rear, at first keeping an alert eye out for any sign of danger. After an hour or two, the lack of any significant event helped him relax slightly. He amused himself by whacking the vegetation with his staff while he walked. He whistled softly, revelling in the wide-open spaces, despite a growing thirst. At length, the dry air and hot sun got the better of him and he called forward to Bertie, suggesting a rest. They sought out the shade under a patch of scrubby acacias and lay in the sand while fanning themselves.

"I really don't want to complain," panted Tilley, "but is there a chance of finding some water soon? My mouth feels like the bottom of a bird cage."

James gave a wry smile, working his mouth so it produced some saliva before answering. "I don't think so. The countryside is getting drier. However, I should be able to find something juicy to eat, with a bit of luck." He got up, groaning slightly, and searched the immediate area. He strode over to a tussock of grass and poked around the base of the clump. He moved on to a second, then a third before he dropped to his knees and started digging with the sharp end of his staff.

When James returned to the others, who waited in the shade, he was carrying several tubers the size of small potatoes. "Desert yams," he explained. He dusted off one of the tubers and bit into it. "Umm. Delicious," he said, with a trickle of juice escaping the corner of his mouth. "Well, perhaps not, but at least it's edible and juicy." He handed over the other tubers and watched everyone tentatively nibble at them then hungrily bite into them. "They're even better roasted," he added when Tilley grimaced at the taste.

Shinara sat looking at the tuber in her hand, making no attempt to eat it.

James reached across and gently pushed her hand close to her mouth. The girl looked at him, then blinked, a small smile flitting across her face. She bit into the yam.

Sam peered about, wiping her mouth with her handkerchief. "I wouldn't have thought there was much to eat out here. I've hardly seen any animals and all the plants look dry and woody."

"Looks can be deceiving, love. I saw a delicious-looking goanna lizard a while ago and some nice crunchy beetles." James grinned at the expressions of horror on Sam and Tilley's faces. "Believe it or not, if you get hungry enough, you'll be fighting to get some. Seriously, though, there are a lot of edible plants here, if you know where to look. Grass seeds, these yams, a type of small tomato, mushrooms, arrowroot, and cycads."

Bertie looked up, surprised. "I thought cycad seeds were poisonous."

"So they are, unless you treat them properly. You can sometimes eat old seeds raw but, to be safe, I don't think we'll risk it."

Sam dragged her fingers through her hair and licked her dry lips. "I don't suppose there's any chance of a drink of water anytime soon?"

"I don't know, love. We'll just have to see what we find. At least the Dwarrah are in the same fix and may lead us to water."

"I've been thinking about that," interjected Bertie after tossing the remains of his tuber into the tall grass. He rapidly blinked in surprise when it was almost immediately covered with insects. He dragged his gaze from the sight then glanced at the others before adding, "We know the Dwarrah live close to the Neanderthal tribe. I can't see two tribes existing together for any length of time in an area this poor in food. There must be more productive land up ahead."

James nodded his agreement after glancing at the place Bertie was staring at again. "Then I suppose the sooner we get through this dry area the better." He glanced at the others, quickly taking in their condition and deciding they could move on again. "Everyone sufficiently recovered? Then let's get going."

They resumed their trek. Bertie once more took the lead, following the faint marks left by the tribesmen and the better-defined trail of their captives.

Bertie continued to point out interesting things in the trail. "See, someone dragged their boot here. Hmm," he said, while poking at a discolored patch of sand with his stick. "Possibly urine." He bent and sniffed. "Yes, but hours old."

Tilley watched her husband loping along the trail, bending and poking with muttered cries of delight. She turned to Shinara and Sam. "I haven't seen him this happy for days. He loves the challenge."

The sun gradually passed overhead and the heat increased in the early afternoon. They stopped in the shade of a jumble of boulders, seeking out the tiny areas of shade cast by the blazing sun.

James found a few more yams and a handful of unripe bush to-matoes. The taste was sour and left an unpleasant aftertaste in the mouth, but at least they supplied needed fluid.

"I think we need to stop here for a while," said James through cracked lips. "We won't be able to function at all unless we can get out of the sun."

"Thank God," muttered Sam.

Tilley wearily nodded her agreement.

Shinara crawled deeper into the shade between the rocks and closed her eyes.

Bertie, looking as alert and refreshed as when he started, leaned back against the rough surface of one of the boulders and closed his eyes. "A bit of a kip wouldn't go amiss, old boy, but we mustn't delay too long. Can't track the blighters in the dark, what?" Before anyone could answer his question, he began to snore.

James dozed, waking every few minutes while the others slept. The sun slowly sank in the west and he felt the air cool slightly. He got up and stretched, then went behind the rocks to relieve himself. Fin-ishing, he bent to examine a narrow but definite trail between the grass clumps, noting the presence of small clawed footprints, scratchings in the sandy soil and chewed grass stems. *Bettong,* he thought, *or possibly a hare-wallaby.* He considered the possibility of constructing and setting a trap but decided against it. *We can't risk a fire, and nobody's going to eat it raw,* he decided with a grimace.

James wandered back around the rocks and woke the others. While they stretched and yawned, he estimated north from the posi-tion of the sun and a guess at the hour. *I could be a hell of a lot more accurate,* he thought, *if those bloody Dwarrah hadn't stolen my watch.* He compared the direction with the trail they were following and nod-ded to himself. *Still travelling a bit south of west. They'll be heading toward the Chillagoe caves, I reckon.*

Shinara, waking, uncurled from the fetal position she'd assumed in the cleft of the rocks. Sam and Tilley caught her attention when they moved round the boulders. She rose gracefully and stepped over a small log wedged between the stones at the rear of the cleft. She glimpsed a movement from the corner of her eye just before some-thing struck her right calf. Shinara stared down at a pale brown snake coiled at her feet, head drawn back poised for another strike. She jumped and cried out. The snake threw back its head, jaws wide, then slumped belly up on the sand, tremors running up and down its body.

Sam and Tilley moved around the rocks to see Shinara standing, trembling, over the body of the snake.

Sam stared horrified from the shock and pain on the girl's face to the snake, then to the two small puncture wounds in her leg. "James!" she screamed. "Quickly! Over here."

James and Bertie ran over to the women, immediately taking in the situation. Bertie caught Shinara as she collapsed, helping her away from the rocks, assisted by Tilley. James bent to examine the snake briefly then walked over and felt the wounds in Shinara's leg. He listened to her breathing and noted the even more pronounced pallor of her face. Already she had lapsed into unconsciousness.

"Shit!" he exclaimed. He rocked back on his haunches and turned a bleak look at the women. "She's been bitten by an eastern brown snake. Possibly the third most poisonous snake in the world." He exhaled noisily. "She needs immediate medical attention, but where the hell is she going to get it?"

Sam looked stricken. "What can we do? There must be something."

"What about cutting her leg and sucking out the poison?" asked Tilley.

Bertie shook his head. "Worst thing you can do, dear. About the only treatment is to bind it firmly, get her to a doctor and let nature take its course." He looked at James hopefully. "I don't suppose you happen to have any antivenin on you, old chum?"

James shook his head. "In my backpack," he said bitterly. "For all the good that's going to do." He looked at his wife, seeing the question in her eyes.

She'll be dead by sunset.

Samantha covered her face and wept, for the first time really feeling a mother's grief for her child.

Chapter Eighteen

Ernie leaned back and belched appreciatively, wiping his greasy fingers on a piece of soft kangaroo leather. He picked up the bowl beside him, the pale brown, scummy liquid slopping over the edge as he did so, and drank from it with gusto. He smacked his lips noisily and belched again before turning to his host.

"Garagh, my friend. Your hospitality is as generous as ever. May the gods forever smile upon you and your people."

Garagh acknowledged the tribute silently, inclining his head toward his guest. He signalled and two old women hurried up, clearing away the bowls and wooden platters, the chewed over bones and remnants of uneaten roots and tubers. One of them offered him a bowl filled with brownish-grey fragments of plant material.

Ernie hesitated a moment then took a small pinch of the material. He spat into his palm and added the fragments to it, mixing it thoroughly. He rolled it into a small lozenge and put it into his mouth, tucking the quid between his cheek and upper gum line. Almost at once he felt a tingling, followed by a slow lightheadedness and growing euphoria. *Pituri,* he thought. *Cured leaves of* Dubiosia hopwoodii *mixed with Acacia wood ash.* He nodded and smiled at Garagh, who grinned in delight, helping himself to a much larger amount of the drug.

Ernie felt troubled. *I hope he knows what he's doing. The nicotine derivatives in this concoction can be deadly...and addictive.* He felt the chemicals coursing through his system and changed them subtly, rendering them relatively harmless. His mind cleared but he leaned back, feigning enjoyment.

Garagh's face lost expression and he collapsed limply against the wall of the cave, giggling softly to himself. After perhaps half an hour he struggled upright and hawked his quid into the fire where it crackled and spat. He reached for the bowl again then hesitated, finally drawing his hand back reluctantly. "Ah, Wandjina. I never dreamed such solace existed for an old man."

"Not so old, my friend. You have the body of a man not far past his prime."

"Yet the mind within it grows weary as the years pass. I thought when I was called south with my people that I would serve my purpose and pass on my leadership to my son." Garagh shook his head sadly. "Yet I have buried sons and grandsons and their sons. Only the bearers of the black stone," he flipped the glistening black pendant hanging around his neck on a leather thong, "have the joys and sorrows of prolonged life." He gave Ernie a quizzical look. "It has been many seasons since first I met you, Wandjina, yet you too seem not to have aged. I can see no black stone around your neck though."

Ernie grunted. "I am not as other men, just as you are different. You were given life whereas I have life within me. The effect is the same, Garagh."

"You have touched on this before, my friend, though your words can be as slippery as eels and as agile as wallabies." Garagh grinned ruefully. "Will you now tell me how you came to be and the story of your days?"

Ernie shook his head. "That would take a lifetime and there are better ways to pass our days."

"Then tell me why you return so soon, old friend. Your presence gladdens me, but I had not thought to see you for many moons. What has happened that brings you back to us?"

Ernie sat and thought about his next words carefully. "Let me ask you something first. You came to this place from the north nearly twenty rains ago with all your people. I would know your plans. Do you stay here or will you move on?"

"You always knew my intentions, Wandjina. Those of us who wear the black stone are called to the south. We journeyed over many lifetimes to reach this land but I feel our journey is not yet over." Garagh scowled, his overhanging eye-ridges almost hiding his eyes. "Others of my tribe believe our travels are over. In deference to their weariness of spirit, I decided to remain here for a time. The land is good, there is much game, many plants for medicines, and good caves large enough for all the tribe."

Ernie nodded. "It is a wise leader who provides for the needs of his people."

"Yes, friend Wandjina," agreed Garagh, "I do all things for my people, and yet they want more. They want to remain here, to intermarry with the tribes of your people and cease our journey." Garagh stood up and punched the air angrily. "This I will not do! I am leader and I say we will move on. The voices have spoken to me and call me south, with my people."

"These voices," said Ernie, "where do they come from? Who is speaking?"

Garagh shrugged. "The gods...or the spirits of our ancestors. They never made that plain. But I hear them with my mind, Wandjina, not with my ears." A fierce expression crossed his face. "They only talk to me, not other wearers of the black stone. They have told me what I must do, and I tell the others." His voice rose to a shout. "I will not be defied!"

Ernie waited silently until Garagh calmed down. "And the voices have told you it is time to move on?"

Garagh chewed his lip pensively. "They have not told me to remain here."

"Then what have they said?"

The old Neanderthal sat silent for a long time. At last he shifted uncomfortably. He poked a finger into the bowl of Pituri and stirred it absently. He made as if to take a pinch then dropped it back into the bowl. "They have not spoken since we crossed the sea on logs from the hot lands to the north," he whispered. "They told me then to move south into the Great Lands and be one with its peoples."

"And how did you interpret this, my friend?"

"I have moved south and we have avoided overt conflict with the tribes we have met. I wait for the voices to guide me further."

"Are you certain the voices should be obeyed?" asked Ernie gently.

Garagh gave Ernie a startled look. "Of course. They gave some of us a great span of days, have shown us new ways of making weapons and guided us unharmed through many, many seasons of travelling. There is great magic here."

Ernie nodded gravely. "Great magic indeed, my friend." He picked up a stick and poked the fire. In a neutral voice, he asked, "And have the voices told you of the purpose for your journey?"

Garagh looked troubled. "They have not revealed it to me yet." He stared moodily at the Pituri bowl again and licked his lips. "I have had visions, images conjured up before me that others cannot see." He fell silent for a long time. "Strange things, though comforting somehow."

Ernie waited. He gently probed Garagh's mind, seeing turmoil and doubt in the man.

"I...I see a strange land, Wandjina. With many people, more than I would believe the land can hold. They live in holes in great rocks and do strange things, things I cannot comprehend. I see many tribes, but they live together without killing and the faces of their children are happy." Garagh looked pleadingly at Ernie. "What is this land, Wandjina? Do you know it?"

"I will tell you a story of my travels, old friend, and you will tell me if I know it." Ernie settled himself comfortably on the ground and sipped from the bowl of drink beside him.

"I knew a man once, Garagh my friend, who was a leader of his people, a great leader. His people loved him and respected him, for he provided all that they needed and he listened to their troubles and concerns. So loved was he that he came to believe he was the chosen of the gods and that he could do no wrong thing. He led his people down false paths and cut himself and his people off from the tribes around him. Though they performed many wondrous things and became a powerful people, it was as if they were ghosts, for none knew of them or knew what they did."

"Haugh! A ghost people," Garagh breathed. He looked uneasily around the cave, at the gathering twilight outside and the flickering shadows cast by the small fire. "Are they here, Wandjina? Is that why you have returned?"

"This leader," went on Ernie, "mistook his own desires for the desires of the gods. He was a good man, but mistaken. His deeds changed the world around him. He was cut off from his people. In turn, his people were cut off from other men, and all men were cut off from the animals, plants, rocks and water. Then all things were cut off from the spirit that gave them life. In time, he came to realize that the evil in the world arose because of wrong actions and selfish desires. He sought to change things and he called on me to aid him."

"This is a great tale, Wandjina, my friend. Did you aid him?"

"I was able to show him that the evil arose from a single action of his, many years before. This action could not be made whole, but must be changed."

Garagh shook his head sadly. "What sorrow there must have been. For how can any man turn back the days to live again? Even the gods cannot do this."

Ernie leaned forward intently. "Did I not say the man and his people became powerful? So powerful was their magic that they could journey without moving; talk over many valleys, even without mind-talk; and made new creatures for their purposes as if they were gods themselves. At last they found a way to turn back the days."

Garagh trembled and looked about him fearfully. "Mighty beings indeed. Are you sure they are not here, Wandjina?"

"I lived with the man and his people for many seasons, residing in his cave, eating at his fire and instructing his children. Together, we traced the paths of evil and goodness until we found the point where all things came together. We found the action that made the evil."

"And what...what was this action?"

"I will come to this. You must understand—the man himself is good, but all men make mistakes. This man had the greatness of spirit to want to change his action, though it might lead into danger."

Garagh nodded sagely. "A true leader will brave danger to do what is right."

Ernie sighed. "Some dangers are unseen. The man bravely returned to his past days to make right his mistake but is no more. The man I knew then is dead."

Garagh sat silently for a few moments. "Dead? Then he has failed? Or will you act for him, Wandjina?"

Ernie shook his head. "Did I not say that only he can change his mistake? I can only advise him, help him."

"Then if he is dead, the thing cannot be changed."

"You can change it, Garagh my friend."

Garagh sat stunned, with his mouth open. He blinked then shut his mouth with a snap. "I? What have I to do with this man? You said only he..."

"Did I not mention his name, old friend? His name is Garagh, son of Uhlaht, of the People of the Forest. He followed voices over many lifetimes from a frozen land in the north to this very spot. Here he made his choice and here you will make it. But this time you can make the right choice."

Chapter Nineteen

Shinara lay in the hot sand, now cooling as the sun set, her body racked with agonized gasps as she fought for life. She was unconscious, her eyes closed, unaware of the men and women beside her.

Sam and Tilley sat red-eyed from weeping, holding the girl's hands and squeezing them in time with her gasps, as if by doing so they could help her breathe. James sat a few feet away hugging his knees and dully staring at the tragic tableau. Bertie paced. Every few minutes he strode out along the track, bending to examine the marks of human passage. He scoured the horizon, shading his eyes with his bony hands. At last he nodded, muttered under his breath and returned to stand over James.

"We have to have water old chap, or none of us will survive," Bertie stated in a low voice.

James did not reply. He continued to sit, rocking gently back and forth and staring at Shinara's struggles.

Bertie's face tightened. "The girl is dying. Do you want to kill your wife too?"

James shuddered and looked up, staring at Bertie. "What the fuck did you say?"

Bertie dropped to his knees beside James. "Sorry, old man. Didn't mean that, but I had to get through to you somehow." He waited for a few moments then asked, "You are listening to me, aren't you?"

James nodded wearily. "Yes, I'm listening. You were saying something about water?"

"We need water, old boy. Your desert fruits and roots have helped, but we'll all die tomorrow if we don't find water." Bertie's voice softened. "Even yon lassie..."

"You don't have to spare my feelings, Bertie," said James softly. "I know she's dying and water won't save her. The venom of the eastern brown snake attacks the nervous system. Her lungs and heart will progressively shut down and she'll die. Even if we managed to get the antivenin in my pack, it would be too late now. Listen to her breathing."

"I know old boy." Bertie put his hand on James's shoulder and squeezed it gently. "But water may ease her passing. Look how dry her lips are."

"All this is academic anyway. There's no water here."

"No, but I think there's a chance of finding some. I've been looking at the slope of the land. It slopes downward, very gradually I admit, but it starts to rise again about a mile away. Over there." Bertie pointed to where the sun hovered just above the horizon. "See how the shadows fall? I didn't spot it earlier, but I think there's a shallow valley. Given the limestone outcrops and the granite bedrock, there's a possibility of a stream, even if we have to dig for it. I think I should go and see if I can find it."

"I can't allow you to go alone. Too much could happen and you'd be without help."

"So come with me. Or Tilley can go if you'd rather stay with your wife." Bertie stood up. "Either way, the sun is setting and we don't have long before it'll be too dark to find anything."

James got up and dusted himself off. "Take Tilley then. I don't think we should leave the ladies alone."

Bertie snorted. "Don't tell me you haven't noticed that either lady is just as capable as us chaps?" He walked over to his wife and squatted beside her. "Fancy a bit of a stroll, my love? It's a lovely evening and I think I know where there might be a bit of water."

Tilley stretched and got up. "I'll be back in a jiffy, Sam," she said. She squeezed the other woman's arm and followed her husband.

Bertie looked back at James. "It'll be dark by the time we return so if you hear us shout, give a coo-ee so we can get home. There's a good chap."

James watched Bertie and Tilley disappear into the scrub, then he walked over to where Sam sat clutching the dying girl. "How are you bearing up, honey?" he asked gently.

Sam shook her head. "When Garagh told us she was our daughter, artificially bred and nurtured, I hated him...and her. When I found out she could kill with her mind, and seemed to enjoy doing so, I was revolted by her." She looked up at her husband. "Now I just feel an enormous loss." Tears welled up in her eyes. "We had Gaia, our beautiful, darling baby, snatched from us after knowing her for only a few short months. When we got here my mind found her for a few wonderful moments before something blocked me and I lost her again. Now we find that this poor girl is our daughter too and we are going to lose..." Sam broke down and, clutching her husband's arm, cried out in agony. "My heart is breaking. I want to fight for my babies but there is nothing I can do."

James sat and comforted his wife, talking softly of shared memories, treasured moments spent with their child. Gradually the cries that tore at his heart eased and they sat quietly in the gathering dusk, listening to the hoarse rattling breaths forced from Shinara's lungs.

The twilight deepened and stars came out in the deep blue night. The air was suddenly filled with the multitudinous chirps and rasping of insects, high-pitched cries of bats foraging high above them and vague slithering and rustling in the grass tussocks around them. The moon rose, a deep yellow in the dusty air, paling as it surged upward.

Sam noticed it first, a small, flickering orange light low to the west, bobbing and weaving on the horizon. "James. What is that?" she asked.

James stared at it for several minutes. "It's coming closer, whatever it is." He continued watching. "I think it's a fire."

Sam looked worried. "Is it those Dwarrah coming back to finish us off?"

James shook his head. "Aborigines don't normally travel by night. On the other hand, who else would have the ability to make fire?" He turned to Sam with a determined look on his face. "Help me get Shinara under cover. It would be wise to remain undiscovered until we know who it is."

He bent and picked up the limp girl but before he could move, a faint "Hello?" came out of the night. He paused and listened. A few moments later the shout was repeated.

"It's them," Sam said with a grin. "It's Tilley and Bertie." She cupped her hands and called out their names. "Over here!"

James put Shinara down again and smoothed her hair from her face tenderly. He straightened and, drawing a deep breath, let out a long "Cooo-eeee!"

He was answered by a shout and a few minutes later Bertie strode out of the scrub, bare to the waist and clutching his bundled shirt. Tilley trotted at his heels, puffing from the exertion and holding aloft a smoking branch.

"Ah, there you are," exclaimed Bertie. "Good news, we found water. Here," he said, thrusting his shirt at Sam. "A lot has dripped out, but it'll wet your whistle anyway."

Sam took the shirt and unfolded it, feeling the cool wetness on her hands. She bent over Shinara and wiped the girl's face, squeezing part of the shirt to dribble a few drops into her mouth. Shinara coughed, choking, her frail body shuddering in great spasms before she settled again, the only sound being her laboured breathing.

Sam sucked on the shirt, her throat working convulsively as she drew out a few small mouthfuls of water. She passed it to James, who squeezed the garment, tilting his head back to let the water trickle into his mouth.

"Damn, but that feels good." James licked his chapped lips. "Any more of that where you came from?" he asked hopefully, passing the shirt back to Bertie.

Bertie shook his shirt out and put it back on. "Yes, we found the stream bed. Dry as it happens, but by good fortune we stumbled on the place where someone, probably those Dwarrah chappies, had stopped to dig a water scrape. Chased off a few wallabies and there we were, plenty of delicious if slightly muddy water." He laughed. "Tried to bring more with us but the only cups we had were C-cups and my good wife," he twinkled at the blushing Tilley, "refused to part with them."

James snorted delightedly and Sam grinned and hugged Tilley. "Men," she murmured. "Only one thought between them."

"Yes," whispered Tilley in reply, "but what a thought that can be!"

Sam's smile faltered. "Oh, God!" she muttered. "What am I doing? I'm making jokes while my...my daughter lies dying." She started weeping again.

"What about the fire?" asked James, putting his arm around his wife. "Where did that come from?"

"Same chappies that dug for water made a campfire. It was out but a few embers were still there. We managed to coax it back to life." Bertie preened himself and twirled his moustache. "I suggest we all relocate to the fire for the night. I heard a few things walking around out there."

"Good suggestion, mate," said James. He picked up Shinara again, holding her thin body close to his. "Lead on MacDuff."

The burning brand Tilley brought was now reduced to a smoking remnant. They stumbled and felt their way through the scrub, the pale light of the moon casting long black shadows ahead of them. Bertie led the small group and, after about half an hour, he stopped and sniffed the air.

"Wood smoke," he said. Bertie glanced at the blackened branch still in Tilley's hand. "Throw that away will you, love?" He sniffed again, then wet a finger and held it up. "Over there." He pointed slightly to the right and set off again.

Within minutes, the land abruptly dropped away into a shallow streambed filled with rills of coarse sand. Bertie grunted in satisfaction and bore to the right again. "Overshot the bloody thing," he muttered.

The small fire, ringed by stones, had burned down and cast only a dull glow by the time they found it. Tilley at once threw on some sticks from a small pile nearby and the fire flared, revealing the scattered sand of the water scrape nearby. James lowered Shinara to the ground and covered her with his soiled safari jacket. He bent over her in concern, making her as comfortable as possible. Sam joined her husband and picked up one of Shinara's hands.

"She's ice-cold, love. Can't we put her nearer the fire?"

James felt her hands, then put his fingers under the angle of her jaw. He bent his head and put his ear on Shinara's chest, after motioning for silence. Bertie and Tilley moved closer, their hands reaching out for each other as they stood and watched.

At last, James straightened slowly. "I can't detect a pulse," he said dully. "Nor any breathing. I'm afraid she's gone."

Bertie put his arm around his wife when she buried her face in his side. James clutched Samantha to him, letting his pent-up emotions flow while he wept inside for his lost daughter.

The pale light of the moon shone down on the cold form of the young girl lying motionless on the river sand in the warm Australian night. Somewhere, across the stream, a dingo howled. Another joined in, then another, until it seemed as if the entire world mourned her passing.

Chapter Twenty

Gaia felt like she was flying. The countryside, glowing in the pale moonlight and splotched in inky darkness, flowed beneath her while she ran through the night. Vaguely, she was aware of her legs moving rhythmically, her arms pumping and the breath rasping in her throat. Spots swayed and danced before her eyes as her heart hammered to pump blood to her starving muscles. She tried to stop but could not, her limbs and will over-ridden by a mind stronger than hers.

Beside her the figure of Ehrich lurched along, clothed in darkness, with a blank expressionless face. His mouth gaped wide, drawing in great gasps of air; his arms flailed, desperately trying to keep his balance, his legs shaking under him. The landscape flowed past them while they ran through scrubland and patches of rainforest, splashing through small streams in deep gullies, where leaf litter lay moist and thick.

At last, the man gave a cry and fell headlong, crashing into the low *Acacia* scrub. He lay there in a heap, panting hoarsely with his legs scrabbling at the dirt, still trying to run.

Gaia raced on for a moment before feeling an irresistible urge to turn back. She stood above the figure of Ehrich, her thin chest heaving. She felt a ripping sensation within her and it seemed as if the moon leapt and cavorted about the sky, sending black shadows skittering about the landscape. Startled, she glanced up but found the moon hung serenely in the starlit sky. Looking down again, she saw the shadows still moving, roiling turgidly around the man.

Ehrich ceased his scrabbling attempts to run and started to cry, great racking sobs of despair and pain bursting from him. Soon, his cries lessened and he rolled over onto his back, clutching his left knee.

"Oh, you bastards," he muttered. "You fuckin' bastards! You promised me. You promised me."

A dry rattling voice, like the passage of snake scales through dead grass, insinuated itself into the minds of the man and the young girl. *Get up. Now!*

"I can't, you bastards," gasped the man. "You've buggered my fuckin' knee. Jesus, it hurts!"

Get up. We do not have the time for your complaints.

Black shadows flowed over Ehrich and his body jerked spasmodically. He rolled over, then rose to his knees and sprang forward. His knee buckled. He gave an agonized cry and collapsed again. Anger crackled in the air as the shadows receded, forming a pulsing circle of darkness around them.

We do not need him. We can control the girl.

Yes, leave him to die.

We can move faster without him.

And when we need physical strength again?

The girl...?

...is weak. We need him still.

Let them rest for a time.

Gaia sank to the ground beside the unconscious body of Ehrich. Tentatively, she reached out with her mind, seeking the signatures of Rima and her mother. Her probe was instantly turned back on her, and the shadows surged forward. Gaia drew into herself with a gasp and the blackness receded again but boiled restlessly around her. She lay down on the ground and huddled into a fetal position when exhaustion overcame her. She stared up at the moon...

...which lurched across the sky. Gaia sat up in wonder then realized she had slept for several hours. She looked around at Ehrich and saw he was awake, sitting up and rubbing his knee gently.

Ehrich looked up and met her eye. He leered at her. "Good morning, little girl. I've been watching you sleep." He winked.

Gaia shivered and drew herself away from the man. Though clad only in a woven grass loin covering, she had never felt unclothed until this moment, even among the youths and men of her adopted tribe. She half-turned away from him, while hunching her shoulders.

"A bit scrawny, aren't you?" he whispered. "Mind you, I rather like 'em like that." He edged closer to Gaia. "Don't be afraid of me, little girl. Us humans have to stick together. I can get you out of here, and we can go off together."

Gaia bowed her head over her drawn up knees and breathed quietly, her shoulders shaking in fear.

Ehrich shrugged and grinned. "Hey, little girl, at least I'm human." He turned away to stare at the encircling shadows moving restlessly about them, then toward the east where the stars were fading. "Better me than these black devils," he muttered.

A few minutes later, he crept closer to Gaia. "Hey, little girl," he whispered. "Look what I've got." He slipped the front of his jacket to one side, revealing the butt of a handgun stuck in his belt.

Gaia looked, curious. "What is it?"

"It's a gun, stupid. Haven't you ever seen one before?" He grinned. "No, I guess not. This little baby will buy me plenty of power in this world. Stick with me and I'll get us out of here when the time is right."

"What about those things, those shadows?" Gaia shuddered at the thought of them invading her flesh and her mind again. "They won't let you."

"Funny thing," Ehrich muttered with a confused crease in his forehead. "They don't seem to be able to access my memories or abilities unless I let them. I haven't told them about my gun and they don't seem to know I've got it…or care."

As the sky lightened, the shadows became less substantial. They surged and flowed, and the dry rustling noise that preceded speech flooded over Gaia and Ehrich.

Get up. Now.

Gaia got up slowly and stood shivering in the pre-dawn chill. Ehrich was slower and a shadow detached itself from the rest and flowed over him. His head jerked back and he cried out.

Get up, or suffer.

"Alright, damn you!" screamed Ehrich. "Just keep your filthy hands off me."

Move or we shall do it for you.

Gaia and Ehrich broke into a stumbling run, their stiff muscles cramping under the strain. The surrounding blackness flowed away ahead of them and closed in behind, ushering them in the chosen direction. They headed north, fleeing the dawn. Gaia looked forward and saw the black outline of a patch of rainforest silhouetted against the greying sky.

The first rays of the new day were touching the tall saplings of the tropical rainforest as the humans, obscured by the black mist around them, entered the tangle of new growth. The shadows poured between the tree trunks and vines, slithering unhindered through thorny vines and palms. Gaia and Ehrich slowed. Their clothes and limbs caught on the barbs, drawing bloody scratches across them. The blackness behind touched them and they pushed forward again with renewed vigor, desperate to escape the tenebrous feel of their captors.

Stop.

The command took them by surprise and they stood uncertainly in the green gloom of the forest.

Sit down. Keep quiet.

Gaia and Ehrich obeyed, Gaia shrinking away from the man's touch as he put his arm around her. The shadows coalesced beside them and the dry scaly noise of their speech reached a crescendo.

We are followed.

By whom?

Who would dare?

The hairy animal that was with the girl and another.

They are no threat.

There is another.

What could threaten us? The old man?

No. They are small and many. They come with the hairy animals.

What are they?

We do not know.

Gaia's heart leapt when she heard the shadow speech. *It could only be Rima, but why do they think there is two of her? And who are these others? Could it be my parents, with friends perhaps?* She listened when the voices spoke again in her head.

Are they a danger?

To such as us?

There was a pause, then a single voice spoke, old and dusty and redolent of decay.

Two of us are no more. They met this threat and are gone.

The silence grew longer, the shadows hanging close to the trees and rocks in the gloom. Gaia listened hard but could only detect a soft whispering, the words, if any, being indistinguishable from the gentle sough of the dawn breeze high above her.

Abruptly, a dark form shot toward the group with a piercing mind cry. *They come!*

The black mass of shadows shattered, rushing apart when two huge, hairy beasts, screaming and brandishing branches ripped from the trees, hurtled into them.

Wulgu and Rima beat the undergrowth fiercely, roaring with rage, trying to hurt their foe. The blackness slipped between them, oozing through the foliage unharmed, circling and taunting the yowies.

"Rima!" cried Gaia, leaping up with excitement.

Ehrich leapt at the girl and clamped a hand over her mouth, bearing her to the ground again. With his other arm, he grasped her around her torso. He grinned as his hand lingered a moment on her bare chest with its tiny breast buds. Ehrich looked around and, choosing his moment, dragged Gaia into the bushes. He straightened up, clutched the struggling girl firmly and limped deeper into the forest.

Rima howled as she heard her name called and swung her head around, trying to find Gaia. The shadows swept over her and she roared again in frustration as her senses were blocked. Rima grabbed at the black forms but they slipped through her grasp. She called out with her mind but only Wulgu's cries of anger answered her.

The shadows withdrew from the rampaging yowies with a howl of demonic laughter.

They cannot touch us.

Where is the girl?

And the man also.

Find them.

The black mist spread outward, flowing around Wulgu and Rima as they vainly sought to come to grips with the insubstantial beings.

Here!

Black shapes flowed into the forest then, suddenly, broke apart again with cries of confusion and pain. Small hairy forms flitted through the undergrowth, snouts bared wide in feral snarls as the small beings that tracked the shadows burst among them. The furry defenders leapt at the vaguely humanoid black forms. Though the attackers passed through the shadows and the shadow beings reformed behind, the occasional shadow being would wither and fall with a despairing, dusty cry.

Rima and Wulgu stopped in their tracks, looking around bewildered as the shadow beings trembled and fled out along the edge of the forest toward a jumble of limestone rocks. The small hairy beings jumped and hooted, brandishing sticks. A few held stone objects that they put carefully into pouches at their waists.

Where is Gaia? asked Rima. *And the bad man? I cannot see them.*

I saw them briefly as we attacked, replied Wulgu. *But I cannot see them now. Call out to her, Rima.*

I have but she does not answer.

She must be close, said Wulgu. *Let us look for their tracks; it is almost day. Perhaps our little friends...*Wulgu looked around. *Where are they?*

Puzzled, Rima looked up. There was no trace of the small hairy beings. They had disappeared into the undergrowth, leaving no trace of their presence.

Chapter Twenty-One

The Dwarrah village was centred on several limestone caves in a verdant valley. Nathan, Ratana and Narahdarn were ushered by their captors into a large area of bare, flattened earth in front of the largest cave and held at spear-point as the tribe excitedly gathered round. The old hunter left them and ran up to the main cave, disappearing inside it.

Nathan and Ratana were both sweating and feeling the effects of exhaustion. They stood bent over, panting and waiting for the spots before their eyes to vanish. Gasping, Nathan reached out for his wife's hand and squeezed it. "Chin up, love. If they wanted to kill us they wouldn't have gone to all this trouble." Ratana could only nod in reply, sweat dripping off her long, black hair.

Narahdarn was in better shape, being slimmer and fitter. He looked around curiously, noting the appearance of the bark shelters and evidence of stone tools around them. He listened absently to the chatter of the tribe, then swung round in surprise as he recognized a phrase. Concentrating, he heard the phrase again, then another one and realized that among the chatter of unknown dialects was one he was familiar with.

He smiled and addressed the old woman that had used the phrase. "Greetings, old mother. May you always find food."

The chatter cut off abruptly and the old woman stared at Narahdarn open-mouthed. She backed into the crowd and disappeared. The other women started pointing at Narahdarn and calling to the hunters, asking questions and making comments in the new dialect.

"Ho, Mulgah, I thought you said they could not be understood?" one woman asked.

"He speaks well and he is handsome," commented a nubile young girl.

"What are those skins they wear, Bulwah?"

"Are they cold that they wear so much?"

"No, they sweat like a kangaroo after a hard chase," one of the hunters stated with a grin.

The young girl who had commented on Narahdarn's speech and looks stepped closer, her firm breasts jiggling as she walked up to him. "This one is handsome though he wears so much it is hard to tell if he is virile." She giggled and flashed Narahdarn a broad grin. "I will take him as mine to warm my bed."

The other women clapped and laughed, bursting into excited chattering again. Some of the men grinned and pointed though a few scowled at Narahdarn.

"I am Budtha," said the girl, stroking Narahdarn's arm. She felt the cloth of his cotton khaki shirt gingerly between finger and thumb. "What is this?" She bent closer to look. "It looks woven as one weaves pandanus leaves or grasses, but much finer. Can I have it?"

Narahdarn smiled and nodded, stripping off his shirt and draping it round the young girl's shoulders. "I am Narahdarn," he replied, "Of the Euahlayi tribe." He took Budtha's shoulders in his hands and looked into her soft dark eyes. "It is not seemly that we talk of mating at this time. That is a matter for the elders to decide," he added firmly.

Budtha smiled and dropped her eyes, folding her hands demurely in front of her tiny loincloth. "I hear you, Narahdarn." She turned away then grinned at the crowd of women, waving the shirt above her head. "I have a gift," she cried. "Know that he is mine." Budtha danced off through the crowd, her almost naked body bouncing delightedly.

Nathan looked at Narahdarn quizzically. "How did you learn their language so fast? Yesterday you were having problems understanding anything more than a few words."

"It's not their language," explained Narahdarn. "I still can't understand the local dialect but what I was speaking was a sort of trading language, used by many tribes."

"Trading? Who are they trading with, and what?" asked Ratana.

Narahdarn shrugged. "Anything, and everything. Seashells, skins, worked tools, pituri, ochre, gum resins. Anything they can make or find, for something useful from their neighbors. Anyway, the point is they need a common language to trade so they've developed one. This one seems to be related to the modern Dyirbal language of northeast Queensland."

"I could catch a bit of it," said Ratana slowly. "Was it wise to give that girl a gift that could be construed as an offer of marriage?"

Narahdarn looked embarrassed. "I doubt it'll come to that. We will be out of here in a few days and besides, the elders will scarcely allow a marriage to a man with no family or proven hunting skills." He shrugged. "In the meantime, we have an ally in their camp." He looked at the crowd, searching for Budtha. *'Strewth, but she's a right beauty,* he thought. *If we were staying…*Narahdarn's thoughts were interrupted by a stir in the crowd.

A body of men emerged from the main cave and strode down to the bare earth arena. An imposing individual led the group, his body and face covered with cicatrices, the ritual mutilations signifying high status. He stood nearly six feet tall, a full head above his companions, and his body was well muscled despite his obvious old age. He faced Nathan, who casually moved in front of Ratana, and spoke a few terse phrases in the unknown dialect.

When no response was forthcoming the man turned and called out a name. The old hunter stepped forward and gesticulated at Nathan and Narahdarn, jabbering away as he did so. The man turned back to Nathan and started yelling at him, waving his arms around and working himself up into frenzy.

Nathan kept his eyes fixed on the leader but spoke to Narahdarn quietly, out of the corner of his mouth. "I can't understand a word. You'd better try talking to him in your trading language. Any idea what he's saying?"

"Sorry mate," replied Narahdarn. "The only thing I'm picking up is his anger. Wait until he pauses for breath." He listened intently, then stepped up alongside Nathan and held up one hand. The torrent of words faltered and Narahdarn broke in quietly in the trading tongue. "Forgive me, old one. Your words are without doubt full of wisdom. Will you tell us your name and how we have offended you?"

The leader stopped talking and considered Narahdarn's words. He spoke the old hunter's name and the man approached. "You did not tell me they could speak Yarraga."

"What does yarraga mean?" whispered Ratana.

"Literally, it means 'spring wind'. I suppose that's when the main trading takes place," replied Narahdarn softly.

The leader faced Narahdarn and drew himself up to his full height, towering over Narahdarn's slight frame. "I am called Kurreah. I am Wirreenun and I speak for the Dwarrah. Who are you?"

Narahdarn inclined his head. "I am Narahdarn, the Bat, of the Euahlayi. We seek only to pass through your hunting lands."

"And who are these other well-fed ones with you?" asked Kurreah.

Narahdarn put his hand on Nathan's shoulder. "This is Narran, the River, also of the Euahlayi. This other is his mate Rana, the Frog, from the Kalaw islands to the north." He lapsed into English and hurriedly whispered an explanation to his friends. "Nathan would be too foreign-sounding, so I have given you a similar name from my tribe. Making you a relative means I can speak for you. You look too different, Ratana, although you are cousins. I couldn't think of a good name off the top of my head so I fell back on my biology lessons." He smiled briefly. "Rana is Latin for frog. I kept your Torres Strait Island family connections though."

"So what's his name? Nathan asked. "I heard him use Kurreah and Wirreenun. Which is it?"

"Kurreah is his name. It means 'crocodile'. Wirreenun is a title of sorts. It means he is a low grade Karadji, a medicine man or a sorcerer. A learned man, anyway," explained Narahdarn.

Kurreah scowled at the whispering. "Why are you in the lands of the Dwarrah?"

Narahdarn spread his arms wide in a slow, exaggerated shrug. "We, and our friends, are on walkabout. We seek to pass through your lands, hunting only for food, as is our right."

"Wurrunnah," Kurreah gestured at the old hunter, "says you travel with white people." A murmur ran through the crowd. "He says you have bonds of friendship with these ones."

"That is true, Kurreah," conceded Narahdarn. "These white people are friends. They come from a far place, seeking their child who is lost."

Several of the old women made sympathetic noises and a babble of conversation arose. Kurreah silenced them with a chopping motion of his arm. "The white ones harm our land. They slaughter our animals without regard for taboo and desecrate our holy places, killing those who protest."

"Shades of white Australia," muttered Narahdarn in English. To Kurreah he said, "We do not know these people of whom you speak. The white ones who travelled with us have a proper regard for the land and her creatures. They break no taboos. We ask that you send us back to them. They were left by your hunters to die in the desert."

"They did well," said Kurreah harshly. "Perhaps if more die, the rest will leave."

"Wirreenun, may I ask who are these white people that desecrate your lands?" asked Narahdarn.

"They come from the north, out of the hot lands. They hunt the game that are the Dwarrah's by right, they pollute the taboo streams and billabongs and they kill and eat babies and young children," spat Kurreah. The women in the crowd made moaning sounds, rocking back and forth on their heels.

Narahdarn quickly translated for Nathan and Ratana. "Doesn't sound like the Neanderthals we know," commented Nathan. "Ask them if they know of Garagh or Ernie."

Kurreah's eyebrows lifted as he caught the whispered conversation. "You use Garagh's name, the evil one who leads the white people. How could you know this unless you are friends of them?"

Narahdarn shook his head. "Our Karadji knows a man of this name and seeks him out. Our Karadji told us to follow him here. Perhaps you know him. He goes by the name of Errnee, or..."

Nathan grabbed Narahdarn's arm. "For God's sake, Narahdarn, remember the hunters' reaction!"

"...Wandjina," finished Narahdarn.

"Shit!" exclaimed Nathan.

"Oh, dear," muttered Ratana.

Several people in the crowd screamed and the mass as a whole drew back. The hunters gave an angry shout and levelled their flint-edged spears at the trio. Kurreah stood impassively, looking at Narahdarn with hooded eyes.

"You dare to use this name of power here?" Kurreah said softly. "You invoke the spirits of the air and water?" He turned to the crowd watching fearfully and raised his arms. "Know this," he called out. "My magic is stronger than this man's. He invokes the dread one but I can nullify his curse. You are safe, my people."

Narahdarn waved his hands in a placating manner. "I invoke no spirit," he said. "I know a man by the name of...by this name. He is a man of our people and he works for the good of our people."

"The Wandjina," Kurreah turned back to the crowd quickly. "I can use his name, my people, as my magic is strong." He dropped his voice, glaring at the trio. "The Wandjina appears as a black man but he aids the Garagh and the white invaders. If you follow the Wandjina, you are my enemy."

Kurreah signalled to his armed hunters. "Take them and bind them. Put them in the small cave and guard them well." He stepped closer to Narahdarn. "I must decide whether it is better to kill you or just let you die." He gestured sharply. "Take them away."

The hunters hustled Narahdarn, Nathan and Ratana up to the cave system and to the mouth of a small cave, the entrance of which was overgrown with ferns. They produced ropes woven from Pandanus fibres and bound them securely by the ankles and wrists. The hunters then dragged them into the cave, stooping to avoid the low ceiling, and threw them roughly onto a pile of refuse at the rear.

When the hunters had left, Nathan rolled over to face Narahdarn. "Nice one, mate. You had to use his bloody name, didn't you?"

"Nathan, love. There's no point in recriminations now." Ratana looked at her husband sadly. "How are we going to get out of this?"

"Don't ask me," snarled Nathan. "Ask the whiz kid here. He seems to want to be in charge. And look where it's got us," he added.

"How securely are you tied?" asked Narahdarn quietly. "I've been trying my bonds but unfortunately they seem quite expert at knots."

Ratana struggled briefly then gave up. "No go, I'm afraid."

Nathan strained for a moment then snorted. "Regular little boy scouts, aren't they?"

Narahdarn shot Ratana a quizzical look then calmly said, "Then we'll have to try guile...unless you'd rather wait and see whether Kurreah decides to let us go?"

"Brilliant deduction! And just what did you have in mind?"

"Please, Nathan," pleaded Ratana. "It's not helping, love. Try to think of something."

They lay in thought, Nathan squirming around, trying to get comfortable and muttering under his breath. After a while, he stated, "My bladder's about to burst. Do you think those bastards would let me relieve myself?"

"Good thought, mate," said Narahdarn with a nod of his head. He struggled to sit up, then called out in the trading language. "Greetings, noble hunter. I request a word with you." He looked apologetically at Ratana. "That sounded terribly formal," he whispered. "But I'm unsure of the casual forms." He repeated his greetings.

A head thrust through the ferns at the entrance to the cave. "Be quiet, devil, or I shall stab you myself."

"I cannot harm you," said Narahdarn soothingly. "I am tied up and your Wirreenun is stronger than I."

"That is true," the guard said while shifting uneasily from one foot to the other. "What do you wish to say?"

"My friend here," Narahdarn nodded toward Nathan, "asks that he be allowed to relieve himself."

The guard shrugged. "He does not need my permission to do so."

"Would you have him soil himself? In decency, unbind his hands that he may attend to this."

"It is all one to me," said the guard, withdrawing from the cave.

Narahdarn sank back onto the refuse. "Well, it was a good idea, mate. Let's see if we can't think up another one."

"That was no ruse, you bastard," grated Nathan. "I bloody well do have to go...oh, shit!" The acrid stench of urine filled the cave as Nathan's bladder let go, staining the front of his khaki slacks. Nathan swore and rolled over until he faced away from the others, toward the cave wall. He lay still, his shoulders shaking slightly.

Ratana rolled over to him and rested her head on his arm. "It's all right, love. No harm done, you're with friends." She hesitated, then whispered, "I'm going to have to go, myself, soon." Nathan lay silent, unresponsive. After a while she sat up and shrugged. "Snap out of it, love. We are in a jam and we need cooperation, not sulks."

Nathan grunted. "Then give that bloody guard some incentive. Offer him your oh-so-lovely body, dear wife. I'm sure he'd untie your legs for his pleasure."

"Jesus, how can you even think I'd do that?" Ratana shot Nathan a look of disgust and rolled away from him. "That's disgusting."

"It's not on, mate," added Narahdarn quietly. He gave Ratana a sympathetic look then sunk his head on his chest to consider the problem.

The heat of the day lessened and the mouth of the cave fell into shadow. Once or twice the guard peered in at them impassively. Near sunset, as the gloom in the cave deepened, they heard voices outside, followed by a different hunter poking his head inside.

"Changing of the guard," commented Narahdarn.

A few minutes later they heard the murmur of voices outside. They strained to hear what was being said but the voices were in Dwarrah and unintelligible. Then a head poked through the ferns again.

Narahdarn recognized the round grinning face of the young girl, Budtha.

"Greetings, my husband," she murmured, as she stepped inside the cave. Narahdarn's khaki shirt was draped around her shoulders but it in no way obscured her jiggling breasts as she dropped down on her knees beside Narahdarn. She glanced at the other two lying there then turned her attention back to Narahdarn.

Budtha's eyes roamed over Narahdarn's supine body, a twinkle in her dark eyes. She reached out and lightly touched his bound arms and legs, running her fingers over the cloth of his vest and shorts. Her hand came to rest on the front of his shorts and she grinned. "Is my husband missing his Budtha?" she asked softly.

"Budtha, can you untie me?" asked Narahdarn.

The girl considered his question. "What would you do if I untied you?"

"We would leave here, Budtha. You would not want us to die, would you?"

Budtha shrugged, her smile replaced by a pout. "Why should I care about these others? But you, my husband..." She smiled again and rubbed his crotch gently.

Narahdarn struggled to maintain his composure. "Budtha, you could come with us."

The girl stopped rubbing Narahdarn and thought about his proposal for several minutes. Then she grinned and started plucking at Narahdarn's belt. "What is this thing? How does it untie?" She tugged at it, working it back and forth until it gave way. Budtha laughed and pulled his shorts and underpants down.

Narahdarn groaned. "For God's sake, Budtha..." He lowered his voice. "We are not alone."

Budtha looked puzzled. "What does that matter, my husband?" She glanced over at Ratana, who was looking away uncomfortably, and at Nathan, who was regarding the scene with a big grin on his face. "Why should I not enjoy myself with you?"

She started stroking and tugging at Narahdarn, cooing with delight when he responded to her touch. "I have a husband who is virile, indeed," she boasted. Budtha quickly straddled Narahdarn's hips. She lifted her loincloth and settled herself, then groaned with delight at the sensation of her man inside her. She slowly rocked back and forth, with a beatific grin on her round face.

Narahdarn groaned. "Budtha, we should not...oh, God!" He tried to suppress his feelings but he looked up at the firm-breasted girl jiggling above him, at the expression of ecstasy on her face, and his loins melted. He felt himself responding to her motions and he gave up the struggle, straining upward to meet the girl.

Nathan stared at the couple avariciously, a gleam in his eye and a small trickle of spittle at the corner of his mouth. "Go, man," he whispered. He panted as he became aroused, and nudged Ratana with his feet. "Why can't you ever do anything like that, wifey?" he grunted.

Ratana turned away and screwed her eyes shut, embarrassed by the sounds of lovemaking and appalled by the crass comments of her husband.

Budtha's and Narahdarn's cries became louder. He shuddered and dropped back exhausted and aching. The girl rocked slowly for a few minutes more then slipped off Narahdarn and lay beside him, adjusting her loincloth. She raised herself on one elbow and looked into his eyes. She nodded in satisfaction and drew a small flint blade from a pouch at her waist.

Budtha rolled Narahdarn over and sawed at his ropes with the flint. After a few seconds, they parted and Narahdarn rolled over and sat up. He rubbed his wrists to restore the circulation, then pulled his shorts up. He reached out and took the blade from the girl's hand. Slashing the ropes around his ankles, he crawled over and released Ratana, then Nathan.

Budtha sat quietly and watched as Narahdarn released the others and they crept slowly to the cave mouth. Narahdarn looked at her and, after a moment's hesitation, held out his hand. She grinned and took it, moving rapidly to his side.

Ratana looked out cautiously, parting the ferns slowly with her hands. She withdrew back into the cave and whispered. "There's only one guard. It is deep twilight and I can't see anyone else."

Nathan picked up a rock and hefted it in his hand. "One blow with this should do him in," he grunted.

Narahdarn shook his head and put a restraining hand on the other man's arm. "We don't kill unless we absolutely have to. The two…three of us can overpower him. We can tie him up and leave him in the cave." He picked up the pieces of rope lying on the ground and started sorting them into lengths.

Budtha looked from one to the other. She tugged at Narahdarn's arm. "Husband, what are you saying?" She shook her head vehemently when Narahdarn told her. "You must not hurt him, he is my brother, Guddah."

"Damn!" muttered Narahdarn. "Now we have to overpower him without hurting him. How the hell are we going to do that? He's not just going to stand around while we tie him up."

"Ask her," urged Ratana. "Perhaps she has an idea."

Budtha motioned them all to remain and stepped out of the cave, ducking under the overhang. She called out softly and a few minutes later the ferns parted again as she led in a reluctant-looking young man. She spoke softly to the man who scowled and shifted his feet uneasily. She spoke again and the man answered her with a torrent of words, his voice rapidly rising in volume. Budtha clapped a hand over the young man's mouth and spoke yet again. The man stood silent for a moment then shrugged and sat down. Budtha signalled to Narahdarn.

"Bind him, my husband," she whispered. "But gently. He will not cry out until dawn."

The four of them slipped out of the cave and, keeping to the rock wall, skirted the main encampment. Several low fires burned outside the main caves and by the grass and bark shelters nearby. A low buzz of conversation interspersed with laughter covered the noise of their passage.

They emerged from the small valley of the Dwarrah as the moon rose, casting its pale yellow light over the stark landscape. Narahdarn brought them to a halt under a tall gum tree. The night was quiet save for the thrum of insects and the distant squabbling of fruit bats at the edge of the forest.

"Okay, we seem to have got out all right. The question is, what now?"

Nathan scowled at Narahdarn. "We don't have much of a bloody choice do we?" he complained. "We either keep wandering or we try and find those Neanderthals. They might protect us from those savages back there."

"We've got to go back and find the others," Ratana protested. "They were left to die out there. We must go and help them."

Narahdarn nodded his agreement. "We must find the Neanderthals because Ernie will be there, but we have a duty to help the others, out of friendship if nothing else." He turned to Budtha. "Where are the white people? Where do they live?"

Budtha shivered. "We don't want to go there, my husband. They are evil people and will kill us. Come away with me and after a while we can return to the Dwarrah." She tugged at his arm.

Narahdarn took her gently by her shoulders. "Budtha, my pretty one. No one shall harm you, but I need to know where they are." He smiled at her. "So that we can avoid them."

The girl put her arm around Narahdarn and rested her head on his shoulder. "I am content," she said. "The white devils live in that direction," she pointed to the west. "About a day's travel."

"That is good, Budtha. I thank you." Narahdarn kissed her forehead. "Now, can you lead us back the way we came, into the desert?"

Budtha grinned. "Oh, yes. My brother Guddah told me exactly where you were found and the way you were brought here." She danced off a few steps. "Come, my husband, I will take you there."

Chapter Twenty-Two

James sat dozing, back pressed against the sandy bank of the dry streambed. His wife, Sam, lay with her head in his lap, sleeping fitfully. Every few minutes she cried out in her sleep and struggled, her limbs flailing before settling down again. A few feet away lay Bertie and Tilley Simpson, curled up and touching. They slept solidly, gentle snores disturbing the peace of the chill dawn air.

James shivered, wishing he had his jacket, then remembering it was still draped over the body of his daughter Shinara, only a few feet away. He raised his head wearily and peered into the darkness. The moon was ghostly pale over the western horizon and the silvery light threw a dark shadow from the stream bank over the place where the body lay. He sighed and lay back, wondering yet again whether there had been any way of avoiding the disasters of the previous days.

A pale pink glow suffused the eastern horizon, washing out the stars. Gradually his eyes made out the feeble attempts they had made the night before to set up some sort of camp. The fire lay inert, only pale, threadlike wisps of smoke showing the presence of live embers beneath the ashes. A faint pungent aroma of burnt *Acacia* tickled his nostrils. He closed his eyes, listening to the dawn chorus of birds starting up in the brush across the stream.

A faint scrabbling sound intruded. James ignored it, thinking about the coming day and their limited choices. The sound came again and he sat very still, listening. After a few moments of silence he went back to his thoughts. His mind slipped away from the decision he knew they would have to make regarding Shinara's body, remembering instead happier moments in the past.

The sound came louder, accompanied by a ripping sound. James sat up. He lifted Sam's head gently from his lap, laying it on the sand. He got up quietly and moved towards the fire. The first rays of the new day lit up a scene that he knew would be with him until he died. Several wild dingoes circled Shinara's body. His jacket lay to the side, ripped to shreds and strips of her pale green dress lay about her in the scattered sand. One dingo held her right hand in its mouth and was tugging at it, growling as it did so.

James let out a horrified shout. The dingo holding Shinara's hand dropped it and bolted. The other three turned toward James and balefully regarded him with pale yellow eyes. He shouted again and waved his arms. Two of the dogs retreated a few steps but the other held its ground. The hair on its back and tail rose and it gave a deep growl. It lowered its muzzle toward the girl again, keeping its eyes fixed on the man as it did so.

James looked about him wildly and grabbed a branch. He swung it over his head and charged the dingoes, screaming as he ran. The two standing farther off broke and ran with their tails between their legs. The leader hesitated then yelped as the branch caught it across its body. It snapped at the branch then ran off, tail held high. It halted by the bushes across the stream and looked back for a moment before slipping into the undergrowth.

A horrified gasp behind him made James swing round. Sam stood clutching Bertie's arm a few paces behind him, staring at the scene of desecration. Tilley bustled up at that moment and, taking in the scene with only a moment's hesitation, dropped to her knees beside Shinara and began pulling the fragments of clothing together over the girl's body. Sam joined her, before tenderly brushing the sand from her limbs.

Bertie put his arm around James's shoulders. "Blasted dogs," he muttered. "Puts us in a bit of a quandary, what?"

James dropped the branch he held and looked up at Bertie with a stunned look on his face. "Sorry, mate, miles away. What did you say?"

Bertie coughed. "Sorry to put it so bluntly, old chap, but, in this heat, we have to do something with the...er, with Shinara." He waited for a response from James. When none was forthcoming, he went on. "We should bury her, old boy, but with those dingoes around we can't do that."

James shuddered and shook his head. "I don't want to leave her," he whispered. He drew in a deep breath and exhaled slowly. He turned to Bertie with a wan smile. "I'm okay, really. I know we have to do something." He looked around. "A cairn of rocks perhaps?"

Sam sat back on her heels and wiped the fresh tears from her eyes. "James, love," she called, "Lend me your hankie, will you? The bites on her hand won't stop bleeding."

"Sure, hang on a moment...ow!"

Bertie gripped James's arm hard. "What did you say, Sam?" He strode forward and squatted by Shinara, holding up her right hand. He took the handkerchief from James's shaking hand and gently wiped away the smears of blood. Immediately, fresh drops oozed from the wounds. He dropped the hankie and pulled the lids of Shinara's eyes up carefully, one after the other, peering closely. He rocked back on his heels and grinned.

"Blow me!" he said. "The lass is alive."

"What?"

Bertie nodded, his grin broadening. "When you said she was bleeding...I mean, corpses don't bleed, old chap. Then I checked her eyes. Should have done it last night but there wasn't enough light and I didn't think of it..." He cut off the flow of his babbling and took a deep breath. "Her pupils show a light response." He saw Tilley's blank look and explained. "The pupils open and close automatically in response to light levels. If they still respond she must be alive."

"But why is she so still and quiet?" asked Sam. "She looks dead."

"I'm not a medic chappie, so I can't say for certain. I think she's shaken off the main effects of the snake bite but it's left her in a coma." Bertie ran his hands through his thinning white hair. "Bit of a turn up for the books, what?"

"So what do we do now?" asked Tilley.

James pursed his lips. "We can't stay here. We don't have food and the water won't last long." He pointed at the water scrape, still damp but already drying in the morning sun. "I think our best bet is to keep following the trail to the Dwarrah." He shrugged. "We may still be able to rescue our friends and the countryside should be more hospitable where they live."

They set out again within the hour, Bertie in the lead, slowly following the signs of human passage. James came next, holding Shinara's frail body close to him, then the two women. The day got hotter as the sun rose and they were forced to stop often, James setting Shinara down carefully before collapsing in exhaustion, sweat streaming off him. He refused all offers of help in carrying the girl, struggling up again within minutes each time.

Toward noon, they sat in the sparse shade of a wizened gum tree, watching the air ripple and move over the hot plains. Sam noticed a tiny black object in the distance, shimmering and dancing. She watched it for a few minutes, then tapped her husband on the arm.

"What's that, love?" she asked, pointing at the object.

James peered intently in the direction she pointed, shading his eyes from the glare. "Probably a mirage. The hot air can take a perfectly ordinary object like a tree stump and make it look as if it's moving." He continued watching and after a few minutes said slowly, "Except, I think it's something alive. It's definitely moving, and there's more than one."

Bertie and Tilley peered at it too. "I'm afraid all I can see is a blur," Tilley apologized. "My eyes are a bit dickey."

Bertie grunted. "Not much to see, my darling. Two or three upright figures moving from left to right in the distance. Though I think they are a bit closer." He glanced at James. "What do you think they are, old boy? People or emus?"

"Emus?" Tilley nervously replied. "Are they dangerous?"

James shook his head. "No, but they are intensely curious birds. They may come and investigate us but they won't hurt us. Don't worry about it."

They continued to watch while the upright figures grew slowly larger, first splitting into several objects then merging again.

"I think they're people," said Bertie quietly. "But are they the Dwarrah, come to finish us off, or someone else?"

The approaching group of people eventually solidified into four definite shapes moving at a slow jog. "Four," said Sam. "So it's not our friends, miraculously freed."

James looked around him helplessly. "Not much cover here. Perhaps if we keep low and remain still, they may pass us by."

"Too late," said Bertie quietly. "The blighters have spotted us."

The figure at the front of the short column of runners pointed and swerved in their direction, followed by the others. They rapidly approached until about fifty yards away the leading figure suddenly stopped and crouched. The other three ran past, waving their hands and shouting.

"'Strewth, it *is* them," cried James, shading his eyes from the glare of the sun. He ran forward and hugged Nathan, then Ratana.

Sam ran up and greeted them, hugging Ratana close to her when they finally reached each other. "Oh, love," she sobbed, "I never thought I'd see you again."

Bertie sauntered up and shook hands with a sweat-soaked Nathan and Narahdarn, who stood panting hard. "Good show, chaps." He nodded in satisfaction and twirled his moustache. "Showed the natives what for, eh?" He looked at Narahdarn who was glancing back at the fourth person still crouching down in the scrub. "Who is the other chap, then?"

"A friend," muttered Narahdarn. "She helped us escape." He turned and ran back to Budtha, who looked increasingly like she was going to run away. He dropped to his knees beside her and reassured her. Reluctantly, she accompanied Narahdarn back to the others.

"I say!" breathed Bertie, when she drew close. "A regular native beauty." He drew himself up and straightened his jacket.

"You just keep your libido under control," growled Tilley, coming up to the group and punching him hard on the arm.

Bertie winced. "Nothing could be further from my mind, love," he protested. "You know you are the guiding star of my life." He waved a hand in the general direction of the girl. "Just an appreciation for the beauty of nature...like a sunset, you know?"

Tilley snorted. "Do you have the same trouble with your man?" she asked Sam.

Sam smiled through her joy. "No. And I know you don't either. I've seen you two together."

Narahdarn spoke quietly to the group, with an arm around Budtha, who stood as close as possible to him. "This is Budtha," he said. "She is Dwarrah but helped us escape. She has...ah...formed an attachment to me..."

"Mating like rabbits, you mean," muttered Nathan. Ratana looked away, embarrassed.

Narahdarn shot him a calculating look then went on. "She is very afraid of white people. The Dwarrah seem to be in fear of the Neanderthal people, who are also white. Please try and be calm and friendly around her until she gets to know you."

Narahdarn lapsed into trading language to introduce his friends. "Budtha, these white people are like family to me." Budtha looked at him quizzically, then at the smiling white faces. Narahdarn pointed at James and Sam. "This one is Yamee, who is like a father to me, and his woman Amantha." He gestured at Bertie and Tilley. "The old man is a Wirreenun, he is called Birra-ti. His woman, who is also wi, is Tee-li. This young woman," Narahdarn brought the reluctant girl round in front of him, "is Budtha." He looked beyond the group, with a puzzled expression on his face.

"Where is Shinara?" he asked James.

"I'm afraid she was bitten by a snake, an eastern brown," James said. He hurried on at the look of horror on Narahdarn's face. "She's alright, mate. I must admit we thought she died but she seems a lot better today. Still unconscious though." He pointed back at the tall gum tree.

Narahdarn ran to the prostate figure of Shinara, dragging Budtha by the arm. He let out a cry when he got close enough to clearly see her condition and dropped to his knees beside her. Budtha sat beside him and glanced from the young girl to Narahdarn then back again.

"Who is this girl my husband sheds tears over?" Budtha asked with a suspicious tone. "She is ugly and has no breasts. I can bear many healthy children. Come away, husband, and leave this girl to die."

Narahdarn faced Budtha and said slowly and clearly, "The elders of my tribe entrusted me with her care. I must look after her as my daughter."

Budtha poked at the ugly double wound in Shinara's leg and shrugged. "Her spirit will soon be with Waddagudjaelwon anyway."

"Be silent, woman," Narahdarn snarled. "I must speak with the spirits and ask Waddagudjaelwon to release this one from her care." He bent over the unconscious girl and reached out with his mind.

Shinara!

Swirling, incoherent thoughts met his.

Shinara!

Who?

Shinara, it is I, Narahdarn.

Narahdarn. Where are you?

Here. Open your eyes, Shinara. Come back to me.

Pain.

It will pass. Put it away from you and come back to me. Open your eyes, Shinara.

The young girl's eyelids trembled and opened. Sam gave a gasp of joy and sat next to the girl before cradling Shinara's head in her arms. The girl looked up at her then returned her gaze to the young man and licked her cracked lips.

Who? she asked Narahdarn.

Narahdarn regarded Sam for a few moments, noting her expression and the thoughts flooding in the forefront of her mind. *Your mother,* he replied. *She loves you.*

Love?

You will learn.

Narahdarn rose and dusted his shorts off. "She will be all right," he said. "Her mind fought the venom. She will be weak for a time, but something cracked in her mind. I believe she will be increasingly responsive."

"Dear God, I don't know what to say." James clapped Narahdarn on the back, sending Budtha nervously skipping away a few paces.

Bertie looked at the women clustered around Shinara, patting her and laughing. "Good show, old boy." He vigorously wrung the young man's hand. "Thought she was a goner."

"Bloody wonder-boy strikes again," muttered Nathan. Aloud, he said, "I don't know whether anyone is interested but those Dwarrah didn't let us go, we escaped. I imagine they're tracking us right now. I, for one, don't want to be captured or killed."

"Yes, you're right, Nathan," agreed James. "We need to get out of here fast, but where to?"

"Well," Bertie replied. "Your friend Ernie seems to have his finger on the pulse of the situation. I think we should find him."

Nathan, Budtha and Shinara expressed no opinion but the others wholeheartedly agreed.

"Oh, jolly good," Bertie exclaimed with a smile. "I really do want to see these Neanderthal chappies. They could answer many questions about their disappearance. I mean, the possibilities..."

James broke in on the archaeologist. "Perhaps we could discuss this another time, mate. A more immediate problem is finding them."

"Budtha knows," Ratana said with a sidelong glance at the native girl.

Narahdarn nodded. "Yes, she's scared to death of them but knows where they live." He turned to the silent girl and held her gaze quietly for a few moments before broaching the idea to her, "Budtha, my desert flower, can you take us back to the edge of the forest outside your valley?"

Budtha nodded with an animated and eager quiver through her

slim body.

"And from there, can you take us to the valley of the white people?"

Budtha recoiled, her contented smile slipping from her face. "Please, my husband, do not take me there. The white devils will kill me and eat my spirit."

Narahdarn enfolded the girl in his arms and spoke softly to her. "I give you my word, Budtha. No one will harm you if you take us there."

The young girl drew back, her eyes searching Narahdarn's face. After a pause, she nodded hesitantly. "If my husband wishes it, I will obey. But it is easier to go directly to the white devils from here, rather than back the way we came first."

"Good girl," smiled Narahdarn. "Can you take us there unseen by the Dwarrah hunters?"

The girl thought for a minute. "Yes, my husband." She hesitantly nodded. "They run like Gheeger, the west wind, and can track Goonur, the kangaroo-rat, over solid rock but I know a way they will hesitate to go." She looked hard at the white people. "Perhaps your Wondah, your white ghosts, know some magic to protect us?"

Nobody laughed at the suggestion.

"Narahdarn," James muttered to get the young man's attention. When they'd moved away from the group far enough for privacy, James put his hand on the man's shoulder and said, "Narahdarn, if you don't mind, I want you to take the lead when we head out."

"But you are our leader, Doctor Hay," the young man protested. "All of them..." he indicated the knot of people talking together, "...look up to you. They trust you. They don't know me that well and I don't have your experience or wisdom."

James chuckled. "My friend, I trust you and, evidently, so did those who know you back at the complex or they wouldn't have put her..." he nodded at Shinara, "...in your care. Besides, you are a native of this country. You speak the language and you are young, strong and fast. I think your experience is what's needed now, not mine," he stated with an amused tone. "I want you to take the point position and lead the way, ready for anything that comes our way. I'll bring up the rear and watch our backs...and the ladies." He winked, trying to defuse the anxiety written all over the young man's face.

Narahdarn searched James's face, then nodded in acceptance. "As you wish, Doctor. But the rear position is very dangerous. How can we help you if *your* back is not covered?"

James slapped him on the shoulder. "No worries, mate, I'll be fine. I'll be watching *all* of our backs, including mine. Let's just get to the village as fast as we can."

When Narahdarn nodded again, James nodded in return then moved toward the group, who silently waited to leave.

They set off at a fast walk, angling toward the east. James carried

Shinara, who, though conscious, was too weak to support herself. Budtha led the party, alongside Narahdarn. She kept breaking into a run then slowing to a walk again, looking back at the straggling group in agitation.

"We must hurry," she whispered to Narahdarn. "The hunters probably left at dawn and our track is easy to follow."

Narahdarn took Shinara from James. "Let me spell you for a bit, mate." He urged the others onward. "We have to pick up the pace. Budtha says the Dwarrah hunters will be close behind us."

They pressed on. The land slowly changed from a flat desert landscape to a broken, densely vegetated area. The group came to the entrance of a shallow canyon that appeared to be carved out of the sandstone by flash floods.

Budtha stopped and turned to Narahdarn. "My husband," she said quietly. "Gnoolooyoundoo lives here. I was here once before with the women of my tribe, seeking medicines. Gnoolooyoundoo devoured three women and his valley is now taboo. The hunters will not follow us through there but I am afraid."

Narahdarn translated for the others. "I must admit I'm worried, and Budtha is scared, but I think we must go through there."

"What is this Gnooloo thingy?" asked Tilley nervously.

"Probably just some mythic character from an old legend," scoffed Nathan. "You know how ignorant these people can be."

"You dishonor your own people," said Ratana angrily. "I don't know why you are acting like this, Nathan. I feel I no longer know you."

"Grow up, woman. This is the real world. Nice people come last, or haven't you noticed?" Nathan turned away and looked back the way they had come.

James gave Nathan an odd look before talking to Narahdarn. "Can you find out a bit more about this monster?"

Narahdarn nodded. "I'll try." He spoke to Budtha again, listening to a long, involved reply, accompanied by much gesturing. At last, he turned back with a shrug. "I would say it's a real animal but it doesn't show itself often. Stripping away the obvious exaggeration, like breath that kills and blazing eyes, I'd say it's a very large monitor lizard."

"Big enough to eat people?" Tilley gasped with incredulity, fear coloring her breathless question.

"This may be only a young girl's fancy but the Komodo dragon to the north of here is known to kill and eat children so it may also be true. I know the Komodo grows to some ten or twelve feet," said James. "There may be a comparably sized monitor lizard here."

"So, do we go in there?" Sam gestured toward the cleft. "Or do we try and go around it?" She stared up at the steep cliffs facing them. "That may be difficult," she added.

"Time's run out," Nathan commented with a note of resignation. "We have company."

They swung round to see a solitary Dwarrah hunter standing several hundred yards away, glaring at them with hatred. He gestured with his spear and gave a bloodcurdling shout. Several other warriors joined him. Together, they started running toward the group gathered in front of the Gnoolooyoundoo's lair.

"Oh shit," Nathan exclaimed.

Chapter Twenty-Three

Ehrich limped further into the dense rainforest, clutching a weakly struggling Gaia. The dim light filtering down through the canopy foliage meant the undergrowth was scarcer and movement was easier between the soaring tree trunks. Sun flecks danced on the thick leaf litter and the humid air was heavy with the scent of decaying vegetation.

Gaia gagged at the odor that seemed to permeate her very being.

After a mile or two, Ehrich released his hand from the girl's mouth and set her down on the ground, running his hands over her body as he did so. He grinned at the cringing girl and licked his lips.

"Nobody to disturb us here, little girl. You can scream and shout all you like but your hairy friends won't be able to find us."

"Rima will find me," whispered Gaia, trying to cover her chest with her thin arms. "And when she does she will kill you if you hurt me."

Ehrich laughed. He pulled out his gun and brandished it. "If I see your hairy friends I'll kill them, and I'll enjoy it." He cocked his head and regarded the girl with glinting, dead eyes. "Besides, little girl, I won't hurt you too much…if you behave." He tucked his gun into his jacket pocket and moved forward.

Gaia backed away, her hands and feet scrabbling in the leaf mould at a frantic pace. She backed up against the moss-covered bark of a small tree and clung to it, crying. "Don't, please!" she sobbed.

Ehrich kept a small smile on his face as he sauntered forward, though his breath came faster. "Oh, that's good, little girl," he whispered in a breathless tone. "Why don't you try and run for it?"

Gaia looked around wildly, then leapt to her feet and darted off to one side. Ehrich lunged and caught her grass loin covering, ripping it off her tiny body. Gaia screamed and ran; Ehrich limped in pursuit, a great grin plastered over his face.

Gaia ran until her lungs felt like they would burst. Then, a great tearing pain in her side doubled her over and she stopped. She crouched behind a fallen tree trunk, trying to keep quiet, but her breath came in great whooping gulps. She listened to the silence of the forest, broken only by the occasional bird cry. A rustling in the leaf litter made her heart race. A small potoroo poked its head out from a clump of ferns. Relieved, she sank back against the log. It sat up on its hind legs like a small, fat wallaby and looked at the frightened girl before suddenly leaping off in alarm.

Gaia cautiously raised her head over the log...and looked directly into Ehrich's eyes. He stood only a few feet away and was grinning at her.

"Peek-a-boo, little girl. Want to try again?" he asked.

She turned and lurched away, holding her side. Ehrich moved around the log and pursued her. He caught her by one arm and pulled her roughly upright. Holding her at arms length, he looked her over slowly while she tried to cover herself with her other hand.

"Just as I like them," he breathed. "Young and defenceless with just a hint of the woman to come." He giggled and drew Gaia close, before running his hand over her naked back and buttocks.

Gaia screamed a thin, piercing scream of anguish. Tears streamed over her grimy face and she struggled to pull away. "No!" she cried. "Please, no!"

Ehrich laughed. His breathing came faster at the sight of the terrified child. "Go, girl. Fight me," he whispered. He lowered his head over hers and planted wet lips on her tear-streaked cheek. His coated tongue lazily traced a path from her cheek to her mouth while his eyes watched her reaction.

Gaia went rigid, her heart raced and her vision dimmed. She closed her eyes. *No!* she screamed in her mind. *No!*

Abruptly, Ehrich's hold on her arm loosened. She opened her eyes and saw him lying on his back in the leaf mould, shaking his head, a stunned look on his face.

"What the fuck...?" he muttered. He struggled to his knees. "You little bitch. You hit me with something."

Gaia backed away a few steps. "Don't come any closer," she threatened with a quavering voice.

"Or what?" the man asked with a sneer. "So you like it rough, do you?" Ehrich clambered to his feet and stood swaying in front of her. "We'll see how you like it now then." He adjusted the tight fabric over his swelling groin and moved forward.

Gaia screamed again, jumped backwards, and gathered herself to run, a look of terror on her face. Ehrich grunted and grabbed for her. She lashed out with her mind, her scream of '*No!*' shooting forward with the force of a lightning bolt.

Ehrich dropped as if pole-axed. He groaned and writhed on the ground, then struggled to his feet again. He clutched his head with both hands. "What did you do to me, you fucking cunt?" he snarled before moaning in pain. He raised his head and stared at Gaia, who stood her ground, wiping her face with the back of her hands. He hesitantly moved a foot forward, then another. "Was that just a fluke?" he asked.

Gaia glared at him and mentally lashed out again.

Ehrich dropped to his knees and retched from the bottom of his bowels. He rolled over with vomit trailing from his chin and forced a shaky hand toward his jacket pocket. Pulling the gun out with the tips of his fingers, he tried to point it at the girl but dropped it. He reached for it but instead fought the urge to vomit again.

Gaia gestured and Ehrich's hand jerked, sending the gun flying.

He moaned, clutching his belly as he fell and vomited again. The sour stench of feces billowed around them both as his bowels let loose.

The girl gagged then stepped back, a look of horror crossing her face. She paused then reluctantly edged forward and picked up her grass loin covering. Then she turned and ran.

She did not look back.

❧❧

Darkness boiled in the clefts and crevices of the limestone rocks left littered by an ancient landslide. The shadows drew back from the harsh sunlight piercing the gloom. Anger pulsed through the vague, formless figures, a primal anger that sought an outlet for its sadistic desires.

The man and the girl escaped.
We can find them…
…and kill them this time.
Yes. Slowly and painfully.
And what of the others—those things that hurt us?
What are they?
Animals.
But…familiar…
??
Their minds resonate with us.
That is why they can unmake us.

The shadows were silent for a time, their thoughts guarded while they contemplated the disaster that had befallen them. Never, in countless centuries, had any force been able to touch them so. Pain they had known, injury even, after a fashion, but never unmaking. An older voice, reeking of time and decay, stirred at last.

The old one, he who opposes us, must be found.
Why?
He is the one all the humans look to for strength.
??
Our sibling who resides within spoke of his findings. The humans seek the old one.
Where is the old one?
Near.

We go there?

No.

Dry, scaly voices rose in a storm, echoing through the cracks and crevices of the rock fall. When the sounds died away, a single voice rasped a query.

Then what?

We seek another people, closer, with one who hates. One who will do our bidding. One who will help us destroy the humans and those who unmake us.

The shadows shivered.

⚬⚬

Wulgu and Rima spread out into the forest, searching for any trace of Gaia. The churned up area where they attacked the shadows was chaotic, a battle scene strewn with broken branches and fern fronds. They cast about in a wider circle, spiralling outward, and, at last, came across the footprints of a man.

Ehrich passed this way, Wulgu exclaimed while giving vent to a hair-prickling growl.

And Gaia? Rima asked, while approaching with a whimper and smelling the track.

Just the man.

Then where is my Gaia? She must be here somewhere. Rima called out to the girl, sending her mental shout into the silence of the rainforest.

Wulgu slowly wandered along the trail of boot prints leading deeper into the forest. He carefully examined them, pressing into the leaf litter with his fingers, sniffing at the ground and the occasional clumps of ferns.

He was injured, Wulgu stated. *See how he favors his left leg. Also he carries something.*

Gaia?

Possibly. Her smell is present, but very faint, Wulgu turned and thoughtfully regarded the other yowie. *It is your choice, Rima. Do we stay and continue to look for the child, or do we follow Ehrich?*

Rima looked about in an agony of indecision. *Follow,* she sighed. *If she is in danger, it is more likely to be from him.*

Wulgu grunted and turned back to the trail, following it slowly, making sure he missed no possible clue. At one point, he gestured at large three-toed prints crossing the path.

Cassowary bird.

The track passed through the forest in a more or less straight line, though it deviated to avoid obstacles like fallen trees and a patch of stinging trees.

He is no longer under the control of those dark things, observed Wulgu. *See how he makes decisions to avoid unnecessary hardships.*

Ah! The girl...

Wulgu stopped and sniffed the ground.

Rima joined him, passing the air of the forest floor over her sensitive scent receptors. She recognized a familiar odor.

Gaia! Rima gave a low gurgling cry of joy that slowly faded when she breathed in again. *I smell fear, Wulgu.*

Wulgu pointed. *He stands here, she over there. She backs away, he follows. She runs, thus...in that direction.* The great male yowie bent down, and gently lifted something in his huge fingers. He placed it in the palm of his hand. *Dried grass?* he asked.

Rima leaned over to examine it. *It is from the garment Gaia wears. It bears the scent of the man.*

Wulgu growled and started forward, following the faint bare footprints of the girl superimposed by the boots of her pursuer. Gaia's footprints led them onward for several hundred yards, her panic and terror evident from the marks of her passage. The yowies noted several places where the moss and lichens were brushed from tree trunks and twice came upon disturbed areas of leaf litter where the girl had fallen. Throughout it all, the man had run on at a constant rate, displaying no sign of urgency.

He follows, but confidently, said Wulgu. *I fear what we may find.*

Wulgu slowed and stopped. *Ehrich stood here,* he said. *He faced that log and on the other side of it...*Wulgu stepped forward hesitantly...*it sheltered the girl.* He breathed out raggedly. *See? They confronted each other.*

Rima's lips curled in disgust. *What is that stench?*

Wulgu poked through the leaf litter with his fingers, then carefully wiped them with moss from a fallen log. *Vomit,* he observed, with a look of distaste, *and human waste. The man lost control of himself for some reason.*

Where is Gaia?

She left. Wulgu pointed to the small footprints. *Hurriedly, but not in panic. He follows once more, but slowly.*

Then we must too, Wulgu. Rima moved off in agitation. *I cannot bear to think of her in danger.*

I am not sure she is in any danger, Wulgu responded with a puzzled tone. *Something struck down the man without hurting her.*

Chapter Twenty-Four

At as fast a pace as the others could tolerate, Narahdarn led the way into the sandstone canyon with Budtha by his side.

Nathan was next in line before pushing past them with an oath. "Get out of my way, assholes!"

Bertie grabbed Tilley and broke into an ungainly trot, determined to keep up. *Bloody hell! I wish I'd joined that group of elderly runners now*, Tilley thought while her husband dragged her quickly behind him.

Sam and Ratana jogged as rapidly as they could while supporting Shinara on either side. By the time they reached the first large boulders scattered over the floor of the narrow valley the others were out of sight.

James trailed behind the women, alternately watching them move toward cover and watching for the hunting party on their heels. He looked back in time to see the first hunters reach the entrance to the canyon. The group of warriors stopped and spread out, watching as Sam, Ratana and Shinara disappeared behind the boulders. The hunter in charge, the older one who captured them before, launched his spear at James. It fell short, clattering off the rocks.

The man broke into a torrent of words, screaming at James and shaking his fist. He began haranguing the other Aboriginal hunters until, reluctantly, they started edging forward, brandishing their weapons and screaming a chant that was indecipherable to James.

Uh-oh, time to go, James thought while he cautiously watched the Aborigines move slowly toward him. *It looks like they're prepared to break the taboo on this place.* He turned and ran into the valley, catching up with the women and Bertie after he came around a tumble of boulders.

"Come on," he cried. "They've decided to follow us."

They ran deeper into the valley, urging Shinara onward. The girl ran, stumbling often and clutching at the others for support. The valley branched off into side channels carved through the crumbling rock, formed by seasonal floods. In the lowest parts of the streambeds grew a variety of low herbaceous plants and a few scraggly shrubs. They sprinted around and through the bushes in a broken field style of defence running.

James lagged a pace behind, constantly watching for the attackers while he ran.

Budtha, Narahdarn and Nathan waited at the junction of the first large side valley. They urgently beckoned the others onward.

Narahdarn put his finger to his lips when they approached. "We must be as quiet as possible from now on," he said. "Budtha says Gnoolooyoundoo lives in one of these side branches but she is not sure which one."

"Yeah, right," muttered Nathan, while kicking a small rock. The rock skittered across the loose scree, sending a cascade of clatters echoing off the canyon walls.

"For God's sake, Nathan!" hissed James. "At least try not to alert it to our presence."

A slithering noise, like dry scales rubbing over loose rocks and sand, echoed down the valley. The group froze, staring into the shadows. The noise grew louder just before a long, thin head emerged from behind a boulder. Yellow-gold reptilian eyes stared at the humans dispassionately while a purplish, forked tongue flicked out, tasting the air. The head sinuously moved up and forward until it cleared the boulder. The neck hung with folds of scaly skin and a barrel-shaped body supported on four clawed legs slowly followed. The snake-like tail lashed from side to side as it advanced. The lizard came to a halt about fifty feet from the humans and raised its head high into the air, its flicking tongue tasting their fear.

"That's the monster?" brayed Nathan. "What a pack of weak Sheilas these ancient Abo's are!"

James grunted. "It's a sand monitor, I think. A large one, perhaps as much as six or seven feet but certainly not big enough to hurt us as long as we stay alert." He turned to Narahdarn. "Is this what Budtha called Gnoolooyoundoo?"

Narahdarn shook his head. "She says this is one of Gnoolooyoundoo's children. She says we must go quickly, before it calls its father."

James pursed his lips. "Okay. It is possible larger monitors could thrive here, so we'll assume she's correct. Which way do we go?"

Budtha pointed up the valley, speaking quietly but urgently.

"There is a path that leads out of the valley at its head. If we do not reach the path before Gnoolooyoundoo comes, we are dead," translated Narahdarn. "I really think we'd better be going."

They set off at a fast walk, watched by the monitor lizard. Nathan picked up a stone and shied it at the animal before he left, sending it running for cover. He laughed again and hurried after his companions.

The floor of the valley grew narrower and more uneven. They

clambered over boulders, helping each other over slopes of loose rock and up steep inclines. Half an hour of walking found them at a sandy, wider area at the junction of three canyons. The land was flatter and scrubby vegetation grew around the edges and up the sides of the valley walls.

"What's that smell?" whispered Sam with an intense look of distaste on her face. "There's something dead around here."

They all stood quietly, listening to the silence, broken only by a muted roaring sound in the direction of one of the side canyons. Bertie moved cautiously toward the entrance, followed by James.

"Don't go, love," called Tilley. "Leave it."

Bertie put his finger to his lips and crept on. "I'll be all right," he whispered with a throat that threatened to close with choking fear. "We need to know what it is."

He pushed through the scrub, then parted it in front of him. At the base of the low cliffs, under a dark, roiling cloud of flies, the corpse of a large animal lay baking in the hot sun. Movement around the scattered edges of the body attracted his attention. Several monitor lizards, ranging from small ones only a foot or two long, to giants in excess of six feet, worried and tore at the skin of the corpse.

Bertie tossed a stone, hitting the body. The flies rose in a dense cloud, and the roar of their buzzing rose in pitch. "A diprotodon," he stated. "A young one but still too large to succumb to these blighters. I wonder what killed it?"

James looked up at the cliffs. "It could have fallen, I suppose." He brushed several flies from his face with an expression of disgust. "Come on, let's get back to the others."

A soft, sibilant hiss stopped James in the act of turning to go. The small lizards around the body stopped feeding and sat stock-still, their heads raised in alertness. The hiss came again, followed by the scrub on the far side of the dead animal waving violently. The monitor lizards scattered, disappearing in moments.

James stared toward the corpse when something rose behind it. A huge, yellow eye regarded him balefully over the body. The hiss was repeated, more loudly this time, and a flickering, forked rope lashed over the top of the animal, disturbing the flies. James backed up slowly until he collided with Bertie. He felt cold, despite the baking heat of the canyon walls.

"My God!" he muttered. "I don't believe it. This can't be real."

Bertie stared goggle-eyed at the emerging creature, taking in the scaly skin and the ropes of saliva trailing from its open jaws—jaws studded with deadly sharp teeth. A belch of foul air blasted over them when the creature lurched forward, one huge clawed foot coming to rest on the diprotodon corpse. It turned its head sideways and watched the two men as they backed away.

"What in God's good name is it?" breathed Bertie.

"It's the extinct giant monitor, *Megalania prisca*," James whispered. "We are in deep shit, my friend."

"What do we do?"

James shook his head. "I don't know." He took a deep breath and mentally reached out to Sam. *Love? Get the others out of here quickly.* Silence roared in the chambers of his head and he cursed silently. *Why is this bloody telepathic power failing us?* He called again, more urgently. *Sam, get out of here, now!*

James, love. What is it? The answer came weakly. *I can hardly hear you.*

The monster, James screamed while sending as much of a mental picture as he could. *It's here. Take the others and get out.*

James gripped Bertie's arm. "Come on, mate, slowly back away. No sudden moves."

The two men withdrew slowly from the scrub and backed to where the others stood watching them in alarm. As they reached the group, the giant monitor burst out of the scrub in front of them and halted, staring across the sandy basin at the humans. The lizard raised itself up to the full length of its forelegs, standing over six feet high as it did so. Its skin hung loosely around its jowls and in folds across its body. The tail whipped from side to side, sending patterns of light and dark scattering over the rich colors of its reticulated skin. It hissed loudly and opened its mouth again in a huge gape.

Sam gasped and clutched Ratana. Tilley screamed and stumbled back, sitting down hard on the hot sand. Shinara stood, swaying slightly and looking at the beast curiously.

Budtha fell to her knees, her arms outstretched toward the monitor. "Gnoolooyoundoo," she cried. "Do not eat me, or my husband, I beg."

"Fuck me," grated Nathan. "That bloody thing's more than thirty feet long." He glanced at Narahdarn. "Well, get us out of this one, wonder boy."

Tilley scrambled up and clung to her husband. She started crying. "What do we do?" she sobbed.

Bertie shook his head while hugging her. "We're in a bit of a jam, love, and no mistake. There's not much we can do." His lips turned up in a wry, crooked smile. "Now might be a good time to start praying."

They started edging toward the far side of the valley, the whole time keeping their gazes locked on the giant reptile. It lowered its head and cocked it to one side, watching them with the intentness of a poised, angry cobra. As they drew away, it lurched forward in a threatening pose, hissing loudly at the same time.

"Ask Budtha where the path out of here is," James whispered to Narahdarn.

Narahdarn gestured with a nod of his head. "Over there, mate.

Beyond the bloody lizard. Unless it moves to let us past, we're stuffed."

They reached the far side of the basin and backed up against the sandstone walls. Budtha huddled against Narahdarn, whimpering softly. The others displayed a variety of emotions, from helplessness to fear and a certain amount of anger. Shinara alone maintained a calm demeanor, her face reflecting puzzlement. If it wasn't for Sam and Ratana pulling her back with them, she would have remained standing in the sandy basin.

The monitor hissed louder than before and advanced in short rushing bursts. It opened its gaping jaws to the limit, saliva dripping from its open mouth and ragged flesh still draped between its teeth.

"Why doesn't it just attack and get it over with?" Nathan snarled while restlessly running his hands over his right thigh, unconsciously searching for the knife he usually carried there.

"We are not running and that is confusing it until it figures out how to react," James stated in a flat tone. "It's whipping itself into a killing frenzy now though." James watched the reptile closely as it glared at them. Its tail whipped back and forth furiously, the muscled rippling under its scaly hide moving like waves of angry water.

A sudden movement at the lower end of the basin caught the reptile's attention as it tensed its muscles for the final rush. The Aboriginal hunters burst from the scrub at a run, spears held ready to throw. They skidded to a stop when they caught sight of the giant lizard and the tableau of humans pressed against the canyon walls. For a long moment, they stood there, frozen, their spears drooping slowly as they stared, open-mouthed. Then, with a loud scream of fear, one of them broke and ran, crashing into one of the other warriors and knocking him to the ground. The monitor gave a deep coughing roar and spun on its hind legs. The long tail lashed past Shinara as it turned. It launched itself down the valley at the hunters when they ran for their lives. Scrub parted before the animal as it vanished from sight. Deep hissing roars mingled with screams of terror faded as the pursuit receded.

James shook the lethargy of fear from his limbs. "Quickly," he grated. "Before it returns. Into the valley." He grabbed Sam by the hand and dragged her forward.

The others followed quickly too, though Ratana had to return after a few paces to urge Shinara onward. They ran up the central valley, passing many crushed and rotting carcasses of kangaroos, diprotodon and other unidentifiable beasts. Passing through this charnel house, they found their path narrowing and angling upward. Soon, they were clambering from rock to rock and, at last, they hauled themselves over the lip of the canyon to fall exhausted at the top.

Reaction to their harrowing experience set in. Overcome by a feeling of lethargy, Bertie sat down hard, leaning against a rock and wiping his face with his large spotted handkerchief. His complexion was pale and he flexed his left arm gently, pain on his face.

"By God," he gasped. "That didn't do the old ticker any good." He waved a hand deprecatingly when Tilley limped over, full of concern. "Not to worry, my love. Lots of life in the old dog yet."

"I don't want to hurry you," James said, "but we can't stop too long. If those hunters got away, they'll be coming after us. It will take them a while to scale the cliffs, but we want to be long gone by the time they do."

"In a moment, James, darling, please," Sam pleaded. "Ratana and I need to rest for a while. I'm sure the others could do with a break too."

James inspected the others as they sat in slumped positions around him. He nodded. "Okay, we'll give it half an hour. Then we have to go." He wandered over to Narahdarn. "Can I have a word?"

"Sure, mate. Pull up a pew," Narahdarn replied with a grin. "What's on your mind?"

James settled himself on the ground next to the young Aboriginal man. Budtha gave him a sour look and huddled close to Narahdarn on the other side. James sat for a moment in silence then jerked his head at Nathan, who was sitting apart from the others.

"How well do you know Nathan?" James asked.

"Not too well," replied Narahdarn. "I've seen him around the complex, you know, in the Glass House Mountains, off and on. He always struck me as a decent bloke." He grimaced. "Until the last couple of days at least. Now I'm not so sure."

James nodded. "I know what you mean. I've known him most of his life and I would have risked my life on his commonsense and decency." He picked up a handful of small stones and started throwing them at a clump of grass a few feet away. "He's the natural grandson of my adoptive grandfather, which sort of makes him a brother or a cousin. I tutored him when he was a youngster and helped get him into James Cook University. I introduced him to Ratana. He has a good mind, though he is a bit headstrong and loves politics more than science." James sighed. "He has changed...or something has changed him."

"Budtha believes he has been put under a spell by a Karadji," said Narahdarn quietly.

James looked up sharply. "Do you believe that sort of thing?"

Narahdarn nodded. "I have trained under Wan...under Ernie. I have seen things I cannot explain."

"I, too, my friend," agreed James. "Even as a sceptical scientist I find it hard to explain away some things." He hesitated. "Last year something similar happened to Nathan."

Narahdarn waited. After a few minutes, James continued in a quiet voice. "Last year a group of scientists and businessmen in America developed a machine capable of altering men's minds at a distance and of releasing vast energies from the Earth's core. They built a working model and used it on the Glass House Mountain complex. Somehow they knew of the existence of Garagh's group and tried to destroy it."

James ran his fingers through his hair. "It turned out that they were under the control of something otherworldly, insubstantial creatures with malefic intent. They appear only as dark and loathsome shadows. They could not perform physical tasks themselves but used humans to do their work. These people were sort of possessed."

James raised his head and looked across at Nathan. "They struck at us by invading Nathan. He unknowingly became a spy for them. For a long time they went undetected and his nature changed for the worse. Ernie was able to detect their presence and cast them out." He looked at Narahdarn with a haggard expression on his face. "I fear that somehow the Shadows are back inside him."

Narahdarn sat silently, absorbing the information. At length he spoke softly. "James, my friend. We will soon be with the great one. If you are right, he cast them out before and can do so again. Do not lose hope."

James smiled and clasped the young man's arm. "Thank you." He got up, dusting off the seat of his trousers. "Get a bit of rest," he added. "We have a way to go yet."

The sun was sinking in the west by the time James roused the group. He watched as, one by one, they fell asleep. He didn't have the heart to wake them, though he felt an increasing tide of urgency rise within him. At last he stirred and roused them, having to shake some of them awake.

They set off again, with Budtha and Narahdarn in the lead. The top of the cliffs they climbed proved to be a plateau, gently sloping away from them down to a distant river clothed in dense riparian forest. The land grew less sandy as they travelled, and the vegetation gradually became more luxuriant, the air more humid.

Finding a small stream at last, they rested to slake their thirsts and to wash the dust out of their hair and outer clothes. They pressed on, though Budtha became increasingly nervous as they neared the river. She clung to Narahdarn's arm and looked fearfully about her, jumping at any small noises in the undergrowth.

"She's in terror of the Neanderthals," Narahdarn explained. "All her life she has heard tales of their ferocity and cruelty. She is literally putting her life in our hands by leading us here."

Pushing through a dense wall of plants, they emerged onto the stony bank of the river. The water ran rapidly and noisily over great boulders, the sound of rocks clattering together in the current a continuous counterpoint to the wash of the waters. The air was cooler by the river, shaded as it was by huge bloodwoods and paperbark trees. Biting insects swarmed and for a while the slap of hands on bare skin and muffled curses interrupted the natural sounds of the river.

Budtha and Narahdarn hunted in the low plants along the water's edge and returned with handfuls of pale yellow-green leaves.

"Here," he said. "Crush these and smear them over your exposed parts. There's a natural repellent oil in them."

Sam smeared the pungent juices over her arms and legs and went to find Shinara to anoint her. She found the girl sitting on a boulder staring out over the water, unconcerned by the attentions of the myriad mosquitoes and gnats. Sam sighed, expecting to find a carpet of little corpses around the girl, a result of Shinara's inclination to kill rather than merely discourage. Instead, her mouth dropped open in surprise.

A grey miasma of tiny insects danced and swirled over the water in front of Shinara. The girl turned to Sam with an open-eyed look of wonder on her face.

"They obey me!" she cried. "I tell them what to do and they do it." She gestured and the insects hovered in front of them, then divided into two roiling swarms and sped off across the river. Shinara clapped her hands in delight and uttered a tinkling laugh. "This is better than killing them. See, they return to do my bidding."

The swarms returned and danced in front of her again. A few fell from the cloud, dropping lifeless into the water. More followed until it became a steady rain of tiny corpses.

"Why are they dying?" cried Shinara. "I do not want them to."

Sam put a hand gently on the girl's arm. "You are making them fly until they are exhausted. Release them and let them rest, Shinara."

The remnants of the swarm dissipated. A few mosquitoes homed in on the warm bodies and began feeding. Sam crushed some more leaves and smeared them over Shinara's arms and legs. The insects flew off.

"This is a better way, love. Only control them when it is really necessary."

Shinara looked up at Sam. "What is this 'love' you call me?"

Sam stroked the hair away from the girl's face and gazed into her eyes. "I am your mother, Shinara, and I..." She paused. "I only found out I was your mother a few days ago. Since then I have come to know you and realize I love you."

The girl's forehead wrinkled. "What is love?"

"Love is what a mother should have for a daughter...and a daughter for a mother," said Sam slowly. "Love is wanting what is best for the other person, even if it means being hurt." She sat collecting her thoughts. "When Narahdarn was taken away, you asked for him. Why, Shinara?"

The girl shook her head. "He's always been with me. Ever since I can remember he has been here, guiding me, telling me when to sit, stand, when to sleep and eat. I felt hollow when he went, as if my insides were gone."

"And now that he has returned?"

"I am happy…I think." Shinara smiled then quickly frowned. "But he is no longer with me, he is with another." Her frown deepened as she struggled to find the words. "She is…I am…I do not know how to say this. I feel his happiness and it makes me happy, but I feel sad too. He no longer tells me what to do."

"You have changed, Shinara. When he went away you were help-less," Sam gave an involuntary shudder as she remembered just how helpless the girl had been, able to kill with a mere glance. "Then you were bitten by the snake. When you recovered, it was as if you woke from a sleep." Sam stroked Shinara's hand, her fingers tracing the barely discernable white scars that were all that remained of the dingo's bite. *She heals incredibly fast,* she thought. She glanced down at the girl's leg, only a faint bruising showing where the eastern brown snake had bitten her.

"Yes. I think I was asleep. I am awake now and everything is wait-ing for me." Shinara sprang to her feet, disturbing the large orange and white butterfly that was sunning itself on a rock nearby. "I must think about love, too. I am not sure why I should want to hurt myself to make another person happy." She ran off along the riverbank, jump-ing at the dragonflies darting above her.

Sam rose to hurry after her. Despite Shinara's powers, the world of ancient Australia was too dangerous to let anyone wander alone in it. The thought made her catch her breath and tears sprang to her eyes. *What of my baby?* she thought. *My own darling Gaia may be wandering alone.* Sam raised her hands to her face. With an effort, she controlled her sobs. *At least Cindy, or rather Rima, is with her.* She smiled through her tears. *Rima would die before letting any-thing even touch Gaia.*

Chapter Twenty-Five

A rosy morning glow touched the Tjalwalbiri village, the rising sun itself lost among the thunderheads gathering far to the east. Men and women had been about their business since first light. Men prepared for the day's hunt, carefully checking over their weapons or sitting in groups two or three and discussing matters of import. Women gathered in small groups around the communal fires, chattering and laughing as they prepared a frugal morning meal. Children scampered around them or chased each other in complex games of tag between the bark and thatch shelters.

Tjimi, the medicine man, or Karadji, a learned man of the highest degree, emerged from his shelter. He stretched then grunted as a small boy cannoned into him. He caught the infant and held him at arms length, frowning. The boy struggled for a moment then muttered an apology. Tjimi smiled and hugged the boy tightly before releasing him. Screaming with laughter again, the boy rejoined his playmates.

Tjimi wandered into the bush to find his usual spot. Scraping a hole in the sandy soil with a stick, he squatted. He cast his mind back over the night and the terrifying dream he had endured, frowning as he contemplated the necessary actions of the coming day. He finished his business and, cleaning himself with a handful of soft grass, walked back to the village.

He nodded at two of the elders sitting cross-legged by a fire, fossicking for remnants of flesh on a well picked over lizard carcass. A woman hurried over to him and pressed a baked yam into his hand. He thanked her and sat down beside the elders.

"Greetings, honored elders," he muttered, before taking a bite of the cold yam.

The elders nodded their greetings in return, wiping their greasy fingers in the soil.

"We see you, Karadji," said one of them. "Will you be joining the hunt today?"

Tjimi shook his head slowly. "There will be no hunt today, Ngarragun. The spirits visited me in the night and we must convene a council."

Ngarragun frowned and shot a look of worry at the other man. "What did they say?" he asked Tjimi.

"I will speak to the whole council of elders together," stated Tjimi, throwing the last bit of yam on the fire. He got up and wandered off, speaking over his shoulder. "Gather the elders and meet at the Spirit Cave when…" he glanced at the eastern horizon, "…the sun emerges from the clouds."

A tenth part of a day later, Tjimi sat beside a small fire ringed in smooth river stones. The Spirit Cave was no more than a deep depression scooped into the sandstone hills, facing away from the prevailing weather. It measured about three man-lengths deep and about six man-lengths from side to side. A small person could stand upright near the rear wall, which was decorated in stylised paintings of emus, kangaroos, lizards and other less recognizable animals and spirit beings in ochre, white and black pigments.

Across from the Karadji, seven elders of the Tjalwalbiri tribe stoically waited for the ritual to begin. 'Elder' was an honorific rather than a descriptive title for the men. Although some wore the grey speckling of advanced years in their black hair, others presented a youthful appearance. All were Wirreenun. However, ones who visited the spirit world at will, communing with the spirits of earth, sky and water, talking to the ancestors, and guiding the tribe through the perils of daily existence were special.

They sat quietly, waiting for the Karadji to begin. None would presume to talk until the Karadji gave permission. Only he, of all the tribe, had slept beside Tjakkan's waterhole and been transported by the rainbow being into the depths. He now carried cords and crystals within his body, enabling him to fly up into the sky, travel across the land as fast as an emu and live underwater. His power was associated with a large black crystal he carried in his totem pouch, along with the flat black obsidianites they all owned.

Tjimi cleared his throat and looked around the semicircle of men facing him. "Last night, I was visited by Tjakkan himself and taken far to the east, to the rainforests along the Gayandi River. I walked among the trees and spoke with the cassowary and the striped dog. They gave me warnings."

The elders leaned forward. "Warnings of what, Karadji?" asked an old man hoarsely.

Tjimi glanced at the other man. "Warnings of the Quinkan, Baimeburra. The Quinkan have come among us and have attacked Guyyah." The Karadji shrugged. "Of itself, it is a source of sorrow only, for the spirits guide us all. I would weep to see Guyyah taken from us but if it is the will of the spirits…However, Tjakkan declares the girl to be under his protection and bids me find her."

The elders frowned and muttered among themselves, remembering the little white girl who had dwelled among them so recently. Her powers were evident and an asset to the tribe. It had been a pity when she left but there was no gainsaying the wishes of the spirits. Her dream was specific and personal and no one, even the Karadji, could forbid her. At least her spirit protector, her soul made visible, the yow-ee, accompanied her.

Collective heads shook. If Guyyah had met the Quinkan, the malicious spirits of the cracks, crevices and other dark places, then her yow-ee would need to be strong.

Tjimi spoke again. "Tjakkan tells me we must come to the aid of Guyyah. I will journey there myself, today. I ask that three of you accompany me." He looked around at the semi-circle of elders. "Ngarragun, one shall be you. Also Njangaringu, for you are a healer." He pondered deeply, bowing his head on his chest. "I think Wiradjerun is the third, for he has spoken to ghosts from far places."

Tjimi rose to his feet. "We four must prepare for our journey. The forest is two day's travel from here and we must be there by nightfall. The rest of you must keep the women and children silent for we must summon the necessary powers with the bullroarer. When we have gone, set Guyyah's likeness on the walls of Spirit Cave, with that of her yow-ee. Draw the Quinkan about her and signs of protection. Go now."

He turned and strode down the hill toward the village and his shelter. After a few moments, the others dispersed, Ngarragun, Njangaringu and Wiradjerun following their Karadji, the rest hurrying off to do the bidding of the spirits.

Silence fell across the small clearing with the scattered shelters, as women and children withdrew from sight. A few babies squalled for a moment before their mother's breasts quieted them. The older children sat quietly, playing with bones and sticks, casting fearful looks at the shelter of their medicine man.

The bullroarer started up. A strong young man stood on a nearby hillock, whirling the grooved stick around his head on a long woven cord of plant fibres. The air hummed and roared, building to an all-pervasive thrumming sound that spread out over the scrubland, summoning the spirits of the tribe.

Tjimi sat with the selected Wirreenun, facing the position of the rising and setting sun, the hot north of ancestral lands and the land of the cool south winds. They intoned deep sonorous phrases, feeling the power of the spirits come upon them. Tjimi took out his black quartz crystal and stared into its glistening depths. He saw Tjakkan stir within it and felt the answering vibration of the crystals set deep within his bones and intestines. The energy and strength of the spirits flowed over him.

"Come," Tjimi said. He rose and tucked the crystal back into his pouch then stepped outside. He and the other three medicine men rose onto the balls of their feet then dropped into a coiled crouch. They leaped forward, their legs pumping fluidly and, within moments, passed from sight.

The bullroarer faltered in its flight, then the sound stuttered and faded. Complete silence fell across the tribal lands for several minutes before the muted sounds of normal daily life slowly resumed.

∽∾

Gaia's panicked flight rapidly turned into a stumbling walk when reaction set in. She halted, holding onto a sapling with one hand, and looked around her as if seeing the forest for the first time. She held her grass skirt up in the other hand and stared at it, like it was an alien creature. After a few moments, she blinked, looked down at her naked body, and wrapped the skirt around her. She tied it with strands of the grass fibre, her fingers slipping and fumbling with the knots.

Her legs shook and the young girl sank to the leaf-strewn forest floor. Tears welled in her eyes and she wiped away a thin trickle of mucus that ran from one nostril. Her lips quivered and a thumb crept slowly into her mouth. Gaia's eyes assumed an unfocused stare as her mind shut down, withdrawing in horror from the harm done to her and by her.

Ehrich slowly limped along the trail. The pain in his left knee forced him to drag his leg when he moved. He grimaced when fresh waves of fecal and vomit stench wafted up at him from his sodden clothing. He gripped the branches and smaller trees with his left hand to support his passage; his right hand hung by his side. In it, he gripped the handgun.

He almost missed Gaia. She was lying curled up in a fetal position under a small tree. Ehrich blinked and moved closer. His lip curled into a snarl while he raised the gun. He hesitated, noting her blank stare and absence of reaction to his presence. Lowering the gun again he squatted beside her. He ran his eyes over her body, smiling at the ragged remnants of the grass skirt imperfectly covering her loins. For an instant, he felt a flash of lust, then he shifted his weight and the cold stickiness of his clothing quelled his urges. The memory of his loss of control swept over him, a flush of shame burning his face.

Rising to his feet again he raised the gun and sighted along it at the untidy and dirty mat of hair falling across Gaia's face.

"What a waste, my dear," he whispered. "I'd love to enjoy you but I really can't take the chance." He cocked the weapon and his finger tensed. After a long pause, he lowered the gun again. "Can't do it, my dear. Not here, not now."

Ehrich turned and limped away. He looked back over his shoulder at the immobile girl. "I will see you again, little girl, make no mistake," he called softly. He continued down the faint trail, eventually disappearing into the green gloom of the rainforest.

The life of the forest resumed after a while. Small marsupials pattered over the leaf litter, nosing into fallen logs after insects or nibbling on seedling leaves. Birds swooped and called. The whip-like crack of the male riflebird rang out as it unobtrusively flitted from bough to branch, announcing its territory. The cassowary that had crossed the path of the young girl earlier in the day returned and stared at her with a glassy eye. It pecked desultorily at fallen blue quandong fruit then strode on its way.

A patch of fern rustled and a long-nosed bandicoot poked its head out. It blinked in the light and half turned to go back to its daytime sleep. It saw the form under the tree and its whiskers quivered. Scuttling forward, the bandicoot nosed around the girl's still body. A sound came from the forest and it jumped, ears pricked forward. The sound came again and the bandicoot exploded into action, dashing back into the cover of the ferns.

A few moments later a brown and tan thylacine, or marsupial wolf, trotted into view. The striped back and hindquarters blended beautifully with the mottles and shadows of the vegetation. It slowed and approached Gaia without any sign of fear. It sniffed her then turned away, settling itself down under a spindly sapling. The thylacine yawned, its jaws spreading wide, then put its head on its forelegs. It fixed Gaia with its stare and waited.

The light flecks on the forest floor shifted slowly as the sun, unseen above the dense green canopy, rose toward noon then fell away. A prowling marsupial lion, the fierce *Thylacoleo*, came across the girl and the thylacine as the day reached its hottest. Although it outweighed the striped dog and could kill it with a blow of its paw or a snap of its long-toothed jaws, it forbore. The lion had gorged the night before on a young Diprotodon and lain up in the densest vine thicket it could find. A growing thirst had sent it out in search of a stream.

The hackles on the thylacine rose as the lion approached. It emitted a deep growl in answer to the whiney singsong of the marsupial cat. For a few moments they each stood their ground and faced each other down. The lion swung its head in indecision then moved cautiously to one side and, keeping its eyes on the dog, swung around it and into the forest. The thylacine stood staring after the lion for a long time, small growls issuing from its throat. Eventually it lay down again though it continued to cast looks at the place where the cat disappeared.

The day crept on. The light flecks vanished and the shadowless forest grew dimmer. Soft footsteps padded up the trail towards the girl and the striped dog. It stood again, facing the approach, its ears forward. With a bound it leapt to one side and slipped into the shadows, where it watched as two mountainous bulks of hair loped rapidly toward the girl.

Rima spotted Gaia first and cried out in joy, uttering a cacophony of hoots and calls. *It is my darling Gaia. We have found you, my child.* The female yowie faltered then gently stroked the immobile child.

What has happened to you? Oh, Wulgu, what is wrong with her?

The other yowie bent over Gaia and poked her gently with a long finger. *Her mind sleeps,* he thought. *Yet, her body is unharmed. I feared for her but the stench of the man is faint.* He snuffed the air and moved around the area. *I was right! She is protected.* Wulgu pointed at the ground. *Both a lion and a dog have approached her yet she suffered no harm.*

And none shall come to her now, growled Rima. *I will die before I let her out of my sight again.* She picked up Gaia, cradling her in her strong hairy arms.

Then we must take her away from this place, said Wulgu. *Her mind is unreachable and unless she awakens, her body will waste away. I cannot wake her and neither can you, but Wandjina can. We must take her to him.*

Rima looked doubtful. *I suppose so.* She hugged Gaia, threatening to crush the frail girl in her arms as she did so. *Where is Wandjina? I do not know where to find him. Do you?*

Wulgu nodded vigorously, the whole front of his body rocking up and his fists slamming into the dead leaves of the forest floor in his enthusiasm. *Yes, Rima. He gave me precise directions. All I need is a star sighting and I can guide us there. That is why we must leave the forest immediately.*

The yowies set off back the way they had come. Wulgu led at a fast pace with Rima keeping up as best she could, cradling Gaia with one arm, and using the other to swing herself along. She resisted any suggestion by Wulgu that he help by carrying the child. Gaia was her child and now that she was found again, nothing and no one was going to separate them again.

Dusk set in, the gloom under the canopy increasing as they hurried back, passing the spot where Gaia and Ehrich had fought. Wulgu cast anxious looks over his shoulder as they ran.

We are being followed.

Who by? Rima asked, worried that she already knew the answer from the scents she'd picked up in the forest.

Not who, what. There is a thylacine about a hundred yards back. It has been following since we found the girl.

Is it dangerous?

To such as us? No. I just do not understand its purpose.

Then ignore it, Wulgu.

They ran on, emerging from the forest proper into dense re-growth forest as night enveloped them. A few minutes later they found themselves in open scrubland with the first stars of the evening winking in the deep purple sky. The yowies stopped and caught their breath. Rima put Gaia down on fern fronds she'd carefully plucked and laid in an open patch of ground. She smoothed the damp hair from the child's eyes and stroked her thin, scratched limbs. Concentrating, she tried to reach into Gaia's mind again but found nothing beyond a few fleeting images shot through with veins of terror. The girl moaned and thrashed her arms and legs weakly. Rima sent a soothing message, hooting softly as she did so. Gaia quieted again and her staring eyes closed.

Wulgu ambled up and pointed into the sky. *There is the Southern Cross. That point there*, he raised Rima's arm, sighting along it, *is south. We must head west again, around the forest, then to the north. The valley of the Neanderthals is within half a night of here if we keep moving.*

"Then it is as well that we have intercepted you now." A deep, measured voice spoke from the shadows in the Tjalwalbiri tongue. "For we cannot allow you to go there."

Chapter Twenty-Six

Kurreah, Wirreenun of the Dwarrah, sat by his fire at the entrance of the main cave. He was in a foul mood, snapping at anyone who ventured into the cave and even knocking aside a succulent haunch of wallaby offered by his youngest wife. He gripped a half-finished flint nodule firmly in his left hand, angling it while he lined up the hammer stone. He struck, knocking off a thin sliver of flint that flew across the fire into the shadows beyond. Kurreah gave a grunt of pleasure. He ran his thumb along the blade, feeling the thinness and sharpness of the edge. He shifted his grip and tapped again, sending another chip arcing into the gloom. Slowly, the spear point took shape.

The Wirreenun imagined the feel of the flint blade slicing into soft flesh, his face twisting into a vicious snarl. *May the spirits guide that young man to me*, he thought, mentally dredging up the image of Narahdarn. *I will teach him to humiliate me.*

Kurreah flushed as he remembered the scene when his hunters returned. Three men lost to the dreaded Gnoolooyoundoo. Even that was acceptable if the people they pursued vanished down the monster's gullet too. He ground his teeth in rage.

My hunters gave up the chase! They admitted defeat and returned to me, as if I would forgive them. And they were aided by that bitch, Budtha. Kurreah scowled as he thought of his revenge. Unable to strike out at Narahdarn and his companions, he had killed the young girl's brother at once, raging at his obvious complicity in their escape.

The bitch is next, he thought. *I will point the bones at her tonight.* He gave a grunt of satisfaction at the thought of Budtha dying in agony within days.

Kurreah set the spearhead carefully to one side and picked up the shaft. He sighted down the long supple piece of wood, running his fingers lightly over the grain, balancing it across the palm of his hand.

I will have to avenge myself. I cannot afford to let them survive.

He pulled a small half-gourd closer to the heat of the fire and stirred the contents with a twig. Lifting a drop of the viscous amber fluid, he rubbed it between a finger and thumb. Satisfied with the stickiness he smoothed the resin liberally on the notch in the head of the spear shaft and set the flint blade firmly into it.

It is clear to me now. They are allies of the white demons. I must find a way to kill them all.

Working swiftly, he pressed the end of a long kangaroo leg sinew into the gum and wound it tightly around the base of the blade and the haft. He set more gum on the sinews, smoothing it over.

I must lead the tribe against them at first light. There will be argument but I am Wirreenun. I will kill any that oppose me.

Kurreah tested the firmness of the blade in its setting then hefted the spear. It felt light and alive, seeming to leap from his hand as he brandished it.

Ayee, Narahdarn. I will pierce your chest with this spear and let your spirit out. Then I will bind your spirit. Kurreah chuckled to himself and set the finished spear against the wall of the cave.

He stretched and got up, wandering outside to the bushes. He urinated, shook himself dry, and re-entered the cave. The Wirreenun stopped dead in his tracks and his hand flew to his totem pouch. The light from the fire sent his shadow dancing over the rear wall of the cave, over the soft skins of his bed. Beside the familiar shape of his body flickered another, sliding and warping over the uneven surface of the rock. The shadow was vaguely man-like in form though its outline wavered as he looked. A dry slithering sound echoed through the cave. Yellow eyes stared back at Kurreah and a wave of malice swept over him.

"Quinkan!" breathed Kurreah. He drew a ragged breath and gripped his totem pouch. "You have no power over me, Quinkan. I am Wirreenun, my spirits are stronger than you."

Think you so?

The question came complete and crystal clear into his mind. Kurreah jumped and looked about him for the speaker. He swung his head back toward the shadow on the back wall. "How is it that you speak and I hear you, though no sound comes to my ears?"

A dry chuckle raised the hairs on the back of his neck. *You profess to speak with the spirits and yet have no knowledge of how spirits converse?* The voice crackled with scorn.

"I speak with the ancestors and the spirit beings who made all things through dreams, not speech, Quinkan."

You are sure I am Quinkan?

"I have never seen one," admitted Kurreah. "Yet you have the form spoken of in fireside tales and I can feel your malice. You come by night into the dark places, seeking to do harm."

Laughter whispered through the air again. *I have not offered you harm, nor will I. I wish only to aid you.*

"Aid me? How?"

You seek to kill a number of humans and those you call the white demons. I can help you do this.

Kurreah smiled, despite his awe of the Quinkan. "Unless you are a very powerful spirit you will not be of much help." He spat into the fire. "And if you were that strong you would not seek me out. What is it you want of me?"

Indeed, you are a wise man. The thought slipped into Kurreah's mind, feeling like the rancid touch of decaying intestines. *It is true that I need something from you.*

The silence dragged on as Kurreah waited, determined not to ask again.

The voice in his head hissed and the shadow glided closer, making Kurreah flinch. *My kind is powerful but we cannot kill unless a man is very afraid. However, we can strengthen a man, we can gift him stamina and endurance. He can become very powerful.*

The voice became softer, persuasiveness oozing into the man's mind. *Let us strengthen you...*

Another voice laid itself over the first. *Our wishes are the same...*

None will be able to resist you... whispered another.

You will avenge your humiliation...

You will kill the white demons...

Kurreah's heart surged. He thought excitedly of the opportunities that lay before him. "I accept your help, spirit. How would you strengthen me?" he asked.

Like this...

The blackness leapt at the man, enveloping him in a foul miasma. The darkness swept into his mouth and nostrils, pervading his lungs and surging into his nervous system. His mind drowned in the terrible flood and Kurreah found his will pinioned as he screamed silently into the void.

His eyes would not obey him and the familiar objects in the cave gleamed with a faint fire. He looked into the night, watched, horrified and helpless, while legions of shadows trooped into the cave, and slipped silently into the cracks and crevices of the rocky walls around him.

⚜ ⚜

Kurreah's youngest wife, Gooma, found him sitting by the smoking remnants of his fire in the predawn chill. She shivered and watched him for a few moments before venturing closer.

"Husband," she whispered. "May I approach you?"

Kurreah continued to sit motionless, his eyes fixed and staring into the night. Gooma crept closer and lifted her hand tentatively to touch him on the arm. He was cold to the touch, his muscles bunched and rigid under his skin. Kurreah's eyes slid over her and his mouth opened. A voice emerged, a scaly rasp totally unlike the deep gruffness of his normal voice.

"Bring the elders to me."

"Now, my husband?" quavered Gooma. "They will be sleeping and..."

"Now!" barked Kurreah. "Obey me or die."

Gooma turned and ran off into the night. Faintly, the sounds of activity from the other caves and bark shelters beneath the towering gums filtered through the night. Minutes later the pattering of feet on the hard packed earth presaged the arrival of the elders.

Four young men moved into the firelight and stood looking down at the cross-legged figure before them. When Kurreah ignored them, one cleared his throat to speak.

"Why have you called us from our warm beds and our wives, Kurreah?"

Kurreah looked up at the speaker. "Nimbun, you will address me respectfully as Wirreenun," he said softly. "I have a task for you and I must give you the strength for it. Do you accept my strength?"

Nimbun bobbed his head. "Yes, Wirreenun."

Kurreah stared at the others, noting the way they looked at each other for support. *Elders,* he thought scornfully. *There is as much wisdom in them as in my wives.* A smile flickered across his face. *I would not have picked them if they were strong,* he reflected. *The strong died and I am left with the power.*

A chorus of acceptance from the elders interrupted him. *My memories and lusts are all that are left to me,* he thought. A shadow fell across his mind, obliterating his bitter reflections.

Kurreah stood, his long legs unfolding. He stretched out his arm toward the four shivering men. "Take then the power of the spirits."

Blackness flowed from the ground, up their legs and enveloped their torsos and heads in an instant. Cries of alarm were extinguished as the shadow beings poured into them, subjugating their will.

The five men stood still in a rough circle around the fire. At length, Kurreah spoke again. "Go. Rouse every man who can walk and bear a spear. Bring every boy too. I have need of all today. Assemble them in the clearing."

The glow of dawn suffused the sky with pink and grey Galah bird feathers of wispy cloud by the time the shifting mass of men and boys came together. The men stood impassively, resting on their spears, or squatting with boomerangs and killing sticks in hand. Boys milled about, chattering excitedly and brandishing sticks. They hushed when Kurreah stepped out of his cave and strode down to meet them.

"Men of the Dwarrah, the spirits visited me in the night and gave me a vision of what must be." Kurreah pitched his voice, letting it carry over the heads of the assembled men and boys. Women and children gathered around the edges of the clearing, listening apprehensively to his words.

"Too long have we allowed the white demons to live alongside us.

The land they live on is ours; the game they hunt is ours. Our ancestors cry out for us to take what is ours and kill the demons...and all who would join with them."

The men started muttering when the direction of Kurreah's speech became clear. The old hunter Wurrunnah pushed his way through the ranks. "We hear you, Wirreenun," he said. "But why should we risk an attack? The white demons have left us alone for many moons and there is plentiful game." Wurrunnah shrugged. "Besides, they are many and strong."

Kurreah snarled. "We will attack because I say so and the spirits are strong in me." He flung out his hand toward the elders, standing impassively to one side. "Ask then of your elders. Nimbun, what say you?"

Nimbun stirred and he spoke without expression. "The spirits have spoken to our Wirreenun. We must attack."

"And you others?" sneered Kurreah.

The other three elders stared straight ahead and added their confirmation. "It is so. Our Wirreenun possesses a very strong spirit."

"Well?" snapped Kurreah. "I require only your consent and the spirits will strengthen you as they do me." A sooty nimbus spilled out around his body. The assembled tribesmen gasped and withdrew a step as the figure of their Wirreenun rose slowly into the air. He hung there, about a foot off the ground, for the space of a dozen breaths then settled to the ground again.

"Do you consent?" asked Kurreah quietly.

"We must think on this," muttered the old hunter.

"Consent," insisted Kurreah. "Or die."

Wurrunnah shook his grey-haired head. "This is a weighty matter. We must discuss it."

Kurreah gestured and a dark bolt flashed across the clearing, dimming the morning light. Inky shadows swam over the old hunter's body and his face twisted in horror. He screamed in terror then gripped his bone knife and plunged it into his own belly, twisting it. He fell in a jerking heap, his blood gushing over the dusty ground.

An answering scream came from the watching women and children. An old woman hobbled forward and dropped to her knees beside the dying man. She raised her voice in howls of anguish. Blackness flowed over her and her screams died away. She clutched at her throat and fell over the corpse of her husband. Her heels drummed in the dust for a few moments before a horrified silence fell over the village.

"Do you consent?" Kurreah mindlessly repeated

The crowd stirred, eyeing the bodies in front of them. "We consent," came the ragged reply.

The Wirreenun bared his teeth in a savage grin. "Then walk into my cave and receive the blessings of the spirits."

Hesitantly, the first men moved towards the cave and entered it. Soon, they emerged and stood silently to one side as others moved forward. Some of the men took their sons by the hand and led them forward, muttering soothing words to the terrified boys. When they came from the cave, the others saw that the spirits had calmed the children, giving them strength of purpose. With more confidence than they felt, the rest of the Dwarrah manhood welcomed their oncoming spirit possession.

Chapter Twenty-Seven

Tjimi, the old Tjalwalbiri Karadji, stepped out of deep shadow. Starlight glistened on his dark skin and the sheen of sweat covering him. Beside him, three dark forms moved on limbs that still shook slightly from the stupendous efforts of the day.

Rima froze in place, recognition washing over her. With a guttural growl and a swiftness surprising for his size, Wulgu placed his huge body in the path of the men who approached.

Tjimi smiled, his white teeth contrasting against his black skin. "Tjakkan has guided us to reach you in time."

Wulgu roared and advanced on the men, his great arms reaching for them.

Wait, Wulgu, Rima cried out. *I know these men. This is Tjimi, the Karadji, and other elders, of the tribe where Gaia and I have lived for many years.*

Then why do they wish to turn us from our path? We must rejoin Wandjina so he can restore the child.

"Wandjina?" Tjimi asked with a startled look. "You converse with Wandjina?"

Perhaps not the one you mean, Rima thought while a chill shivered up her spine. *I see a great spirit being in your mind when you use his name. The one I know is a man, though he possesses great power and wisdom.*

"No matter," Tjimi replied. "The spirits instructed us to find you and keep you from other humans for a time. This, we will do," he insisted with a firmness in his words that breached any argument.

I am stronger than you, Tjimi, for all your powers, growled Wulgu.

"That is true," conceded Tjimi. "And I am pleased that the child Guyyah has such powerful protection." He bent and laid his spear on the ground beside him, then straightened. "I will not fight you, yow-ee. If I cannot convince you that the child must not join the other humans then I have failed Tjakkan and you may take her."

Convince us then, medicine man.

"First, yow-ee, answer me this." Tjimi gestured at Rima, who still clutched Gaia in her strong arms, shielding her frail body with hers. "I know the soul of Guyyah manifests itself as the being she calls Rima. That is well known. But whose soul are you? What man stands so close to the child?"

Wulgu's mind radiated amusement. *You have a lot to learn about our kind, Tjimi. I am not a soul of any man. I am a sentient being like you, independent in thought and action. Rima is the same; she is not part of the child.*

Tjimi's eyebrows shot up then he frowned. "If what you say is true then my belief in souls is shaken. You are truly beings like men?"

Yes.

"Then where are your people? In the years that Guyyah and Rima lived with us I saw no other yow-ee...you *are* yow-ee?"

We are known by that name but in all the lands there are but the two of us. We were created by ones who would seem as gods to you and brought to this place as protectors...for the child and others. Wulgu sat down on his haunches, bringing his huge head on a level with the man. He bared his long canines in a grimace. *Enough of this, medicine man. Convince me.*

Tjimi smiled and sat down, folding his long legs beneath him. He signalled the other men to sit also. "Very well, then. I will tell you of the vision sent to me by Tjakkan." He sat silent for a long while, until Wulgu started fidgeting. Then in a low, singsong voice Tjimi started his narration.

"I am Tjimi, son of Nahwalbun, son of Weenun. I am Karadji of the Tjalwalbiri peoples. I became Wirreenun when I entered manhood. I have fasted and visited the spirits in the high places and in the great deserts. I have slept by the waterholes and braved the great serpents that dwell within them to learn from the spirits. At last, I entered the domain of Tjakkan, who took me up to the heavens. There, he killed me and cut me open, inserting the magic cords and crystals within my bones and my intestines. He brought me back to life and I became Karadji. I can fly through the sky, I can run across the land like the emu without tiring, I can swim to the bottom of waterholes and rivers and talk with the spirits."

The three men behind him twice clapped their hands in unison. "It is so," they chanted.

"And though it was as if I was gone but a night within the belly of Tjakkan, when I walked the earth once more, a season had passed and my people mourned me as truly dead."

The Wirreenun clapped again. "It is so."

"Last night," Tjimi went on, "Tjakkan called to me through the black crystal he gave me and I left my hut and flew to him. I flew up into the heavens until the stars ceased to wink but stared at me hard and cold. The land of my ancestors spread out beneath me like a round river pebble. I came to Tjakkan in his shining hut far above the land I knew and he spoke to me."

Tjimi took a deep breath and his limbs trembled. "He sent his servants to me, small and hairless were they, long of limb with no faces save for huge black eyes. They did not need mouths for they spoke through the crystal and I heard them as I hear you, yow-ee."

"Haugh!" muttered the three men. "Strange are the ways of the spirits."

"Tjakkan spoke to me through his servants and I saw a vision that troubled me," Tjimi went on. "I saw men numbered as gum nuts in the forest or as hairs on the kangaroo. They built great huts, fought, and destroyed each other's huts. They cut down trees and killed the animals and the land itself died. The medicine men were powerful for they carved great huts out of wood and shining stone and moved them by magic through the air and over water and land."

Tears glistened on the old man's face as he recalled his vision. "I asked the great spirit Tjakkan why he allowed men to so ruin the land. He answered that he desired it not and he wished to change the vision. I saw then many men again but living in peace with other men, respecting the land and the animals. The land was green and fruitful."

The Wirreenun nodded to each other. "This vision is a good one," they agreed.

"I asked Tjakkan to create the second vision. He replied that the child Guyyah was to be mother to this world. He instructed me to find her and keep her from the Wandjina for six days." Tjimi shook his head. "I did not understand this for surely Wandjina is a good and powerful spirit? Tjakkan told me Wandjina has come down to dwell with men for a time, with white men like unto the child Guyyah."

The old Karadji fell silent.

Rima stirred and asked, *How can Gaia...Guyyah...be a mother to this world? She is but on the threshold of womanhood and cannot yet conceive.*

"I know not," admitted Tjimi. "It was not revealed to me." He raised his head and looked up at the shaggy face of Wulgu. "So, yow-ee. Have I convinced you?"

Wulgu rumbled deep in his chest. *My name is Wulgu, old man. I must think on this.* He dropped his head in thought and projected to Rima. *What do you think, Rima?*

I leave the decision in your hands, Rima replied. *As long as my Gaia is safe it does not matter whether we are with these men or with Wandjina. Only...Wandjina could heal this hurt that keeps her sleeping.*

Wulgu raised his head again. *Old man, your first vision is a true one.* He sighed deeply. *I too would see the second one come true. We will stay with you for six days...provided you can heal the child.*

Tjimi smiled. He beckoned to one of the Wirreenun behind him. "This is Njangaringu," he said. "He is a healer and skilled in driving out evil spirits."

Njangaringu dropped to his knees beside Rima and held out his hand toward Gaia. Rima frowned, hesitating, then laid the girl gently on the ground, adjusting her ragged grass skirt modestly.

One of the other men, Ngarragun, pulled a flat piece of wood out of his pouch, then a sharp stick and a sinew. Working deftly, he wrapped the sinew around the stick, placed it point down in a depression in the flat wood and started spinning it rapidly. Within moments, a curl of smoke spiralled upward. He dropped some fine dried grass on the wood and blew on it gently. A small flame sprang up. He added tiny twigs and resin and minutes later he nursed it to a healthy blaze, sending a rosy glow over the small group. He carefully added small gum branches to the crackling fire.

The healer examined the girl carefully, lifting her eyelids and probing her mouth, nostrils and ears with his fingers. He ran his hands down over her body and limbs, muttering to himself as he did so. He sat back and called out, "Guyyah, open your eyes." After a minute, he repeated the command and with a flutter, the girl's eyelids opened. She stared at the medicine man without recognition or expression.

"Good," Njangaringu said with satisfaction. "Rima yow-ee, support the girl in a half-sitting position." He rummaged in his pouch and drew out half a dozen shiny quartz pebbles. He pressed them in turn to parts of Gaia's head and body, holding them in place for a few moments as he muttered beneath his breath. Then he leapt up and ran over to the far side of the small clearing, keeping in clear sight of Gaia's face.

Njangaringu leaned forward with a fierce expression on his face, drew his hand back and hurled a quartz pebble directly at Gaia's head.

Wulgu gasped and started to reach forward, knowing he could not move fast enough to intercept the missile. He saw the pebble leave the man's hand, spiralling while it flew in a dead straight line toward the girl...then, nothing. The stone failed to land. There was no sound of it striking the child, the ground or anything else. Wulgu drew his hand back in astonishment, his jaw hanging open.

The healer moved across the clearing, lifting his knees high, thudding them against his chest as he walked, stamping hard on the ground. When he resumed his place in front of the girl he selected another stone and hurled it at Gaia's chest. Again, Wulgu saw it in the air, then it disappeared. The performance was repeated four more times, with the quartz pebbles directed at the points Njangaringu pressed them to earlier.

The Wirreenun ran forward and dropped to his knees beside the listless girl. He quickly searched her small belly and pressed his finger to a spot left of her bellybutton.

"Here," he said with a nod. "The spirit resides here."

He bent and pressed his lips to the spot and sucked hard. Gaia moaned and weakly writhed against the ground. Njangaringu sucked again then suddenly sat back. He spat something into his hand and grinned.

"I have removed the spirit." Njangaringu held up a grey quartz crystal veined with black. It glistened wetly in the firelight. He passed it around then, taking it back, he carefully wrapped it in a piece of tanned skin and placed it in his pouch. He turned back to Gaia, who still lay unmoving. "You may get up now, child," he said casually.

Gaia's gaze moved and fastened on Njangaringu's face. "Hello," she said. "What are you doing here?" She glanced over at the other men, her face crinkling into a broad smile. "Tjimi! And Ngarragun, and Wiradjerun! How lovely to see you." She twisted, looking around the small fire. "Is the rest of the tribe here?"

Gaia rested her hand on Rima's great hairy hand and peered up into her huge face. "Rima, you won't believe what a horrible dream I've had! I dreamed we were attacked by Quinkan and a dreadful man who…" Her voice trailed off and she became very still. "It wasn't a dream, was it?" she whispered. "I remember now. I was very frightened and I thought the man was going to kill me or…" Gaia drew a shuddering breath. "Then a voice told me to be strong and that I must become an adult very fast. It sent a striped dog with a big mouth to watch over me. The voice told me things."

"What things, child?" asked Tjimi quietly.

Gaia shook her head. "Things about me and what I must do. I don't understand, but the voice told me I would when the time came."

The girl struggled to sit up. "Who is that, Rima?" she asked, pointing at Wulgu.

That is Wulgu, my child. He came back with your mother to find you. He is a strong and faithful friend.

Only a friend, Rima? Gaia's amused thought drifted into her mind. *I think he means a bit more to you.*

Rima blushed and averted her eyes. Wulgu hooted softly and laughter cascaded over everyone's minds.

"My mother?" Gaia asked aloud. "You know my mother? Where is she?"

Not far from here child. In six days I will take you to Wandjina, who will bring you to her.

Gaia nodded. "I am dying to see her but I shall be patient, Wulgu." She laughed. "Don't look so astonished, Rima. I have grown up a lot in these last few days and I can see there is a proper time for everything." She turned back to Tjimi. "Is there any food, Tjimi? I am starving."

Chapter Twenty-Eight

"That is the valley of the white demons," Budtha said, pointing toward a faint trail that disappeared into a jumbled field of rock. "I have never seen it, for what woman would be allowed near? But I know it well." She tightly gripped Narahdarn's arm and whispered up at him. "Come away with me husband. Leave these strange white people here and let us find our own place. I will have many babies and you…" Her slim body shook while she spoke.

"Hush, woman. These are my people, black and white alike. I will not abandon them," Narahdarn growled at her, a glare emphasizing his irritation. "Do not speak of it to me again. If you want to be my woman, you will be strong and brave."

He started down the trail leading to the valley. Early morning light made the land glow with vitality after the rains of the night before. The riparian forest by the fast flowing river provided shelter from the storm and a selection of palatable fruits and tubers.

They camped for the night well off the path, denying themselves the comfort of a fire in case the Dwarrah hunters escaped the giant monitor and continued their pursuit. Despite their tribulations and uncertainty they slept well and were in a buoyant mood when they woke.

Narahdarn looked back at his small party of travellers. Immediately behind him and Budtha, the two aging archaeologists laboured to keep up. *The old man is holding up well*, he thought, *but the woman looks tired and worn*.

Next came Nathan and Ratana—he with his usual grumpy expression, she talking quietly to him. Samantha and Shinara followed, though the young girl was a far cry from the withdrawn, almost autistic girl of a few days ago. She skipped and chattered with her mother, bursting into peals of laughter. James brought up the rear, a grin on his face as he watched his wife and newfound daughter.

The valley walls slowly rose beside them, as they pressed onward. The clay soil was dry, despite the overnight rains, and fell away in small landslides, revealing limestone bedrock in places. A small stream gurgled and rippled through the centre of the valley, no more than three feet across even at the mouth of the valley. Grass grew abundantly near the stream and was dotted with wildflowers. Scores of butterflies, mostly small yellows but also several tiny brilliant blue ones, danced above the thick, green growth. A flock of rainbow lorikeets flew overhead, screeching raucously, and a small mob of wallabies stared with curiosity from the rocks near the far wall of the valley. A heavy scent of eucalyptus oil lent a blue haze to the air.

Narahdarn grinned with delight. *Truly an idyllic spot,* he thought. *These Neanderthals chose well. Speaking of which...*He signalled a halt and silently gestured for James and Bertie to join him.

"I don't want to alarm you but we are being watched," he said.

Bertie peered around the site. "I don't see anyone. Are you sure?"

"Over there," James said, tilting his head toward the spot. "In that clump of *Acacia* near the valley wall."

"You've got bloody sharp eyes, old boy. Yes, I see him now. What do we do?"

"Nothing," replied Narahdarn. "Keep your hands empty and in sight, talk and laugh if you can and think happy thoughts." He caught the quizzical look on Bertie's face and added, "They're telepathic, remember?"

Bertie looked sceptical. "Ah, yes. So you said." He snorted then marched back to his wife.

Narahdarn grinned. "Boy, has he got a surprise coming."

They resumed their journey into the valley. They passed the clump of *Acacia* without incident, the watcher withdrawing from sight. The group fell silent, apprehensive of the coming meeting and hopeful that Ernie preceded them. Even Shinara became quiet and held on to Sam's hand.

Bertie looked about him with great interest, pointing things out to his wife. "Look, my love, see those cuts on the trees? Made with stone tools. I can't wait to see first-hand how they make them. It certainly beats holding an old weapon or tool from a dig."

They crossed, then re-crossed the stream. "Thal means valley, you know," Bertie chirped in his lecturer's voice. "They first found fossils of ancient man in the valley of the Neander River in Germany, hence the name Neanderthal. I'll never forget my first visit there. It was back in 1952, and it was..."

"I know, you idiot," smiled Tilley, squeezing his hand. "I was there, remember? It was our honeymoon and it was 1953, dear."

Bertie blushed and fingered his moustache frantically. "By Jove! You're right, my love. Funny how the mind plays tricks on you, what?" He coughed, then went on. "The stream put me in mind of it. I spent my whole adult life chasing fossils of these extinct cavemen only to find them living in another valley at the far ends of the earth." He shook his head with a smile.

The valley walls grew closer together and they wound their way carefully through a massive rockslide. A section of the valley wall had collapsed and scattered rubble almost across to the far wall. The scree slope rose to a massive gouge in the valley rim, allowing access to the upper slopes of the range of hills.

Emerging from the rockslide, they found the valley opened out once more. They came across the first definite signs of habitation. Several rough lean-to shelters nestled under a grove of tall gum trees. As they approached, a figure stepped out of one and walked into the open. He carried a long, stone-tipped spear in one hand, the other held up at shoulder height, palm spread toward them.

Narahdarn walked up to the man, stopping ten paces away. James, Bertie, Nathan and Ratana joined him. Budtha shrank back, joining the other women by the stream.

"We come in friendship," said Narahdarn. He waited, with a smile on his face.

The man facing him was built like a wrestler, a short stocky body perched on muscular thighs, the whole covered in a fine pelt of dark hair. A hide loin piece secured by a thin cord around his ample waist covered his genitals. The arm holding the spear bulged with muscles too; the hand held high showed large calluses. The head was distinctly different. The forehead sloped backward from huge eye ridges. The cheekbones were sunken, with a squat nose and protruding upper jaw. The lower jaw receded under a straggly beard, giving the appearance of a pronounced snout. His head was perched on a huge neck, angled forward, giving him a pugnacious look, as if he was about to spring forward.

"As I live and breathe," muttered Bertie, his eyes darting over the man. "A bloody living Neanderthal. Look at that skull, the length of his forearms and shins. My God, he's an ugly chappie. I wouldn't want to meet him on a dark night."

The silence that followed Narahdarn's words extended into an uneasy vacuum. The man shifted his stance and cleared his throat. He barked out a phrase, unintelligible to everyone except Narahdarn, who smiled again and nodded, then added a few phrases of his own in the same language.

Narahdarn turned to the others with a translation. "He was waiting for our response to his mental queries. He lost patience and asked who we were. I'm just grateful for the good grounding Garagh gave me in his language before we left."

"I thought you said they are telepathic," said Bertie. "Couldn't he just read our minds instead of asking questions?"

"It doesn't work like that, mate," replied Narahdarn. "He can read our minds but it's difficult until he's built up a sort of set of mental coordinates. Once he has those, he can have a conversation with just one person or many. The problem is, he's got hold of a lot of subconscious thoughts from our minds but it confuses him." He grinned.

"You'll have to stop thinking twentieth century thoughts."

The Neanderthal spoke again and Narahdarn translated. "He wants us to go on up to the caves. Everyone is waiting for us there. He says he has spoken to Garagh and Wandjina and that we are welcome."

"Garagh!" exclaimed James. "Garagh's here? Thank God, I thought we'd lost him."

"So did I. I wonder where he went?"

The caveman turned and trotted up the well-worn path ahead of them. They broke free of a belt of trees and came out into a large open space in front of a series of caves worn out of the limestone rock. A mixed crowd of men, women and children stood around the clearing, silent, except for the chatter and laughter of small children. The adults and older children maintained a fixed concentration on the group of newcomers.

James had never encountered more than a handful of telepaths at a time and was aware of intense mental probing that resulted in a faint tickling sensation at the back of his head. He concentrated on friendly thoughts and pleasant incidents from his past.

Bertie and Tilley were in ecstasy. They pointed and stared, babbling to each other, Bertie making notes in his battered notebook with a blunt stub of a pencil. So intent were they on seeing everything there was to be seen that they failed to notice the others had come to a halt. Tilley bumped into Ratana, stepped back hurriedly and collided with an off-balance Bertie, who fell hard on his posterior. A ripple of laughter washed over the watching crowd.

"I say," said Bertie, climbing to his feet with a grimace. "Laughing at one's misfortune? Not on, old boy, not on." He shook his head and glared at the Neanderthals.

"It's okay, mate," said Narahdarn softly. "They thought you did it on purpose to lighten a serious moment. It seems they rather enjoy what we'd call slapstick humor."

"Really?" said Bertie, brightening. He beamed and waved.

"There's Ernie...and Garagh," called Sam. She ran toward the figures standing in front of the largest cave. Drawing near, her step faltered. Ernie, yes it was Ernie, though he looked younger, more dynamic...Ernie smiled at her but Garagh was looking downright embarrassed. He glanced over at Ernie and took a step backward. Sam stopped a few feet away and stood looking at the pair while the others advanced.

"You're not Garagh, are you?" she said softly. "You look like him, but you're not."

A look of confusion came over the Neanderthal. "What is she saying, Wandjina? I can see myself in her mind...and in the mind of these others but I am doing things I have never done." He looked at Ernie anxiously. "Are they casting a spell on me?"

Ernie shook his head and put his hand on the other man's shoulder. "No, my friend. They intend nothing but good for you and your people. These are the ones I told you about. They are friends you will have in days yet unborn. They have memories of great deeds you have yet to perform."

"Haugh!" Garagh shook his head. "You tell me but I do not understand. One thing I can grasp, Wandjina. If they are friends of yours, they are friends of mine." He was silent for a moment then the whole crowd burst out in a buzz of conversation, smiling and laughing. Garagh went on, "Come, my new friends, let us eat."

The crowd of onlookers broke up and went about their business, leaving the small group to wend its way into the large cave where several women tended to roasted meats and tubers.

James touched Ernie's arm and drew him to one side. "It's good to see you again. I'm afraid we got rather lost that first day."

"No matter," Ernie smiled. "You are here now, unharmed I see. You must tell me what has befallen you."

"I will, but I want to ask you about Nathan first." James paused, uncertain how to broach the subject. "Ernie, read my mind as I talk, please. Remember when those shadow creatures attacked Nathan last year, how his behaviour changed for the worse? Well, it's happening again, impossibly, as those devils aren't here in our past."

"I'm rather afraid they are here," said Ernie calmly. "Somehow they came back with us. If you say Nathan is infected then it's possible he acted as the conduit for their travel."

"Shit! Can anything be done?"

"Yes, I removed a number of them before but I must have missed one," Ernie muttered. "Let me think on this a while, my friend."

He steered James back to the others, who had started to eat their first decent meal in days. After the first hunger pains were assuaged, they got to talking, catching up on the events that had befallen the groups over the last few days. While the adults talked, Shinara played with a small group of adolescent boys and girls in one corner of the cave. Despite the lack of a common spoken language, sufficient mental connection was made to allow play.

Budtha clung to Narahdarn's arm, peering suspiciously at the food handed her by the Neanderthal women, shrinking back whenever Garagh looked in her direction. She was equally alarmed by the presence of what she perceived as the other great danger, the feared demon Wandjina.

Narahdarn explained the problem to Ernie. "The Dwarrah Wirreenun believes you to be basically demonic and she thinks Neanderthals kill and eat babies." He smiled wryly. "Sort of has a familiar ring to it."

Ernie nodded. "Propaganda." He smiled kindly at Budtha who edged behind her man. "How receptive is she?"

Narahdarn shrugged. "I have tried. I can sense emotions and occasionally flashes of half-formed pictures but she does not receive me."

"May I?" asked Ernie. He probed gently for a few minutes then withdrew. "Her beliefs are based only on what she has been told. Her father and brother saw the body of a child killed by a fallen tree near this valley. Scavengers had eaten part of the body and there was a knife cut opening up the chest and body cavity. They assumed Neanderthals had killed and eaten parts of the child."

"Why did they cut the body open?"

"Neanderthals view it as a kindness. They believe the soul must have a passage to escape the body, so they made one. They also smeared ochre on the head and feet and left it that way, since they didn't know the funerary rites of his people. They have a strong belief in the afterlife and have a set of definite customs regarding funerals."

"Fascinating, old boy!" chipped in Bertie, who had listened in on the conversation. "I hope I can get to see a real Neanderthal funeral instead of just excavating one."

"I sincerely hope you don't get to see one," stated Ernie. "We should be out of here in a couple of days and I'd rather leave the tribe intact. Try and keep your professional curiosity within the bounds of decency, professor."

Bertie flushed. "Sorry, old chap, didn't mean to sound heartless. It's just so overwhelming. D'yer think these chappies would mind if I nosed around a bit? I'd hate to leave without seeing everything I could. This'll make a fascinating paper when we get back."

Ernie smiled and nodded. "I'm sure they won't. You made a bit of a hit with your comedy routine out there. Just don't go into any cave or hut without being asked. Don't talk to the women without a husband or father present..."

"I know, I know, the whole anthropological routine. I won't forget." Bertie got up and, with Tilley in tow, bustled out of the cave.

"Now, to return to our other problem," said Ernie. He addressed Budtha in the Dwarrah language. "Child, your Wirreenun was right in one aspect. Just as a Karadji is far above a mere Wirreenun, so am I far above a Karadji-man. I have powers that would make any medicine man afraid." He smiled as Budtha paled. "But you have nothing to fear from me. This man," he laid his hand on Narahdarn's knee, "whom you have taken as a husband, is like a son to me. I welcome you as a daughter, Budtha."

As he spoke, Ernie's mind probed gently at Budtha's memories and ingrained fears, weakening some, strengthening others and building up her own confidence. At his final words the girl flashed Ernie a quick smile and buried her head behind Narahdarn's shoulder.

"She will fear me less now. You must talk to her of the reasons behind the child's mutilations, though. She will believe you." Ernie stared hard at Narahdarn. "She also believes you to be her husband. No, I have not probed at the reason for this belief, but I am concerned for her. What will she do when it is time for you to leave?"

"I have thought about this, Wandjina. I would bring her with us if I could. I have...feelings for her."

"She would be lost in your modern world. It would not be a kindness to subject her to that. If you leave her, I will see she is married off to a good man, Narahdarn, for I will be staying."

"I...I don't know, Wandjina. I must think about this." Narahdarn got up in a hurry, looking flustered, and left with Budtha.

Ernie sighed and turned to Ratana and Nathan. "And you, my dear daughter, how are you faring?"

Ratana bobbed her head. "I am well, Wandjina, though..." Her voice trailed off.

"And you, Nathan?"

Nathan scowled. "Okay, I suppose. I'm sick of this wandering about the countryside, being a target for any demented idiot with a grudge. The sooner we can conclude this business and get out of here, the better."

"I learned a little game here with the Neanderthals, Nathan," said Ernie softly. "Perhaps you'd like to try it, it's very simple." He went on without waiting for Nathan's response. "You slap your knee with your palm, then make a fist, fingers down and hit your knee again. Then you turn your hand on edge, open your fingers and chop down on your knee. The purpose is to see who can do it longest." Ernie gave Nathan a searching look. "Try it with me."

"You *are* kidding, I hope?"

"No. Humor me, Nathan. Try it with me."

Ernie started slapping his knee, making a fist then turning his hand. He repeated it two or three times before Nathan reluctantly followed suit. Nathan managed it twice then turned his hand before making a fist. He hesitated, started again, then lost control all together.

"Fuckin' stupid game! I've got better things to do," he snarled and walked away.

"What was that all about?" asked James.

"A psychological test I picked up a few years back," smiled Ernie. "It looks deceptively simple but it displays the functioning of brain activity. It shows me there is a subtle interference with his motor control." He reached out and squeezed Ratana's hand. "The news is not good, daughter. The shadow beings are still within him. This explains how they got back to the past but I wish I knew why they came. What do they hope to achieve?"

"Revenge maybe, or to stop you changing the world?" guessed Sam. "Perhaps they won't exist if you change things."

"It is possible. I am curious, too, as to where they originated. When I was here last I lived through events the long way." Ernie smiled. "There was no evidence of them then, though their mental signatures are strangely familiar." He shook his head. "It will come to me. In the meantime, if I knew a way to restrain them and question them I would. I fear the most I can do is evict them and I may not even be able to do that."

Ratana looked into Ernie's eyes with tears glistening. "Please try, Wandjina. I don't know my own husband now."

"I will try, daughter." Ernie patted Ratana's hand. "Now, Sam, James, I have news of your daughter, Gaia."

James leapt up with a start; Sam dropped to her knees in front of Ernie with a gasp. "Tell me," she said. "Is she safe? Where is she? When can I see her?"

Ernie grinned. "She is safe. Near here. Soon." He laughed at their expressions. "I really don't know much more than you." He held up a hand to quell further expostulations. "I got a hurried and rather mysterious call from Wulgu. He found Gaia and Rima, then he had a bad run in with those shadow beings but got through it all right. He was going to be here by now but was stopped by the elders of the tribe Gaia's been living with."

"Why did they stop her?" asked Sam anxiously. "Are they holding her captive or something?"

"I'm not sure. Wulgu couldn't maintain the contact. I've noticed our mental contacts are weakening. Anyway, the elders had a dream or something about preventing her from joining us for another five days. Now that concerns me. Garagh here," he clapped a hand on the Neanderthal's broad shoulder, "has agreed to change his plans. That means the future could change any time. When it starts, old Xanatuo will begin the recall procedure. We must have everyone together as soon as possible."

"My God," said James. "What can we do? Did Wulgu say where they were? Can we go and fetch them?"

"He gave me directions but you and Sam will stay here. I will find out myself why they prohibit her contacting us. Garagh will come with me. We leave immediately. I think time is short."

Ernie and Garagh got to their feet. Garagh picked up his spear and a small bag of food. Ernie looked pensive for a moment then said, "Garagh is leaving his great-grandson Uhlaht in charge. Anything you need, get Narahdarn to translate. I think you'll find you can generally make yourself understood though. Don't make the mistake of thinking they are stupid because they are primitive."

He turned and ran to the cave entrance with Garagh. "Look for us by nightfall." Ernie softened his gaze when he turned to Ratana. "I'm sorry, daughter. I will attempt to cure Nathan when I return. Be strong for him."

Without a backwards glance, Ernie sped after Garagh, catching up with him as they disappeared into the trees at the far end of the clearing.

Chapter Twenty-Nine

The day passed quickly in the Neanderthal village. The customs and artifacts of the friendly people fascinated all of them. After some initial awkwardness, Bertie found that his wishes were being anticipated; the men invited him into their huts or showed him how they fashioned their tools. The women quickly separated off Sam, Ratana, Shinara and Tilley from the men folk and hustled them off up the valley.

When James expressed some concern at the separation, Sam's only comment was "Women's business," and he had to be content with it. He busied himself examining some of the local art, images of the local wildlife painted on a rock wall deep inside one of the caverns. The images reminded him of photographs he had seen of the cave art of Europe, though the subject animals were typically Australian. The artists beamed at him when he traced the outlines with his finger, nodding his appreciation.

Shortly, the artists drifted away, caught up in their own affairs and the daily necessity of providing for their families. James remained, puttering around the cave, examining the paintings, the pigment pots and the style of crude brushes used. For the most part these were merely chewed twigs, though he found two small tufts of kangaroo fur bound to a short stick. Another exciting find for the scientist was the presence of large flat wicker baskets, filled with a selection of dried herbs. He hummed to himself while he investigated, so preoccupied that he did not notice the time slipping by.

Lengthening shadows from the cave entrance intruded on him, causing him to finally check the time. He cursed when he remembered the Dwarrah had stolen his watch. He put down a crude clay bowl smeared with pigment and got up, stretching. He wandered to the cave mouth where he stopped, aghast at the sight that met his eyes.

Neanderthal men and boys streamed back from the trees on the far side of the clearing, running for the caves. Others burst out of the huts, milling about in confusion. James saw a man fall, and he stared in disbelief at the long spear that impaled him. Another fell, though for no apparent reason. This man rose to his knees, then collapsed again when several objects raised plumes of dust near him.

James caught sight of black figures moving in the bushes near the trees. An Aboriginal warrior ran out, hurled a spear at the retreating Neanderthals and ducked for cover. Another trotted out and threw a killing stick that hit a small boy with an audible thump. The boy fell and the warrior gave a yell, running up to the boy screaming on the ground and hitting him with a club.

Some Neanderthals grabbed weapons and charged the first wave of Aborigines, brandishing spears and stones. More Aborigines ran out of the trees, showering the approaching Neanderthals with a hail of stones. People fell to the ground, clutching heads and limbs. Screams and moans filled the air, mingling with the triumphant shouts of the Aborigines pushing the Neanderthals back across the clearing.

James heard his name called. Narahdarn waved at him from another cave then dashed across to join him, Budtha right behind him. "It's the Dwarrah," Narahdarn panted. "The others are in the main cave. Come on, we've got to get over there. Uhlaht's organizing the defence."

They ran toward the main cave, trying to keep to the rock wall of the valley rather than risk the open space. James was appalled to see that in the last few minutes the Dwarrah warriors had gained a complete ascendancy over their opponents. Bodies littered the clearing, most of them white though in the increasingly bitter fighting close to the caves, numerous Aborigines had fallen.

The situation inside the main cave was utter chaos. Young children were screaming and crying, older boys stood around ashen-faced, clutching sticks or crude fire-hardened spears. Men milled around near the entrance in comparative silence though James could physically feel the mental energy pouring out all around him.

Abruptly, half the men rushed to the entrance and, taking cover behind a mound of large boulders, began throwing a rain of small stones at the advancing Aborigines. Howling with rage and pain, the Dwarrah ran for cover, sheltering behind trees and in folds of the land.

The other Neanderthal men rapidly collected up all the spears and set them carefully to the sides of the entrance, within easy reach of the defenders. Children were hustled to the rear of the deep cave, watched and guarded by several older or wounded men. The youths started searching for rocks, digging in the soil to unearth them or prying them off the rocky walls.

After the Dwarrah men took cover from the hail of stones, the noise of the fighting died down. Uhlaht, Garagh's great-grandson, scrambled over to where James, Nathan, Narahdarn, Budtha and Bertie stood, trying to keep out of the way. He barked a few phrases, listened to Narahdarn's reply, then went into a long rambling monologue. Eventually, Uhlaht turned on his heel and walked back to direct the defence of the cave. Narahdarn turned to the others with a quick translation.

"Uhlaht is unsure of our loyalty. I assured him we would help defend the tribe and reminded him of our friend Wandjina's friendship with his people. He accepted our offer of help."

"Oh, great!" muttered Nathan. "Not content with taking us on this stupid expedition, now we're being forced into battle. Talk about being caught between those black devils and a hard place!" He looked around at the rocky walls of the cave and tittered.

"Nobody's forcing you," grated James. "If you don't want to help, go and sit with the children." He turned his back on Nathan.

"To continue," went on Narahdarn. "Uhlaht is concerned. We have limited supplies and weapons in this cave. Unless we can break out we will be in a very serious situation. Furthermore, as you may have noticed, with the exception of Budtha here, there are no women or girls present. All of the women went to the cave of the Mother this morning, further up the valley. The Dwarrah have not attacked them but that may only be because they are unaware of them. Uhlaht has told them to hide in the cave."

"What the hell can we do?" asked James. "I won't be content until I know Sam and Shinara are safe." He glanced at the others. "I'm sure Bertie and Nathan feel the same."

"Spot on, old boy," agreed Bertie. "Women and children first and all that. Let's go give these blighters the old what for, eh?"

"Jesus!" muttered Nathan. "What a load of crap from an old fart."

Bertie rounded on Nathan, his eyes glittering. "You have a foul mouth and a nasty mind. If you insist on continuing in this unseemly manner, I assure you this old fart will be happy to teach you some proper manners. Now sit down and desist!"

Nathan took a step back, opened his mouth then thought better of it. He sat down on a boulder and put his head in his hands.

Narahdarn nodded. "That's all very well, sir, but I'm not sure how we can help the situation. We are only four men without any real experience with fighting or killing."

"Hmm. On the other hand, we are heirs to thirty thousand years of culture and organized warfare. Surely we can come up with some winning tactics?" Bertie twirled his moustache fiercely.

"A few modern weapons wouldn't go amiss either," James responded. "Okay, wishful thinking apart, let's try and analyse our situation logically. We have to attack the Dwarrah and break out before they find the women and children. We lack much in the way of weapons and don't have the means of making others. Where does that leave us?"

"Up shit creek," muttered Nathan.

The others ignored him. Narahdarn nodded slowly, turning James's words over in his mind. "The Dwarrah and the Neanderthals are probably fairly similar in fighting ability. The numbers are about equal as far as I can tell. Weapons are the same, skill the same, numbers similar, so where can we get an edge?"

"Tactics, maybe...or discipline?" put in Bertie. "This puts me in mind of the ancient Greeks and Romans. They'd form a disciplined battle line. They could withstand repeated attacks by superior mobs of barbarians. Of course, they had armor. Pity we don't have metal-working capability."

Renewed shouting broke out at the cave entrance when a shower of missiles cracked off the boulders and walls. Muffled cries told of bruises and other injuries. The rocks were gathered up and thrown back. They could hear them clattering on tree trunks outside, amid jeers from the untouched warriors.

"Pity we don't have some of those tree trunks in here," said Bertie. "We could fashion a good old Roman 'tortoise' and attack under cover."

"Damn, there's something at the back of my mind that I can't quite..." complained James. "It'll come to me." He turned away and wandered back into the cave, picking his way through the crying children.

"What about this Ernie chappie? Can you contact him with your telepathy?"

"I've tried," said Narahdarn. "So has Uhlaht. He's also tried to contact Garagh but without success."

Uhlaht moved over to them again. He spoke briefly to Narahdarn then went back to help his fellow tribesmen break up more rocks for missiles. Narahdarn immediately passed on the message.

"The Dwarrah are lighting fires to smoke us out. Uhlaht says that if we can conjure up some magic then now is the time to do so."

James wandered back again, deep in thought. "Narahdarn," he asked. "Can you read what is in my mind? The thing I can't quite put into words."

"I doubt it," said Narahdarn with a grimace. "I usually need a directed thought. We can give it a try, though. Hold on." He concentrated hard, emptying his mind of all conscious thought while James contemplated the problem facing them. Sweat poured from the young man's face before he broke off.

"Sorry, doctor. It's times like these I could use a Vulcan mind-meld," he grinned. "All I can get is half-formed images of paintings, paint pots and dry plants."

"Never mind, it was worth a try...hang on, yes! Oh, shit, yes! Listen. These guys are all natural telepaths, right?" James babbled. "Well, that means they can get disciplined very fast. One person could give them the control to act like an army instead of a rabble."

"There's still the problem that they are not well armed," stated Bertie. "A spear in the guts will rapidly destroy a person's concentration."

"No, no! That's where my idea comes in. The plants these people use for their dyes are dried in large shallow wicker baskets—you saw them Narahdarn—we could use those as shields. Put a bit of hide over them, fix a strap or two..."

"By Jove, you've got a point. Stand shoulder to shoulder with a shield guarding your left side and a trusty spear in your right hand and the line is well nigh impregnable, as long as you can control them..."

"...Which Uhlaht can!" completed James. "What do you think?" he asked anxiously.

"I think we need to get Uhlaht over here immediately."

"Won't work," muttered Nathan. The others ignored him again.

Uhlaht got very excited when Narahdarn explained the concept to him. Bertie and James attempted to hold a clear image of what they meant while the Neanderthal delved into their conscious thoughts. He nodded vigorously then looked crestfallen. He explained through Narahdarn that most of the baskets were in the huts below or in the cave of pictures. Only a few were kept in the main cave as food containers.

The first billows of smoke rolled into the cave entrance before the eight wicker baskets were collected. Under instructions relayed through James and Narahdarn, Uhlaht set a group of men to work attaching sinews to act as thongs and draping thick kangaroo hide leather over them. Coughing from the smoke, Uhlaht held up the first shield. It covered his body and left arm completely, stretching from neck to waist. He brandished his spear and gave a loud cry of exultation. Quickly, the other shields were finished.

Uhlaht selected seven men and formed them into a line, explaining what he wanted them to do, showing them in mental visions the task ahead. Within minutes, their actions became coordinated.

Meanwhile, the crackling of the flames became louder and waves of smoke hung like a pall in the still air, gradually drifting downward. Paroxysms of coughing broke out from the rear of the cave where the children, the old and the wounded huddled.

Uhlaht gestured and the seven men joined with him to form a line. They stepped over the boulders heaped defensively at the cave mouth and advanced into the smoke between the two raging fires. For a moment all was silent, then a ragged scream rent the air, followed by shouting and the sound of spears and rocks hitting the shields.

"What's happening?" asked James. "I can't see a thing."

Narahdarn tapped a man on the shoulder and asked a question. "He says one man is down but their spears do not penetrate the shields easily. They have killed many."

"What are they doing now?"

The man listened and spoke again.

"They have reached the cave of pictures. They are bringing many baskets back."

Minutes later, four weary figures stepped through the smoke, which was thinning out as the fires died down for lack of tending, with two men loaded down with baskets. Uhlaht grinned and wiped the sweat and grime from his face. Men leapt forward to take the baskets and, working from experience, rapidly transformed them into new shields.

Nathan sat apart from the others with a sulky expression on his face. Every now then a horrified look would pass over him, only to be replaced by his usual petulance. Several times, he struggled to open his mouth, fighting for control of his own body. Blackness seemed to sweep over him from outside the cave. He leapt to his feet with a strangled cry.

"Up the...no, you bastards...they are further up...oh, Jesus, help...women, up the valley." Nathan collapsed, weeping.

Narahdarn strode over to him and half lifted the man by the collar of his shirt. "What are you saying?" he demanded.

Nathan's tears shut off like a tap. "You can't win, you know," he said calmly. "We will kill them all."

Narahdarn lifted his hand to strike him. James took his arm. "It's not Nathan talking," he said quietly. "Leave him. We have to get out of here."

Uhlaht gave a great cry of distress, soon echoed by all the other men. The children started wailing and one fled from the cave. A thump and a scream told of his fate.

Narahdarn paled as he listened to the cries and babble. "The women have seen Dwarrah warriors on the cliffs above them. There is a way down to the valley floor only a hundred yards from the cave of the Mother."

Chapter Thirty

Ernie and Garagh found Gaia by mid-afternoon. The two men lay on their bellies in the dust, looking over the lip of a low ridge at the billabong with its ring of scrubby vegetation. A thin trickle of smoke betrayed the presence of humans somewhere near the edge of the water. Garagh shaded his eyes, looking beyond the waterhole. The strip of dark forest along the river captured his attention.

"Too close to the river for my liking," he grunted. "There are beasts in that river I would not care to meet."

Ernie nodded absently, his senses probing the area below them.

"So what do we do, Wandjina? Wait for dark and try and sneak up on them?"

Ernie smiled. "They already know we are here. That's a Karadji-man down there, remember?" He rose, dusting himself off and picking up his spear. "Come on."

He dropped from the lip of the rise and trotted down the gentle slope to the billabong, Garagh following close behind. When they reached the scrub, the bushes parted and Tjimi stepped out. He stood facing them, leaning on a long thin spear with his left leg nonchalantly bent and resting against his right knee.

After a long pause, Tjimi stroked his ragged, grey beard with one hand and spoke. "I see you, he who is called Wandjina."

Ernie nodded. "Greetings, Tjimi, Karadji of the Tjalwalbiri. You are a long way from your home lands."

"By all accounts, so are you...Wandjina." He inclined his head toward Garagh. "Who is your companion? He is pale like a ghost."

"He is Garagh, leader of the Urgah, the People of the Northern Forests. He is my friend."

"I do not know this people. They must be from far away."

"Further indeed than you can imagine, Tjimi."

The silence dragged out. Tjimi calmly contemplated the men in front of him; Ernie waited patiently, determined not to break the silence first. At length, Tjimi sighed and lowered his leg. "Why have you come, Wandjina?" he asked.

"For the girl."

Tjimi raised an eyebrow. "What girl would this be?"

"Do not play with me, Tjimi. You know well who the girl is. The yowies have told me."

"I suspected as much," said the Karadji grimly. "I cannot let you take the girl, Wandjina."

Ernie calmly regarded the man. "Do you think you can stop me?" he whispered. His outline shimmered as he felt his power mounting.

Tjimi shrugged. "I will try, for Tjakkan has bid me do so."

"Tjakkan?"

Tjimi nodded. "It is his power that runs in my intestines and strengthens my bones. He speaks to me in dreams and I obey his voice."

Garagh looked troubled. "This Tjakkan," he asked. "Does he live in the sky in a shining hut?"

Tjimi raised both eyebrows. "You know him too?"

Garagh fingered the black stone around his neck. "He is of the 'Others'," he muttered to Ernie.

"Aaah! That explains a lot, my friend." Ernie faced Tjimi again. "I will not contest you for the girl, Karadji, but I must satisfy myself as to her safety."

Tjimi's eyes searched the faces of the men in front of him. He nodded. "You are welcome at my fire. What hospitality I can offer, I do so freely," he said, using the formal words of greeting. He led the way back through the scrub to the bank of the billabong and the small fire beside it. Tjimi introduced the three men standing alertly in the clearing, adding, "They are all Wirreenun of the Tjalwalbiri." Then he introduced the visitors.

Wulgu ambled forward and embraced Ernie clumsily with one enormous arm.

Welcome Wandjina. My heart is glad you have come.

Gaia got up from the ground where she was playing with Rima. She walked over to Ernie and Garagh and regarded them solemnly. Ernie looked back with a small smile on his otherwise impassive face, but Garagh looked increasingly ill at ease.

"I know you, Ernie, or is it Wandjina?" she said. Ernie inclined his head. "I remember my parents talking about you when I was a baby. You look different, not older but younger." She cocked her head to one side. "Your inner flame gives you away, Wandjina."

Gaia turned to Garagh. "I remember you too. Yet, the Garagh I knew is not you. Time is a funny thing, isn't it?"

"Yes, child," said Ernie gently. "We came back here to change time. I knew my purpose but it seems there is another." He sighed deeply then looked from Gaia to the dense bushes near the edge of the water and back again. "Do you know yet your part in this?"

"Yes, Wandjina. That is why I must remain here for a time. I cannot say why because knowing may induce you to try to change events."

Gaia stepped forward and laid her hand on Garagh's arm. "I wish I could have got to know you better, Garagh. You are a good man."

Gaia stepped back then turned and lightly ran back past Tjimi and the Wirreenun, away from the yowies, to the dense bushes near the billabong. She turned to face the group and shivered slightly.

The bushes rustled and parted as Ehrich pushed his way out. One arm went around Gaia's throat and he pointed a gun at the men with the other.

"Thank you, little girl," he smirked. "I was wondering how to get close to you."

Wulgu bounded forward with a roar as Rima launched herself toward the man. The crack of the gun was heard in the din just before Rima collapsed to the ground. A scarlet stain spread over her chest. Wulgu reached for the man but the man responded by clutching Gaia tightly and grinding the barrel of the gun to the side of her head.

"Another step and she dies," said Ehrich. He grinned. "What have I got to lose? Understand me, ape?"

Wulgu halted, his eyes blazing with anger, the hair on his head and shoulders erect.

"Move back, with the others, ape."

Ehrich waited while Wulgu slowly retreated, his eyes fixed on the man as he did so. A series of intimidating growls reverberated from his chest and his muscles quivered with the strain of holding himself back.

"Please, Wulgu," said Gaia in a small voice. "Look after Rima. I'll never forgive myself if she dies." A tear rolled slowly down her cheek.

"All right, ape, that's far enough. Now sit down on the ground. Do it!" he snapped. He pointed the gun back at the men. "Okay, now you bloody Abo's and you, whoever you are, you ugly brute," he waved the gun at Garagh. "Drop your spears."

Tjimi and the Wirreenun stood unmoving, a questioning expression on their faces. Garagh also looked puzzled. Ernie translated in their respective languages and they complied, albeit reluctantly.

"Now," said Ehrich. "The girl and I have some unfinished business. We'll be leaving now and none of you better follow. If you do," he brandished the gun again and fired above their heads, "you'll end up like that ape, savvy?" He pointed the gun at Ernie. "Translate for the savages, you black bastard. I don't want them getting any noble ideas."

Ehrich dragged a non-protesting Gaia across the end of the clearing to a point where the scrub was thin. He glanced over the open ground toward the river. "We are crossing that empty space. If as much as one of you sets foot outside this billabong while we are in sight, I'll kill the girl at once. Got it?"

Ehrich backed out of the vegetation and disappeared with his arm still around Gaia's throat. Wulgu at once moved after him with a savage growl.

"Stay!" snapped Ernie. "You are not to follow." He ran over to Rima and squatted beside her. He listened to her hoarse breathing and took her pulse under her jaw. "She will live," he grunted. "Wulgu, you will attend to your mate." Ernie glanced at Tjimi. "I would deem it a favor if you would assist the yowies."

Tjimi inclined his head. "If her yow-ee is hurt, then Guyyah is in danger. We will do our part by helping her. Will you seek the child herself?"

Ernie nodded. "I will."

"And will you do Tjakkan's bidding by returning her to our care?"

"We shall see." Ernie turned, saying, "Come Garagh, let us see whether it is safe to follow them yet...Garagh?" He leapt to his feet with a curse and pushed cautiously through the bushes.

The long stretch of bare ground between the billabong and the river forest appeared empty and flat at first glance. Shading his eyes, Ernie could just pick out the figure of Ehrich jogging toward the forest, dragging Gaia by one arm. He looked for Garagh and saw him, bent double, using the slight depression of an old streambed for cover, running after them. The streambed angled away from the direction taken by Ehrich. Garagh lifted his head every few moments to check their whereabouts.

When the man and the girl vanished into the forest, Garagh came out of cover and raced across the open ground. Ernie cursed again and ran out into the open, knowing there was no hope of reaching his friend in time.

Ernie reached the forest feeling no effects from his exertion. He altered the blood supply to his leg muscles, raising its oxygen content. He wondered briefly whether he should use more radical changes to his body in order to catch up sooner but decided against it. The girl knew Ehrich was there and put herself in his power anyway.

Why?

The trail Ehrich and Gaia took was plain in the soft earth of the riverbank. Garagh's footprints overlaid the boot prints. Their passage was so recent that leaves they'd crushed underfoot were still springing back up. Ernie followed at a run, sensing the direction rather than looking for visual clues. He came to the river, far below the point where it ran noisily over a boulder-strewn bed. Here it moved slowly through a large pooled area, with an oily, heavy look. He saw clawed prints in the mud of the bank and a smooth muddy track where something large had recently slipped into the murky depths. Ripples still crossed and re-crossed the pool.

A shout startled Ernie and he saw Garagh diving for cover behind a log about a hundred yards away. The sound of a shot echoed across the pool, deadened by the paperbark trees.

Garagh scrambled up, ducked under a vine and ran forward to throw one of his spears at Ehrich. Ernie moved closer and saw Ehrich push Gaia to the ground before firing at Garagh, missing him. Garagh's spear fell short, landing deeply embedded in the sand in front of Ehrich's feet. Ehrich laughed, firing off another two shots at Garagh. The Neanderthal threw again, this time hitting Ehrich in the thigh. He screamed and fell to the ground, squeezing off another shot as he did so.

Garagh quickly covered the ground between his adversary and himself. He grappled with Ehrich in a fierce grip. The brute force of the Neanderthal swiftly overcame his opponent but the spear still sticking in the man's thigh got in the way, preventing Garagh from pinning Ehrich to the ground. He shifted his grip and Ehrich, blood pouring from his wound, pressed the gun into Garagh's side and pulled the trigger.

Ernie's first impulse was to rush forward and aid his friend but he kept his human impulses in check. *This is his destiny. It must play out*, he thought with deep sadness as he watched his friend fall.

Garagh collapsed with a cry then pulled himself up on one knee, his eyes glazed with pain. Ehrich wrenched the spear from his leg and limped over to Gaia, who was still sprawled on the ground near the edge of the water. He stood above her and lowered the gun, pointing its deadly muzzle directly at her forehead.

Ernie stood undecided. *Just how important is she? Should I do nothing and trust to the 'Others' or act on my own?*

He cursed and raised his spear, knowing the distance was probably too great, even for him. A movement in the water stopped him. He watched a slow swirling as something on the surface dipped under water and lazily moved toward the shore. Ernie dragged his concentration back to Ehrich and Gaia, steadied himself, and threw.

"That's it, little girl," Ehrich said through clenched teeth. "I wanted to play but the big boys wouldn't let me. Besides, if they're afraid of you then I want you gone too." He laughed and aimed the gun. "Goodbye, my sweet."

Ernie threw his spear. The spear fell short and thudded to the ground fifteen feet in front of Ehrich, causing him to jerk at the same moment he pulled the trigger. The bullet missed Gaia and splashed into the water.

The next moment Garagh crashed awkwardly into Ehrich, knocking him down and sending the gun spinning into the water. He teetered on the edge, then his eyes rolled in his head and he fell into the river. A wave washed over Gaia as a giant scaly hide rushed past her and huge jaws closed over the lifeless body of Garagh. The water swirled violently then gradually stilled. Nothing moved on the surface of the river.

Ernie ran up, grabbing his spear from the ground as he did so. He stood over the groaning Ehrich and put his spear to the man's throat. "I should kill you," Ernie whispered. "Garagh was my friend."

He closed his eyes as grief overcame him and he tensed for the kill.

Gaia put her hand on Ernie's arm. "Do not kill him. It is not necessary. Your friend Garagh did what needed to be done." She gazed into the terrified eyes of the man lying on the ground. "Let this world claim him," she said. "He can do no more harm." She turned and, leading Ernie by the hand, walked down the river and out of sight, not looking back.

⁂

The life of the river forest, stilled by the gunshots and noise, slowly returned. The cicadas started their monotonous thrumming, followed a few hesitant minutes later by birds crying and frogs ratcheting in the shallows. Ehrich stirred and sat up. He ripped his shirt into strips and bound his wound tightly until the blood only oozed through the cloth. He felt lightheaded and his leg ached abominably.

"Bastards," he muttered. "So I'm harmless am I? We'll see about that."

He struggled to his feet and lurched off down river. The heat of the day lessened as he limped on, the first mosquitoes and biting flies of the evening putting in an appearance. He brushed them away and overbalanced, falling heavily. He lay there for a moment then forced himself to his feet.

The undergrowth rustled, parting in front of him. The striped face of a large cat peered at him, sniffing the scent of fresh blood. Ehrich backed away, looking with horror as the long, muscled body of a *Thylacoleo* flowed into view. The marsupial cat yawned, displaying huge canine teeth. It yowled, its cry rising to a scream that raised the hair on Ehrich's neck. He gave a whimpering cry, turned and ran. Within a dozen paces his leg failed him and he plunged headlong to the ground. He looked back over his shoulder just in time to see the pink maw of the cat as it sprang. It sank its teeth into Ehrich's back and a long bubbling scream of pain and terror erupted from him.

Far away, in the open land between the river and the billabong, Gaia and Ernie paused, listening to the faint echoes of a scream, which ended abruptly.

"The world has claimed him," Gaia said softly.

Chapter Thirty-One

Uhlaht immediately organized his strongest men, equipping them with the makeshift wicker shields. Other men thrust spears into the hands of the picked warriors, exhorting them to hurry and kill the Dwarrah. Narahdarn argued briefly with Budtha, telling her to wait for him at the back of the cave while he consulted with James and Bertie.

"We must go with them," he said. "They intend a break out to rescue the women."

"Agreed," said James. "We won't have shields but if we keep alert behind the warriors we should be able to get through. I don't know what'll happen when we get to the women's cave though."

"We will think of something I'm sure, old boy," affirmed Bertie.

"You're bloody mad, the lot of you." Nathan gave a snort of derision. "I reckon you must be a couple of sandwiches short of a picnic if you think we can calmly walk through a pitched battle. Lead us to our deaths more like."

"Don't you have any concern for Ratana?" James said in a biting voice. "Even taken over as you are, you must have some love left for her."

Nathan's lip trembled. "Help me, Doctor Hay," he whispered. He opened his mouth in a loud, braying laugh. "Let the bitch look after herself, I say!"

Uhlaht gave a command and twenty men stepped out into the smoke in two ragged lines. Behind them poured perhaps twice as many, unshielded and armed only with sticks, clubs and handfuls of rocks. They charged forward, crashing into a number of Aboriginal fighters. Shouts and screams arose when the spears rose and fell, killing those under their deadly rain.

James, Narahdarn, Nathan and Bertie dashed out of the cave on the heels of the Neanderthal fighters. James found himself grappling with a Dwarrah man almost at once. The man moved with the precision of an automaton and displayed great strength but his actions were slightly hesitant, as if each movement was thought about and considered before being put into effect. James slammed his fist into the man's ribcage, following it up with a knee to the groin. The man grunted, grabbing hold of James's shirt as he fell, dragging him to the ground. They scrabbled in the dust before Bertie knocked the man on the head with a rock.

"Rum bunch of coves, what?" he said cheerfully. "Lots of the blighters but they're moving about like puppets. Come on, old man." He bent down and grabbed James's hand, hauling him to his feet.

James clapped Bertie on the shoulder in thanks and pointed to their left. They ran around the main melee, where the line of Neanderthal men, protected by their wicker shields, slowly advanced into the main clearing. Hordes of black Dwarrah tribesmen leapt and cavorted in front of them, dashing in to jab a spear at the line, then duck away again. Others pelted the Neanderthals with a steady rain of missiles. Several of Uhlaht's men lay still but, as one spearman fell, another took his place. Boys followed, rocks gripped tightly in sweaty hands, dispatching the wounded Dwarrah and dragging the injured Neanderthals back toward the main cave. The litter of fallen bodies was mainly black, though death and the pall of dust clinging to everything reduced the difference between friend and foe.

The four ducked and weaved, avoiding the odd rock that came their way, and leapt over dead bodies. They broke away from the area of conflict into an undisturbed part of the valley. The path up the valley was broad, showing the evidence of much recent usage. They jogged up the track, anxiety lending them strength, the sounds of fighting falling away behind them.

The valley walls drew in again, rising on either side, leaving the floor of the valley with its now diminished brook in heavy shade. Half a kilometre further on they came across another open area, much smaller than the main clearing lower down. The small stream was dammed, forming a large shallow pool. The land sloped up on the far side of the pool, ending at a narrow cleft in the rock wall.

A crowd of men milled around the entrance to the cave, brandishing spears and hurling threats and imprecations at the defenders. A sporadic rain of rocks flew from the cave mouth, preventing the attackers from closing in. While they watched, a man edged along the cliff face. He reached into the entrance and hauled a screaming woman from her sanctuary, hurling her to the ground. At once, several spears impaled her and a shout of triumph rose in counterpoint to the ululating wails from the cave.

"Dear God," muttered Bertie. "Can't we do something?"

"Yeah, mate, you're the scientist here. Think of something," Narahdarn snapped while staring at the cave mouth and flinching at the shrieks of terror emanating from it.

James drew him back into the cover of the trees, franticly searching for any idea that would help. He thought of several solutions but rejected them all since they involved some aspect of modern technol-

ogy unavailable to them in this time. In desperation, he shouted at
Narahdarn. "I can't think of anything we can do. There's only the four
of us and there must be a couple of dozen of them."

"They're led by that bugger, Kurreah," Narahdarn growled. "See,
over there on the left, whipping his bloody troops into a blood lust."

Kurreah turned and stared across the pool at the trees where
they stood hidden, as if he had heard his name spoken. Nathan gasped
and his hands flew to his head, grasping the sides with white knuck-
led fingers. His face contorted and his eyes bulged as he clenched his
teeth against the words forcing their way out of him.

"Yes," he grated. "They are…oh, God, help me…he is here, the
one…who…shamed." Nathan fell to his knees and started screaming.
Moments later, his voice became more normal but his speech was
garbled, as if he were engaged in more than one conversation. "They
are here indeed…remember the wallaby…in the trees by the
pool…contact her…only four of them, no three…her!"

"Shut him up!" hissed Narahdarn.

"Too late," observed Bertie. "Here comes trouble."

Kurreah shouted at his men and pointed down the valley at the
trees. He and five others broke away from the main group storming
the cave and loped rapidly towards the pool.

"Narahdarn, he's right." James spun the young man around.
"Nathan is trying to tell us something. Can you reach Shinara? Remember the wallaby, the dead wallaby? Oh, quickly, man!"

"I can try," he said. He leaned against a tree trunk, concentrating
and ignoring the green ants swarming over it.

"Come on, Bertie," cried James. "We've got to buy him some time."
He ripped a heavy branch from a tree and started stripping the leaves
from it.

Bertie scanned the area and finally picked up a fallen branch. He
whacked it against a tree experimentally, then shook his hand in pain
from the reverberations. He shrugged his shoulders and marched out
into the open, James beside him.

Kurreah and the five Dwarrah warriors leapt the stream below
the dam, circling round to meet the pair. The Wirreenun hesitated at
the sight of the two men standing in front of him with branches in
their hands, then signalled two of his men to circle around them.

Bertie scuffed in the soil with his foot, then bent and picked up a
round stone. He hefted it in one hand then fired it straight at the
leading warrior. The man ducked to one side and the stone hit the
next man in the jaw. He dropped as if pole-axed.

"Howzat?" screamed Bertie, raising both arms in the air.

James grinned despite the peril. "I might have known you were a
cricket player!"

The next moment they were fighting for their lives. A Dwarrah
pushed forward, jabbing at James with his obsidian-tipped spear.

James managed to fend off the jabs, deflecting them with his branch. He retreated slowly into the trees. Bertie fought silently. He cracked a man across the ribs with his stick then stumbled back as a spearhead traced a line of blood along his forearm. Another jab pierced his thigh and he fell to one knee. James leapt to his side and, swinging his branch defensively, put his hand under the older man's arm and hauled him upright again.

Kurreah yelled at the four remaining tribesmen and they pressed forward with renewed vigor. Bertie and James retreated into the trees where Nathan leaned against a tree, watching. Narahdarn looked up, sweat dripping from his brow, as the battle disturbed his mental conversation.

Shinara, you must do something.

I have told you, I cannot kill. Their lives are not mine to take, dear friend.

Despair. *So we must die?*

Agony. *I cannot kill.*

Then do not kill, but do something. Hurry! Aah, too late.

Narahdarn? Narahdarn! Answer me.

Narahdarn dodged a blow and leapt back. He ducked another one, retreating alongside Bertie and James. A warrior lunged with his spear and Narahdarn darted forward, grabbing the shaft just behind the head. The man pulled back instinctively and as he did Narahdarn pushed hard. The man fell backward, dropping the spear to break his fall. Narahdarn swung the spear, catching another man across the knee. The man howled with pain and danced back.

"Good show...old boy," panted Bertie. The old man wheezed with the effort of fending off the warriors. His face and neck flushed scarlet and his shirt dripped with sweat. He clutched his side with one hand, swinging the branch with his free hand. Blood coursed down his leg and the cut on his arm spattered the man in front of him.

James doggedly retreated before the onslaught. His shoulders ached and he knew that soon now the warriors would break through his defence. *Damn!* he thought. *So bloody near.*

A stone hit him on the leg and he winced, then another cracked him on the side of the head and he went down on his hands and knees. *Oh, God! Sam...*

A distant shout filtered through the hazy redness as he knelt, waiting for the final blow. The shouts turned to screams and he raised his head. The Dwarrah warriors streamed out of the cave and ran in all directions across the valley.

Something moved in the cave mouth, something long and monstrous. Impossibly, the form of a huge brown and yellow snake issued forth, curling itself into knots and hissing like an old steam train. It reared up with long, shining fangs extended from its open maw, its head level with the rim of the valley. Then it silently slithered to the ground. Its yellow reptilian eyes stared relentlessly at the group of attackers.

"Bubbur! Bubbur!" shouted the Dwarrah, throwing down their spears and grovelling on the ground. Kurreah stared at the giant snake, his face ashen. He raised his arms above his head and started chanting, stamping his feet rhythmically. The warriors with him edged away then turned and ran down the valley, screaming in fear.

"Fools! Come back!" cried Kurreah. "It is a trick. I am Wirreenun and I speak with the spirits. This is not Bubbur." He whirled to the attack again, raining a flurry of blows at James and Bertie in his fury.

The shaft of his spear caught James across the temple, breaking the skin and knocking him unconscious to the ground. Kurreah swung again and the blade sliced through Bertie's shirt, glancing off his ribs. Bertie fell to the ground, clutching his side.

"So, demon friend," hissed Kurreah as he crouched in front of Narahdarn. "We meet again, and this time you will die." He circled the young man, placing his feet carefully in the sandy soil, his eyes watching his enemy's every movement.

Narahdarn wiped the sweat from his eyes with the back of a hand, his other hand gripping the long spear he took from a downed Dwarrah warrior. He circled the older man, aware that his fighting skills were paltry compared to the everyday life and death experience of the Dwarrah. He stabbed at Kurreah, only to have him knock the spear contemptuously aside.

Kurreah feinted to the left, stepped swiftly to the right and swung his spear haft hard at Narahdarn's head. Only the youth and fast reflexes of the younger man saved him, though the blow caught him on the shoulder, numbing his arm. He stumbled back while Kurreah lunged forward with the tip of his spear inches from Narahdarn's belly. The young man tripped and fell, rolling frantically as the spear dug into the ground behind him.

Narahdarn sprang to his feet, breathing hard.

Kurreah smirked and advanced again.

"You are a child, playing at being a man," Kurreah scoffed. "I will kill you, your friends and your woman." With a swift double motion, the spear haft flew by Narahdarn's head, followed by the blade, which scored a bloody line across his chest. "Even now, my men are slaughtering the white devils."

"You think so?" panted Narahdarn. "When I left the big cave your men were running."

Kurreah's eyes narrowed and he snarled. He feinted again then drew back, half stumbling.

Narahdarn eagerly pressed forward, his spear probing for an opening in the older man's defences. Kurreah straightened, slammed his spear down on Narahdarn's weapon, knocking it from his grip. The Dwarrah swung again and his spear caught Narahdarn on the tip of his jaw, snapping his head back.

The young Aborigine's legs crumpled and he fell on his side. He groaned and the muscles in his legs cramped with spasms when he tried to get up.

Kurreah pushed Narahdarn over on his back with one foot and stood over him with the spear balanced in his hand ready to thrust downward. "My spirits have conquered your demons," he grated. He raised his spear but plunged the point into the ground mere inches from Narahdarn's side when someone hit him from behind.

Nathan screamed and held his head in both hands while he knelt on the ground beside the sprawling Dwarrah warrior. "Get out of here! Run!" he screamed at his companions. "I can't shut it out forever...oh, God, it hurts." Saliva drooled from his mouth and his limbs jerked.

"Sweet Jesus," Bertie muttered, clutching his bloody side and struggling to his feet.

"Let's get out of here, mate," Narahdarn yelled as he struggled to rise. James rushed to help him.

"Too late, you fucks!" Nathan staggered, with a wild look in his eyes.

Narahdarn, Bertie and James froze in place.

Kurreah grunted, staggered to his feet and reached for his spear. He yanked the weapon from the ground and faced the swaying figure of Nathan. For a moment, a dry, rustling sound filled the hot evening air.

"Fool!" Kurreah bellowed. Before any of them could move, he thrust the spear deep into Nathan's chest and twisted.

Nathan gave a gurgling cry and dropped like a stone. The old Wirreenun put his foot on Nathan's chest and tugged. The spear came free with a sucking sound, the air whistling wetly from Nathan's side. A bloody froth bubbled on Nathan's mouth and his body jerked with pain.

Kurreah spat on the ground and turned back to finish off Narahdarn. The black shadow of a fist flitted past his head when he turned and, in the next moment, he fell, with Narahdarn on top of him. The young man's fists pounded into Kurreah's side, forcing the air out of the older man's lungs.

He gasped for breath, his fingers seeking Narahdarn's throat. They found it but slipped on a slick of blood. Narahdarn drew his hand back and chopped down hard with the side of his hand under Kurreah's nose. The thin skull bones splintered and the man gave a choking cry. Kurreah's hands scrabbled briefly at Narahdarn's face while he held both of his hands clamped firmly around Kurreah's neck. Slowly, the older man's hands weakened, fluttered in the air then fell limply to the ground.

Narahdarn rolled off the man's body and lay panting until the spots and lights before his eyes faded. He sat up when Kurreah's body shuddered and a belch of gas escaped his flaccid mouth. A barely seen miasma seeped out of the man and fluttered into the gathering darkness beneath the trees.

Narahdarn shuddered and crawled over to Nathan, where Bertie and James squatted, helplessly trying to stem the flow of blood gushing from Nathan's torso.

The bloody foam around Nathan's mouth frothed and surged as he fought for breath.

Bertie dabbed at Nathan's mouth with a dirty rag he pulled from his pocket. "Poor bugger," he muttered. He glanced over at James, who held his hands on the packed wound, trying to staunch the flow of blood, watching his friend dying. "He won't make it, James. The wound is too bad." Bertie watched the wadded up strip of cloth James packed into the boy's wound begin to dribble blood when it became soaked.

"Lie still, Nathan," James said while putting more pressure on the bloody rag.

Narahdarn watched as the other man tensed, his muscles tautening in a rictus of agony. He coughed, and a familiar black mist oozed from his nose and mouth. It disappeared into the darkness too. With a groan, Nathan's hand crept over Narahdarn's and squeezed it gently.

"I'm sorry, Narahdarn," Nathan whispered. He shifted his gaze and his eyes beseeched James to understand. "I tried to resist but it was too strong." He drew another ragged breath, which sent the hole in his chest fluttering.

A movement drew Narahdarn's attention and he turned to face Bertie. Nathan's eyes flickered with a faint recognition then returned to James's agonized face. "Sorry, Uncle. I let you down."

"Nonsense," James said, gulping down his despair. "You came through in the end, despite everything. Now lie still and we'll get you fixed up in a jiffy."

Nathan coughed, spattering bloody foam over Bertie as he cradled his head. "Can't fool me, mate." He drew another shallow breath and let it out slowly. "I really wish I could see Ratana." The breath rattled faintly in his throat. "Tell her I love her, Uncle. I've been a real shit but I do love..." Nathan jerked and the breath soughed out of him. Slowly, the bloody bubbles burst around his mouth and his body went limp.

James took Nathan's hand and pressed it to his lips. "Goodbye, son." Tears welled as he sat with head bowed in the still twilight. He rocked slowly, remembering the young man he knew from better days rather than the twisted man he became.

After drawing a deep breath and slowly letting it ease from his mouth, James dried his eyes and got up. "Come on, we need to get up to those caves."

Bertie put his arm around James's shoulders. "Are you going to be all right, old boy?"

James nodded. "Leave him here for now. In a way, it is fitting that he lie beside his fallen enemy. He has nothing to be ashamed of."

They walked slowly and painfully up the slope in the gathering darkness, with blood drying and crackling in their clothing and on their skin. The shouts and screaming from the cave of the Mother sank to a low, piteous wailing when they approached. Women gathered outside in small knots, kneeling by prostrate figures, tearing at their hair and throwing handfuls of dust into the air.

James saw one group of women clothed in modern attire kneeling by a body and he felt his heart clench. He leapt forward with a low cry of anguish. A woman from the group turned and with a cry of happiness, leapt to her feet.

"James! Oh, God, thank you!" Sam threw herself into his arms, hugging and sobbing.

James kissed her then looked past her. "Who...?"

Ratana turned with the pale figure of Shinara beside her, hugging her fiercely. "Uncle," she said. "How do we tell Bertie?"

James stood helpless when Bertie pushed past and hobbled over to the women. Bertie looked down at his wife, lying still on the ground. He dropped to his knees beside her, reaching out hesitantly. In complete silence he stroked her hair and his eyes wandered over her body. His hand drew back when he touched the bloody cloth of her shirt and a shuddering sob racked his body. Bertie raised his head, tears streaming down his face, and he howled as if the light had gone out of his world.

Chapter Thirty-Two

A small fire crackled and hissed by the billabong near the river forest. A green stick, charred at the tip, poked into the hot ashes to one side of the main fire. Impaled on its end were the curled remains of several small lizards. Tjimi pulled the stick out of the ashes and tapped the tiny corpses with a gnarled fingertip, dislodging ash and flakes of charred scales. He nodded and grinned, pulling one of the cooked lizards off the stick and handing it to the young girl sitting next to him.

Gaia took the offering and pulled off a leg. A tiny burst of steam escaped the white meat beneath the burnt exterior and she bit into it gingerly. She savored the taste and grinned in satisfaction.

"Very nice, Tjimi," she said. "The women of the Tjalwalbiri could learn cooking from you."

Tjimi grinned in return and, keeping one back, passed the other lizards to Ernie and the three Wirreenun: Ngarragun, Wiradjerun and Njangaringu. They accepted with thanks and started eating. Tjimi did not offer any to the two yowies sitting behind the girl, as he knew that spirit creatures like the yow-ee did not eat food like mortal creatures. He was surprised to see them eating leaves plucked from the branch lying between them.

Tjimi admitted to himself that he was confused. The yow-ee of the girl Guyyah, the one she insisted on calling Rima, was evidently mortal. Though what else could the creature be but the soul of the child? The wound inflicted by the evil man the night before was not serious but it had drawn blood. The invisible spear, accompanied by its own thunder under a strong spell, had bounced from a rib on the yow-ee, inflicting only a flesh wound. Even so, its vitality was more than human. The yow-ee was now almost recovered. Despite the blood, it must be a spirit. This mixture of earthly and spirit was something new to him. The Karadji tucked his thoughts away and turned his attention back to the conversation of Wandjina and Guyyah.

"I am still mystified by the origins of these Shadow beings," Wandjina said. "I used to think they came from some alternate reality, drawn over when that Vox Dei machine weakened the boundaries between realities."

"I don't think so," replied Gaia. "When they were within me," she shuddered, "they felt foul but also natural. They are a part of this world."

"Then where are they from? I was here a long, long time, both before 'now' and after 'now' and I have never come across them until recently." Ernie smiled. "Time is confusing when you put it into words."

"Ehrich and I were both taken over and used. They seem to need some sort of acceptance of them before they can do it. I suppose I was just in great need of someone to look after me." She turned and squeezed Rima's massive foot.

Rima rumbled gently and her thoughts reached out to embrace the girl. *I love you, child. I will always be with you.*

Gaia gathered up the tiny bones and remnants of skin from the lizard she ate. She cupped them in her hand, squeezed gently, then opened her hand and dusted it off on her knee. There was no trace of the remains.

"What else can you do, child?" asked Ernie quietly.

"I don't know until I try it," Gaia replied. She pointed at a fly buzzing around the remains of the Tjimi's meal. She concentrated and the fly landed and started walking in circles. "I could kill it too, but I'd rather not if I didn't have to." Gaia frowned. "I could have killed Ehrich or just hurt him when he kidnapped me yesterday. After he hurt me I wanted to, but now I see it is better not to." She looked up at Ernie, a sad expression on her face. "I'm sorry your friend Garagh died. I would have saved him but Tjakkan told me not to."

"I am saddened by his loss, child, and I shall mourn him in time." Ernie pursed his lips. "You talk with Tjakkan?"

"Oh, yes!" Gaia laughed. "He asked me not to tell you but I only said I'd consider his request."

"How long have you talked with him?"

Gaia looked thoughtful. "I think all my life but only in dreams. Since Njangaringu," she waved at the Wirreenun listening gravely to their conversation, "put the crystals in my body when he healed me, I can hear him any time I want. I can still only visit him in my dreams though."

Ernie leaned forward intently. "Where is Tjakkan when you visit him."

"In his ship."

"Ship?"

"Well, I call it a ship. I suppose Tjimi would call it a shining hut, but in reality, it is a gravo-magnetic mechanism. It's in a geo-stationary orbit above us right now." Gaia looked up, thought for a moment, and pointed. "About there, I think."

"And who is Tjakkan? Do you know?"

"Well, I know he's not human," Gaia grinned. "As to where he's from…I've never asked."

"Why is he here?"

Gaia shrugged, raising her arms high in an exaggerated fashion. "He…manages things. He's been here a long time though I don't think he thinks of time the same way we do."

Ernie opened his mouth, then shut it. He pondered the girl's answer then asked curiously, "How do you know these things, Gaia? You have lived almost your whole life in ancient Australia. How is it you are familiar with these concepts and words?"

"I read my parents' minds when I was a baby. Anything they knew, I knew. Of course, I had to wait a bit before I understood it all."

"And do you know your purpose back here?" asked Ernie. "I thought, when we returned, that finding you was important mainly to your mother and father. I had another agenda, but I'm finding that the two are intertwined. Possibly mine is less important."

Gaia nodded her head solemnly. "Yes, I know it, Wandjina, but that bit of information from Tjakkan I think I will keep secret. You'll find out soon enough anyway."

The fly buzzed weakly and fell over. "Oh, dear. I've been neglecting my demonstration." Gaia smiled and the fly fanned its wings and flew off. "Control can be useful sometimes."

"Indeed," agreed Ernie. "Is it limited to animate objects?"

Gaia grinned. The sand started moving near the man's foot, swirling and rising. Gaia gestured and the sand froze in place, several inches above the ground. She snapped her fingers and it fell, all at once. "I can only manage little things so far, but I'm working on it."

"How long have you been aware of these abilities, child?"

"I've always been able to make people and animals see what I wanted them to. My ability to make objects do what I want only started after Wulgu and Rima rescued me from the Shadows. And those little furry things, of course."

"What were these other creatures you came across? The little furry things?" asked Ernie.

"You'll need to ask Rima and Wulgu about those. I only saw them briefly when they attacked the Shadows."

Small, thought Wulgu, *and humanoid.*

Intelligent, added Rima, *with a language of their own.*

They reminded me of monkeys, Wulgu rumbled. *Yet I know this land has never produced primates. All native animals are marsupials, the pouched animals, or egg-layers.*

"It is interesting," said Ernie. "Australia has produced marsupials that mimic placental animals found in other parts of the world. Kangaroos and wallabies are grazing animals like sheep and cows, the thylacine and thylacoleo are predators like the wolf and lion, and there are many marsupial equivalents of rats and mice. Yet there has never been a marsupial monkey or ape, unless you count creatures like the tree-kangaroo." He shrugged. "Similar ecological niches produce similar functions I guess, though Australia only had marsupials to work with."

"Did they have pouches, Rima?" queried Gaia.

I'm not sure. They carried things near their waists but with all the hair, it was hard to see.

"Like you, Rima, they were naturally clothed," Gaia laughed.

"If they had pouches, they may be a sort of marsupial monkey, unfortunately now extinct," said Ernie. He addressed Rima again. *You say they were intelligent? What were their minds like?*

Fuzzy, Rima promptly replied *But nice. There was a love of family and a hatred of the Shadows, but no words, only emotions.*

What was interesting, said Wulgu slowly, *was a feeling of similarity with the minds of the Shadows. They had the same basic texture.* He shook his massive head. *All creatures feel different mentally, yet the feel of their minds had a definite affinity with the Shadow beings.*

Ernie turned to Tjimi and the three Wirreenun. "Do you or your people know of a race of small, hairy men?"

Tjimi conferred briefly with the Wirreenun in a low voice before replying. "We are aware of these people. They call themselves Winambuu. They keep to themselves for the most part, living within the deep forest and dark places of the earth."

"Are they dangerous?" asked Ernie.

"A man would be wise not to anger them if he found himself in their lands," replied Tjimi cautiously.

"Wulgu, you said earlier these…Winambuu…managed to kill the Shadows?"

Yes, Wandjina. At least that is what I think happened. Neither Rima nor I could hurt them yet these little furry creatures wielded a stone and we heard the death cries of the evil ones.

Ernie nodded and sat in thought for a long time. The fire died down to glowing embers and the sun slowly crossed the skies, sending the shade of the gum trees creeping across the sandy soil as if avoiding its harsh rays. Gaia and the yowies moved with the shade, seeking out the coolest spots. At length Ernie spoke again.

"I have brought these Shadow beings to a time when they did not exist. I fear that they will wreak their evil on the people of this time, yet I am powerless to do more than cast them out. I cannot destroy them, nor can I take them back to their own time." Ernie looked up at Tjimi. "I ask you to contact the Winambuu and seek their help in this matter."

Wiradjerun stirred and replied to Ernie's request. "It is not easy to contact these beings, for they are spirit. Yet if anyone can do so, I can, for I am 'he who talks with ghosts'. I will dream tonight and ask them to consider your request, Wandjina."

Ernie inclined his head. "I thank you," he said formally.

Wiradjerun tapped Tjimi on the arm and bent his head close to the Karadji's ear in a whisper. Tjimi started then turned his head to regard a bare patch of ground close to the edge of the scrub. "There is one who would speak with you, Wandjina," he said. "See, he comes."

Ernie turned to regard the indicated ground. His face crumpled as he looked, and he shook his head as if by doing so he could deny the evidence of his senses.

"Oh, Nathan, my son," Ernie muttered. "What has happened while I was gone?"

Wulgu looked from the bare patch to Rima and back again. *What do they look at?*

I do not know, Wulgu. I cannot see anything and Wandjina's thoughts are hidden.

Gaia watched curiously then communicated with the yowies. *I can see a somewhat misty shimmering over there. It is colder, as if the heat of the day is being sucked away to produce this thing.* Gaia listened and pondered. *Wulgu, does Wandjina have a son called Nathan?*

No, child. The only Nathan I know returned with us to this time. He helps Wandjina but he is with your parents and the others at Garagh's home.

Ernie groaned, pressing the palms of his hands against his eyes. He rose to his feet. "I must leave at once. Something terrible has happened at the caves." He put his hand on Gaia's head and stroked it gently. "Your parents are safe, child. Do not fear for them."

Turning to Tjimi, Ernie said, "I am reassured by your concern for Guyyah. Please bring her when you feel it is time. I must return to the caves now." He glanced at the three medicine men sitting beside him. I ask that Ngarragun accompany me. I have need of him."

"I am honored that I can help you, Wandjina," Ngarragun said, rising. "I shall accompany you."

Ernie picked up his long spear and, after a last ruffling of the young girl's hair, rose on his toes and set out at a fast pace. Ngarragun ran easily beside him, with his spear in hand. Within minutes, the two men were distant dark specks moving over the desert lands in a small storm of dust.

Chapter Thirty-Three

The scene at the Neanderthal village was one of devastation and ruin. Though the survivors worked all through the night by the light of large fires, the sight that greeted James the next morning thoroughly depressed him. The Neanderthals had come through the attack by the Dwarrah relatively unscathed considering the ferocity of the fighting. Eleven Neanderthals lay dead, the bodies arrayed under the tall gum trees near the stream. Their female relatives had washed the bodies and the rites of mourning were in full swing. Groups of women and girls sat around the bodies, slowly rocking in time to a low, sonorous chant. Men and boys sat further off, listening as one after another got up to speak. They praised the dead men and boys, reciting their deeds and nodding agreement.

It was fortunate that only three women died during the attack. This would not have been the case had Sam, Tilley, Ratana and Shinara not accompanied the Neanderthal females to the Cave of Women earlier. James recalled the awestruck tones as the women described what happened when the Dwarrah warriors at last entered the cave. They told how Sam and Ratana had thrown themselves at the warriors, how Tilley fought the man trying to stab a young girl, how she threw him down and how she died at the hands of another warrior. They told how Shinara had conjured the great snake Imboolath from the underworld and sent it against the Dwarrah men, thus saving all their lives.

Tilley now lay within the small cave on the far side of the valley. She lay in honor, attended by the girl she saved and the senior women of the tribe. Bertie sat with her too, refusing to leave her side, though it went against all custom for a man to attend the death sleep of a woman. By custom, a husband only came close when the time arrived to bury her.

Poor Bertie, James thought. *I don't know how I'd react if my Sam had been taken from me. And Ratana. She's holding up far better than I thought she would.*

Nathan's body lay in another small cave about half a mile down the valley. Ratana, Narahdarn and Budtha had washed him and clothed his body in a soft kangaroo skin. The Neanderthals had been unsure how to treat the dead Aboriginal man. On the one hand, he was an attendant on the great Wandjina, held in high regard by their leader; on the other hand, they remembered his foul mouth and uncooperative attitude. The action that led to his death, saving his friend Narahdarn, had tipped the balance. It was now obvious that just as evil spirits had possessed the Dwarrah, so too had Nathan been possessed. In death, he and the Dwarrah men were free of the evil influence.

The Dwarrah suffered far more at the hands of the Neanderthals in the battle. Despite the initially superior numbers of Aborigines, the defensive tactics utilized had turned the tide. Forty-seven Dwarrah men lay dead, the bodies lying neatly, but unattended, beyond the screen of trees at the lower end of the valley, well away from human habitation.

Earlier that morning, Budtha, supported by Narahdarn, examined the dead men carefully. Budtha managed to identify each corpse and had been extremely relieved to find that neither her father nor her brother was numbered among them. The large number of corpses defied efforts to prepare them adequately for burial however, so the Neanderthals were content to just arrange them neatly and cover them with fresh green eucalyptus branches.

James turned at the sound of a soft footfall behind him. Uhlaht, Garagh's great-grandson, who led the Neanderthals so successfully in the battle, looked weary. Unsure of how to talk with James in the absence of an interpreter, he resorted to loud simple language, as if talking to a child.

"We bury men, women, ours, when sun reach there." He pointed to the western sky about halfway between the horizon and the zenith. "We bury woman your too?"

James nodded, marshalling his meagre horde of Neanderthal words to express his thoughts. "Thank you, Uhlaht. We grateful are honor for," he stumbled.

Uhlaht put his hand on James's shoulder and peered into his eyes from under his own huge eye-ridges. "Us honor. Woman brave. Honor bury with People."

James nodded again. "And Nathan? We bury friend too?"

Uhlaht looked uncomfortable, not meeting James's eyes. "We not know customs black people." He hesitated and half-turned away. "Not proper bury black person in valley our." He waved at the aftermath of the battle with his hands. "Black people cause hurt much, not forget. Not want bury black people here."

James sighed. "Nathan friend. We take Nathan out valley, bury with black man custom."

Uhlaht smiled. "Yes, you do. Soon?"

James pointed to the sky, low down in the west. "When sun there."

He turned on his heel and walked away.

The rites of mourning carried on unabated all morning. The chanting of the women continued, occasionally interspersed by periods of wailing. Following each episode of grief, the women painted another of the bodies in intricate patterns with red ochre. Towards noon the women suddenly stopped their crying and singing and started preparing food. As the sun slowly started its downward path, the women passed around the village, handing roasted meats to the now silent men and boys under the trees. Others packed baskets made of woven grasses with meats and baked roots, setting them to one side. Having distributed the food, they sat in the shade of the trees on the other side of the clearing from the men, staring at the reddened bodies of the fallen Neanderthals.

The sun continued to sink toward the valley rim. Uhlaht strode into the clear area and cried out in a ringing voice for all to prepare.

"Our men have died to give us life," he cried.

"We honor them," a low response from around the clearing answered.

"They are one with our ancestors."

"Let us honor them," droned the tribe.

"We must send them to the afterlife so they can live among us again."

"So let it be."

Everyone got to their feet. The men picked up prepared stretchers of branches and woven pandanus leaves, gently lifting the bodies onto them. The women picked up the baskets of food and fell into line behind the men as they set off up the valley. At the same time, two men took a stretcher and ran up to the small cave where the body of Tilley lay. A few minutes later they came out with the women clustered around her. James supported Bertie, who now looked every bit of his seventy-five years. Gone was the robust and lively man of the last few days; a gaunt cadaver, who stumbled and clutched at those around him for support, replaced him. Sam and Shinara followed, helping Bertie negotiate the rough path.

The two processions, one large, encompassing most of the tribe, and the other tiny, with its few followers, wended its way slowly up the valley. They passed through the gum trees, splashing through the shallow waters of the dammed stream, past the Cave of Women and into an area of bare rock and earth. Close to the valley walls lay two freshly dug pits, yawning ever wider as they approached. The tribe gathered around the larger pit, into which the bodies of the eleven Neanderthal men, boys and women were placed. Men jumped down into the shallow pit and swiftly bound the limbs of the bodies, curling them as much as possible into a semblance of a fetal position. They placed them on their left sides, orienting their faces to the east and covering their features with supple skins of opossum and wallaby.

Taking gourds of red ochre, they sprinkled the bodies liberally with the pigment, followed by a splashing of water fresh from the stream. Youths stepped forward, relatives of each of the dead men and women, and handed down weapons and tools to the men in the grave, which they placed alongside each body. Baskets of food were set in the grave within easy reach of the bodies. The women now approached, sprinkling flowers picked from the valley floor.

Clambering out, the men stood to one side, having made themselves ritually unclean by their association with the bodies. Uhlaht addressed the tribe again.

"Let us remember these men. Talk of them often, use their names that we do not forget their deeds and that our ancestors will send them back to us again."

A murmur of assent ran through the crowd. Uhlaht signalled to the burial squad standing to one side and they began scraping the loose earth and rubble back into the grave. When the grave was full and heaped, they tumbled large rocks onto the site.

Uhlaht now turned to the small group around the other pit. Several Neanderthal women clambered into the grave and gently lowered Tilley's body into it. They manipulated her corpse onto its left side, binding her knees up under her chin and covering her completely with a soft kangaroo skin. Ochre and water followed, with a shower of flowers that mounded over the body. Next they placed food and utensils, carved bone needles, coiled sinews, stone scrapers and knives.

Bertie sat nearby on a flat rock, watching the proceedings. James and Sam sat alongside him, holding his hands as his thin body shook with sobs. As the women clambered from the grave, James squeezed Bertie's hand and got up. He moved to the graveside, standing for a moment with head bent, then he threw a spray of bottlebrush flowers into the grave. He returned to Bertie and held him while Sam gave her last respects.

Uhlaht cleared his throat and addressed the tribe once more. "We bury here a woman who was a stranger but who gave her life for the People. Honor her and remember her name."

"We will remember," said the tribe.

"Let her name be used for girl-children that her spirit may be one with the tribe. Let her join our ancestors and one day return to us through a child named for her. Let the name of Teelee live on."

Uhlaht signalled to the men who moved forward with their earthscrapers.

"Wait," croaked Bertie. He hauled himself to his feet, shaking off James and Sam. He staggered to the side of the pit and stood swaying, looking down into the grave. He wiped the tears from his eyes with his shaking hands. "Well, old girl," he muttered. "We had a good run, didn't we?" He ran his fingers through his hair and let out a long quavering sigh. "I always hoped we'd go together, love. Together in death as we were in life. Not to be, old girl, not to be."

Bertie shook his head and drew himself up straight. "Can't think of a better send-off for you, though. You'll sleep with some old friends for a little while until I can join you, Tilley my love." He snapped off a salute. "Keep the home fires burning, old girl." He rummaged in the pocket of his shorts and took out an old battered lighter. He flicked it several times before it lit, then he held it out over the grave. "Use this to guide me home, love." Bertie dropped the lighter onto the mound of flowers in the grave and turned away, tears streaming down his face again.

Behind him the tribe muttered. "Haugh," one voice cried. "He gives the gift of fire."

Bertie walked back to James and Sam. He managed a weak smile through his tears then blew his nose noisily on his dirty handkerchief. "Well, life goes on, old chums." He looked around. "Where are the others? I thought they might have come to see the old girl off at least."

"They wanted to," said James quietly. "But there's a bit off ill-feeling towards Aborigines at the moment and we agreed it would be better for them to keep a low profile."

Bertie nodded. "Understandable, old boy." He took a few deep breaths and brushed his clothes down, glancing at the men rapidly filling in the small grave. "She would be happy to know she had a real Neanderthal burial, you know. We had just uncovered the grave of a woman before you lot snatched us away. Tilley thought the remains of the flowers were quite beautiful and..."

Bertie paled and sat down quickly on the rock. "Oh my God," he breathed. "I knew there was something anomalous about the skeleton in that grave. It was *Homo sapiens* in a Neanderthal grave..." His voice trailed off.

James looked at Sam in horror. *Digging up the grave of his wife?* he thought.

Sam put her arm around Bertie and hugged him. "At least you know she rested peacefully for thirty thousand years, Bertie. And it was you who found her, not a stranger."

Bertie smiled. "The situation has a certain irony to it, doesn't it?" He looked up at James's horrified face. "Oh, don't worry, old boy. I am not upset. I'm just interested in knowing who is buried next to her...closer than these chaps." Bertie waved a hand at the large grave mound. "There were indications of another body lying in the same grave but the old girl and I ignored them. Thought it was an animal or sacrifice. Never considered a human, for some reason"

He grinned. "Perhaps it was me!"

After a brief pause, Bertie frowned. "No, that couldn't be, unless I die in the next couple of days. I shall have to go back and finish up the excavation and find out who or what it is," he finished brightly.

The crowd of mourners drifted away as the last great rocks were placed on the grave mounds. Bertie, Sam and James joined them as the Neanderthals wandered back down the valley, chattering quietly. Narahdarn met them at the big cave.

"Wandjina's here," he said quietly. "He arrived while everybody was at the funeral." Narahdarn hugged Bertie. "I'm sorry we couldn't be there, mate. Did James explain?"

Bertie nodded. "Yes. Thank you, old man. How is Ratana holding up?"

"As well as can be expected." He gestured off down the valley. "Can you all come? Wandjina wants to talk to us."

"Is...is Gaia with him?" asked Sam.

Narahdarn shook his head. "No. I'll let him explain...but she's fine, don't worry," he added, seeing her expression.

James heard the bodies of the Dwarrah men before he saw them. The heat of the day, now thankfully easing, drew flies in great seething swarms toward the bodies tucked away in a stand of gum trees at the entrance to the valley. Off to one side, a small group of Aborigines stood around, waiting for them.

James greeted Ernie with a handshake and a clasp of his shoulder. "Where's Garagh?" he asked.

Ernie shook his head. "Garagh is dead," he said simply. "He died saving your daughter."

James looked stunned. "I'm sorry," he said. "He was your friend a long time."

"That is true," admitted Ernie. "Yet he was not the friend we all knew."

"Where is she?" broke in Sam.

"She is safe, Samantha," answered Ernie. "She is in the care of Tjimi, a powerful Karadji, a wizard you might call him. She will come to no harm."

"When can we see her, Ernie?"

"Soon. Be patient. This whole venture is turning out to be more complex than even I thought." Ernie turned to the two Aborigines standing behind him, leaning on their spears.

"This is Ngarragun of the Tjalwalbiri. He is a Wirreenun, or medicine man, and represents the tribe that Gaia lives with." Ernie gestured at the old grey-haired man. "Gubbeah, here, is a Dwarrah. We met him this afternoon as he journeyed here to ask for the bodies of his tribesmen."

"It is important that we say the correct words and that the men are buried. Otherwise, their spirits will wander, causing trouble for the living." Ernie spoke seriously, looking at each person in turn.

James shifted uncomfortably. "Granted, but there's going to be a problem. We can't possibly dig forty-seven graves, or even one big one. And given the circumstances, I don't think the Neanderthals will help us."

"That is why I have agreed to help," Ernie said. "I dislike intervening in the affairs of mankind more than I have to but I see the necessity. We must dispose of the bodies yet allow some part of them to be
taken back to the Dwarrah village for burial. The heads, I think."

Sam looked sick. "Remove their heads? Gross."

Ernie smiled. "Perhaps, but necessary." He turned and walked
up to the grove of trees where the Dwarrah dead lay stretched out in
rows, covered by green gum branches. The old man, Gubbeah, limped
beside him. They stood at the edge of the massed bodies for a moment, then started moving among them, chanting. Ernie picked up
two small pieces of wood and clapped them together rhythmically,
constructing a simple percussion base for the old man's song. The
chant rose and fell for many minutes before the two fell silent. They
walked back to the watchers.

Ernie turned back to the grove with its silent inhabitants and
raised his arms. A wisp of smoke sprang up on the chest of the dead
Wirreenun, Kurreah, followed by a brightly glowing fire. The flames
grew and leapt from body to body until the whole stand of trees blazed
from one end to the other. Billows of white smoke rose into the sky,
amid great cracklings and roaring of the flames. Roils of black smoke
curled within as the bodies burned. The watchers drew back several
yards, the heat blasting their faces. Only Ernie stood, apparently unaffected, close to the inferno.

So fierce were the flames and so rapid the spread through the
grove that within thirty minutes the trees were reduced to smoking
blackened stumps, the ashes picked up by the breeze and scattered
across the land.

Ernie turned to Gubbeah and spoke quietly. The old man nodded
and trotted off slowly.

"He will collect the skulls and carry them back to the village for
burial," Ernie said. "He goes to make a woven bag for them. Come," he
added. "We have one more task ahead of us."

Ernie walked over to the body of Nathan lying under soft kangaroo skins on the other side of the stream. When they arrived, he embraced Ratana, who knelt silently beside the body of her husband.
Although she was shaking, the girl gave no other outward indication
of her grief.

"Courage, daughter. He died bravely and his spirit lives on."

"I know, Wandjina," Ratana replied in a quiet voice. "But if only
you had driven out the Shadow inside him this may never have happened." Her voice trembled. "I lost a husband and a friend. I lost my
world and my future." Her large, expressive brown eyes bored into
Ernie's while she asked, "What shall I do, Wandjina? Where shall I
go?"

"There is work for you here, daughter, if you are strong enough.
There are things in store for you that are important. I will be with you

and, in time, you will see that Nathan is here too." He held her at arm's length and looked into her eyes. "We must give him the rites, daughter, that he may join the spirits and be at peace."

Ratana nodded and crossed to Sam, then hugged her. She squeezed Bertie's hand and watched as Ernie stooped and seemingly without effort picked up the large-framed body of Nathan. He crossed to the valley wall and laid the body close to the sheer rock face. He stepped back and started a high-pitched chanting. Ngarragun dug into a small pouch and sprinkled ashes and red ochre over the kangaroo furs, joining his voice to Ernie's.

When the death chant was finished, they fell silent, stepped back, then turned and walked back across the stream to the others.

James looked troubled. "We can't just leave him like that. At least we ought to..."

A low rumbling came from beneath them, soon building to a roar. The water in the stream shivered and the leaves on the trees whipped as if a strong wind blew. The ground trembled and with a ripping, tearing noise, a section of the cliff face collapsed in a cloud of dust.

The ground stilled and the dust cleared. The body of Nathan lay beneath the shattered bones of the broken hills.

"Come," said Ernie. "We have much to do before we leave, and we must talk with Uhlaht. He leads the tribe now."

Chapter Thirty-Four

"No! I will not listen to you, Wandjina. You are not of our people. We will move south tomorrow, as my father Garagh wished." Uhlaht, great-grandson of the recently devoured leader of the Australian Neanderthals, glared at Wandjina and his friends.

"Garagh changed his mind, Uhlaht," interjected Ernie quietly. "I spoke with him at length on the day I arrived, a mere five days ago, and he decided then to stay here."

"And two days ago he died, after telling me we would go," hissed Uhlaht. "He always intended to move south. You know as well as I do that he stayed here only to strengthen those weak ones among us. My father was a great leader of his people and I will follow his desires, not those of a black man who *says* he is a friend."

James listened to the conversation. Although not fluent in the Neanderthal language, he knew enough to follow most of what they said. Narahdarn sat beside him, following the argument on a mental level, as well as an audible one. He whispered a quick translation where he felt James needed help. Bertie understood less, his grasp of a new language at his age being less than easy. Even he could sense something was wrong, although, still burdened with his wife's death, he only listlessly followed what was going on anyway.

"Why does Uhlaht refer to Garagh as father?" James whispered to the young man next to him. "I thought he was a grandfather or something."

"Great-grandfather," muttered Narahdarn in reply. "It's a generic term covering all generations."

Uhlaht shot a savage look at Narahdarn, pointedly waiting for him to fall silent before continuing. "Listen, then, Wandjina and I will say it again for you. The tribe moves south tomorrow because the 'Others' wish it, because my father wished it, and because I wish it. Further, the attack by the Dwarrah proves this place is not safe for my people. We will find a safe place. That is my final word." Uhlaht stood up and stalked from the cave, shouting for the heads of each family.

Ernie grimaced and scratched his head. "I think that's it," he said. "Before the attack I was doing so well. I know I had Garagh convinced to stay here. Now he's dead and his bloody grandson is undoing all my work."

"Is it so important?" asked Bertie, plucking at the large tear in his shirt and the thick makeshift bandage underneath.

"Yes, it is," Ernie replied. "The time we come from is an accident, an aberration of the space-time continuum. Scientists discovered the movement of this tribe from this spot, at this time, resulted in a disruption that cascaded down the millennia. It could spell the end of life on the planet." Ernie scowled. "I persuaded him. I had the rift healed, then he risked himself and lost...everything." He stared at James, then past him at Sam, Shinara, Budtha and Ratana sitting against the wall of the cave. "I am sorry, James...Samantha...but if Garagh had not risked his life to save your daughter then he would be alive today and the disruption healed."

James looked uncomfortable. "I understand your feelings, Ernie, but I'm glad he saved Gaia's life."

"Yes. I am too, James," Ernie sighed.

"I mourn his death Ernie, but at least he gave his life to save one who can save many more," Ratana added. Sam smiled at her and nodded.

"Perhaps another opportunity will arise. Give him a couple of days to cool off and realize he's no longer in any danger from the Dwarrah, and he may agree to move back," Bertie offered after perking up a bit to the conversation.

Ernie shook his head. "I doubt it. I scanned his mind at a deep level while he talked. He fears the Aboriginal tribes now, where before he only felt a mild distrust. Even if the Dwarrah were all dead, he would fear the next tribe he encountered."

"Could you top the blighter?" asked Bertie. "I mean, remove him as leader. Maybe his replacement would be more pliable."

Ernie glared at him. "I sincerely hope that was not meant seriously. I will not, nor allow any of you to, harm these people. And before you ask, I will not force a change by controlling his mind either."

"Sorry, Ernie," said Bertie, casting his eyes down and again playing with the bandage under what was left of his shirt. "I was just exploring the options, not really advocating mayhem—mental or otherwise."

"Okay, mate. Apology accepted." Ernie picked up a baked root cooling beside the low fire and peeled the charred rind off. He picked at the yellow flesh within, deep in thought. After a pause, he sighed and added, "And we still have the problem of the Dwarrah."

"Let them rot," said Ratana quietly.

Bertie coughed. "In the light of my recent chastisement I feel reluctant to open my mouth again, but I must say I agree. I think those devils should be left alone to whatever fate awaits them. I hope the whole damned tribe perishes in a bloody disaster." The last sentence he said came out as a growl of rage.

"The fault was not entirely theirs," observed Ernie. "The only real failing they showed as a people was weakness. They let a strong man, Kurreah, dictate to them, rather than listening to the collective wisdom of a body of elders. Then the Shadow beings possessed them, blocking whatever hope they had of proper guidance."

"The women and children are innocent too," said Narahdarn. He beckoned Budtha over to him and put his arm around her. She looked up at him adoringly.

"I have said before that I loath interference with a culture, but I fear that it is needed in this case," went on Ernie. "Without able-bodied men and a body of medicine men, the Dwarrah will starve or succumb to the elements."

"How can we change that?" asked James. "You're not advocating another time travel are you?"

"Even if it was possible, I wouldn't recommend it." Ernie smiled. "However, there are alternatives. I had a long talk with the old Dwarrah man, Gubbeah, yesterday. He favors incorporation into another tribe. He thinks some of the old men may object, and the handful of survivors from the battle, but now that the evil spirits have departed they can think for themselves again."

"Interesting idea, old man," commented Bertie, taking an interest again. "But what tribe could they join?"

"The Tjalwalbiri," answered Ernie. "Ngarragun here is in favor, and believes the Karadji of the tribe, Tjimi, will agree too." The old Aborigine's teeth gleamed as he grinned. "They lived with a white girl for ten years and they are not at all racist. I think they will accept the remnants of the Dwarrah and remain on good terms with this Neanderthal tribe if we can only persuade them to stay."

"Could all blow up later, though," said Bertie gloomily. "What's to prevent them falling out once we've gone?"

"I will keep them to their word," said Ernie. "If we can persuade them I will remain when the rest of you return to your time. This is my place and I feel more at home here than in the twentieth century."

"Me too," said Narahdarn quietly. "And I have a reason to stay now." He smiled at Budtha. "Besides, what sort of a man would I be if I ran out on my kid?"

"Kid?" goggled James. "You're...good God! Hey, congrats, mate!"

Sam looked puzzled. "How can you tell? You've only been with her a few days, it's far too early for any signs."

Narahdarn's grin grew broader. "Ms. Hay, from what I've heard, you should know all about the phenomenon. An early fetus has a quite distinctive life signal. Too early for mind, but a tiny blaze of being, thirsting for life."

"I am happy for you," said Ratana. "I wish Nathan and I..." She broke off and sat silently.

Shinara put her arm around her. "Be content to live life one day at a time, Ratana," said the young girl. "Life will present you with much happiness if you give it a chance."

Ratana smiled, holding back her tears. "I think perhaps I might remain too. Nathan and I came to help Wandjina with his work. We haven't done much of that yet, so I will stay and help him now."

"Your help will be much appreciated, daughter."

A noisy hubbub erupted outside the cave. Voices raised and cries of joy and fear mixed with the sounds of children screaming. Ernie rose and left the cave. The others quickly followed. A crowd of men and women milled around the clear area beside the bark huts, with more running toward it every moment.

"What's happening?" asked Sam. "They look awfully upset about something."

Narahdarn stopped a man and fired questions at him before listening intently to the hurried answers. He turned to the others with a puzzled expression. "A hunting party saw a ghost." He listened again. "Down near the river…a phantom of Garagh, they claim."

"Could he be alive?" asked James. "Perhaps he survived the crocodile."

Ernie shook his head. "I'm sorry, but I felt his life force depart. Whatever this is, it's not the man who left here two days ago."

"You can't feel him now? Mentally, I mean," asked James.

"No." Ernie pursed his lips with concentration. "There is something over toward the river but I don't recognize it."

"Perhaps it is really a ghost," whispered Budtha, drawing closer to Narahdarn. "There are spirits all around us."

"Whatever it is," said Ernie, "We shall find out soon enough. It is coming this way."

Chapter Thirty-Five

An hour later the milling crowd of Neanderthal men and women fell silent. Discussion of the meaning of Garagh's ghost had occupied the whole tribe since news of the sighting first broke. Opinion was divided about the meaning. A few believed that no phantom was seen and that the hunting party made a mistake. The majority, however, raised in an environment where spirit creatures seemed as real as fleshly ones, believed it was perfectly reasonable to have ghosts walking abroad.

Those who strongly supported the move south saw in Garagh's spectre their dead leader's determination to move them along faster. On the other hand, those who supported staying where they were recognized the ghost's presence as a sign that the tribe's roots now lay in this valley. Both sides felt vindicated and arguments became louder as time went on, almost leading to blows.

Then a young man raced into the clearing with the news that the ghost was coming. Even now he walked up the path beside the stream, through the groves of eucalyptus trees and meadows filled with grass and wildflowers. The crowd shivered and drew apart, leaving a wide avenue down which the restless spirit stalked.

Ernie watched it approach while searching the figure's mind for familiar thoughts.

The ghost certainly resembles Garagh, though its features look older, wiser, and more bowed by years and experiences no living man could endure. Surely, the days spent in the spirit world marked this ghost. Yet, there are marks of life about it too, he thought while inspecting the figure as it came closer. He squinted, intently capturing every detail of the man. *It casts a shadow in the late afternoon sun, dust rises when its feet fall and, yes, there...it scratched its leg as if some insect was biting it.*

The ghost moved up the long avenue toward the main cave where a small group of men and women waited for it, eagerness and trepidation warring within them. Uhlaht, great-grandson of the ghost, stood in front, with Wandjina and James just behind him.

The spectre stopped and looked at the young Neanderthal man

for a few moments. The young man paled and stepped aside, his limbs shaking. The phantom looked past Uhlaht to the others. A grin appeared on its face and it spoke.

"Gidday, mates! Bloody good day for a stroll, isn't it?"

Ernie's rugged features cracked wide. "Garagh, my friend. It really is you. I hoped but...you have changed. Your mind is different."

James nodded, grinning delightedly. "You beaut!" he cried. "Can't keep a good man down, eh?"

The others crowded forward, smiling and reaching out to touch their friend. Sam and Ratana hugged him in turn, Narahdarn shook his hand delightedly, then pulled Budtha forward, introducing her. The young Aboriginal girl bobbed her head shyly, then ducked behind Narahdarn again. Bertie edged forward and stuck out his hand after everyone else finished their greetings.

"Glad to make your acquaintance, sir. I have heard a lot about you. My name is Bertrand Simpson, erstwhile Professor of Archaeology."

Garagh smiled as he shook Bertie's hand. "Er, delighted," he said, with a puzzled look at Ernie.

"I'll explain later." Ernie gripped Garagh's forearms firmly. "It is really you, isn't it? Where have you been these last few days?"

Garagh shook his head. "I don't know. I remember the flash of light as we travelled the interstices, then nothing. I dreamed strange dreams, but cannot remember what I dreamed. Two days ago I found myself in an opening in the rainforest, the ashes of an old fire at my feet and the footprints of people wearing shoes. I knew that if we became separated you would try to fulfil the mission, so I came here. What has happened, Wandjina? Have you brought about the change? Why do I see the scars of battle?"

"I had changed the future," said Ernie. "I found your former self here and persuaded him to stay. Then the Dwarrah attacked and were repulsed, though at some cost. You lost your life saving Gaia. Eaten by a crocodile, actually." He grinned.

"Gaia? She is here?" Garagh looked around.

"Close. She will arrive soon."

"I feel there is a lot more to this story," Garagh commented.

"I will tell you later. The most disturbing thing is that your great-grandson is now determined to take the tribe south. It seems your esteemed former self changed his mind again."

"Incredible," said James. "Evidently some sort of paradox avoidance."

Sam grimaced. "Speak English, love. For the rest of us."

"I wondered about that before we left. Garagh was returning to a time when he already existed. Could he be in two places at once? Evidently not, the universe cancelled one out...or rather, suspended one until the other one died. Weird!"

"What about Wandjina then?" asked Ratana slowly. "He lived in this time too. Why didn't he disappear?"

"I am not really human," said Ernie quietly. "I appear to be but I am not ruled by time as others are."

Bertie raised an eyebrow. "Hmm. ET, no less!"

Ernie grinned. "No. Not an alien. I am of this planet as surely as you." He looked serious, though his dark eyes twinkled with mirth. "The real aliens are something quite different."

Uhlaht forced himself to speak. It came out as a croaking whisper that shook with fear. "Respected ancestor, father…what purpose brings you from the land of the dead? Are you reborn or do you seek vengeance?"

"Neither, my son." Garagh turned and raised his voice to reach all his people. "I have returned from the land of the spirits as my work is not yet accomplished. For countless years and generations, the People of the Forest have travelled south, following the wishes of the 'Others'. We stayed in this valley teeming with animals and filled with the goodness of the earth to rest before moving on."

Garagh moved out into the middle of the clear area, the people of his tribe moving closer around him as he spoke more quietly and earnestly. "The 'Others' revealed themselves to me as the spirits of our ancestors. They wish us to remain here in this valley."

A muttering swept through the crowd. A few voices raised above the noise.

"What of the Dwarrah?"

"It is too dangerous to stay."

"We must leave."

Garagh held up his hands until silence gripped the crowd again. "I am your leader. I hold the black rock as a sign from the 'Others', giving me immortality. I died in the jaws of the crocodile and returned to you alive. Do you dispute my decision?"

The men and women looked at each other, a low murmur rippling through them. Uhlaht forced his way through the crowd and stood out alongside Garagh.

"Garagh is our leader," Uhlaht declared. "If he says we stay, we stay."

≈≈

Dr. Xanatuo raced through the vast caverns and passageways of the underground complex in the Glass House Mountains. The insistent ringing of the alarm bell still sounded in his ears, fragments of his dream of ancient oceans and the boom and crash of surf still flitted behind his huge black eyes. He ran with a supple and fluid grace, his grey body rippling, his vast domed head surging forward as if breaking through waves. Despite his humanoid shape and mental abilities, the moments after awakening from sleep betrayed his dolphin origins.

He entered the cavern filled with complex machinery and banks of computers. Clouds of vapor billowed around the super-cooled circuitry. Small greys bustled about, adjusting coils, maintaining the multitudinous dials and liquid crystal displays in a state of relative constancy.

An air of expectancy and tension filled the spaces between the equipment, dampening the vibrations generated by the humming machinery.

Xanatuo stopped and fired a mental question at a passing grey. It raised its head and regarded the tall thin scientist solemnly through its dark oval eyes for a moment, then pointed across the cavern. Xanatuo moved over to stand behind another grey that peered intently at a computer screen. A complex series of colored lines marched across the display, forming and dissipating under the influence of unseen forces.

"Is it time, Zeratu?" asked the scientist.

"I am not sure," replied the grey technician, without turning round. He made some fine adjustments to a series of knobs. "There was a surge an hour or so ago, then nothing."

"Why was I not called?"

"By the time we reacted, it was over," stated Zeratu. "You can see the surge on the printout." He gestured at a coil of paper slowly spooling into a plastic container below the workbench.

Xanatuo picked up the paper and worked rapidly back through it until he found the savage spikes stabbing upward for an instant before settling back into an uneasy tremor. "And this time?" he asked. "Are the humans closer to accomplishing their purpose?" Mentioning the humans sent Xanatuo's mind back to his meetings with them before they left. He was relieved he no longer had to speak in that atrociously sibilant language. Although they had not actually said anything, he still smarted from their clumsily hidden amusement at his speech impediment.

"There was another surge, then a slow rise to a level where we expected the generators to cut in," explained Zeratu. "We called you as soon as we saw what was happening. You can see the printout spooling through now."

"So why haven't the generators started operating?"

"The levels remained just below the critical level, sir," said Zeratu. "Something has stopped the reaction." The grey technician shivered. "Reality quivers all about us and non-existence beckons. I am afraid, sir."

"Nonsense. We are professionals. Do your job and all will be well, Zeratu." He stalked away to the other side of the chamber and busied himself with an unnecessary inspection of the cooling system around the quantum generator.

The short tropical twilight slipped gracefully into night. Stars lit, becoming brighter as light drained from the sky, the Southern Cross dominating the darkness. Objects in the night assumed various shades of black, bushes and trees became inky pools against the sooty ground. Within one such pool of stygian darkness lay a still body of water, reflecting the cold white scintillation of heavenly fire. Beside the water, another small fire, hot and red, crackled bravely, throwing back the onslaught of evening.

Creatures moved in the firelight, vaguely human in shape. The glint of an eye, the flash of teeth, the warm glow of orange light on flesh, outlined limbs and features starkly, casting the distal portions of anatomies into obscurity. A murmur spread outward and ripples of light spread through the silent darkness.

Beyond the firelight, past the point where even photons gave up the uneven struggle with darkness, lay things blacker than anything nature could conceive. A susurration, like a mild breeze through dry grasses, filled the still night air. Small burrowing, hopping, slithering creatures froze in place, senses flaring, huddling motionless in terror. The dry slithering grew louder, more menacing and, had any human ears been there to hear, more intelligible.

She is the key.

What of the old man?

He, too, is important.

Destroy one or both and their plan fails.

Why then the girl?

He is...not human. We fear him.

A sense of fear washed through the darkness, followed by a growing anger. It grew until the fur on the tiny creatures huddling in the shelter of vegetation and rock stood on end. Yellow eyes glowed balefully in the deepening shadows.

The girl cannot be touched by mind. She has an aura of strength about her.

So, too, the beasts. Their minds are impenetrable.

The older man resists. His flame is strong.

Too strong.

The other two men. One is at rest; the other's mind is elsewhere.

They will not accept us.

We need only force ourselves in for seconds.

We must act quickly, before her protectors can react...

...and kill her.

Yessss...

Blackness flowed toward the tiny fire, filled with rage and desperation.

Gaia laughed, a high-pitched tinkling laugh. Tjimi smiled and continued the story of his first hunt as a boy. When he finished with the description of the kangaroo hopping off into the scrub with his loincloth caught on its foot, appreciative chuckles erupted from Njangaringu, listening from the far side of the fire.

The two yowies looked at each other, puzzlement obvious on their features, despite their non-human faces.

Where is the humor in the story? Wulgu asked with a puzzled frown.

Rima had more experience of the Aboriginal mind, having lived with Gaia in Tjimi's village for over a decade. *I think in the fact that the kangaroo lived,* she thought doubtfully.

Why is that funny? I would not want to be killed and eaten.

Nor I. Rima shook her large head vigorously. *Most humor seems to be dependent on someone being hurt or embarrassed. I have often wondered...Wulgu, what is wrong with Njangaringu?*

The Aboriginal elder was on his feet, swaying and clutching his head. He gave a great cry of anguish. "Karadji!" he screamed. "Quinkan attack me."

From the shadows at the other side of the clearing came an answering cry. Wiradjerun staggered into the firelight, a veil of blackness over his head and shoulders. He scraped at the intangible shadows, scoring the flesh of his face with ragged fingernails. Wiradjerun groaned. "Winambuu, they are here, I..." He fell to his knees, digging his hands into the sandy soil. "I will not!" he screamed. "Leave me, Quinkan." The blackness writhed and thickened about the man's head.

Tjimi leapt to his feet, throwing himself on the struggling man, yelling to Wulgu to restrain Njangaringu as he did so. The Shadows attacked Tjimi, fighting to keep control of the Aboriginal man and fight off the far more powerful Karadji-man at the same time. A nimbus of pearly light flared around Tjimi's head, searing the darkness, forcing it back. The darkness rallied, formed a spear point of deepest night and hurled itself at Tjimi. The spear met Tjimi's chest in a coruscation of color, shot through with muddiness and decay.

Wulgu launched himself at Njangaringu but the man moved preternaturally fast, sidestepping the huge yowie and sweeping Tjimi's spear from beside the fire. He whirled on one foot, steadied himself and hurled the spear at Gaia, who still sat calmly by the fire. Rima howled, throwing herself forward, knowing she was too far away. The spear slashed across the fire, its flint point catching the firelight. In a fraction of a second it crossed the intervening space between the fire and the girl's body then fell apart in a storm of dust that covered Gaia in a pall of grey.

For a moment it seemed as if all were frozen, then Gaia sneezed and motion returned. Rima collided violently with Gaia, sending her tumbling. Wulgu threw Njangaringu to the ground and fell on him.

Tjimi met the Shadow spear with his pearly light again, hurling it off Wiradjerun. The Shadows melted and flowed from both men, gathering themselves, poised to attack once more.

A shadow flitted into the clearing, then another. More followed, small hairy bodies hurling themselves at the Shadow beings, small dark crystals clutched in hairy paws. Where the crystals touched, Shadows died. They flowed and writhed; desperately trying to escape the leaping forms.

As suddenly as they appeared, the Shadows were gone. The clearing emptied of the small hairy beings except one who stood dimly visible near the bushes. It raised a hand and a clear voice rang in all their heads.

We heard the call of that one and came, it said, pointing at the prostrate Wiradjerun. *We shall hunt them down and kill them.*

Tjimi got to his feet and faced the Winambuu. *Why would you do this?* he asked.

These creatures are our future, it softly responded. *We saw it in their minds. Their evil shames us so we shall atone by killing our descendants.*

Future days can change, Tjimi quickly replied. *Tjakkan assured me of this.*

Tjakkan?

Tjimi formed an image in his mind, then held it.

Aaah! the tiny creature sighed with awe.

Wulgu rolled off the half-crushed form of Njangaringu and got to his feet. He broke in on the conversation, with a startled look on his face. *You can mind-talk!*

The Winambuu turned and stared up at the giant yowie. *We are a secret people. We did not know if we could trust you.*

The tiny form stepped back and disappeared into the bushes with no more of a rustle than an insect makes clambering up a paperbark tree.

Wiradjerun sat up, gingerly holding his head.

Wulgu bent to examine Njangaringu, feeling his limbs carefully. *He will live. Are you sure the devils have gone?* he asked Tjimi.

"Quite sure. With the Winambuu after them, they are doomed."

Rima shuffled into the light, holding Gaia tightly. She looked around suspiciously before relaxing. She dusted the child off with tender sweeps of her huge hands.

I told you I would protect you, she thought.

Gaia smiled and squeezed the yowie's arm. "So you did, Rima. Thank you."

Tjimi gazed unsmilingly at Gaia. "It is time, child. At first light we take you to meet your parents."

Chapter Thirty-Six

The day dawned hot and bright, though clouds started gathering low on the eastern horizon. As the day progressed, clouds thickened and rolled slowly over the sky, blotting out the sun by mid-morning. Despite the cover, the heat increased, the still air holding the humidity close to the ground like a suffocating blanket.

"Storm weather," observed Garagh, sitting outside his cave and cleaning his spear. "My bones tell me we're in for a bad one before the day is out."

Ernie looked up at the clouds. "A bit late in the season for a cyclone but I can feel the pressure dropping."

"Do you think it's a natural storm or is the weather reacting to the change?"

"I haven't seen any evidence of a change yet," said Ernie. "I expected something by now. After all, the tribe stays put rather than moving south, as we intended. Reality has been changed if our calculations are correct."

"What of Gaia?" asked Garagh. "Why should Tjimi claim this Tjakkan has a hand in the future and is using the girl?"

"Tjakkan belongs to Aboriginal mythology," answered Ernie. "Of course, most aspects of mythology have their roots in real events, as you are well aware, old friend. This Tjakkan really exists. He is not a supernatural spirit being, though he can manifest himself that way. Rather, he is what you call an 'Other', a guide from elsewhere."

"An alien?" The Neanderthal showed no surprise at the notion but stopped rubbing a rough cloth over his spear shaft.

"Perhaps. Out of elsewhere or elsewhen. Maybe both. He exists out of time even more than I do," Ernie answered while continuing to scan the sky.

"Why is he so interested in Gaia, Wandjina?"

Ernie pondered the question, then shook his head. "I don't know. He insisted that Gaia remain apart from her parents until the time is right." He rubbed a sore spot on his side and added, "Perhaps it's not her parents. Why should they be important in the larger scheme of things? Who else?" he mused. "We know it's not me, and you were not in the picture. Shinara perhaps?" Ernie stared at Garagh. "You never told me. Why did you create Shinara in the first place? And why bring her along with us?"

"No great mystery, my friend," replied Garagh. "I had instructions from the 'Others', perhaps even this Tjakkan of yours."

"Interesting. We must talk more on this another time. Anyway, that time has now come, my friend. Gaia and Tjimi are on their way. They will be here about noon."

"Today? What will happen?"

"She will no doubt have a tearful reunion with her parents," said Ernie dryly. "As to the rest, we shall just have to wait and see."

As if on cue, the sky darkened and distant thunder reverberated against the valley walls. Soon, word passed up the valley that strangers approached. Garagh ambled down to the village to reassure his people.

Ernie rose, found his friends inside the cave then spoke quietly to James and Sam. He did his best to prepare them, warning them not to expect the baby they had seen only six subjective months ago, but a young girl teetering on the brink of womanhood. Ratana knew Gaia from infancy but the others—Narahdarn, Budtha and Bertie— had never seen her and were intensely curious. They anxiously hovered in the background.

Shinara was absent. The pale young girl disappeared up the valley earlier in the day and was still missing. Garagh sent two men to look for her.

Lightning cracked in the hills behind the valley, followed by a long rumble. A small group of people walked out of the trees at the lower end of the clearing. The Neanderthals moaned in fear and drew back from the two huge, shaggy monsters flanking the little girl.

An imposing Aboriginal man walked in front of her, unarmed but holding himself erect and proud, secure in the knowledge of his great power. Another walked behind her, carrying several spears held point down. Garagh sent out a calming message to his people, reassuring them, explaining that the yowies were protective spirits and would harm no one, provided the young girl was not molested.

The group marched up to the people standing outside the cave. Sam inspected her daughter as Gaia approached. Tears of happiness flooded her eyes and she ran out to her, sweeping the slim girl into her arms, then hugging and kissing her face in an avalanche of emotion. James followed a moment later, grinning broadly, and embraced mother and daughter.

Gaia gave both Sam and James a tight hug in return, then stepped back and stared at them solemnly. "Mother," she said. "Father. I..." She burst into tears and ran into their arms again. "Oh, Mummy, Daddy," she sobbed, "You came for me."

"Of course we did, my love," cried Sam, clutching Gaia tightly.

"How could you ever doubt it?"

James looked across at Rima, who stood forlornly behind Gaia. "Cindy," he said. "We have you to thank for keeping her safe all this time."

Wulgu rumbled. *Rima, her name is Rima, Doctor Hay.*

James nodded solemnly, holding back the mirth he could feel bubbling up inside. "Of course. Rima...thank you." He hugged the huge yowie, his six-foot frame dwarfed by her massive stature.

Ratana came up and joined in the greetings and soon another pair of eyes anointed the young girl with tears. James introduced the others and Gaia solemnly greeted each person, shaking hands with Bertie and reaching up to touch foreheads with Narahdarn and Budtha. Stepping back, Gaia smiled and looked around.

"Where is she?" she asked.

"Who, love?" asked Sam, putting her arm around the young girl.

"I don't know her name. The young girl like me."

"You must mean Shinara," explained James. "She was here earlier. I expect she'll be along soon."

Gaia's face fell. "I must see her, soon."

Ernie and Garagh exchanged meaningful looks at this interchange.

Lightning flashed, followed immediately by a thunderous roar as the heavens opened, sending torrents of water cascading down. Everyone scattered with cries of alarm mixed with laughter. Mothers herded youngsters into huts, assiduously striving to prevent the children enjoying themselves in the downpour.

Sam grabbed Gaia's hand and ran for the main cave. The others followed. They gathered within the entrance, laughing and shaking the water from them as the temperature dropped and a fresh breeze swept through the valley.

The heavy rain churned the soil into mud, washing it away in rivulets that leapt and danced down the hillside toward the stream, which was already a muddy torrent. Gaia laughed and screamed excitedly at every crack of thunder and actinic flash of light. Her enjoyment was infectious and soon everyone was laughing and hugging, chattering enthusiastically, all worries and woes forgotten.

The thunderstorm passed, the rain easing to light drizzle after an hour. The clouds remained heavy and black above them and slowly the heat built up again. The cool freshness that swept through the valley during the storm dissipated as the humidity increased.

Garagh looked up at the lowering clouds, feeling the electricity in the air. "The storm's not over," he muttered.

Ratana dug into her backpack. The surviving Dwarrah had sent back the possessions they stole, along with a gift of food, the day before. She pulled out a pair of khaki shorts and an old James Cook University tee shirt. She gave them to Gaia with a smile.

"We've got to make you look decent for the return journey," she said. "And we'll have to do something about your hair." Ratana shook her head as she tugged at the little girl's tangles.

Sam took her to the back of the cave and helped her to dress, tackling Gaia's matted hair with a plastic comb Bertie had in his pocket. Gaia chattered and laughed as her mother worked on her hair, catching up on the past decade by describing the minutiae of tribal life. Sam worked silently for the most part, encouraging her daughter to talk, soaking in the sight of her, touching her and smelling the strange but so familiar odors of unwashed girl. She wiped away tears with the back of her hands but smiled contentedly.

Gaia paused in the middle of an enthusiastic description of how beetle grubs were cooked and cocked her head on one side. "She comes," she stated quietly and got up. She pushed past a startled Sam and ran out of the cave.

Gaia stood outside the cave looking down at the sodden Neanderthal village and the bare ground now scarred from the rain. A girl walked out from the trees, along the path leading up the valley, with Garagh's men ambling behind.

Shinara walked into the clearing and stopped, looking up at the cave and the tiny figure in front of it. She shivered despite the heat, the shredded pale green dress she wore clinging damply from the rain. She raised a hand in greeting and moved forward.

Sam and James ran out of the cave after Gaia. Sam put her hand on the girl's shoulder but Gaia shook it off. "Please wait, mother," said Gaia in a distant voice. "I must meet Shinara alone."

Gaia walked slowly down the slope. Electricity flashed in the lowering clouds above; hair on both girls' heads flew outward as static charges crackled about them. The dark clouds moved slowly above the two girls, the motion gentle and random at first but soon becoming more violent. Sam called out in alarm but Ernie held her back, his dark face alive with interest and anticipation.

The motion of the clouds increased, swirling into a vortex. A black funnel dropped from the roiling cloud base, shot through with bluewhite lightning discharges. The crack of thunder became continuous, a deep rolling cacophony that set the rocks about them vibrating.

The girls walked slowly toward one another. When they stood only a few feet apart they stopped. Shinara's dress flapped violently in the rushing updraught, her hair streaming upward. Gaia's tee shirt and shorts rippled too as gusts of wind swept over her. Gaia smiled and reached out her left hand. Shinara followed suit a moment later, extending her right hand. Their fingers touched and locked. For a long moment the two girls stood and stared at each other, the now continuous lightning flashes turning Shinara's pale skin to a corpselike pallor. Gaia's tanned skin seemed to deepen in hue, as if the brilliant light from the vortex above was augmenting the pigment in her skin. Shinara opened her mouth and a silvery cloud poured out of it.

So brilliant were the electrical discharges playing about the two girls, however, that the silvery cloud seemed dark by comparison.

Outside the cave, Sam screamed in anguish. "The Shadows, they are taking my babies!" James tensed then relaxed, gripping his wife's arm and pointing.

"It's not Shadows, love...look." The silvery cloud dispersed and as it did so sparkles shot through it until it seemed as if a myriad cloud of tiny particles of mica whirled in the air around them, lit by some ethereal inner light. Gaia, too, opened her mouth and a gush of a deeper red-gold light poured from her. The golden light shivered and dispersed into a cloud around the two, swirling and mixing with the silvery discharge. Thunder crashed repeatedly, and the earth it-self groaned in reply. A shudder ran through the rock floor of the valley. People fell to the ground in the village, screaming in fear. The rim of the valley glowed with a pearly electrical discharge and several sections crumbled and fell.

The darkness grew deeper, the clouds thickening above them. The gold and silver cloud that immersed Gaia and Shinara grew denser, obscuring the figures of the girls, who still stood with linked hands and locked gazes. Then the sun moved. Everyone gasped as the dim glow of light showing through the clouds shifted, slowly at first, then gathering speed. It spun and danced above the clouds, lighting them with a white glow, before darkening to yellow and orange and bright-ening again. The two young girls remained in place, their heads turned toward the sky and their eyes following the light while it moved in intricate patterns above them.

The vortex of the black swirling cloud veined with storm-light grew larger, sucking the gold and silver light up into its maelstrom. The storm surge burst upward, ripping sand and leaves from the ground as it howled. Gold and silver light that intertwined, undulated and writhed into the atmosphere now suffused the black clouds. The noise of the tornado and the thunder rose to a crescendo then abruptly halted. The dark clouds were sucked skyward, hurled into the upper atmosphere and spread out in a huge umbrella of vapor and dust, shot through with glistening rivers of gold and silver. A glowing disc hung above them.

Sam screamed a long wail of heartbreak. James stared open-mouthed at the scene below him in the Neanderthal village. Only mo-ments before his two young daughters had stood, light erupting from their bodies in the clearing below the cave. Now, the clearing was empty, stripped even of the village huts. Gum trees stood bare, their leaves ripped and scattered.

James turned wildly to Ernie. "Where the hell are they?" he yelled.

Ernie shook his head and pointed up above him. "Look," he said quietly. "It is not yet over."

Dark clouds thinned and streamed away, though the sky remained dark. Stars shone despite the presence of the pale, washed out circle of the sun low over the western rim of the valley. The glowing disc above them pulsed through the spectrum. The gold and silver streams thinned too, spreading out in all directions, moving with ever-increasing speed, as if caught up in violent jet streams, until the entire sky was filled with sparkling light.

For several minutes silence reigned in the heavens. The glow of light that originated from the two girls disappeared, and the sun slowly grew in brightness. Then the sun dimmed again and a distant indistinct motion was seen in the sky. The motion grew swifter, more definite. A swirling vapor poured earthward into the valley, rushing downward to the ground, where it thickened and darkened.

A voice invaded their minds, gentle but forceful. Bertie gasped and tapped the side of his head in disbelief.

It is accomplished, the voice said. *Within you resides a virus. Not one to cause disease but rather 'ease'. In time, it will heal the world. Mankind took a wrong path once, at this very place. Two species should have lived as one, interbreeding and mixing their considerable genetic potentials for the good of the planet. Instead, one killed the other and the balance was lost. This is now corrected. The genetic makeup of the girls Shinara and Gaia created this virus. Even now, it infects all intelligent creatures on this planet, Neanderthal, human, dolphin, whale, ape and more. Together, Gaia and Shinara will be mother to all intelligent life that is, and is to come.*

The mental voice faded. The shining disc hung in the air, slowly spinning in place. Then it rose into the heavens so fast that it left a vacuum behind for a fraction of a second. The air filled the gap with a crack and a long drawn out rumble. The dense mist that covered the ground outside the cave swept upward, a vapor trail in the wake of the departing craft.

Two small girls stood in the midst of the clearing, looking up at the sky. Gaia turned to look at Shinara and smiled delightedly. "It's like a looking glass," she cried. "You look just like me!"

Shinara grinned back at her sister. Both girls were now identical; their genetic makeup was blended and balanced. Blue eyes looked back at blue eyes, tanned healthy skin touched its like and red-gold hair intermingled as twins embraced.

The noise released the people from their frozen stance. The Neanderthals immediately started chattering and shouting, arguing about the meaning of the strange words. Narahdarn and Budtha gazed upward, anguish in their faces, hoping for another glimpse of the shining disc.

Bertie grinned broadly and hugged Ratana. "A bloody UFO!" he snorted.

Sam, James and Ratana approached the two girls with joy, and a touch of awe. Both girls smiled up at their parents then shifted their gaze to the now blue sky.

Sam placed a loving hand on each of the girl's slim shoulders then looked at James. "What did the voice mean," she asked, "saying this virus will heal the world? I don't feel any different."

"I don't know, love," he replied. "Whatever it is, we can only hope for the best."

Gaia stepped back from her identical sister and looked at her shyly. "Do you want to explore?"

Shinara nodded. "I think there are some little stone dolls in the big cave. The dolls are beautifully made. Shall we go and look?" She took Gaia's hand and together the little girls ran up the slope, past their parents, laughing gaily.

∽∽

Alarm bells sounded in the Glass House Mountains, echoing through the hollows and caverns. Dr. Xanatuo darted in from the adjacent cavern where he was sipping appreciatively on some hot fish broth.

"What?" he yelled. "Zeratu, what is happening?"

"A spike, sir, followed by a steady rise!" squeaked the grey technician who manned the monitor. "It's happening sir, it's really happening."

Xanatuo grabbed paper spooling from the printer and scanned the rising lines. "I agree. We must..."

A gentle swaying of the rock floor beneath his feet interrupted him. He staggered, then steadied himself by holding on to the workbench until the wave passed.

Zeratu paled and looked up at Xanatuo. "Already? I thought reality had a better grip on us."

"Turn the main generators on," Xanatuo ordered. "We must start the recall procedure immediately." He gripped the bench again as another ripple passed through the complex. He walked unsteadily to a bank of computers and began tapping on a keyboard. "Tie in the main electricity grid for the East Coast. If our power goes down, we may need it."

The pressure in Xanatuo's internal ears altered. He looked around, noting with astonishment that there was now no way out of the cavern. The huge portals carved in the solid rock that led to other parts of the complex had disappeared. For a brief moment he panicked, envisaging a lingering death in a sealed tomb. He grimaced, showing his rows of peg-like teeth. "Reality unravels," he muttered.

The giant apparatus in the centre of the cavern still glowed, energy pouring in from somewhere, despite the cables leading from the room that ended in solid granite.

"Power levels sufficient to bring them back, doctor," observed

Zeratu, with a quaver.

The alarm bell abruptly shut off and the lights flickered.

"Doctor," urged Zeratu. "We may not have much time."

"Do so," said Xanatuo. He grinned at the technician. "Beam them up, Scotty!" He let out a long warbling laugh.

Zeratu gave the doctor a very strange look then snapped the switch. The apparatus roared as vast energies hurtled into its miles of coiled wires, vacuum tubes and capacitors. Liquid helium poured through conduits into the machinery, sending the temperature plummeting. Lasers groaned as light itself slowed. The air rippled and the cavern flattened, the roof flowing and dipping down. A light grew rapidly brighter, filling the cavern with a pearly glow.

Unseen by either scientist or technician, a similar glow grew in a small clearing in the Atherton Tableland of Australia's far north.

Abruptly the noise and glow ceased, cut off as if it never was. Xanatuo saw that the apparatus and all its concomitant hardware—the computers, cables and benches—had gone. Xanatuo and Zeratu found themselves in a completely empty cavern.

Zeratu gave a sob. "I'm afraid, sir. Will it hurt?"

Xanatuo shook his head. "No need to be afraid, technician. You will just cease…"

Zeratu winked out of existence.

"…to be." Xanatuo smiled. His last thought was one of pride that his calculations worked.

The Glass House Mountains stood still and serene. The solid granite of their peaks resulted from the eroded plugs of ancient volcanoes. No caverns, natural or otherwise, existed in the seamless rock.

⁊ ⁊

"Is that all there is to it?" asked James. "It seems to me that changing the future should somehow be more spectacular."

"I say," Bertie exclaimed. "Did you call that show unspectacular?"

"No, of course not. I just expected things to be suddenly different. Everything looks the same." James looked at Ernie. "Are you sure you have succeeded?"

"Almost certain," smiled Ernie. "I've never actually done this before so I don't really know what to expect." He leaned forward, the smile disappearing. "By now, the change will have rippled through to the twentieth century. Old Xanatuo will be trying to recall us before the reality bubble collapses. Give it time, after all, thirty thousand years must take a while to change."

"So in the meantime we need to stay close to Sam?" said James.

Ernie nodded. "Sam, through her sister Andi, possesses the strongest ties to the future. When the bubble bursts, she will be snapped back like a rubber band to the starting point, focusing in on her sister. Anyone or anything touching her will be drawn back too."

"Perhaps we'd better practice," said Sam nervously. "Come on, children." She held out her hands to Gaia and Shinara. "You too, love. And you, Bertie."

Bertie shook his head. "I've decided to stay," he said. "I'd rather be here than thirty thousand years away from my Tilley. Remember, we studied Neanderthals all of our adult lives and now she has in a sense, become one. If I stay, I'll be with friends. I can continue my studies and go and sit on her grave and tell her all about my findings." He smiled sadly. "Really, I'd rather be close to her here than alone in a changed world."

"Don't worry, Samantha," said Ernie gently. "We will look after him."

"So everyone else is staying?" asked James.

"I will stay with Garagh for a time," Ernie said. "Narahdarn will take Budtha back to her tribe and help Tjimi merge the Dwarrah with the Tjalwalbiri. I think the virus may help that merger somewhat. Ratana will help me here until I leave, then she will join the others."

"Mummy," whispered Gaia. "What's that?" She tugged on Sam's arm and pointed across the cave.

A large patch on the cave wall drifted out of focus. An image appeared briefly, then vanished. Budtha whimpered and hid behind her husband. The wall looked normal again.

"That looked like an old camper van," observed Bertie. "In fact, I remember one rather like that a few days ago."

"I don't feel well," complained Shinara. She buried her face in Sam's side.

Sam stroked her hair soothingly. "I don't feel well, either. I feel sort of dizzy and it's affecting my sight."

Ernie shot to his feet. "It's happening," he cried. "If you are saying good-byes, now is the time to do it."

Bertie clapped James on the shoulder, squeezed Sam's arm and ruffled the girls' hair. "Goodbye, chaps. It has been a real pleasure knowing you. Safe landings." He stepped back.

Ratana gave Sam a hug, then kissed James on the cheek. "Goodbye, uncle. Say a prayer for Nathan and me some time." James nodded, trying to hide the tears in his eyes.

Narahdarn shook hands all round. "Hooray, mate." Budtha smiled shyly at James and gave the girls and Sam quick hugs before rejoining her husband.

Garagh raised a hand in silent farewell, standing before the impassive figure of Ernie.

"Goodbye, Ernie...Garagh. It's been a real education." James smiled at both men. "I wouldn't have missed it for the world."

Reality clamped down on Sam and the girls. Sam screamed and grabbed at James, clutching him in a death grip. The feeling relaxed.

"Will I ever see you two again?" James asked.

Garagh smiled. "As Tjakkan wills."

Ernie grinned at him. "I'm not sure I'm up to another thirty thousand years of living just to see you again, mate. Let's just wait and see."

"Oh, God!" cried Sam. "I feel awful." Her vision blurred. She saw the group of men and women around her go out of focus, though James, Gaia and Shinara remained unchanged. She heard a far-off twittering as darkness descended, recognizing dimly the last farewells of her friends. A dreadful pulling sensation gripped all parts of her body, ripping her in all directions. Reality yawned and tore apart. Sam tumbled through the interstices of the universe, dragging her family with her.

Chapter Thirty-Seven

The sound of running feet sank through James's fuzzy perceptions. He lay on the ground with his nose pressed into the dirt, aching
all over and waves of nausea sweeping over him. His vision swam then
cleared abruptly, his eyes focusing on a large ant sitting on a twig. He
looked at it curiously, wondering why he was lying on the ground in
such an uncomfortable position to study ants. *Camponotus,* he decided, making a stab at the identification, *but I don't know what species.*

The nausea lessened and he rolled over and sat up. He saw a
woman and two young girls sprawled beside him. The girls were crying, tears pressing out from between screwed up eyelids. He reached
out to comfort them and memory flooded back.

"Oh, God, Sam!" he cried, "Gaia, Shinara. Are you all right? Say
something."

At the sound of his voice, Sam opened her eyes. She cried out
and scooted over to her husband and the girls, hugging them. The
girls immediately stopped crying and looked about with the stunned
expressions of two normal little girls.

"This place…" James peered at the two girls then the surroundings. "…and time. It's different and so are the girls."

"Where are we?" asked Sam. "Are we back?"

Before James could answer, the sound of running feet translated
into two people bursting through the bushes into the small clearing
where James and his family sat.

"Sam!" screamed the figure in front. "You're here."

Sam scrambled to her feet. "Andi? Oh, it's so good to see you."
She glanced beyond the dark-haired young woman to the man grinning behind her. "Marc. It's good to see you too."

James got up and greeted the two with warm hugs and handshakes.

Andi and Sam were talking, each filled with the events of the past
few days, intent on sharing news and trivia rather than listening to the
other.

"What was that you said, Andi?" queried Sam.

"I only said I liked your hair that color," replied Andi. "I think red suits you."

Sam looked puzzled. "It's always been that color, Andi. What do you mean?"

Andi laughed uneasily. "Come on, sis. You don't have to keep pulling my leg." She caught sight of Gaia and Shinara standing to one side and hurriedly changed the subject. "So who are these lovely young girls?" she asked.

James took the girls by the hand and drew them forward. "These are Gaia...and Shinara, our daughters," he said simply. "Girls, meet your Aunt Andi and Uncle Marc."

"Hello," they said in unison.

"Goodness me," breathed Marc. "I didn't realize it had been so long since we last saw you. I remember Gaia as a baby and Shinara not at all." He shook his head ruefully. "I thought it was only months since..." Marc's voice trailed away.

Andi forced some life back into her voice. "So tell me girls, did you enjoy your camping trip?"

Gaia looked at Shinara. "I am not sure what you mean,Auntie," she said. Shinara just shook her head.

Andi turned to James. "Your camping trip. That's what you came up here for, wasn't it?" She looked around the clearing. "Where's all your gear?"

"Don't have any," said James, waving his hands around vaguely. "Perhaps you could give us all a lift back to town? I think we could all do with a shower and a hot meal." He rubbed his hand over his chin. "And a shave," he added.

"Yes. Yes, of course," Marc said, seizing on something normal in the conversation. He led the way in silence through the eucalyptus and *Acacia* scrub to the road. He opened the camper van doors and ushered them inside, clambering into the driver's seat. Gaia and Shinara insisted on riding in the front seat, running their hands over the panelling and upholstery with cries of delight.

Marc frowned. "You'd think they'd never seen a vehicle before," he muttered.

He let out the clutch and eased the van into the dirt road. "Yungaburra, I think. There is a nice motel there. Quiet, with friendly owners."

"Anyone want a drink?" Andi asked, opening a cooler.

"Thanks," answered Sam. "I could murder a Pepsi."

"Pepsi?" Andi looked and sounded puzzled again. "I don't think..."

Sam shrugged. "Just a Coke then, sis."

Andi took a deep breath and smiled weakly. "All we have is a really good selection of the normal fruit juices. I guess we haven't stocked up on those Australian drinks yet."

Sam accepted a 'Pear Delight', giving James a long hard look. He raised a finger to his lips as a caution, taking and tasting his oddly flavored 'Walnut Fizz'.

The girls accepted drinks but after a few sips, put them aside, lost in the sensation of flying above the road without effort. They screamed with delight at each new sight or as the van bounced in the potholes. They stopped at the intersection with a paved road, where Gaia saw a movement in the shrubbery. A long, thin face pushed through, scanned the road with intelligent eyes then trotted into view.

"It's a thylacine," gasped Gaia. "Look!"

James leapt forward, shouldering Marc aside to peer through the windscreen. "Dear, God! It is!" He tore his eyes from the creature calmly crossing the road in front of them. "Quick, Andi, have you got a camera?"

"Somewhere around here, I think," she answered. "Why?"

James stared at her open-mouthed. "To take a picture of it. Jesus, it's unheard of. They're supposed to be extinct." He turned back in time to see the thickset striped hindquarters and tail disappear into the bushes.

Marc laughed. "Extinct? Come on. They're quite common around here. I've seen them many times." He grunted, turning the van into the main road toward the towns of Atherton and Yungaburra. "A bit of a pest in towns, I've heard. Knock over trash cans and chase cats, that sort of thing."

The rest of the journey passed uneventfully, though James kept his face glued to the window in the hope of seeing another thylacine. He commandeered the camera and sat with it poised in his lap, finger on the button, all the way into Yungaburra. It was early evening by the time they arrived.

Yungaburra was a small town on the rolling farmland of the Atherton Tableland above the city of Cairns. Small tracts of tropical rainforest were scattered over the Tableland, the remnants of a greater forest severely milled in the last century. Therefore, James was surprised to see miles of rainforest, dense and dark, on their approach to the town.

Never approached it from this direction, he thought. *That must be it.*

Marc drove the van through the centre of town, past the pub with its bright lights and the noisy conviviality of a farming community taking its ease. "Good pub," he said. "We can try it tomorrow night if you're up to it."

He pulled into an overgrown drive and bumped up to the motel office. "Wait here," Marc said. "I'll get us some rooms." He was back in a few minutes waving two sets of keys. "Units five and six. Five has two bedrooms so we'll put you lot in there."

An hour later everyone was showered and changed. Marc and Andi passed out items of their own clothing. "We will go shopping in the morning, sis," said Andi. "It's a small town but I'm sure we can find enough to tide you over until you get home."

Sam nodded her head sleepily. "Whatever you say." She yawned. "I think I'm going to turn in." She pushed her plate away, littered with the remnants of a first class meal of fish and chips.

James nodded. "The girls are already asleep, love. You go ahead, I'll put them to bed."

Andi and Marc said their goodnights and closed the door behind them. James turned off the TV and picked up Shinara. He carried her into the darkened bedroom and tucked her into one of the twin beds. He did the same with Gaia, then, leaving the bedroom door ajar and the kitchenette light on, he went in to his bedroom. Sam was already asleep, snoring softly. James undressed and lay down beside her.

James thought back over the last few days. *That was quite a "Boy's Own" adventure,* he thought sleepily. *I wonder if anyone will believe us. No matter, we can always take them and show them...what? What have we been doing on our camping trip?* He closed his eyes. *Tomorrow, I'll think of it tomorrow.*

They slept in the next day, finally leaving the motel just before noon. James persuaded Marc to drive them all down to Cairns, as the shopping would be cheaper down there and the selection much greater.

The drive down to Gordonvale then along the coast road was quiet. Andi grinned and hugged her sister. "Sorry I was being such a goose yesterday, sis. It must have been the combination of the light and dust. I could have sworn your hair was red...and longer."

James reached over and stroked his wife's short dark brown curls. "I'd never look at a redhead, even if it is a rare color," he grinned. "Give me a sultry brunette every time."

Traffic was heavy as they entered the city of Cairns, Capital City of the state of North Queensland. There were many pedestrians and the movement of the cars slow as they weaved their way through the bustle. James caught sight of an old, full-blooded Aboriginal man leaning up against a lamppost as they sat at traffic lights. The old man caught his gaze and smiled. He winked an eye at James before turning and ambling into the crowd.

"That man," cried James, twisting in his seat. "He looks familiar."

"What man, dear?" asked Sam.

"He was a full-blood Aborigine; that's why he stood out. He winked at me."

"I'm sure you're mistaken, love. There haven't been any full-blooded Aboriginal people for decades. Think how divisive it would be if some people were black and some white instead of all a lovely coffee color." She shuddered, putting her light brown arm around James. "I don't want a return to the Stone Age, thank you very much."

"Mummy," piped up Shinara. "Can I have a thylacine puppy when we get home?"

"Oh, yes, me too," cried Gaia. "Can we, daddy, please?"

Sam, they're acting like normal kids now. Did you notice? James sent the thought while watching the animated, but very young, faces of his daughters.

Sam met James' glance and nodded, a smile of relief on her face. "Whatever your dad says is okay with me," she replied.

James' smile matched hers while he answered, "Why not? I had one when I was a boy. I think every kid should have his or her own marsupial pet. Teaches them responsibility."

James leaned back in his seat as the van moved forward again, its electric motor humming softly. He looked out the window at the crowds of contented people, who walked all manner of exotic pets on the streets, and the large green parks spread throughout the city. He drew a lungful of clean air, savoring the fresh smells. He smiled contentedly.

Damn, it's good to be home again, he thought. *Camping is all very well but I'll be glad to get back to work and...home.* The word resonated inside his mind with a comforting gentleness.

He smiled at his wife then his two daughters and headed home.

Epilogue

The room pulsed softly with a glowing pearly light. No boundaries to the room were discernible, nor any furnishings that would give clues to its size or purpose. A soft hum pervaded the air and a sensitive individual standing in the room may just have been able to detect a faint vibration. There were no windows, nothing to suggest that hard vacuum surrounded it, or that the room itself moved in orbit high above the Earth.

Despite the apparent emptiness of the room, it surged with activity. A careful observer would see brighter areas that moved slowly through the air and a listener with ears attuned to a higher pitch than most humans may just have caught fragments of a conversation.

One who was sometimes known as Tjakkan spoke, "The ripples in the continuum are settling about as fast as expected. The future shape of the human unity has changed, though perhaps not as dramatically as we thought it might."

"What are you saying?" asked one who had been known as Yahweh. "Is another interference warranted?"

"Surely the virus is now cosmopolitan?" queried Brahma. "It was engineered most carefully to attach itself to the human genetic code."

"That is, in part, the problem," iterated Tjakkan. "The virus has affected the human genes more than the Neanderthal component. Neanderthal genes are present in over eighty-five percent of people alive today, but they have limited effect."

"Yahweh is right," stated the one known as Hera. You *do* want another insertion. The world and all its components must be balanced—good and evil, negative and positive. It is the nature of life itself, or it will fail."

"Yes. I believe with proper planning we can increase the strength of the Neanderthal component," Kali added.

A murmur of agreement swept through the many listeners.

"When?" asked Odin. "And where?"

"I cannot be certain yet, but about two hundred thousand years ago, in northern Africa."

"Always further back," Yahweh sighed. "Operations were simpler when Odin or myself controlled matters."

"And look where your operation got us," complained Baal. "Religious wars swept the planet."

"Please, let us not argue," said Tjakkan. "We need to study the matter carefully. After all, we have all the time in the world to work with."

The glows drifted together and merged, the many identities subsumed into one. The multi-colored light pondered the on-going problem of humankind while the world turned slowly beneath it.

Scientific Notes

Much of the action in this and the other two books in the trilogy take place in Australia. Both Ariana and I lived in north Queensland for several years and have travelled over the areas covered by James, Sam and the others. Consequently, the general landforms and vegetation types our characters encounter are accurate. Additionally, much research has gone into making sure Aboriginal mythology, beliefs, languages and rituals, as well as prehistoric animals, are portrayed as accurately as possible. However, information about the Neanderthal people is open for debate.

Whether you have read just *Looking Glass* or the preceding two books, *Glass House* and *A Glass Darkly* as well, you will be aware of the central premise of the trilogy: that Neanderthals are alive and well and living in mountain hideaways somewhere near you. So who are these mysterious Neanderthals?

Neanderthal is the common name for a subspecies of the human race. Modern humans like you and me are graced with the scientific name of *Homo sapiens sapiens*. Our cousins the Neanderthals are known in scientific circles as *Homo sapiens neanderthalensis*.

In 1856, limestone quarrymen in the Neander valley in Germany discovered the bones of an ancient man in a cave. Originally thought to be an arthritic soldier from Napoleon's army, he quickly had the epithet 'caveman' attached to him, together with a whole range of misconceptions. Neanderthals traditionally are depicted as shambling subhumans who represented a low form of humanity. Supposedly, the upright, handsome, intelligent, modern man quickly replaced them at the end-point of the evolutionary ladder. In recent years, Neanderthals have undergone considerable rehabilitation. New discoveries throughout Europe and the Middle East show that Neanderthal Man was in fact an intelligent subspecies that cared for its infants and old people. They used fire and stone weapons. They even performed elaborate burial ceremonies that showed they embraced the concept of an afterlife. Certainly Neanderthals had bigger muscles, a heavier bone structure and lacked a chin. But they also had a larger brain than modern man!

The physical differences between modern humans and our ancient cousins are relatively slight. In fact, William Straus and A. J. Cave, two recent researchers, said that "if he could be reincarnated and placed in a New York subway—provided he were bathed, shaved, and dressed in modern clothing—it is doubtful whether he would attract any more attention than some of its other denizens."

Whether or not Neanderthals possessed a language is still hotly debated. The soft parts of the throat like the vocal cords and larynx, or the speech centres of the brain, that might tell us these things, do not usually fossilize. Other structures like the hyoid bone that anchors the muscles controlling the tongue, larynx and jaw would tell us something, but hyoid bones are fragile and, until recently, had not turned up in the fossil remains. We now know they definitely possessed a hyoid bone, removing any reason for them not to have a language.

What then, of their large brain? While the brain itself does not fossilize, we can generalize about it. Evolution dictates that you don't evolve a large brain if you don't use it. It appears from the shape of the brain case that the Neanderthal brain was put together in much the same way as modern humans. Various authors, such as Jean Auel, argued that Neanderthals had other 'talents' in their large brains. Whatever the truth of the matter, a mental ability is not likely to be revealed through a study of their bones.

Put their large brain together with their physical strength and they appear to be a superbly adapted species. Yet, something happened to this superbly adapted human species that removed it from the face of the earth. The disappearance of the Neanderthals is an enigma. Some scientists argue that a more violent subspecies (our own) wiped them out; others say that modern humans mated with Neanderthals and removed them as a separate subspecies by swamping their gene pool. Whatever the reason, we know that about thirty thousand years ago, a very successful subspecies of human vanished suddenly, to be replaced by the subspecies that has spread throughout the world and brought so much ruination to it.

The Australia of thirty thousand years ago was very different from today. What is now a lush tropical rainforest was then a drier sclerophyll forest dominated by gums, she-oak and *Acacia* trees. Rainforest was limited to river valleys and the eastern slopes of mountain ranges where rainfall was higher.

The fauna was very different also. The Pleistocene extinction that removed many of the large animals in other parts of the world also took its toll in Australia. Just as woolly mammoths, sabre-tooth tigers and dire wolves disappeared from North America, so did Australia lose its mega-fauna. Diprotodons were rhinoceros-sized relatives of the modern wombat, a burrowing marsupial. The giant crocodiles once existed, as did the giant monitor lizard, *Megalania prisca*. Huge pythons, dwarfing today's snakes, show up in the fossil record. One fossil site near the Riverslea property in Queensland has yielded a monstrous python that revels in the name of *Montypythonoides riversleaensis*. The marsupial lion, *Thylacoleo*, once roamed Australia, assuming the same role as its placental counterparts in other continents. The thylacine, or Tasmanian Tiger or Wolf, originally inhabited most of Australia. By the time of the European settlers, it was limited to the island of Tasmania, where they hunted it to extinction. Interestingly, people still claim to see them from time to time.

Australia has been inhabited by the Aborigines for at least forty thousand years. In this time, many languages and dialects have evolved or vanished. At least two hundred and fifty Aboriginal languages existed when the white man invaded Australia in 1788, though only about thirty now survive. Geographically adjacent tribes often shared elements of their languages. Extensive evidence of trading between tribes has been discovered and it is reasonable to assume a common trading language existed. Many modern Europeans are bilingual, speaking their own native tongue and today's 'trading' language, English. Most Australian Aborigines are bilingual or even multilingual, and given the propensity for travel and trade, it is certain that people from one part of the continent could make themselves understood in another part. Rather than complicate the story with many languages and dialects, we decided to base the Aboriginal words used in *Looking Glass* on the Euahlayi dialect. The language as written by Europeans is largely phonetic and varies considerably in spelling. The names of the people in the story are, for the most part, actual Aboriginal names.

Reference is made to the 'Dreamtime'. In Aboriginal mythology, the Dreamtime is the oral tradition of an ancient people, passed down in song and dance, by pictographs on cave walls and rocks. The traditions tell of the Creation, of the origins of man and animal, and of how the natural features of the Australian continent came into being. In many of these tales, giant spirit beings called Wandjina soared over the land, creating thunder and lightning. The gigantic Rainbow Serpent writhed across the land, forcing her way through rock and soil, carving out the rivers and canyons.

Other Dreamtime creatures are said to still exist today. The Winambuu are a race of small humanoid beings, secretive and shy. Modern-day sightings describe them as monkey-like or bear-like, neither animal being found in Australia. More sinister are the Quinkan. These black spirits live in crevices, cracks in rocks and dense vegetation. They are said to venture out only to cause harm to humans.

Aboriginal perspectives on spiritual matters such as beliefs, healing, death and magic are not clearly understood by white people. I know from personal experience that many Aborigines do not fully understand these aspects either. Rather than rely on invention I have followed the scholarship of Professor A. P. Elkin who studied Aboriginal society over the period 1927 to 1972. In his book *Aboriginal Men of High Degree* he discusses the nature of medicine men and their powers. Most Aborigines were initiated into at least some degree of spiritualism and magic, though fewer rose to become "clever-men" or Wirreenun; and fewer still aspired to the highest rank of Karadji.

Medicine men make great use of quartz crystals and believe that in their spirit encounters crystals embedded within their bodies give them power. The healing of Gaia is a description of an actual ceremony using quartz crystals.

So much has been written on the subject of manlike animals that I do not intend to go into the arguments for and against their existence here. Well-read people worldwide have heard of such creatures as Bigfoot, Yeti and Sasquatch. Fewer, though, would realize that creatures like these are known all over the globe under a variety of names. The Australian equivalent is the Yowie. This manlike beast has been reported along the whole East Coast of Australia, though the sightings are concentrated in areas such as the Blue Mountains behind Sydney, and the Glass House Mountains north of Brisbane.

Many scientists discount sightings of Bigfoot and his cousins as hallucination, hoaxes or misreporting of sightings of ordinary animals. Some researchers are convinced of the existence of something out of the ordinary, though exactly what is being seen is another matter altogether. Often these sightings are reported by people who we would have no hesitation in believing had they reported something else. Every researcher into the subject has his favorite theory. Some argue that the creatures are prehistoric survivors of some early ape such as *Gigantopithecus.* Others feel they are more human and represent another species of man. A few even regard them as a psychic manifestation having no real existence outside the human mind. Certainly, the literature reveals cases where the beast in question has left no footprints in soft earth, or has just "evaporated" in front of startled witnesses.

Interestingly, sightings of Unidentified Flying Objects (UFO's) often occur at the same time, and in the same area as Bigfoot sightings. Although there is only one (suspect) report of a Bigfoot actually getting out of a UFO, there are many instances of people seeing them near where a UFO has been reported. Janet and Colin Bord, two researchers into these and other mysteries, argue that it is possible that atmospheric and electromagnetic fluxes create an image in the minds of susceptible people that is interpreted in different ways. It is interesting to speculate that if it was possible to manipulate electromagnetic forces precisely enough, one could actually influence what people saw.

There are many reports from around the world of unknown creatures. In past times, these reports was dismissed as mistaken identity or hoaxes perpetrated on gullible visitors by the inhabitants of far-off places. This last century, however, has seen a large number of new animals discovered, from the okapi and the mountain gorilla, to the Blue Ox and the Vietnamese goat. It is certainly possible that there are other creatures waiting to be found. The science of cryptozoology deals with the study of unknown animals. For many researchers in this field, the main avenues of research are old reports, or vague sightings, perhaps backed up by the occasional footprint or dead domestic animal. Other researchers, such as Tim 'the Yowie Man' in Australia, seek evidence in the field, trying to track the beast down, or spending days, months or years in the pursuit. Not every unknown animal is an exciting one like a Nessie or a Bigfoot though. Equally valid unknowns are the myriad of insects or deep-sea creatures waiting to be discovered by some industrious worker in the field.

Time travel is a contentious subject and I refuse to be drawn into an argument on paradox. The question must always remain...if time travel is possible, can one go back and alter the past in such a way as to exclude one's own future existence? On the other hand, will some cosmic censor prevent such problems? Another way out is by the creation of "alternate realities". Quantum mechanics allow unobserved electrons to be in two places at once. The act of observation forces them to choose one position or another. Some people theorize that whole new universes are created, one where the electron took one position, another where it was forced into the other position.

None of the known laws of physics actually forbids time travel, and in theory, it should not be too difficult. In practice, though, you need an awful lot of energy. Ronald Mallett, Professor of theoretical physics at Connecticut University, believes he can devise a working model that utilizes slow light. If you want to know more, I suggest you go and read his paper on the subject.

To what extent is this story fiction versus fact? The characters are fictional for the main part, though my first name is James, my mother had the surname Hay, I recently worked at James Cook University in Townsville as a biologist, and I have Aboriginal friends called Ratana and Nathan. Ariana's birth initials are S.L., like the heroine, she is American, and she came to Australia, fell in love with and married the hero. So I'm afraid you must make up your own mind. If you think the information on Yowies, Karadjis and the like are too unbelievable, read some of the books and journals listed below before you decide. Whatever your decision, I hope you enjoyed the story!

Max Overton, M.Sc. (Hons), G.C.E.T.
Botanist, Biologist, Cryptozoologist
Formerly of Townsville, Queensland, Australia
and of Collinsville, Illinois, U.S.A.
Currently residing where the mysteries exist.

References

Out of the Shadows by Tony Healy and Paul Cropper, 1994. Ironbark by Pan Macmillan Australia Pty Ltd

Cryptozoology A to Z by Loren Coleman and Jerome Clark, 1999. Fireside by Simon & Schuster, New York, USA

The Field Guide to Bigfoot, Yeti, and Other Mystery Primates Worldwide by Loren Coleman & Patrick Huyghe, 1999. Avon Books, USA

Cryptozoology: the Interdisciplinary Journal of the International Society of Cryptozoology Allen Press Inc, USA

Alien Animals by Janet and Colin Bord, 1985. Panther Books, Grenada Publishing, Great Britain

The Neanderthal Enigma by James Shreeve, 1995. William Morrow and Co. Inc, USA

In Search of Prehistoric Survivors by Karl P. N. Shuker, 1995. Blandford, Great Britain

Aboriginal Men of High Degree by A. P. Elkin, 1994. University of Queensland Press, Australia

Archaeology of the Dreamtime by Josephine Flood, 1999. Angus & Robertson, HarperCollins Publishers, Australia

Prehistory of Australia by John Mulvaney & Johan Kamminga, 1999. Allen & Unwin Pty Ltd, Australia

Australian Legendary Tales by K. Langloh Parker, 1953. Angus & Robertson, Australia

Gaia: A New Look at Life on Earth by James Lovelock, 1979. Oxford University Press, Great Britain

The Fabric of Reality by David Deutsch, 1997. Allen Lane, The Penguin Press, USA

Time Travellers from our Future: an Explanation of Alien Abductions by Bruce Goldberg, 1998. Llewellyn Publications, USA

Complete Book of Australian Mammals The Australian Museum, 1983. CollinsAngus & Robertson, Australia

Origins Reconsidered by Richard Leakey & Roger Lewin, 1992. Little, Brown and Co. Ltd, Great Britain

"Time Twister" by Michael Brooks (describes the work of Ronald Mallett) *New Scientist*, 27 January 2001, p. 4

Printed in the United States
59668LVS00003B/223